OUR STORIES CARRIED US HERE:
A GRAPHIC NOVEL ANTHOLOGY

Zaynab Abdi, Aziz Kamal, Craig Moodie, Karelin, Ruth Mekoulom, Alex Tsipenyuk, Zurya Anjum, Sergio Cenoch & Mary Anne Quiroz, Vy Luong, Amara Solomon Kamara

STORYTELLERS

Ashraf El-Attar, sunshine gao, Ana Hinojosa, Mike Centeno, Hop (Guy Bertin "BG" Beyem Gouong, Sandjock Likinè, Gérard Nyunai Ngan), Tom Kaczynski, Toufic El Rassi, Camilo Aguirre, Cori Nakamura Lin, Hamid Ibrahim and the Kugali Team

ILLUSTRATORS

Julie Vang, Tea Rozman, Tom Kaczynski

EDITORS

Hardcover ISBN 13: 978-1-949523-17-1
Paperback ISBN 13: 978-1-949523-22-5
eISBN 13: 978-1-949523-10-2
LCCN: 2018932723

Printed in the United States of America
First Printing: 2021
20   19   18   17   16   5   4   3   2   1

Edited by Julie Vang, Tea Rozman, Tom Kaczynski

Cover design by Nate Powell
Interior design by Shiney Chi-la Her

Photography, videography by Media Active: Youth Produced Media

Green Card Voices
2611 1st Avenue South
Minneapolis, MN 55408
www.greencardvoices.org

Consortium Book Sales & Distribution
34 Thirteenth Avenue NE, Suite 101
Minneapolis, MN 55413-1007
www.cbsd.com

We dedicate this book to all the people who had to endure education inequality and systematic displacement, and whose lives have been negatively impacted by hate, fear, prejudice and xenophobia.

By buying this book you are directly supporting the mission of Green Card Voices.

"*Our Stories Carried Us Here* is a powerful collaboration between storytellers and illustrators from around the country, speaking to the forces that uproot us and send us to each other. The collection is a testament to the power of language as vessels for carrying our memories, to the power of images in holding fast the boundaries of who we were and who we will be."
—**Kao Kalia Yang, author of *Somewhere in the Unknown World***

"*Our Stories Carried Us Here* is a collection of compelling and emotional journeys that reminds us of why the greatest destination humanity can strive for is a world where each of us can safely make our home and belong. This book and the storytellers it features offer a profound gift—the ability to step into the many worlds they bring to life and to step out with the insights needed to better meet the challenges of the communities, schools, workplaces, and democracy we shape together, not as strangers but as neighbors."
—**Rachel Perić, executive director, Welcoming America**

"Once again, Green Card Voices has produced a piece of historical art through storytelling. While reading, I found myself empathizing, crying, laughing, and graphically interpreting a glimpse into the immigrant experience of so many. The experiences are so unique yet remind me that we need to constantly be sharing these stories. The series is an archive of our lived experiences and part of the racial justice movement."
—**Nausheena Hussain, executive director of Reviving the Islamic Sisterhood for Empowerment (RISE)**

"What struck me most about this book was seeing images of what my students have gone through. As an ESL writing teacher, I have read countless journals/memoirs/poems describing my ELs' painful and harrowing life experiences. No two are the same, but they connect through common themes. This book makes their experiences more concrete, less abstract, in terms of the heroes they all truly are. For that, I am thankful."
—**Dr. Amy Hewett-Olatunde, EdD, EdS, ESL teacher, teacher educator, freelance writer, advocate, 2015 Minnesota Teacher of the Year**

"This book is a beautiful, accessible, and heart-expanding invitation for us to learn the stories of some of our neighbors. I hope that many will accept this invitation and channel the understanding and care that is sure to follow into becoming better listeners, community members, and neighbors who welcome and support one another."
—**Alyssa Tsagong, director of education, PBS Wisconsin**

"Filled with compassion and insight into the immigrant experience, *Our Stories Carried Us Here: A Graphic Novel Anthology* is a must read for educators."
—**Jennifer Raponi, professional development specialist and ELL coach, New York State Mid-West Regional Bilingual Education Resource Network**

"*Our Stories Carried Us Here* is a stunning example of the power of comics to uplift the stories that most need telling. In a precarious moment for refugees and immigrants across the world, Green Card Voices has curated an incredible anthology, filled with experiences both told and illustrated by people whose creative work is rarely centered and whose voices we will all be better for listening to."
—**Oriana Leckert, director of publishing and comics outreach at Kickstarter**

"*Our Stories Carried Us Here: A Graphic Novel Anthology* is a beautiful representation of how powerful the intersection of art and storytelling can be. It offers such a critically humanizing perspective that the reader can't help but love, rally around, and stand up for the storytellers, and it encourages the reader to take action in real life. To me, that's what this book is all about."
—**Christine Her, executive director of ArtForce Iowa**

"*Our Stories Carried Us Here* is an infinitely powerful collection of immigrant voices unlike anything we've seen. One cannot comprehend the bravery, trauma, sadness, and triumph of emigrating from one country to another as a young person, yet this anthology captures both the unimaginable journey and the humanity of young immigrants. From the storytellers to the artists, the reader is immersed in a page-turning narrative that gives you chills and arrests your notions of what it means to leave one country behind in pursuit of a different one. Our Stories Carried Us Here is remarkable and is destined to become a beloved classic that belongs in every classroom, library, and bookshelf."
—**Dara Beevas, publisher, and author of *Amina of Zaria: The Warrior Queen***

"An important collection of beautiful work that effectively communicates the genuine and diverse experiences of long-overdue voices."
—**Louis Leung, novelist**

"*Our Stories Carried Us Here*, is an incredible collaboration of authors and illustrators that illuminates the experience of otherness felt by immigrants and refugees. This graphic novel is a powerful affirmation of the way stories foster empathy and connection and provides a greater sense of how to understand and welcome our new neighbors."
—**Molly Hill, editor of Blue Marble Review: A Literary Journal for Young Writers**

"This is an authentic piece of work that has married harrowing stories of our refugee and immigrant youth with beautiful artwork from a diverse group of artists from around the country. *Our Stories Carried Us Here: A Graphic Novel Anthology* shares these important and meaningful stories of our nation's refugee and immigrant students by making them accessible to a wider population through beautiful and powerful images."
—**Leah Juelke, MEd, English teacher, EL specialist, literacy coach, 2020 Global Teacher Prize finalist, 2018 North Dakota Teacher of the Year**

"Will strongly evoke both thought-provoking insights and empathy."

"Eleven storytellers chronicle their journeys from places all over the world—including Guatemala, Chad, Vietnam, and Kazakhstan—to the United States.

Each story compellingly details a variety of experiences the individual **immigrant or refugee** had, highlighting differences between stories that too often are lumped together or not given an opportunity to be heard. **Each storyteller was paired with an illustrator from a similar linguistic and cultural heritage.** The thoughtfulness of the matches shines through, as every panel authentically conveys the narrators' poignant and emotional memories, highlighting the beauty of their homelands and the cultures they still identify with. The narratives show the **struggles and triumphs** of acclimating to a new language, culture, and worldview as well as dealing with obstacles like **racism and microaggressions**. Readers meet remarkable people like Zaynab Abdi from Yemen, whose story is illustrated by Egyptian American artist Ashraf El-Attar in stark black and white. Her harrowing journey was filled with sorrow and trauma yet, when she finally settled in Minnesota, she found purpose and opportunity through hard work and activism, speaking at the United Nations about girls' education in Yemen. Each profile opens with brief biographies and photos or drawings of the storytellers and artists along with website URLs for learning more about them. Glossaries following many of the stories define potentially unfamiliar terms. The vibrant diversity of artistic styles offers pleasing variety within the unifying thematic framework of the volume."

(Graphic nonfiction. 12-16)

—*Kirkus Reviews* **(starred review)**

TABLE OF CONTENTS

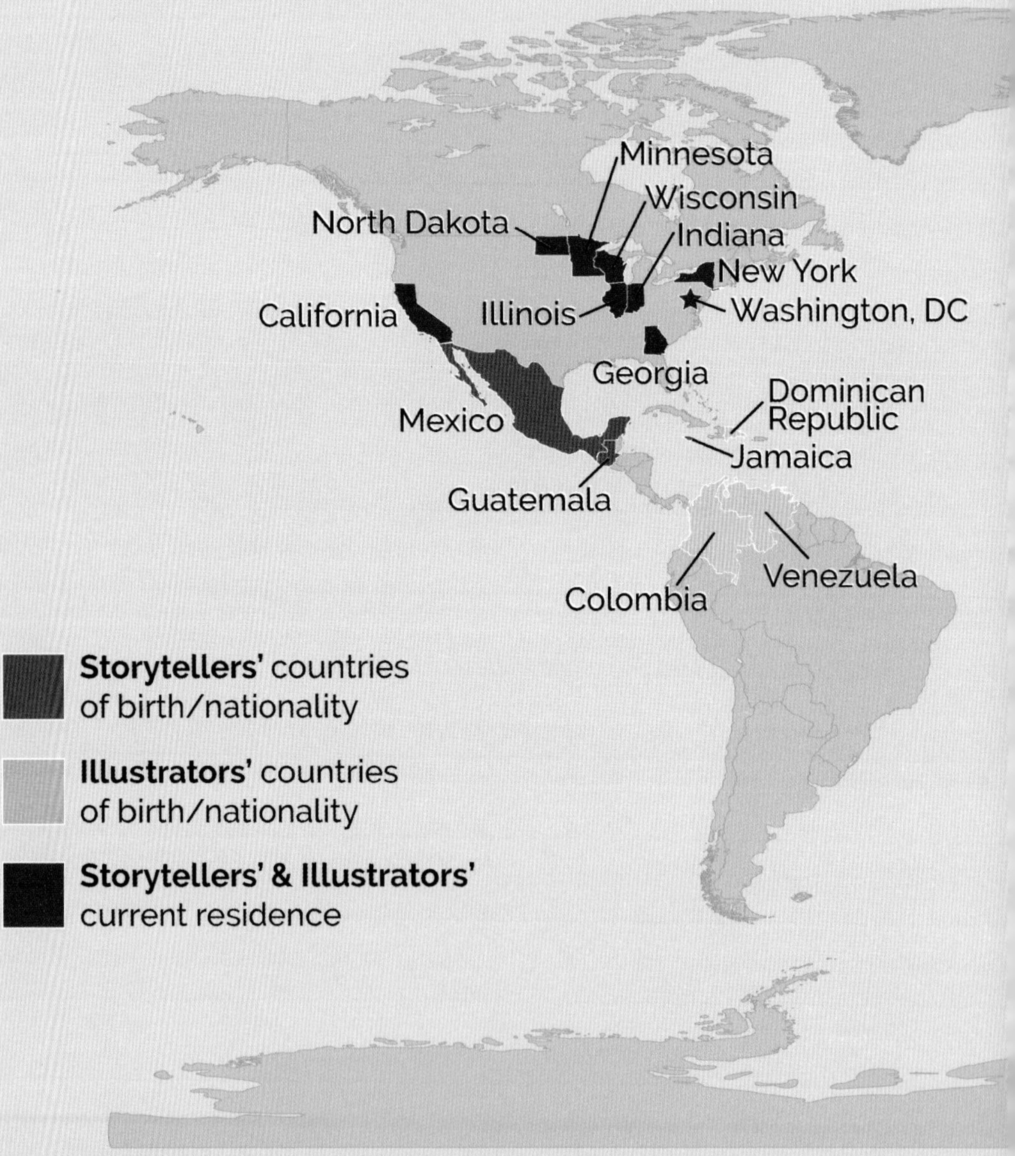
Minnesota
Wisconsin
North Dakota
Indiana
New York
Washington, DC
California
Illinois
Georgia
Dominican Republic
Mexico
Jamaica
Guatemala
Venezuela
Colombia
Storytellers' countries of birth/nationality
Illustrators' countries of birth/nationality
Storytellers' & Illustrators' current residence

WORLD MAP

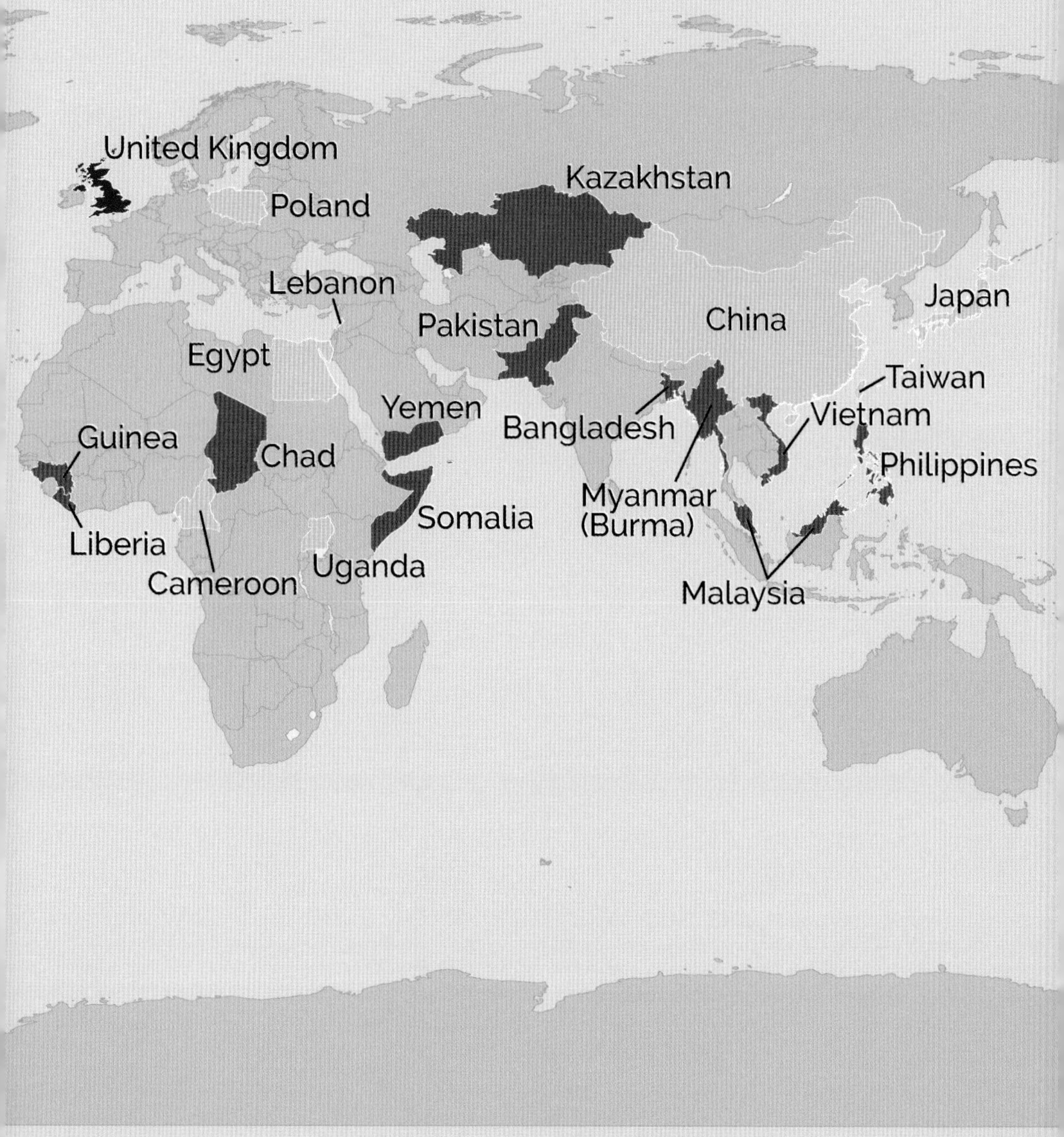
United Kingdom
Poland
Kazakhstan
Lebanon
Japan
China
Pakistan
Egypt
Taiwan
Yemen
Bangladesh
Vietnam
Guinea
Chad
Philippines
Myanmar
(Burma)
Somalia
Liberia
Uganda
Cameroon
Malaysia

FOREWORD

Thi Bui

Author of *The Best We Could Do*
Oakland, California

I don't know who needs to hear this, but the United States of America is not the center of the world. It's not the greatest country in the world, either. I'm not sure any country deserves to call itself that. Sometimes people simply move here to be with their loved ones, like Amara Solomon Kamara and his family did.

Neither is America the "melting pot" of the world, as you'll see in Amara's depiction of being the darker half of an interracial couple in Guinea or Craig Moodie's fond memories of his childhood in Jamaica. Black immigrants often comment that they feel different only after they come to America, where racial discrimination and being boxed into a stereotype because of their skin color is a phenomenon that attaches itself, unwanted, onto their identity and the way they must behave just to get through the day.

At a very basic level, America is the less real part of a recent immigrant's experience. We see this through Ruth Mekolum's art. Her story deftly conveys the difference in experience between a child who is Deaf and her family members who are not, while her art subtly contrasts the rich detail of her memories in Chad and Cameroon with a rough, less colorful impression of Fargo, North Dakota. As she observes, with an expression that is pensive and perhaps full of longing for the old home, "Everything is different."

Why does America have such a high view of itself? Perhaps one reason is that it has been a sought-after destination for a long time, and refugees and immigrants, by virtue of needing documents to cross borders, arrive with the disadvantage of needing permission to simply be human beings with human rights. It's a power dynamic set up for continued imbalance. But more often than not, refugees and immigrants have lived many lifetimes before arriving in this country. You wouldn't know it from their limited English, their humble appearance, or the quiet way many navigate their lives here. They are superheroes who walk among us, disguised as day laborers, fruit pickers, office cleaners, nail-salon workers, students, mental-health providers, people riding the bus, people walking by on the street. You never know if the woman learning how to drive in the next lane used to be a doctor in her home country, having already overcome much greater obstacles than a driving test to do that. Zurya Anjum's comic reminds me of a story my father told me about starting over in the US. He was trying to learn how to continue his work as an educator, but the US didn't recognize his degree. At the school district office, he ran into a fellow refugee. This man had been a famous actor in Viet Nam, but in the US, he was scraping by as a teacher's assistant.

Aziz Kamal's story of being a Rohingya refugee from Myanmar details the grueling journey that many people have gone through just to get here—the dangers, uncertainties, and indignities of leaving a bad situation and the sheer bureaucracy of the screening and admissions process to get to a better situation.

One feels the motif of the American Dream throughout this book—not as the universal truth it is usually painted as, but as a trope that some of the authors would very much like to undo to get at a more personal truth closer to their own experience. "While I'm grateful for the opportunities I've been granted, the road I was on never became easier," writes Karelin, a DACAmented student at Emory University. "This country has given me many opportunities, but it has done so with reservations."

Alex Tsipenyuk, whose family won the Diversity Immigrant Visa lottery, is perhaps the most open of these authors to the notion of America, the country of opportunity. But when one considers the nature of the lottery program, and how many people vie for those 55,000 green cards, one realizes how rare this American Dream is. And for Alex, who benefits from it, there are still the mundane realities of needing to learn a new language and getting used to a new school, new friends, a new culture—and leaving behind what he has always known.

Vy Luong's story follows a hopeful climb to success, but also very matter-of-factly observes, "Now, I have realized that I would still have to earn the riches everybody in Vietnam assumed all Americans have…and many groups of people are still fighting for human rights."

In Mary Anne and Sergio's story, the gloves come off. We see an immigrant narrative become a story of community building as resistance to the white supremacy hinted at in the other stories. This comic is an anthem, and I am ready for it.

I was not ready for the tears that Zaynab Abdi's story pulled from me. Such fierceness on top of resilience! Her leadership and advocacy inspire me and fill my heart with gladness, because there are more and more times as I get older, and this year especially, when I feel my mortality…and I am ever so glad that younger people like her remain.

What do refugees and immigrants fight for? It is not for the jobs of other Americans. It is not to take over this country. It is, as Zurya's story states simply, so that refugees and immigrants can live a life just like anyone else. That is all. In the simplicity of the ask, one sees the beauty of what people seek when they cross the world in search of a new home, of what people who have peace take for granted.

I am reminded of a poem, "For Peshawar," by Fatima Asghar:

> *I wish them a mundane life.*
> *Arguments with parents. Groundings.*
>
> *Chasing a budding love around the playground.*
> *Iced mango slices in the hot summer.*
>
> . . . .
>
> *Loneliness in a bookstore. Gold chapals.*
> *Red kurtas. Walking home, sun*
>
> *at their back. Searching the street*
> *for a missing glove. Nothing glorious.*
>
> *A life. Alive. I promise.*

THE STORIES

ZAYNAB ABDI

Born: Aden, Yemen
Current: Minneapolis, Minnesota

Zaynab Abdi is a Black, Muslim, Middle Eastern, and Immigrant woman who is passionate about social justice and advocacy. She graduated magna cum laude from St. Catherine University with triple majors in political science, international studies, and philosophy. She will be starting Columbia University in the Fall of 2021. Zaynab works alongside the youngest-ever Nobel Peace Prize winner, Malala Yousafzai, as a youth advocate for girls' education. She has spoken at the United Nations several times, and her story was featured in Malala's book *We Are Displaced*. Zaynab was appointed by Minnesota Governor Tim Walz's office to serve in the 2019 Young Women's Cabinet. In her free time, Zaynab enjoys playing soccer, biking, and mentoring young leaders to be civically engaged.

www.greencardvoices.org/speakers/zaynab-abdi

ASHRAF EL-ATTAR

Born: Egypt
Current: Washington, D.C.

Ashraf El-Attar is an illustrator from Egypt. He currently resides in Washington, DC. He earned his MFA in Illustration from Savannah College of Art and Design with a full scholarship from the Ford Foundation. His children's books and graphic novels have been published in the United States and around the world. His work has also appeared in several magazines such as *Baystate Parent* and *Washingtonian*. His preferred medium is traditional ink and paper.

www.linkedin.com/in/ashraf-attar-73006053

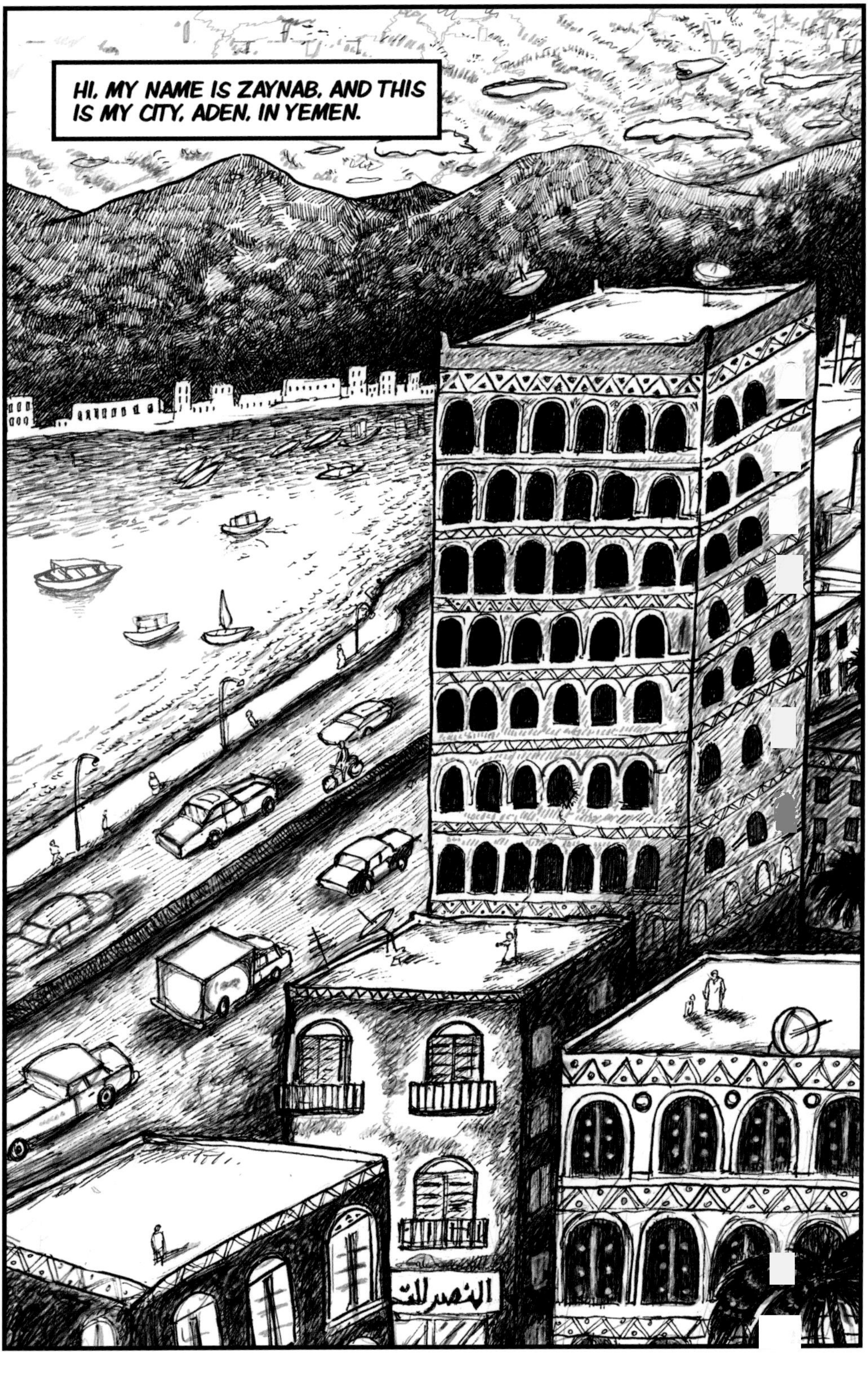
HI, MY NAME IS ZAYNAB, AND THIS IS MY CITY, ADEN, IN YEMEN.

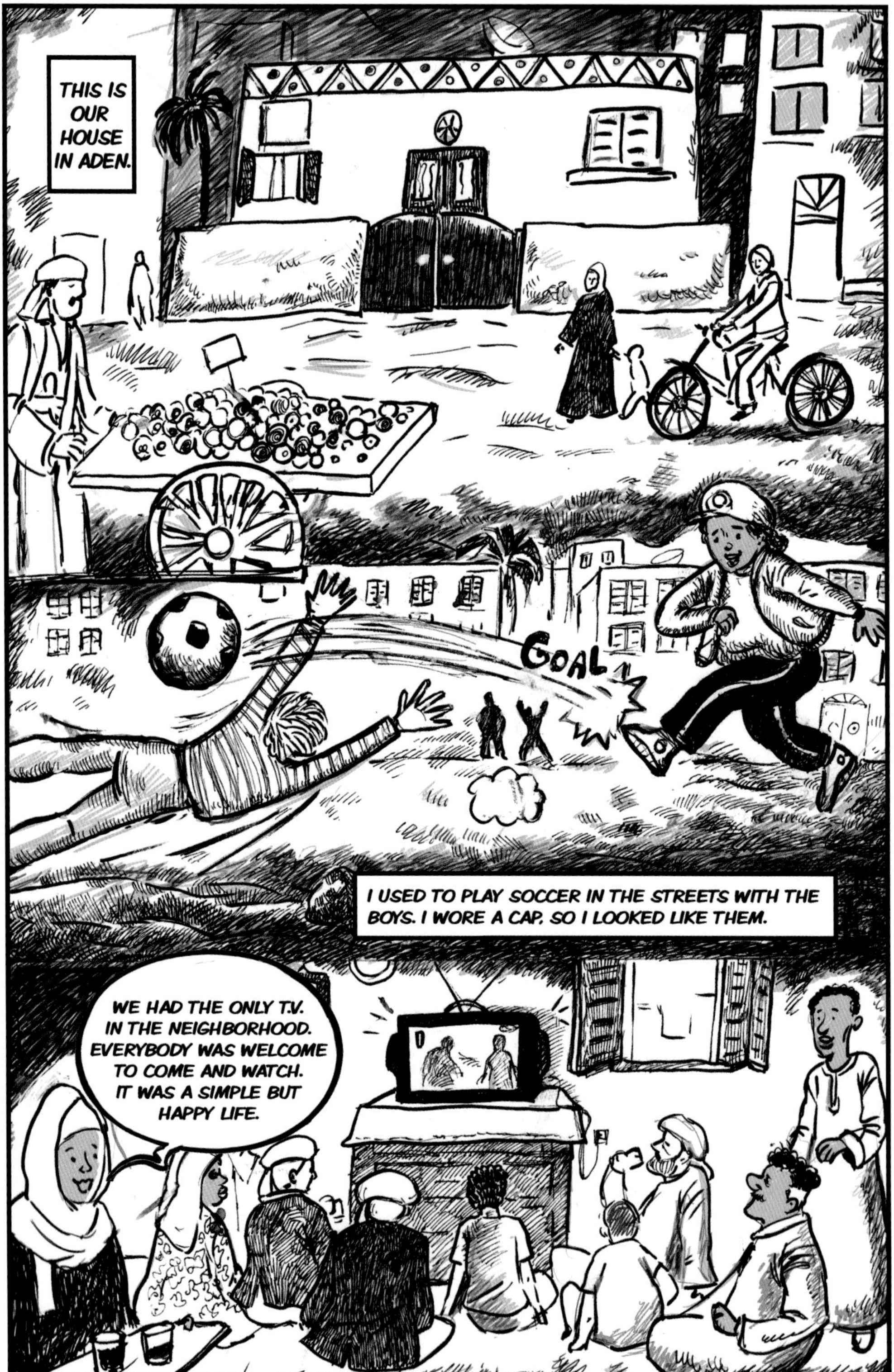
THIS IS OUR HOUSE IN ADEN.
GOAL
I USED TO PLAY SOCCER IN THE STREETS WITH THE BOYS. I WORE A CAP, SO I LOOKED LIKE THEM.
WE HAD THE ONLY T.V. IN THE NEIGHBORHOOD. EVERYBODY WAS WELCOME TO COME AND WATCH. IT WAS A SIMPLE BUT HAPPY LIFE.

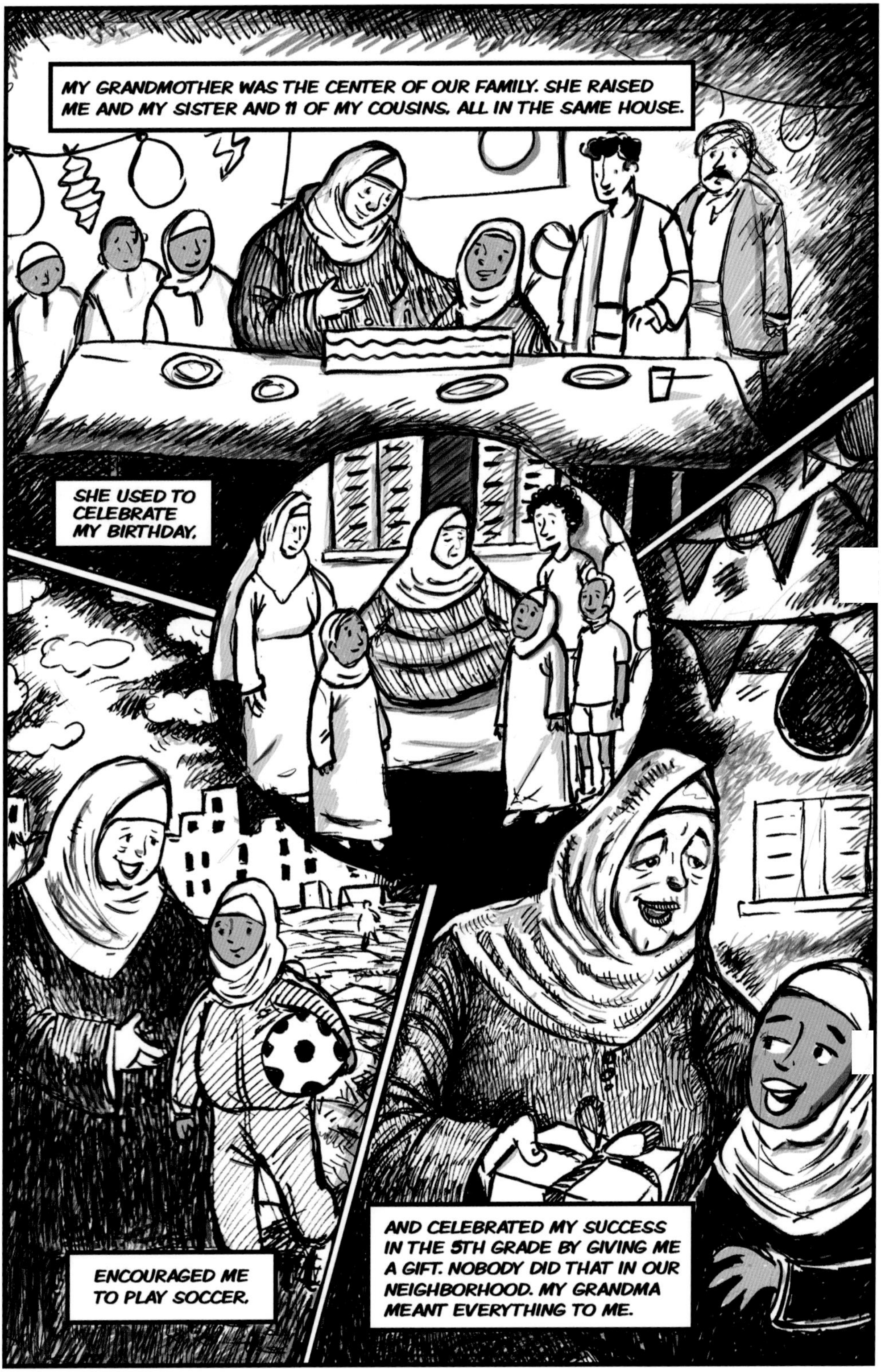
MY GRANDMOTHER WAS THE CENTER OF OUR FAMILY. SHE RAISED ME AND MY SISTER AND 11 OF MY COUSINS, ALL IN THE SAME HOUSE.
SHE USED TO CELEBRATE MY BIRTHDAY,
ENCOURAGED ME TO PLAY SOCCER,
AND CELEBRATED MY SUCCESS IN THE 5TH GRADE BY GIVING ME A GIFT. NOBODY DID THAT IN OUR NEIGHBORHOOD. MY GRANDMA MEANT EVERYTHING TO ME.

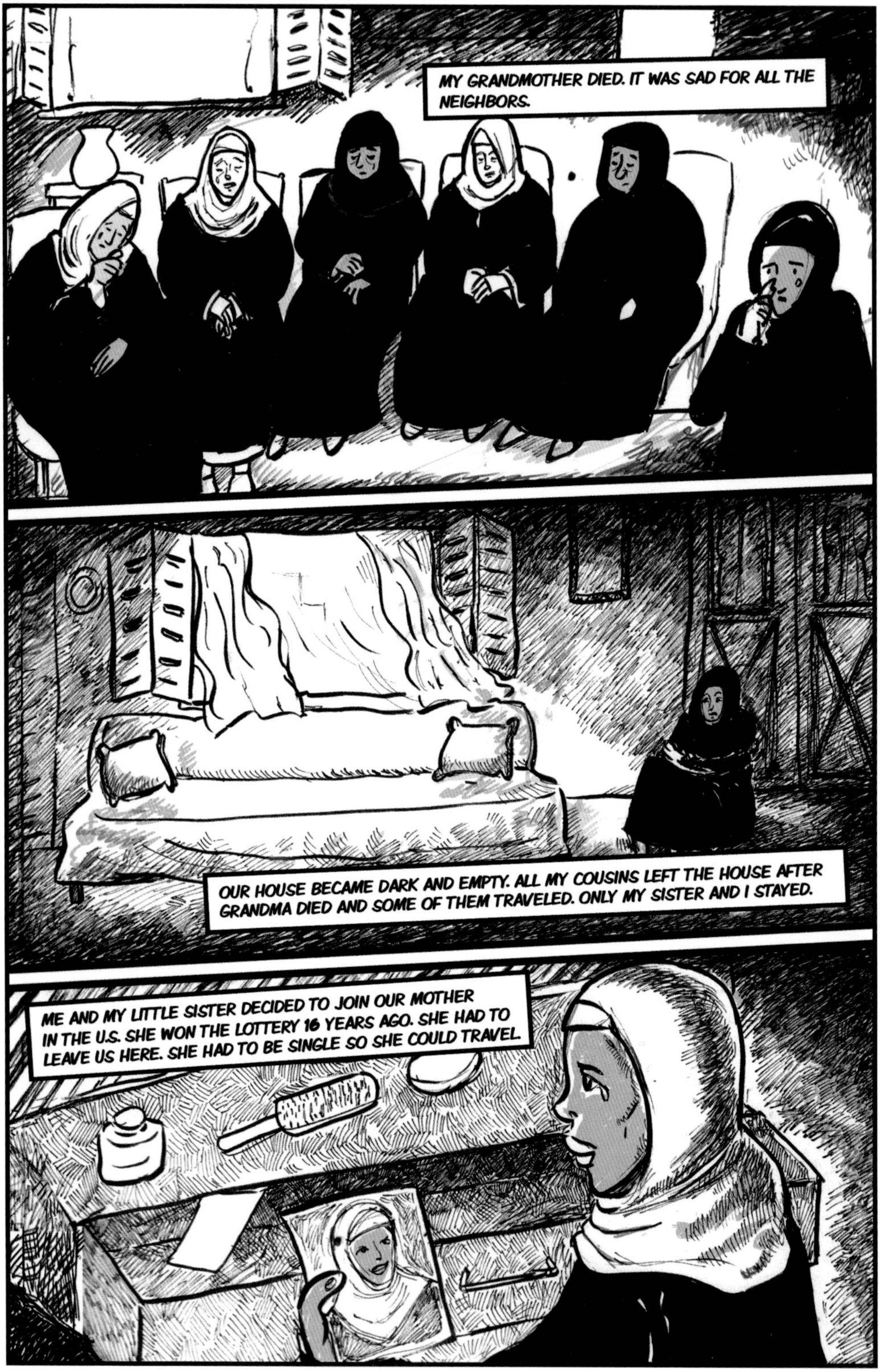
MY GRANDMOTHER DIED. IT WAS SAD FOR ALL THE NEIGHBORS.
OUR HOUSE BECAME DARK AND EMPTY. ALL MY COUSINS LEFT THE HOUSE AFTER GRANDMA DIED AND SOME OF THEM TRAVELED. ONLY MY SISTER AND I STAYED.
ME AND MY LITTLE SISTER DECIDED TO JOIN OUR MOTHER IN THE U.S. SHE WON THE LOTTERY 16 YEARS AGO. SHE HAD TO LEAVE US HERE. SHE HAD TO BE SINGLE SO SHE COULD TRAVEL.

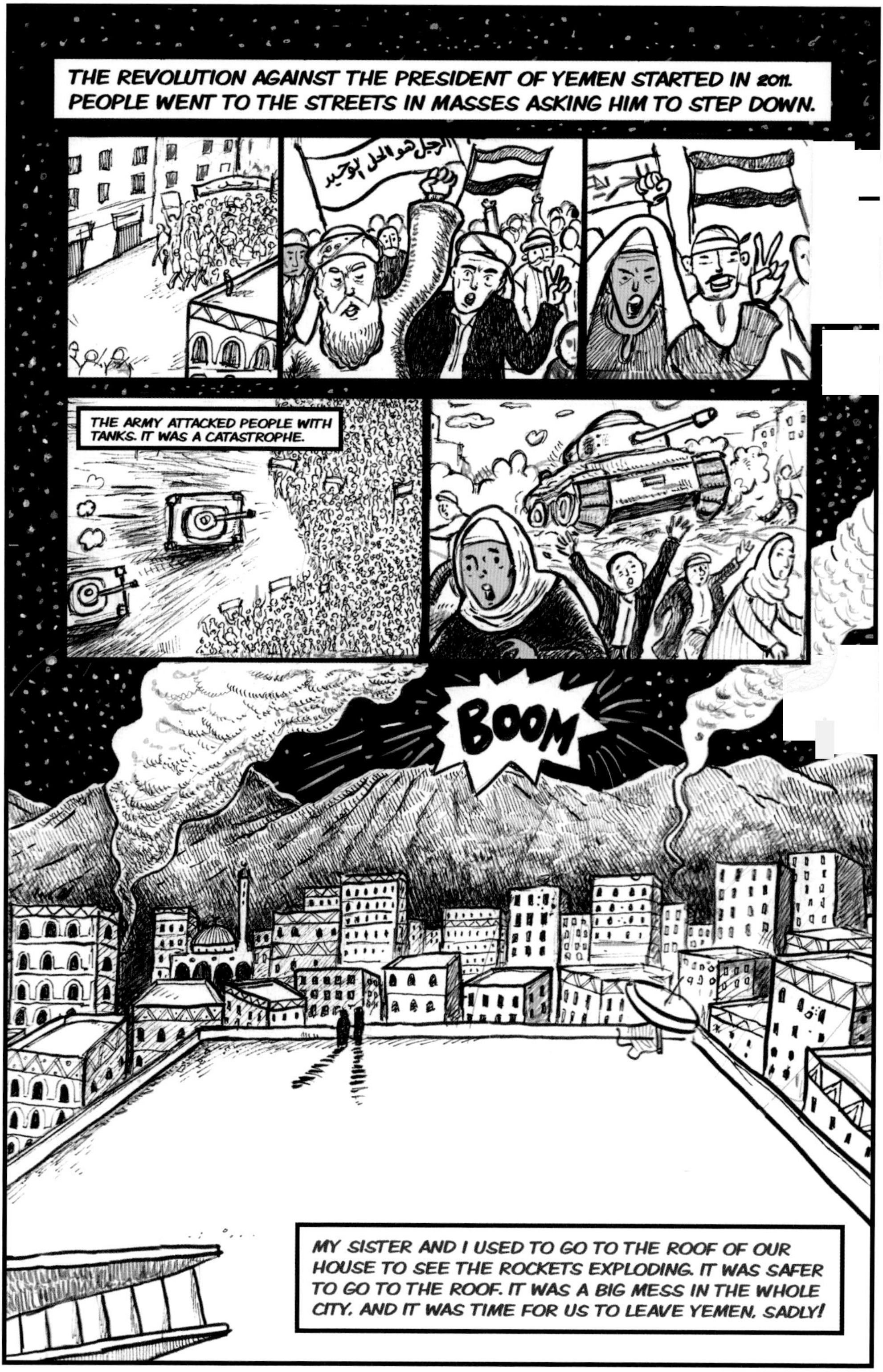
THE REVOLUTION AGAINST THE PRESIDENT OF YEMEN STARTED IN 2011. PEOPLE WENT TO THE STREETS IN MASSES ASKING HIM TO STEP DOWN.
THE ARMY ATTACKED PEOPLE WITH TANKS. IT WAS A CATASTROPHE.
BOOM
MY SISTER AND I USED TO GO TO THE ROOF OF OUR HOUSE TO SEE THE ROCKETS EXPLODING. IT WAS SAFER TO GO TO THE ROOF. IT WAS A BIG MESS IN THE WHOLE CITY. AND IT WAS TIME FOR US TO LEAVE YEMEN. SADLY!

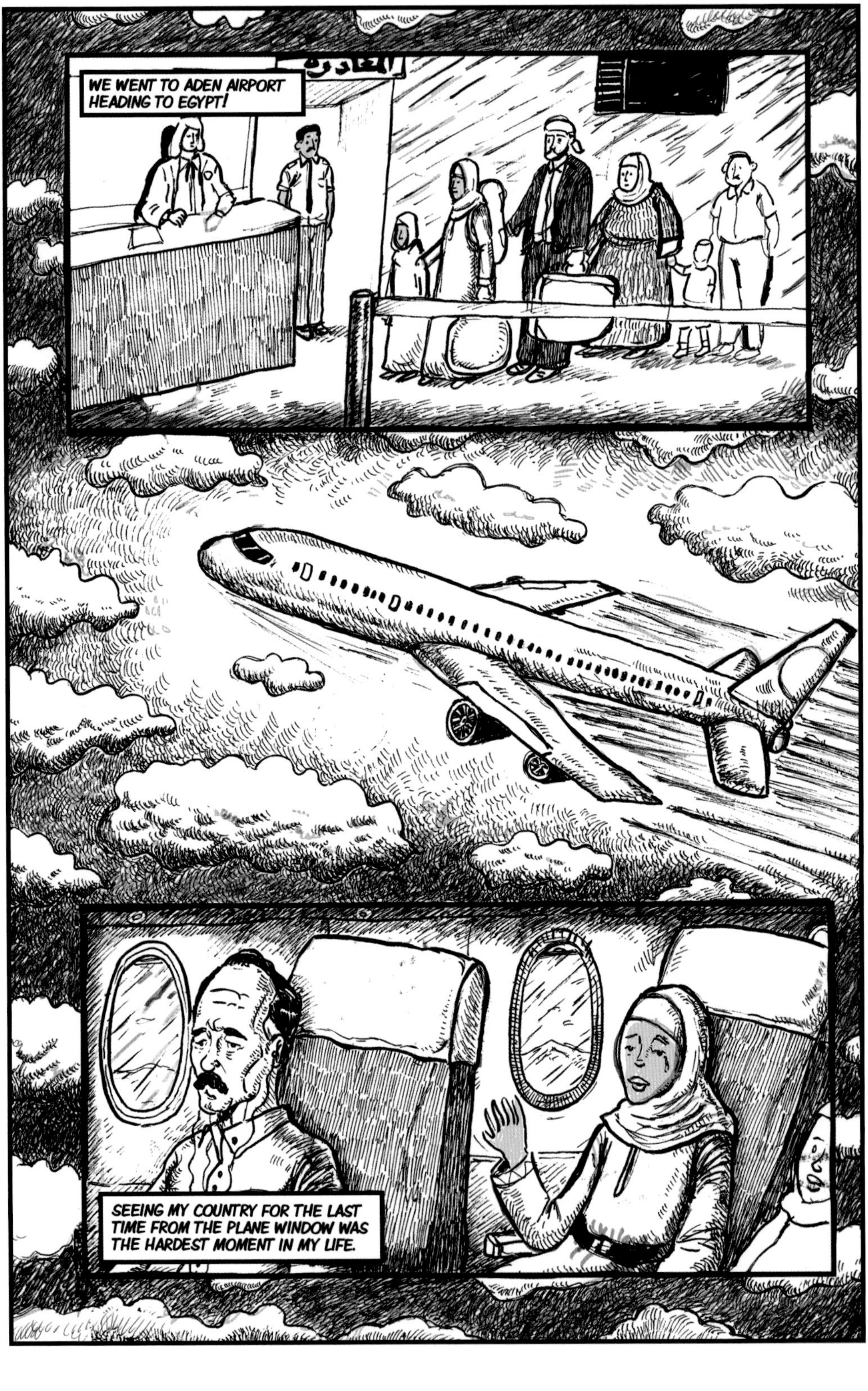
WE WENT TO ADEN AIRPORT HEADING TO EGYPT!
SEEING MY COUNTRY FOR THE LAST TIME FROM THE PLANE WINDOW WAS THE HARDEST MOMENT IN MY LIFE.

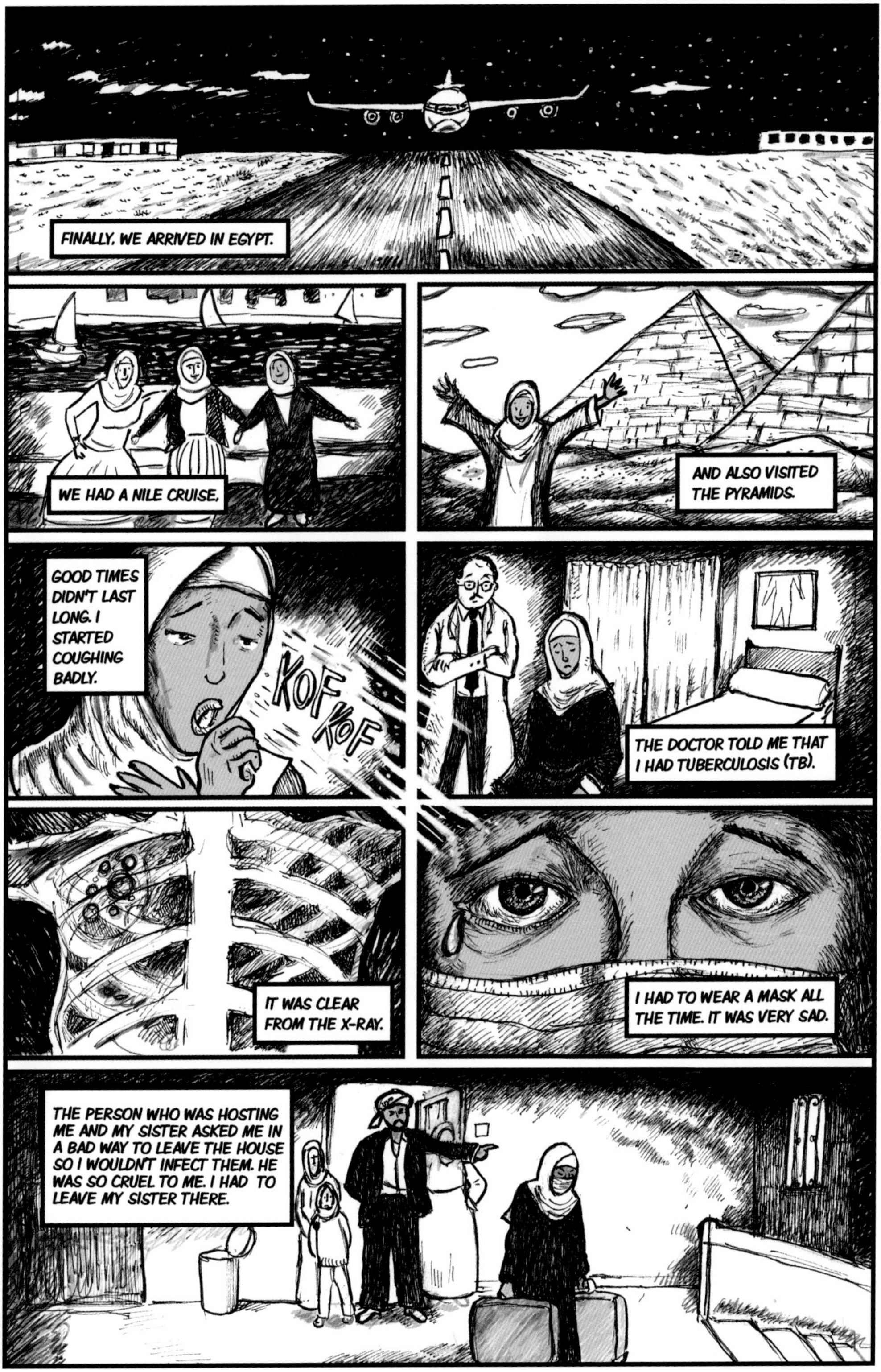
FINALLY, WE ARRIVED IN EGYPT.
WE HAD A NILE CRUISE,
AND ALSO VISITED THE PYRAMIDS.
GOOD TIMES DIDN'T LAST LONG. I STARTED COUGHING BADLY.
KOF KOF
THE DOCTOR TOLD ME THAT I HAD TUBERCULOSIS (TB).
IT WAS CLEAR FROM THE X-RAY.
I HAD TO WEAR A MASK ALL THE TIME. IT WAS VERY SAD.
THE PERSON WHO WAS HOSTING ME AND MY SISTER ASKED ME IN A BAD WAY TO LEAVE THE HOUSE SO I WOULDN'T INFECT THEM. HE WAS SO CRUEL TO ME. I HAD TO LEAVE MY SISTER THERE.

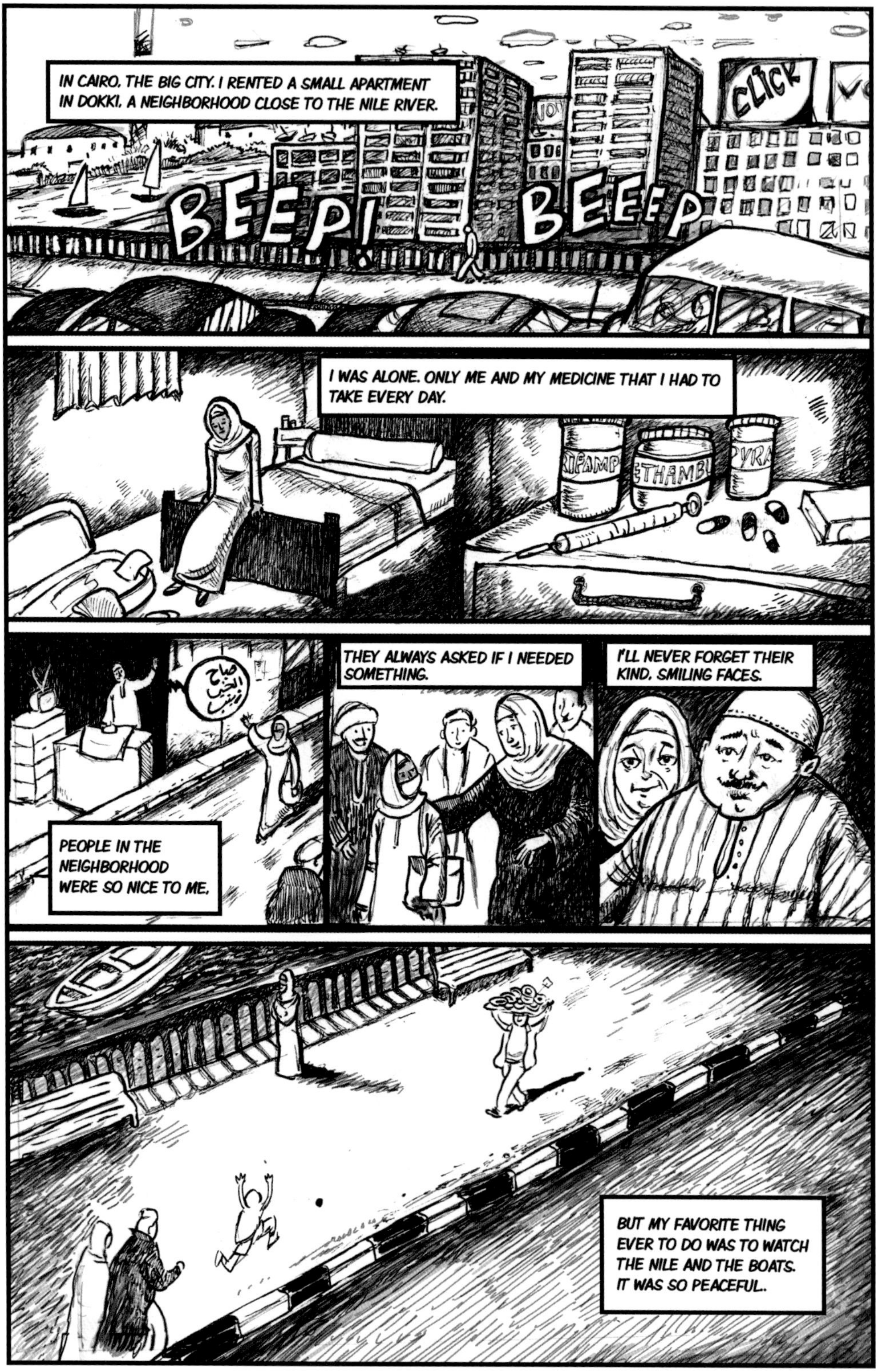
IN CAIRO, THE BIG CITY, I RENTED A SMALL APARTMENT IN DOKKI, A NEIGHBORHOOD CLOSE TO THE NILE RIVER.
CLICK
BEEP! BEEEP
I WAS ALONE. ONLY ME AND MY MEDICINE THAT I HAD TO TAKE EVERY DAY.
RIFAMP
ETHAMB
PYRA
صباح الخير زينب
PEOPLE IN THE NEIGHBORHOOD WERE SO NICE TO ME.
THEY ALWAYS ASKED IF I NEEDED SOMETHING.
I'LL NEVER FORGET THEIR KIND, SMILING FACES.
BUT MY FAVORITE THING EVER TO DO WAS TO WATCH THE NILE AND THE BOATS. IT WAS SO PEACEFUL.

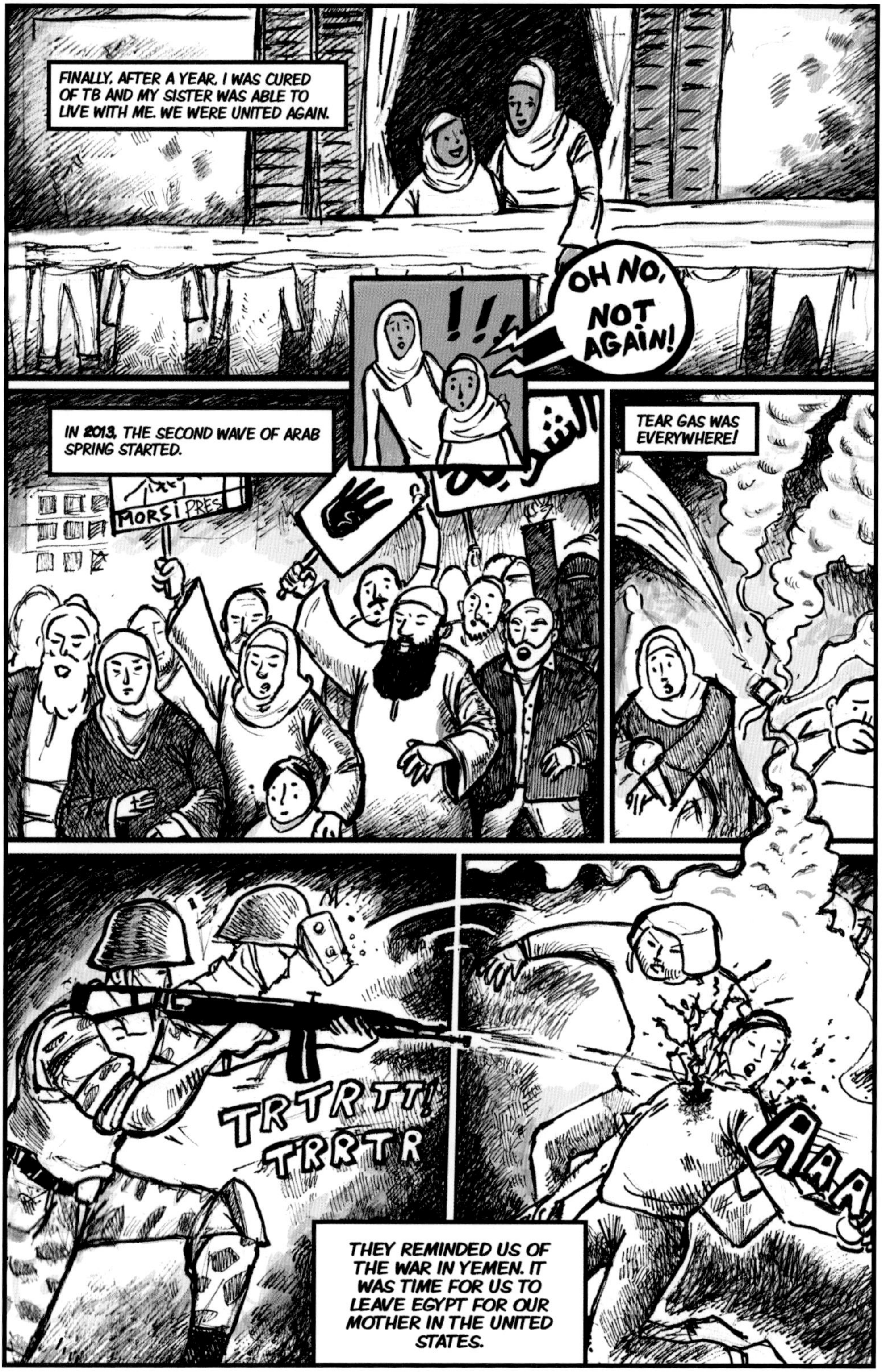
FINALLY, AFTER A YEAR, I WAS CURED OF TB AND MY SISTER WAS ABLE TO LIVE WITH ME. WE WERE UNITED AGAIN.
!!!
OH NO, NOT AGAIN!
IN 2013, THE SECOND WAVE OF ARAB SPRING STARTED.
MORSI PRES
TEAR GAS WAS EVERYWHERE!
TRTRTT! TRRTR
AAAA
THEY REMINDED US OF THE WAR IN YEMEN. IT WAS TIME FOR US TO LEAVE EGYPT FOR OUR MOTHER IN THE UNITED STATES.

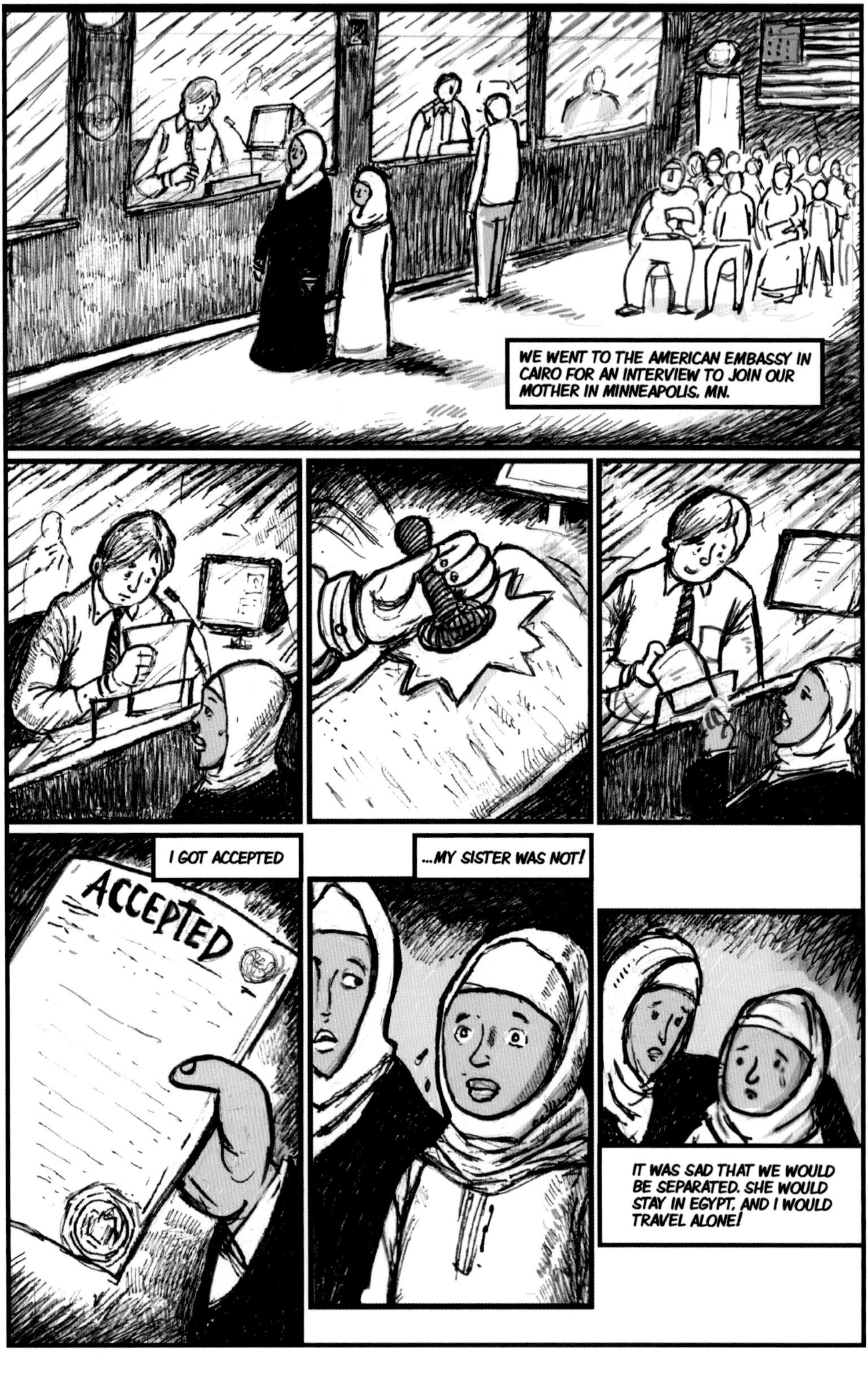
WE WENT TO THE AMERICAN EMBASSY IN CAIRO FOR AN INTERVIEW TO JOIN OUR MOTHER IN MINNEAPOLIS, MN.
I GOT ACCEPTED
ACCEPTED
...MY SISTER WAS NOT!
IT WAS SAD THAT WE WOULD BE SEPARATED. SHE WOULD STAY IN EGYPT, AND I WOULD TRAVEL ALONE!

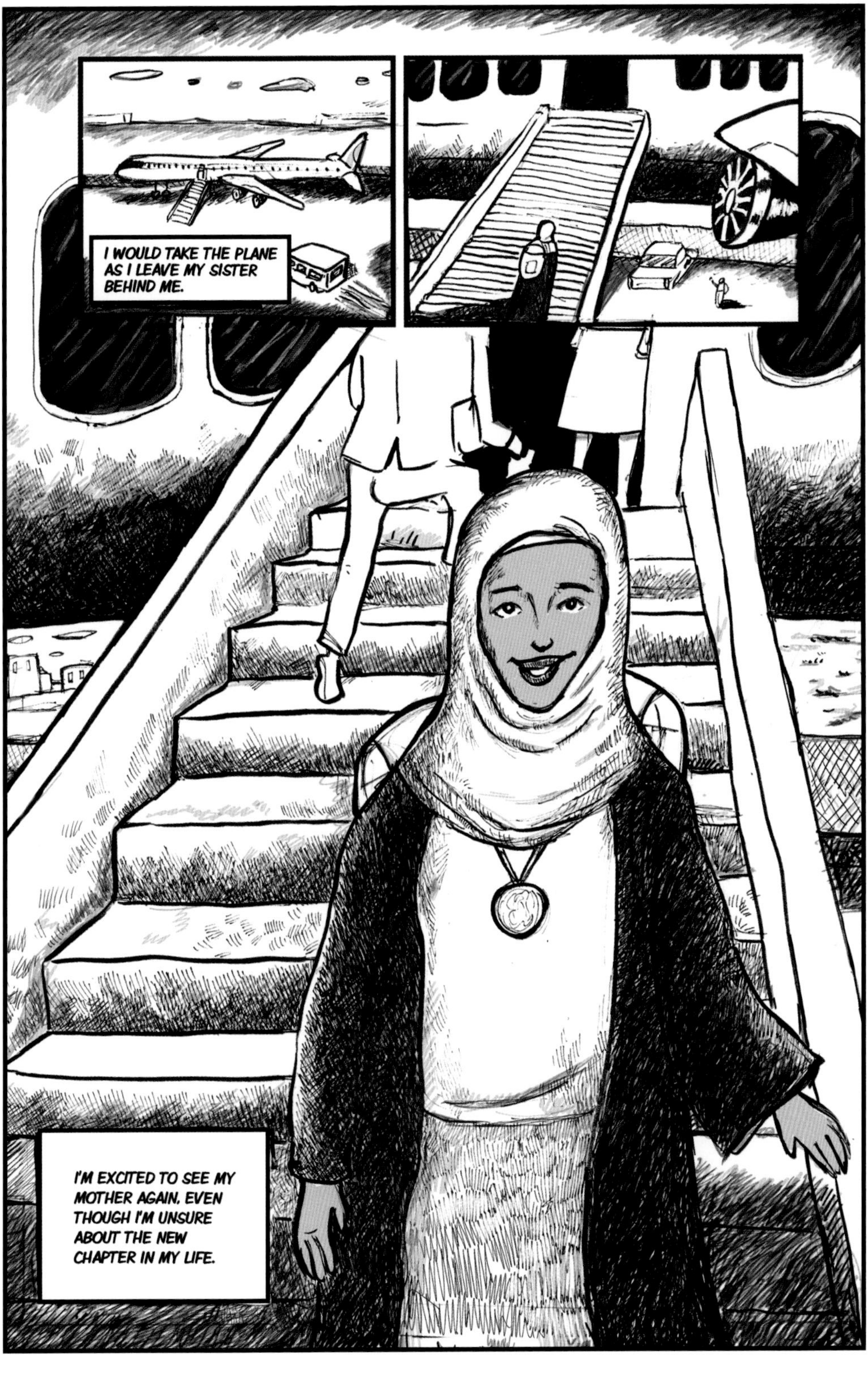
I WOULD TAKE THE PLANE AS I LEAVE MY SISTER BEHIND ME.
I'M EXCITED TO SEE MY MOTHER AGAIN, EVEN THOUGH I'M UNSURE ABOUT THE NEW CHAPTER IN MY LIFE.

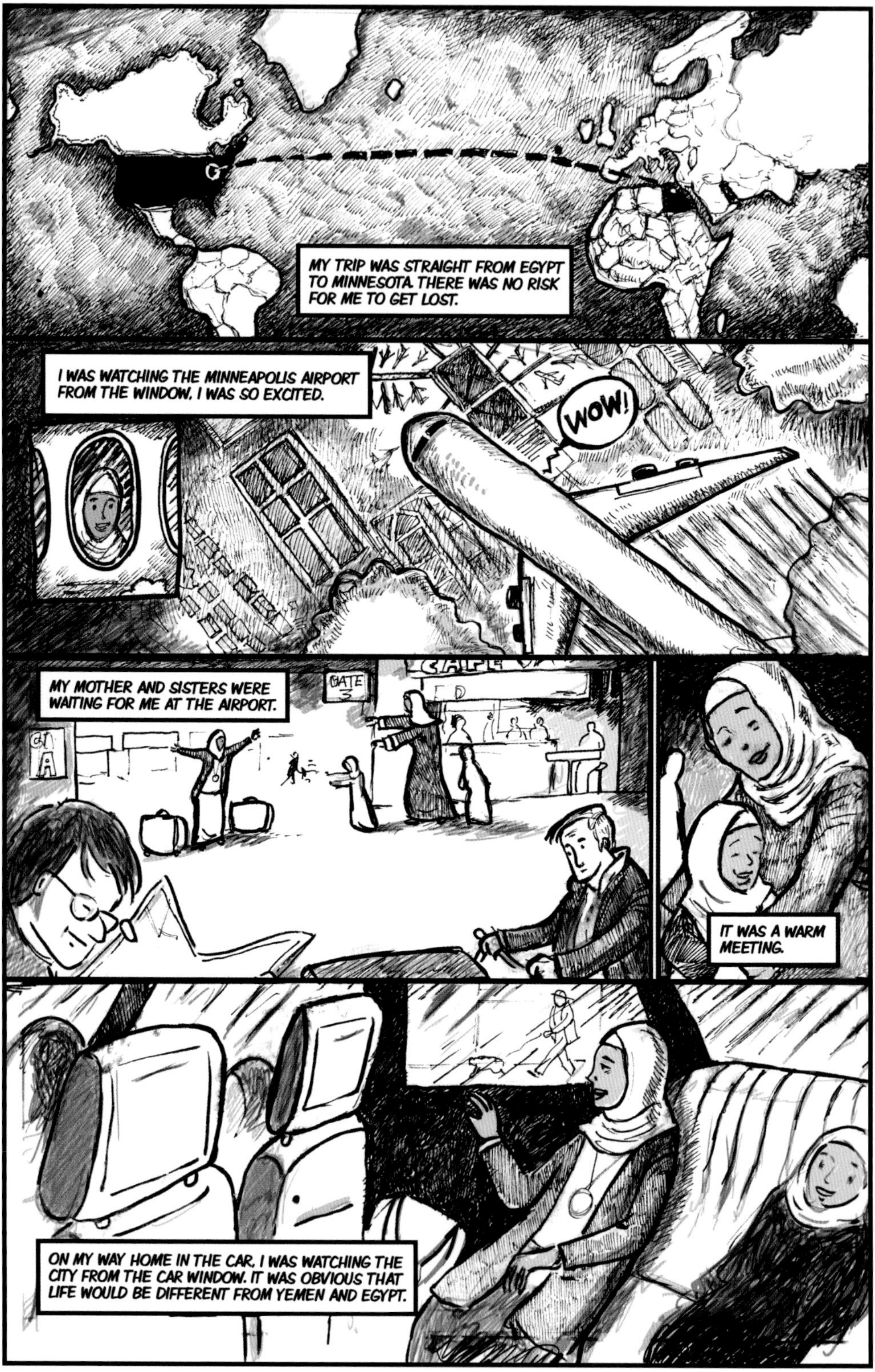
MY TRIP WAS STRAIGHT FROM EGYPT TO MINNESOTA. THERE WAS NO RISK FOR ME TO GET LOST.
I WAS WATCHING THE MINNEAPOLIS AIRPORT FROM THE WINDOW. I WAS SO EXCITED.
WOW!
MY MOTHER AND SISTERS WERE WAITING FOR ME AT THE AIRPORT.
GATE 3
IT WAS A WARM MEETING.
ON MY WAY HOME IN THE CAR, I WAS WATCHING THE CITY FROM THE CAR WINDOW. IT WAS OBVIOUS THAT LIFE WOULD BE DIFFERENT FROM YEMEN AND EGYPT.

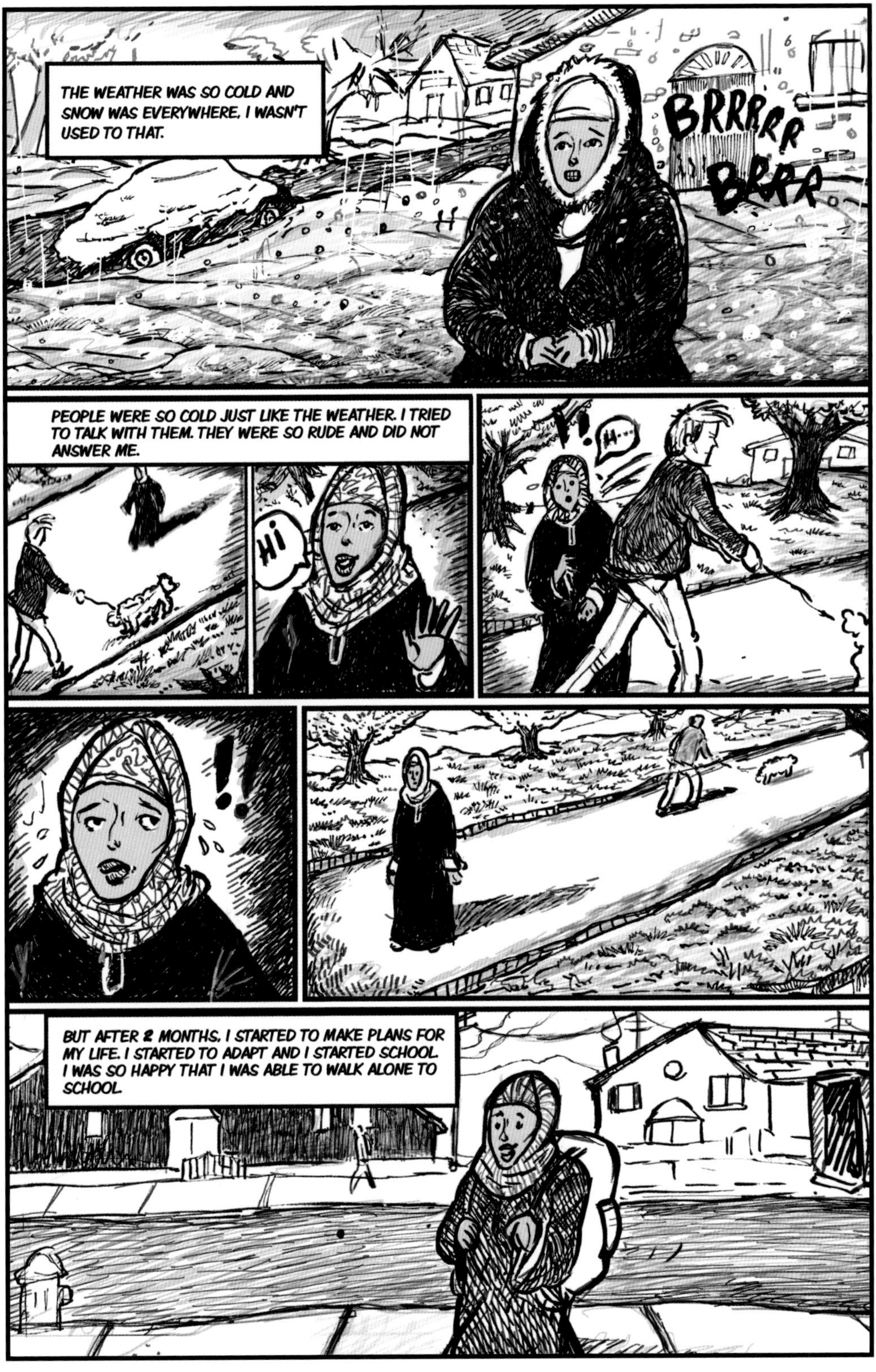
THE WEATHER WAS SO COLD AND SNOW WAS EVERYWHERE. I WASN'T USED TO THAT.
BRRRRR BRRR
PEOPLE WERE SO COLD JUST LIKE THE WEATHER. I TRIED TO TALK WITH THEM. THEY WERE SO RUDE AND DID NOT ANSWER ME.
HI
!
H...
!!
BUT AFTER 2 MONTHS, I STARTED TO MAKE PLANS FOR MY LIFE. I STARTED TO ADAPT AND I STARTED SCHOOL. I WAS SO HAPPY THAT I WAS ABLE TO WALK ALONE TO SCHOOL.

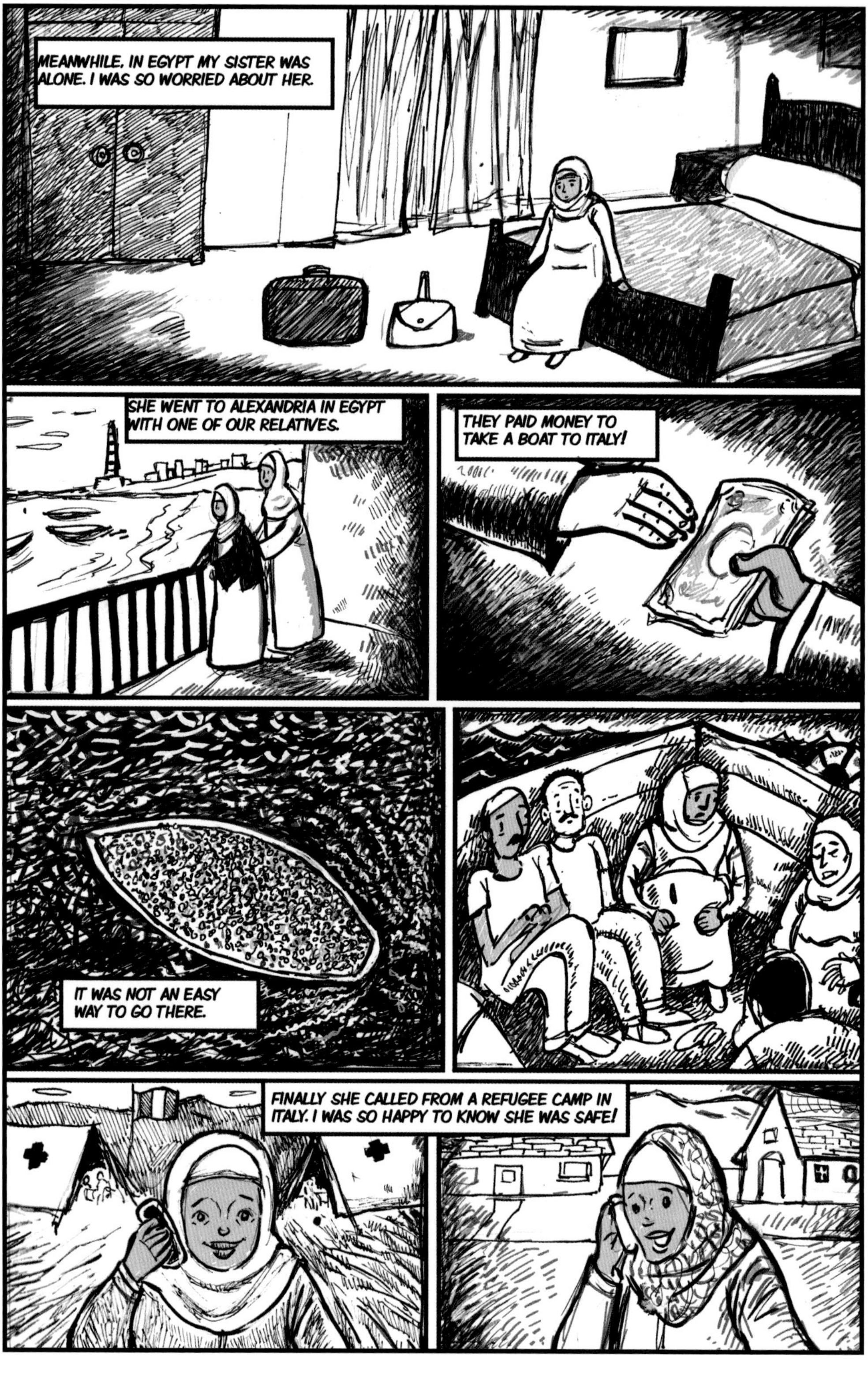
MEANWHILE, IN EGYPT MY SISTER WAS ALONE. I WAS SO WORRIED ABOUT HER.
SHE WENT TO ALEXANDRIA IN EGYPT WITH ONE OF OUR RELATIVES.
THEY PAID MONEY TO TAKE A BOAT TO ITALY!
IT WAS NOT AN EASY WAY TO GO THERE.
FINALLY SHE CALLED FROM A REFUGEE CAMP IN ITALY. I WAS SO HAPPY TO KNOW SHE WAS SAFE!

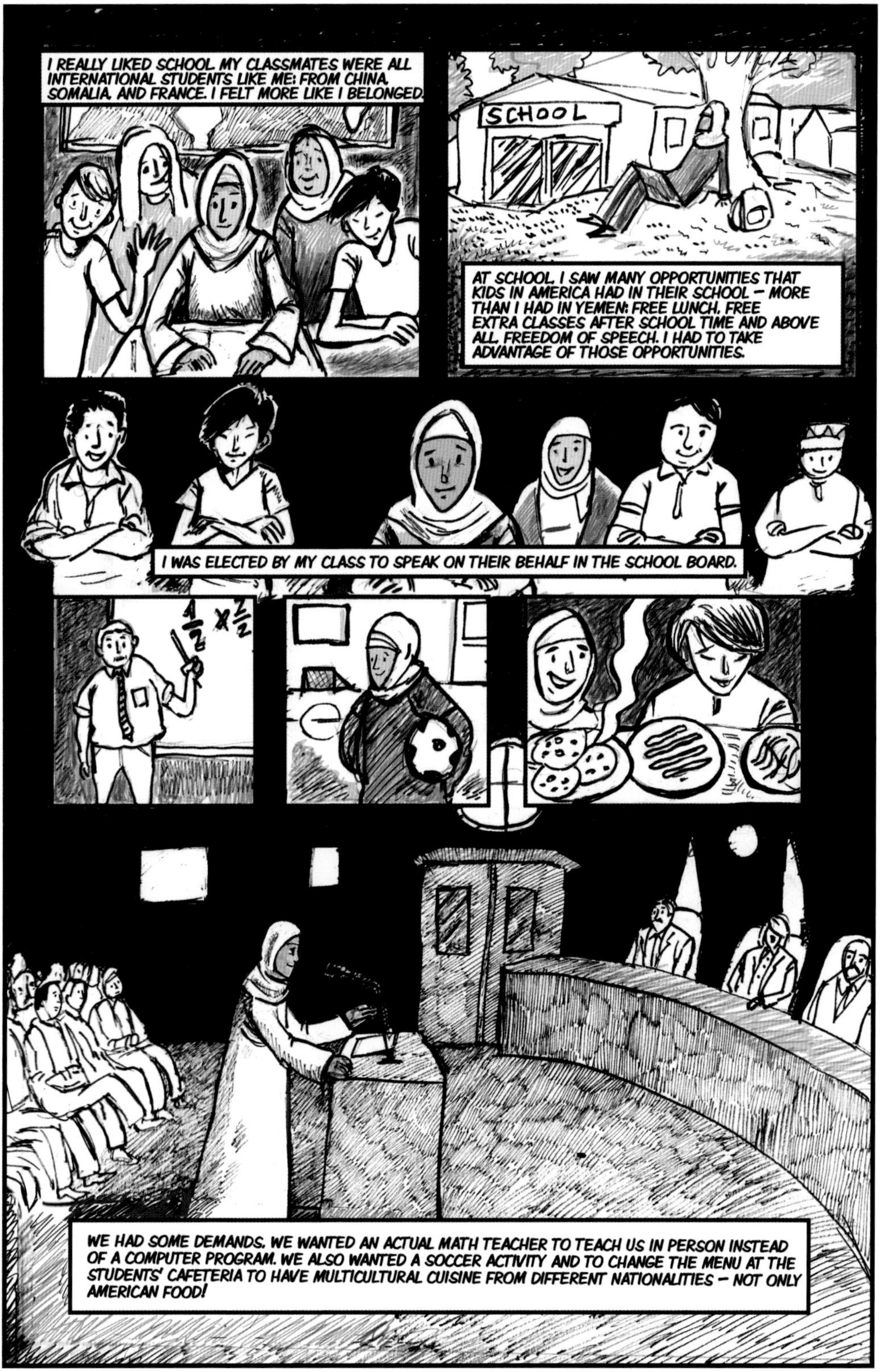
I REALLY LIKED SCHOOL. MY CLASSMATES WERE ALL INTERNATIONAL STUDENTS LIKE ME: FROM CHINA, SOMALIA, AND FRANCE. I FELT MORE LIKE I BELONGED.
SCHOOL
AT SCHOOL, I SAW MANY OPPORTUNITIES THAT KIDS IN AMERICA HAD IN THEIR SCHOOL – MORE THAN I HAD IN YEMEN: FREE LUNCH, FREE EXTRA CLASSES AFTER SCHOOL TIME AND ABOVE ALL, FREEDOM OF SPEECH. I HAD TO TAKE ADVANTAGE OF THOSE OPPORTUNITIES.
I WAS ELECTED BY MY CLASS TO SPEAK ON THEIR BEHALF IN THE SCHOOL BOARD.
WE HAD SOME DEMANDS. WE WANTED AN ACTUAL MATH TEACHER TO TEACH US IN PERSON INSTEAD OF A COMPUTER PROGRAM. WE ALSO WANTED A SOCCER ACTIVITY AND TO CHANGE THE MENU AT THE STUDENTS' CAFETERIA TO HAVE MULTICULTURAL CUISINE FROM DIFFERENT NATIONALITIES – NOT ONLY AMERICAN FOOD!

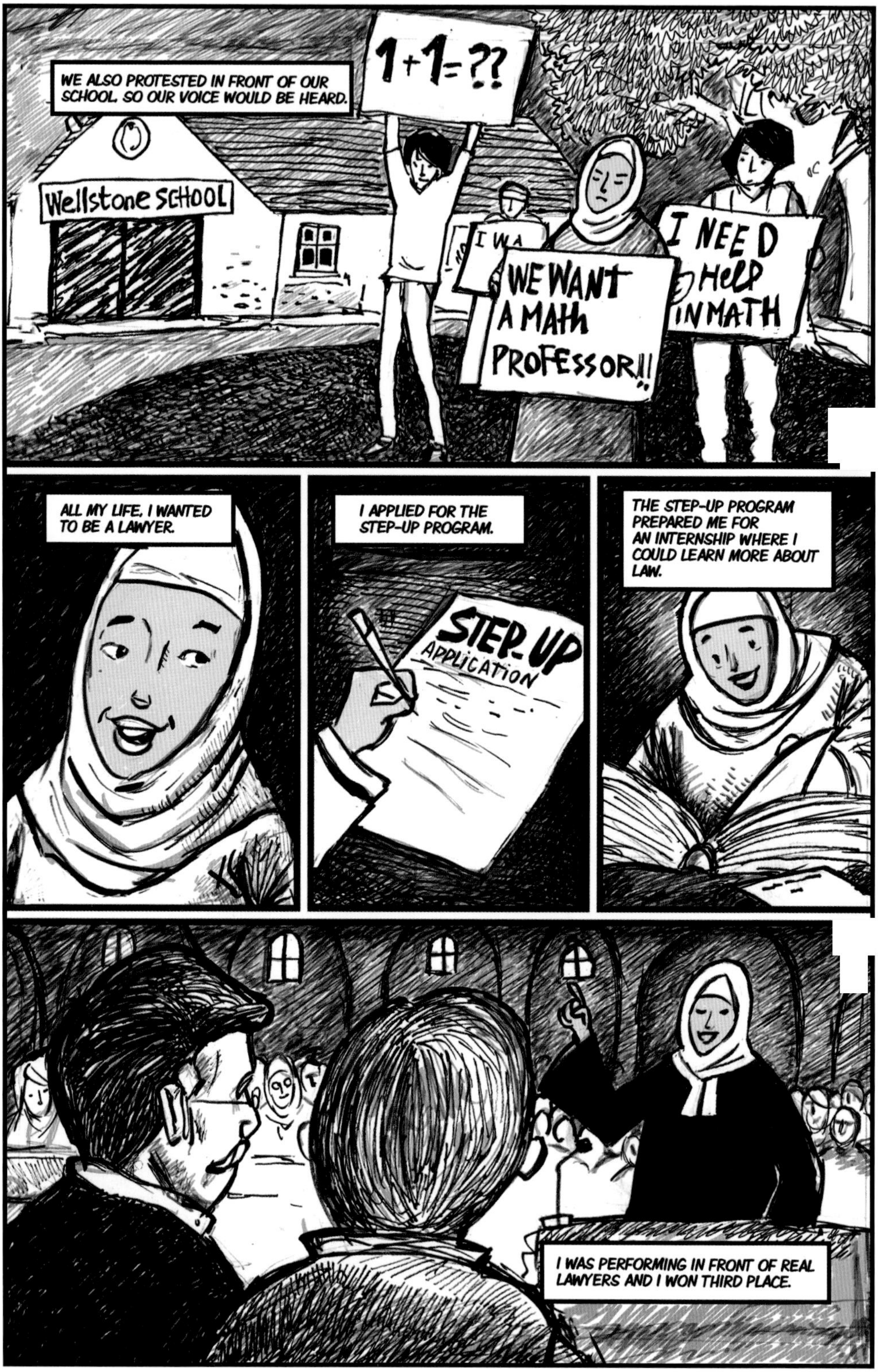
WE ALSO PROTESTED IN FRONT OF OUR SCHOOL, SO OUR VOICE WOULD BE HEARD.
1+1=??
Wellstone SCHOOL
I WA
WE WANT A MATH PROFESSOR!!
I NEED HELP IN MATH
ALL MY LIFE, I WANTED TO BE A LAWYER.
I APPLIED FOR THE STEP-UP PROGRAM.
STEP-UP APPLICATION
THE STEP-UP PROGRAM PREPARED ME FOR AN INTERNSHIP WHERE I COULD LEARN MORE ABOUT LAW.
I WAS PERFORMING IN FRONT OF REAL LAWYERS AND I WON THIRD PLACE.

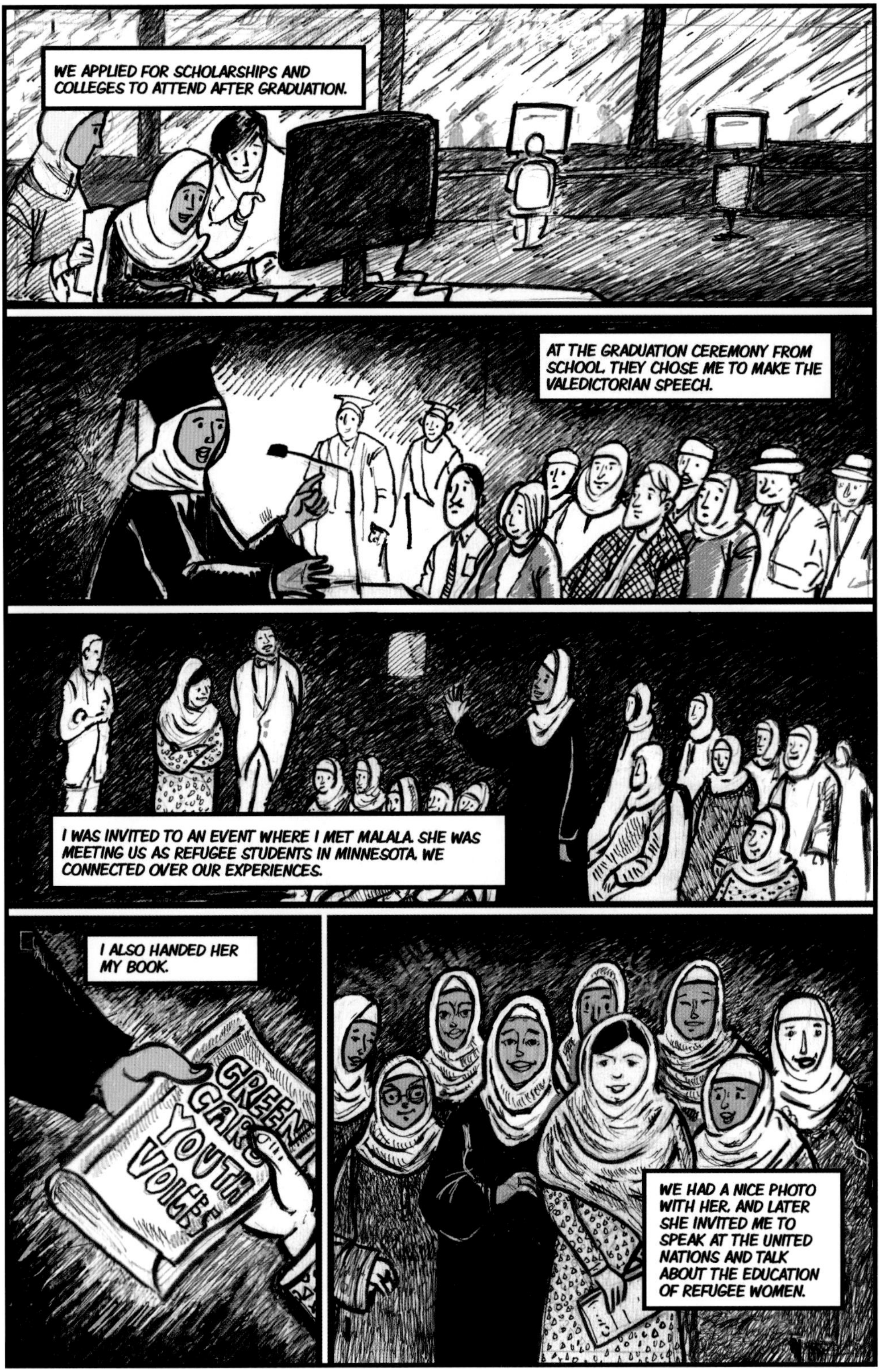
WE APPLIED FOR SCHOLARSHIPS AND COLLEGES TO ATTEND AFTER GRADUATION.
AT THE GRADUATION CEREMONY FROM SCHOOL, THEY CHOSE ME TO MAKE THE VALEDICTORIAN SPEECH.
I WAS INVITED TO AN EVENT WHERE I MET MALALA. SHE WAS MEETING US AS REFUGEE STUDENTS IN MINNESOTA. WE CONNECTED OVER OUR EXPERIENCES.
I ALSO HANDED HER MY BOOK.
GREEN CARD YOUTH VOICES
WE HAD A NICE PHOTO WITH HER, AND LATER SHE INVITED ME TO SPEAK AT THE UNITED NATIONS AND TALK ABOUT THE EDUCATION OF REFUGEE WOMEN.

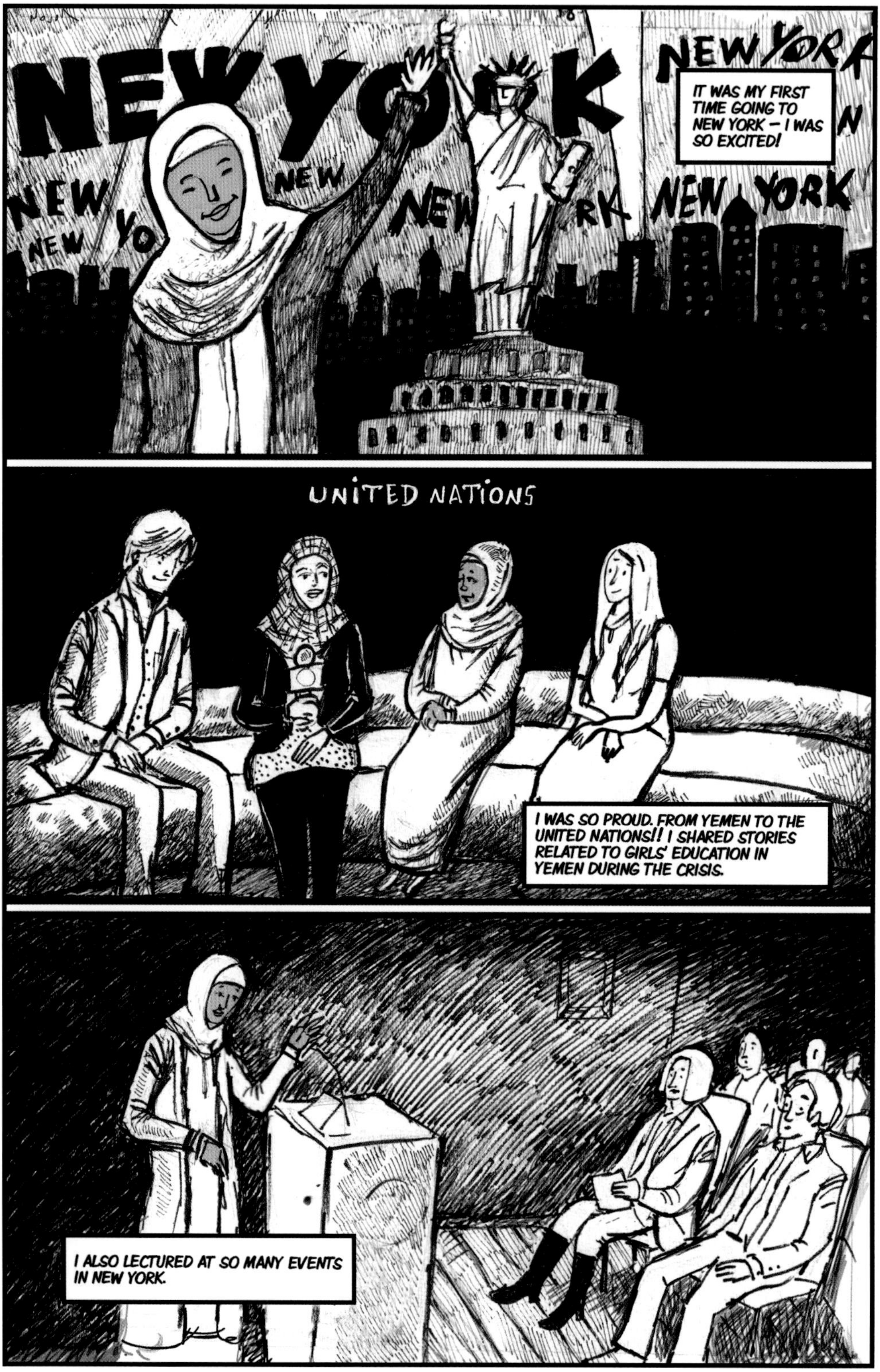
NEW YORK
NEW YORK
IT WAS MY FIRST TIME GOING TO NEW YORK — I WAS SO EXCITED!
UNITED NATIONS
I WAS SO PROUD. FROM YEMEN TO THE UNITED NATIONS!! I SHARED STORIES RELATED TO GIRLS' EDUCATION IN YEMEN DURING THE CRISIS.
I ALSO LECTURED AT SO MANY EVENTS IN NEW YORK.

I GOT ACCEPTED TO ST. CATHERINE UNIVERSITY. DURING MY JUNIOR YEAR, I WAS ELECTED STUDENT SENATE PRESIDENT. I MANAGED TO CHANGE A LOT OF THINGS. I SUCCEEDED IN CANCELING THE ACT TEST. IT IS NO LONGER REQUIRED FOR ESL STUDENTS TO PASS IN ORDER TO GO TO COLLEGE. I ALSO CREATED A SPACE FOR STUDENTS TO MEET IN ONE OF THE COLLEGE BUILDINGS — AND, OF COURSE, I CREATED A SOCCER TEAM AND ACTIVITY FOR THE STUDENTS.

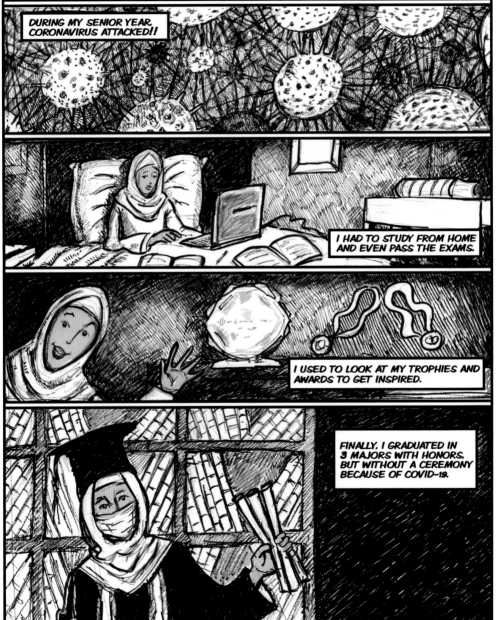

DURING MY SENIOR YEAR, CORONAVIRUS ATTACKED!!

I HAD TO STUDY FROM HOME AND EVEN PASS THE EXAMS.

I USED TO LOOK AT MY TROPHIES AND AWARDS TO GET INSPIRED.

FINALLY, I GRADUATED IN 3 MAJORS WITH HONORS. BUT WITHOUT A CEREMONY BECAUSE OF COVID-19.

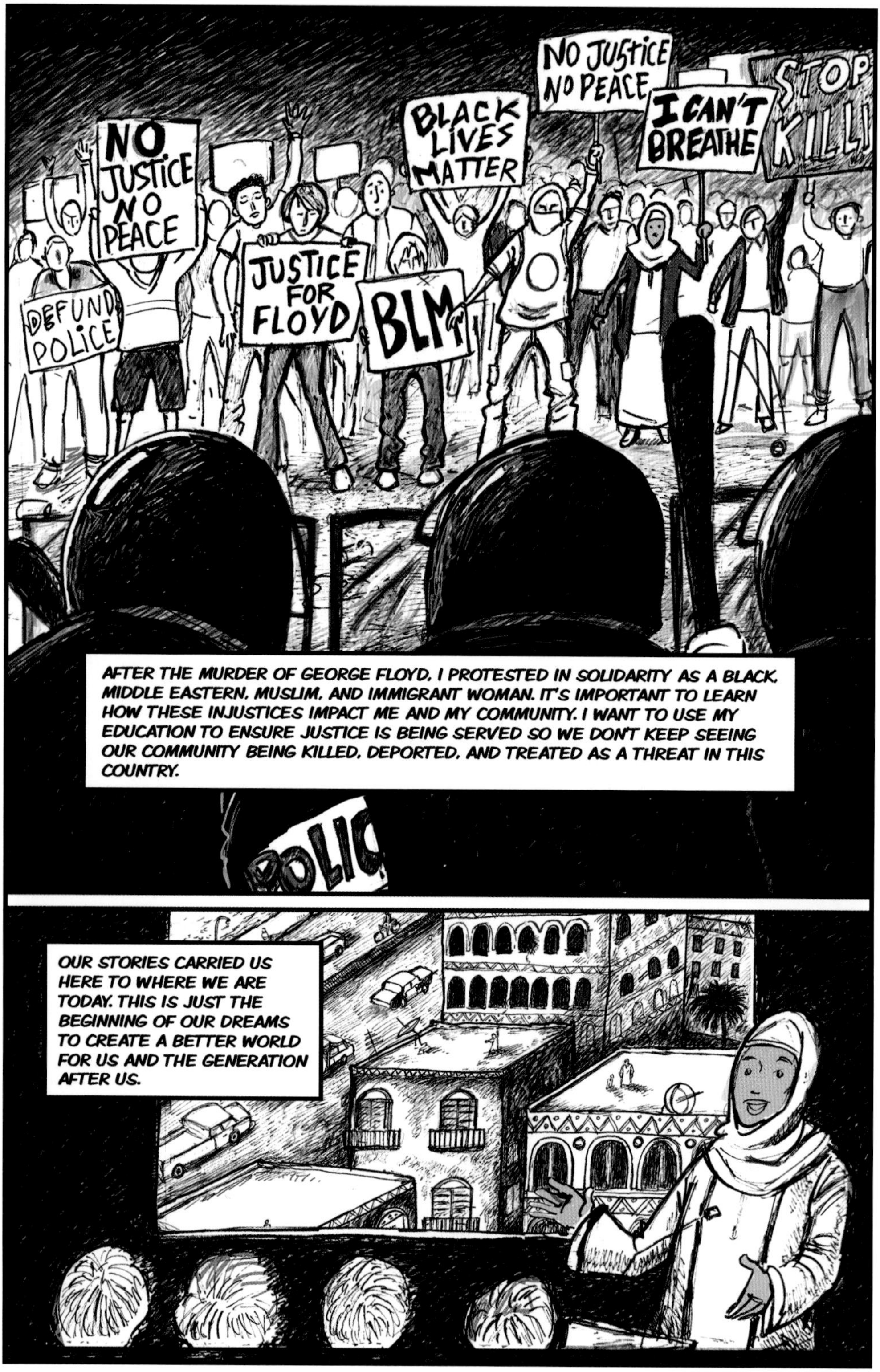
NO JUSTICE NO PEACE
BLACK LIVES MATTER
NO JUSTICE NO PEACE
I CAN'T BREATHE
STOP
DEFUND POLICE
JUSTICE FOR FLOYD
BLM
AFTER THE MURDER OF GEORGE FLOYD, I PROTESTED IN SOLIDARITY AS A BLACK, MIDDLE EASTERN, MUSLIM, AND IMMIGRANT WOMAN. IT'S IMPORTANT TO LEARN HOW THESE INJUSTICES IMPACT ME AND MY COMMUNITY. I WANT TO USE MY EDUCATION TO ENSURE JUSTICE IS BEING SERVED SO WE DON'T KEEP SEEING OUR COMMUNITY BEING KILLED, DEPORTED, AND TREATED AS A THREAT IN THIS COUNTRY.
OUR STORIES CARRIED US HERE TO WHERE WE ARE TODAY. THIS IS JUST THE BEGINNING OF OUR DREAMS TO CREATE A BETTER WORLD FOR US AND THE GENERATION AFTER US.

GLOSSARY

ACT: The ACT is a standardized test used for college admissions in the United States. It is currently administered by ACT, a nonprofit organization of the same name.

DV (Diversity Visa): The Diversity Immigrant Visa Program (DV Program) makes up to fifty thousand immigrant visas available annually, drawn from a random selection among all entries to individuals who are from countries with low rates of immigration to the United States. The DV Program is administered by the US Department of State (DOS). Commonly called the Green Card Lottery, it is a United States congressionally mandated lottery program for receiving a United States Permanent Resident Card (also referred to as a "green card").

Green Card: A commonly used name for a Lawful Permanent Resident Card. Generally denotes that the person carrying it has Lawful Permanent Resident status.

Green Card Lottery: A drawing of chance that selects people to receive diversity visas for the US.

School board: The board of directors or board of trustees of a school, local school district or equivalent. The elected council determines the educational policy in a small regional area, such as a city, county, state, or province.

STEP-UP: A nationally recognized youth employment model that trains and matches Minneapolis youth ages fourteen to twenty-one with paid summer internships.

The Arab Spring: A series of anti-government protests, uprisings, and armed rebellions that spread across much of the Arab world in the early 2010s. It began in response to oppressive regimes and a low standard of living, starting with protests in Tunisia, Libya, Egypt, Yemen, Syria, and Bahrain, to name a few.

Tuberculosis (TB): A disease caused by bacteria called Mycobacterium tuberculosis. The bacteria usually attack the lungs, but they can also damage other parts of the body. TB spreads through the air when a person with TB of the lungs or throat coughs, sneezes, or talks.

Valedictorian: An academic title of success used for the student who delivers the closing or farewell statement at a graduation ceremony (called a valediction). The valedictorian is traditionally the student with the highest academic standing among their graduating class.

AZIZ KAMAL

Born: Sittwe, Myanmar
Current: Milwaukee, Wisconsin

Aziz Kamal is Rohingya and is the fifth son in his family. Aziz is a sophomore at the University of Wisconsin-Milwaukee studying business accounting. His long-term goal is to get a master's degree in business and start his own company. In his free time, Aziz enjoys helping people at the Rohingya American Society Center. Aziz is happy being in the U.S. because he couldn't attend or complete middle school in Myanmar and Malaysia. His hobby is learning new things, traveling, and meeting different people.

www.greencardvoices.org/speakers/aziz-kamal

SUNSHINE GAO

Born: China
Current: Minneapolis, Minnesota

sunshine gao was born in China and raised in Indiana and Kentucky. Once, they studied moral philosophy and ecology; cooked noodles; and sold produce. Now, they draw stories about home—in all its forms, with all its complications. In spite of everything, they believe the world can be made a beautiful place.

www.sunshine-gao.com

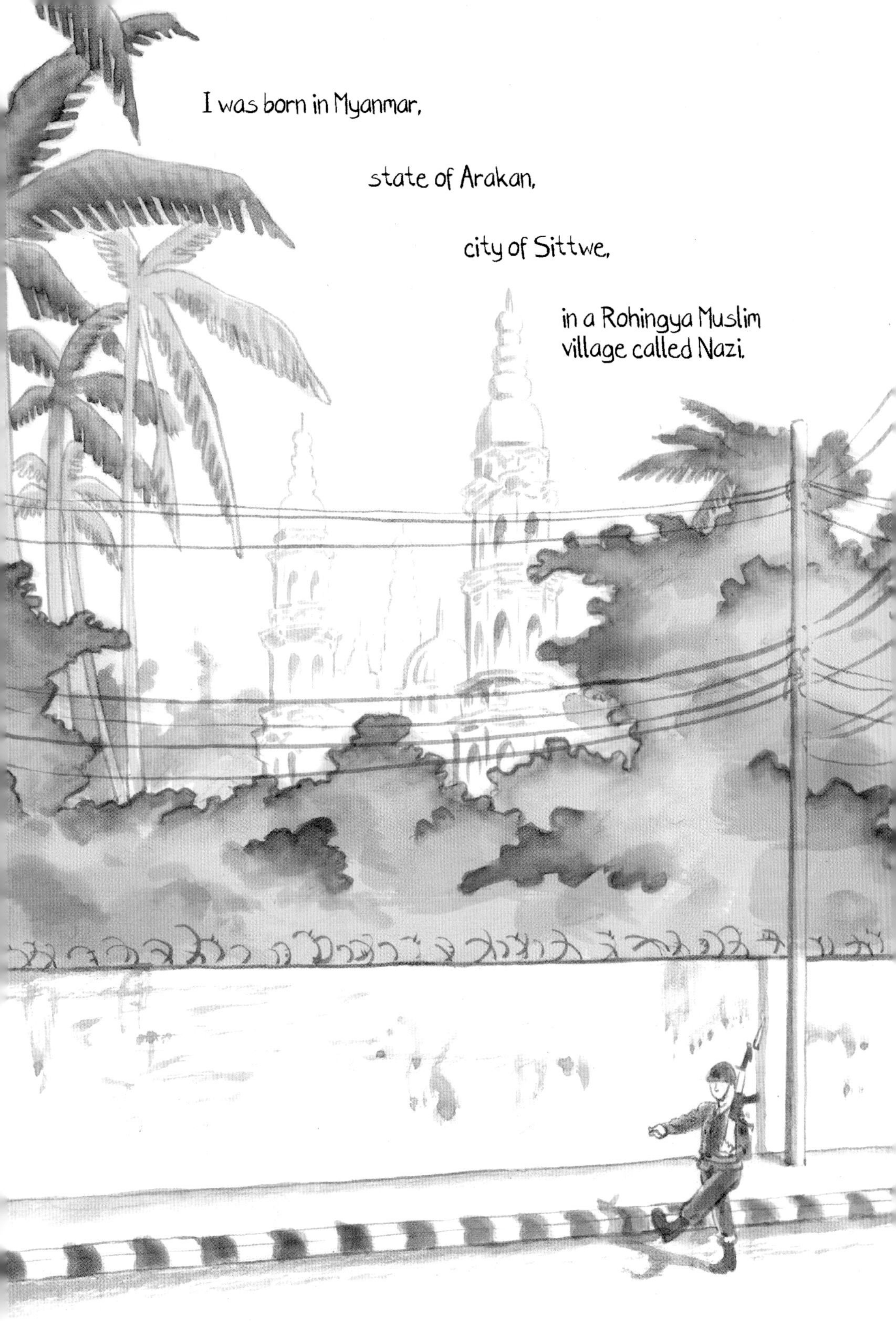
I was born in Myanmar,
state of Arakan,
city of Sittwe,
in a Rohingya Muslim village called Nazi.

My family has six brothers, one sister. I am the fifth brother.

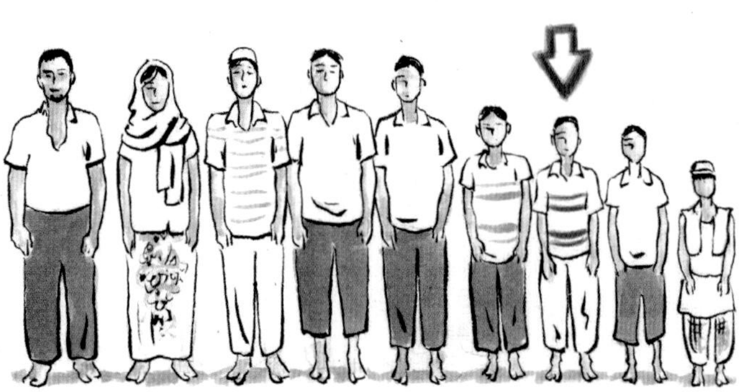

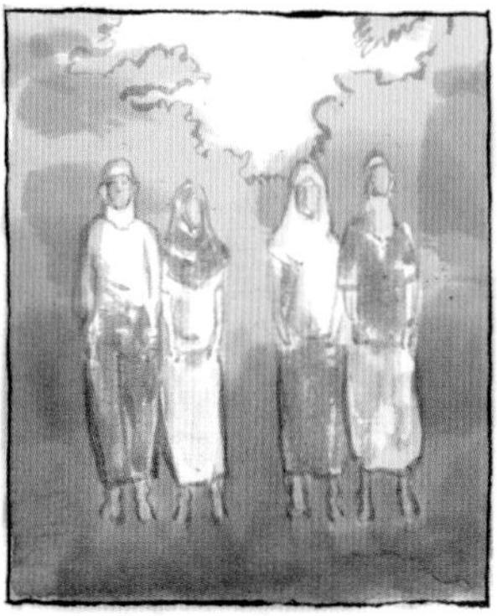

Our grandparents lived in the countryside outside Sittwe. But we were not allowed to visit them.

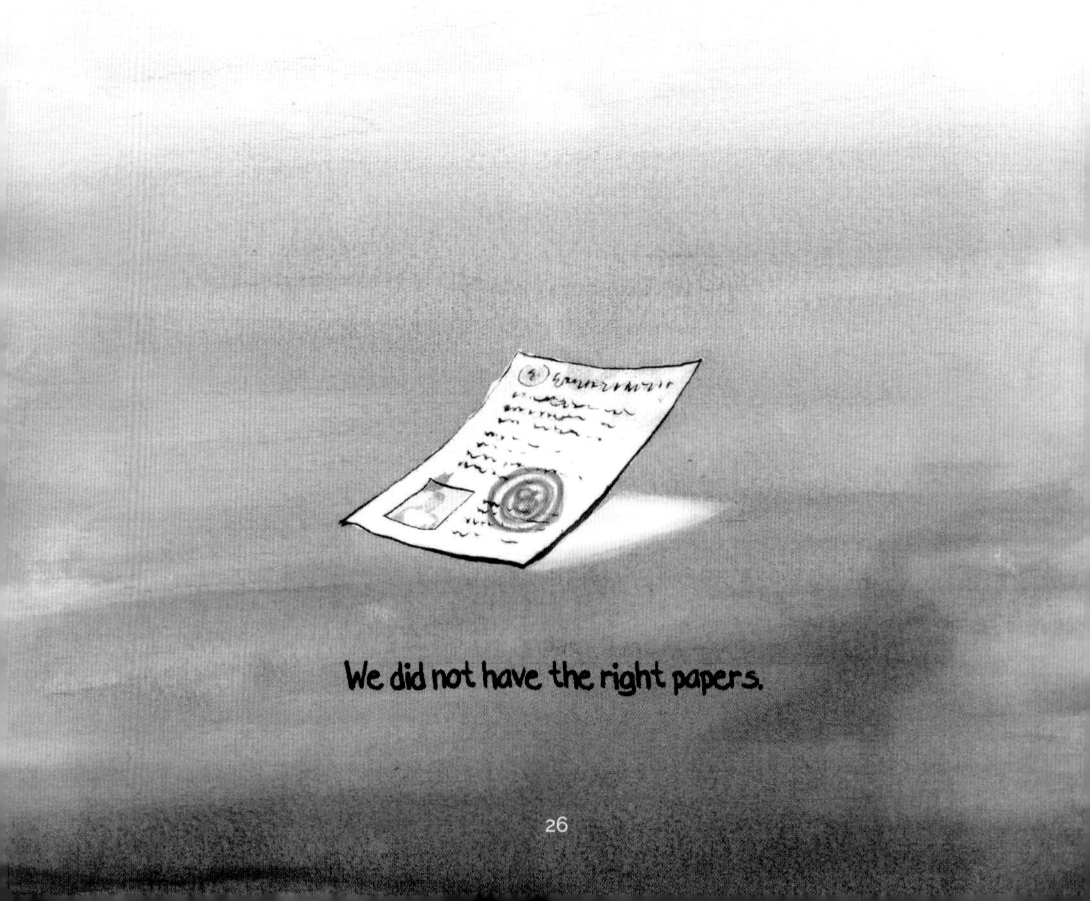
We did not have the right papers.

Muslims and Buddhists (and others) lived together peacefully in Myanmar before. But for many years now, it is bad.

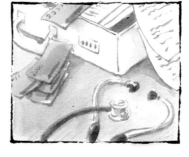

The Burmese government passed a law in 1982 that did not allow Rohingya Muslims to be citizens.

We could not travel in Myanmar without documents.

We could not become doctors or businessmen.

We could not marry if we did not get permission from the government.

We could not vote.

When I was five years old, I first went to school, but I could not finish middle school.

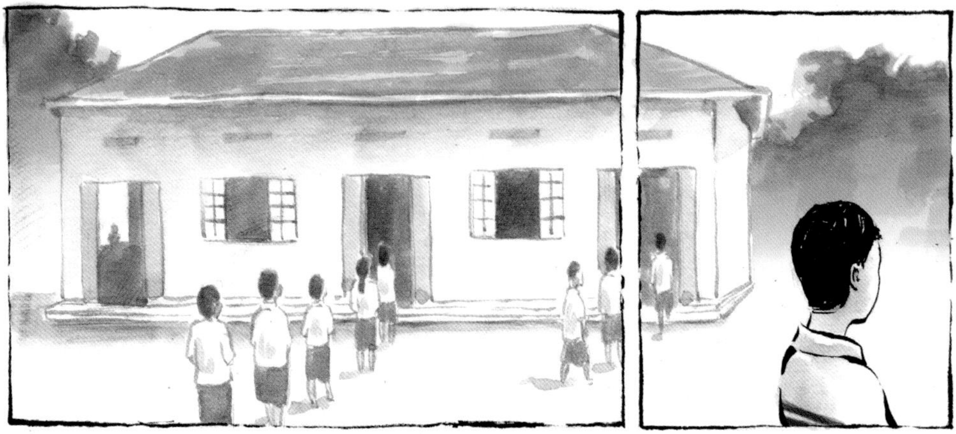

Buddhists could go to school for free. But Rohingya had to pay a lot of money to go to school, and that's why I left.

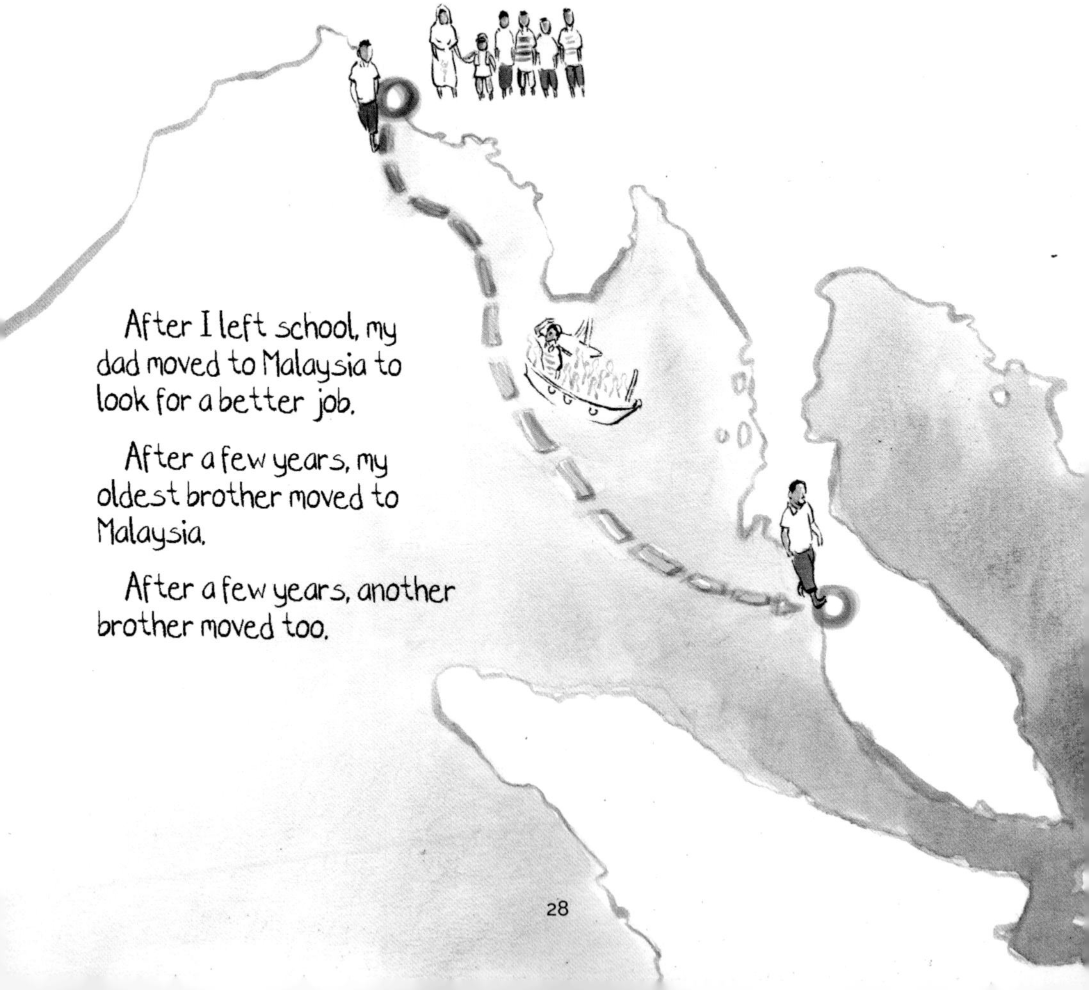

After I left school, my dad moved to Malaysia to look for a better job.

After a few years, my oldest brother moved to Malaysia.

After a few years, another brother moved too.

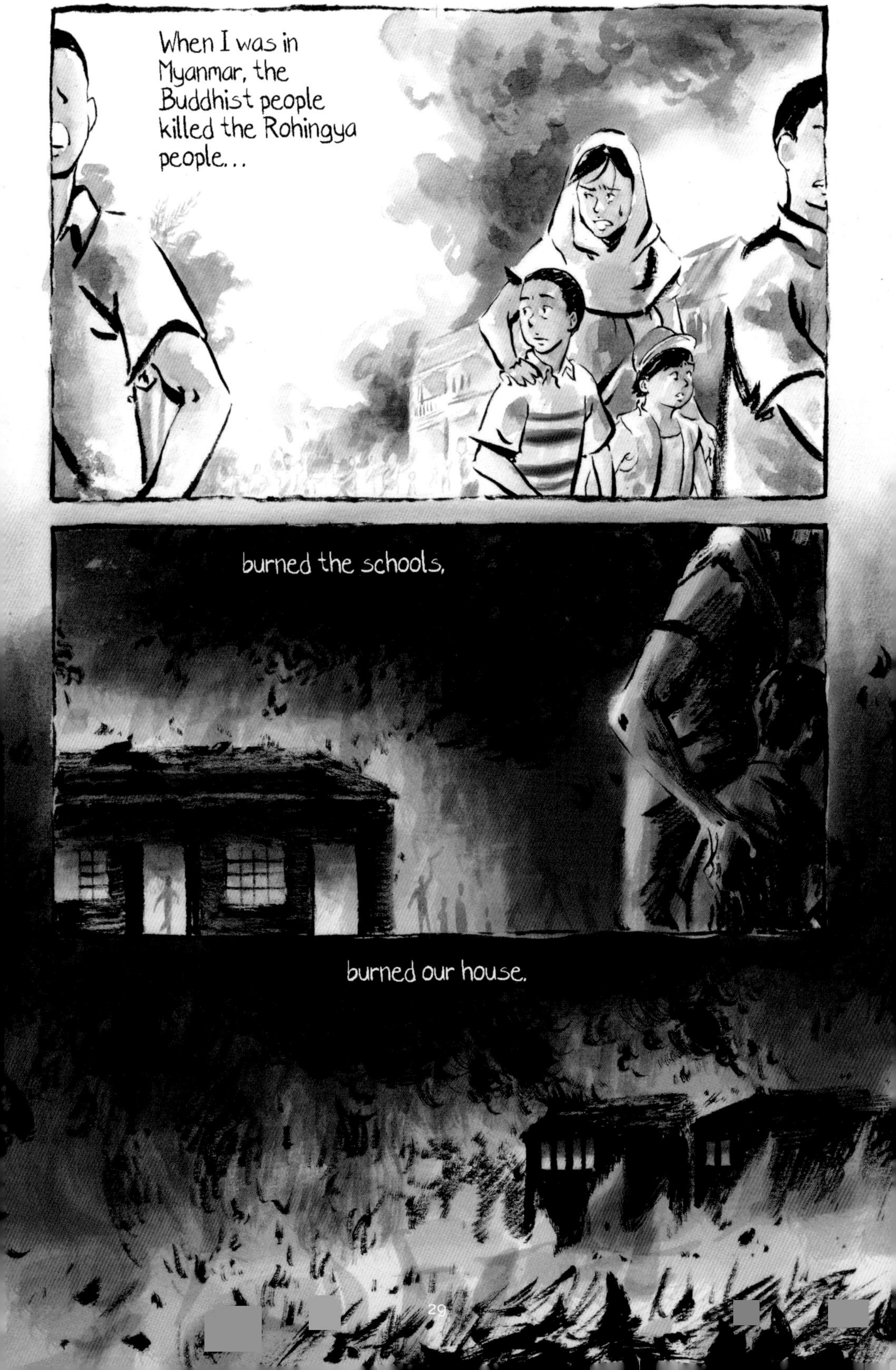
When I was in Myanmar, the Buddhist people killed the Rohingya people...
burned the schools,
burned our house.

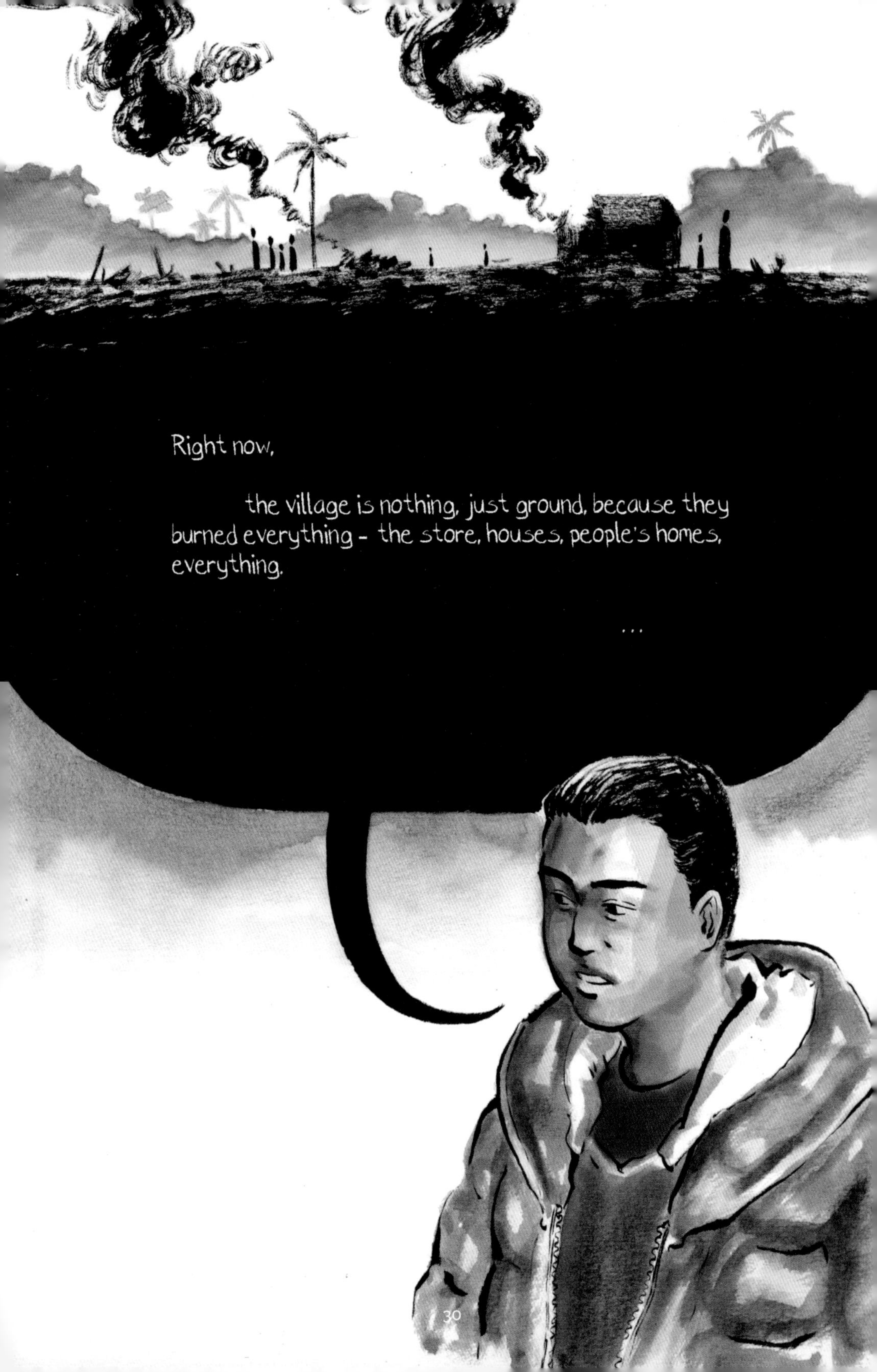
Right now,
the village is nothing, just ground, because they burned everything - the store, houses, people's homes, everything.
...

After that, we lived in camps.

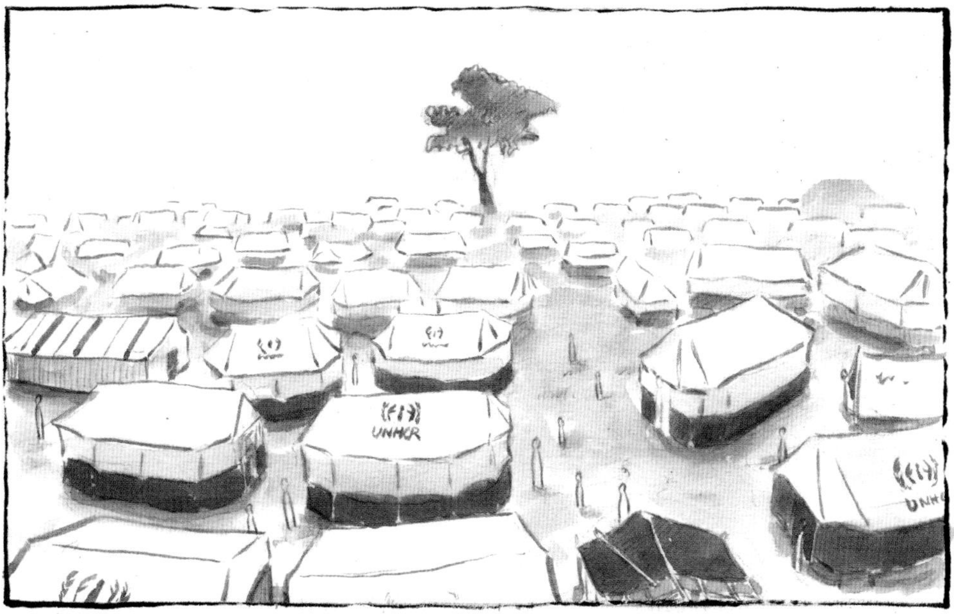
UNHCR
UNHC

The camps were from the United Nations. The United Nations gave each family one tent, and so my family lived in one.

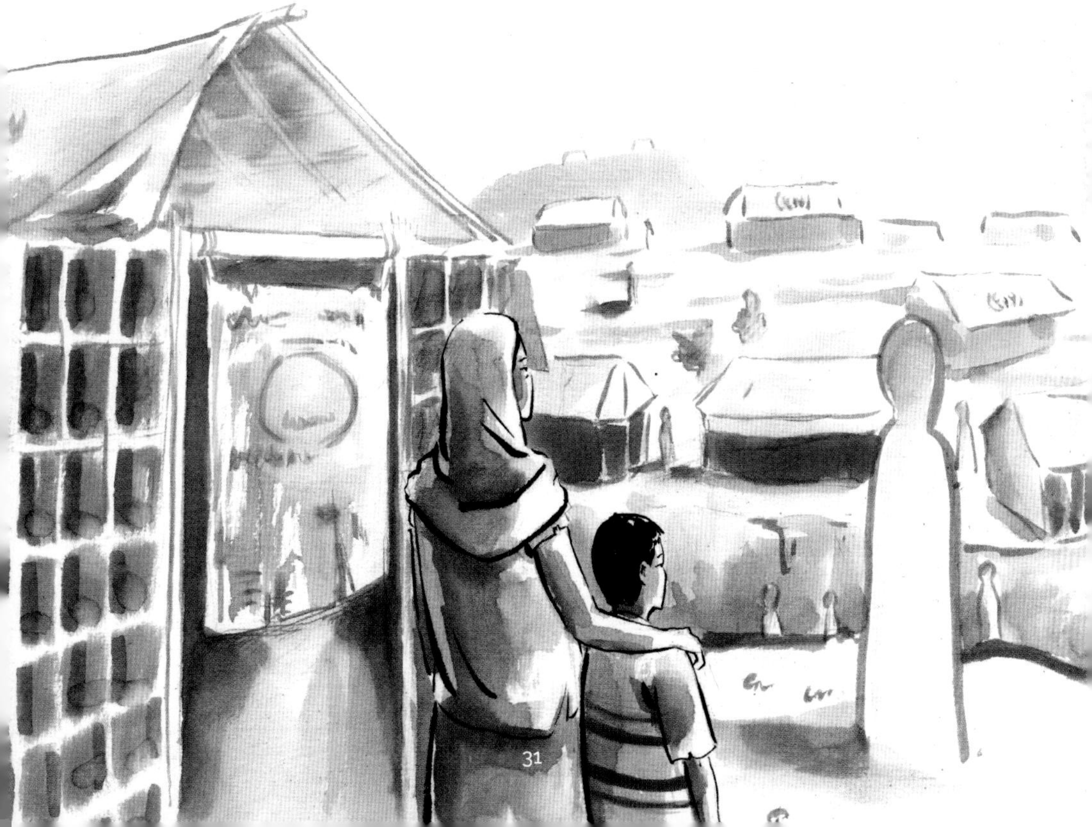

A lot of people died when we lived in the camps. There was not enough food or water. There were diseases.

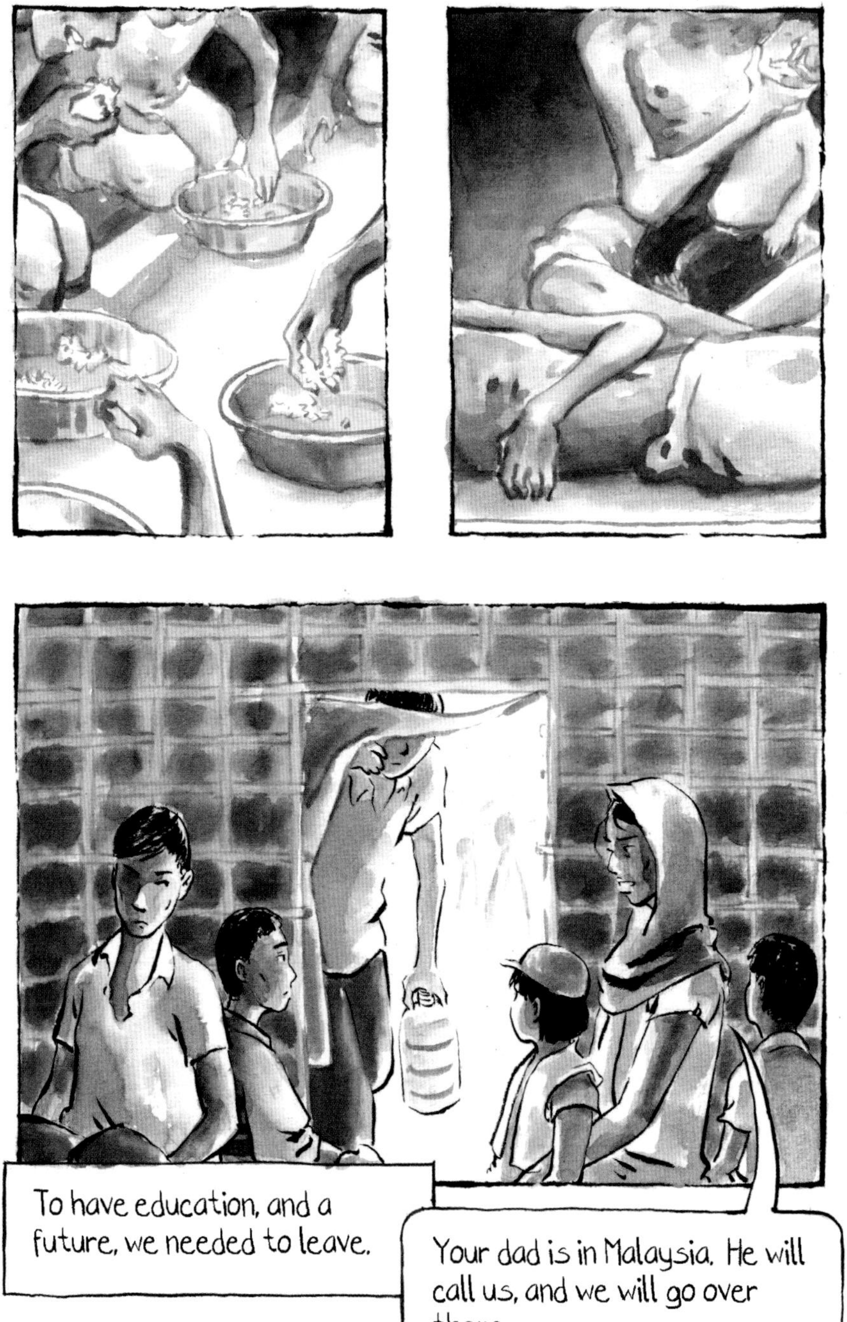
To have education, and a future, we needed to leave.
Your dad is in Malaysia. He will call us, and we will go over there.

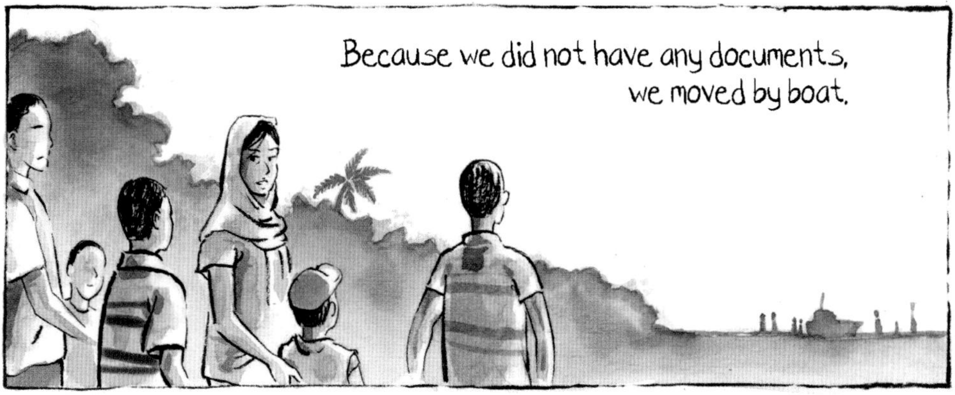
Because we did not have any documents,
we moved by boat.

When we left from Sittwe, my mom talked to the smugglers and the smugglers said only our family will go on the boat.

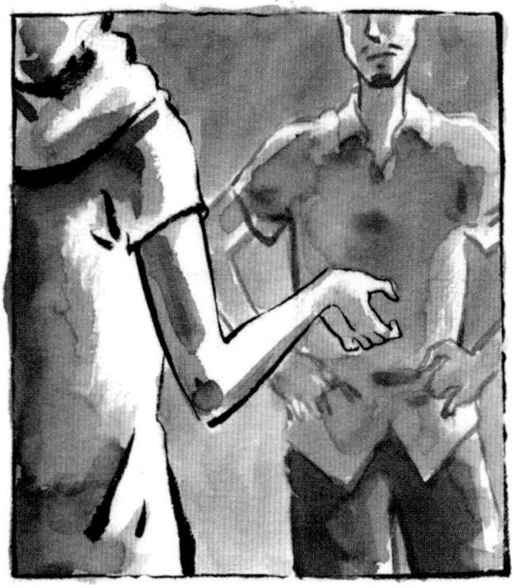

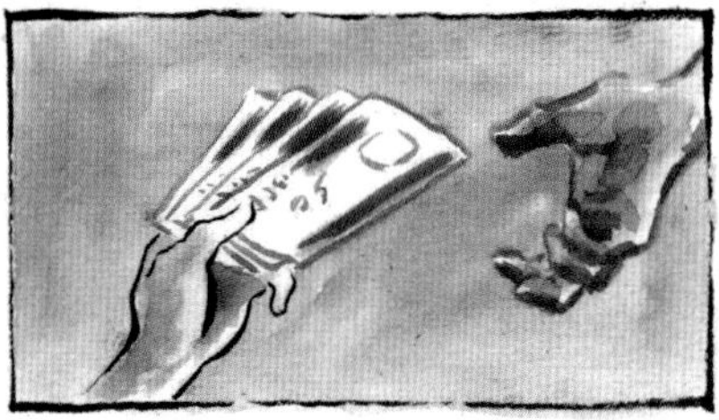

After a few days, my mom gave money to the smugglers.

And when we got to the boat, we saw a lot of people.

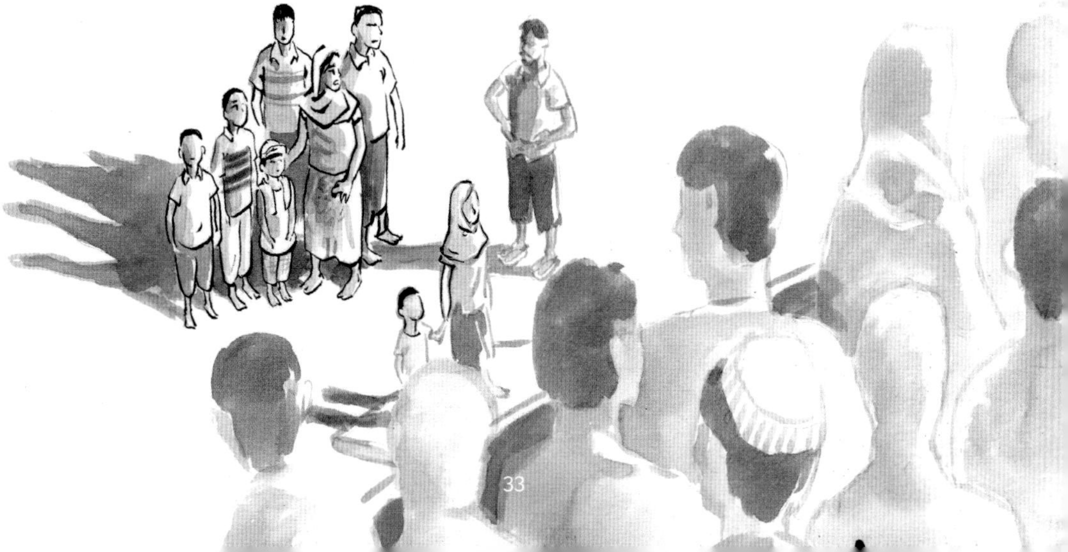

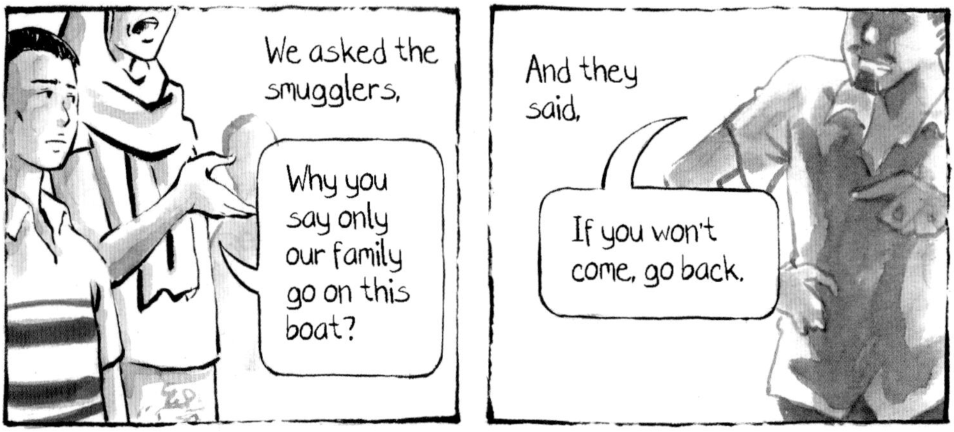
We asked the smugglers,
Why you say only our family go on this boat?
And they said,
If you won't come, go back.

But if we go back, my mom will lose our money, because the smugglers would not give it back.

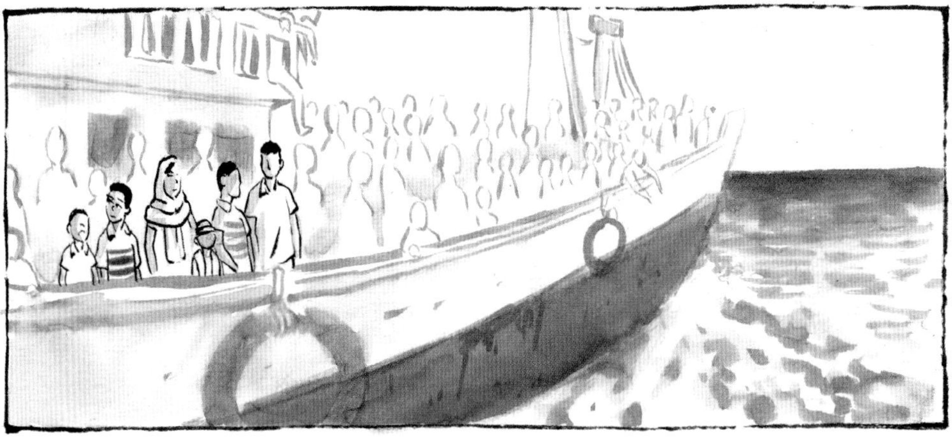

That's why we got in the boat. And there was not enough food for one month's journey in the boat. A lot of people died.

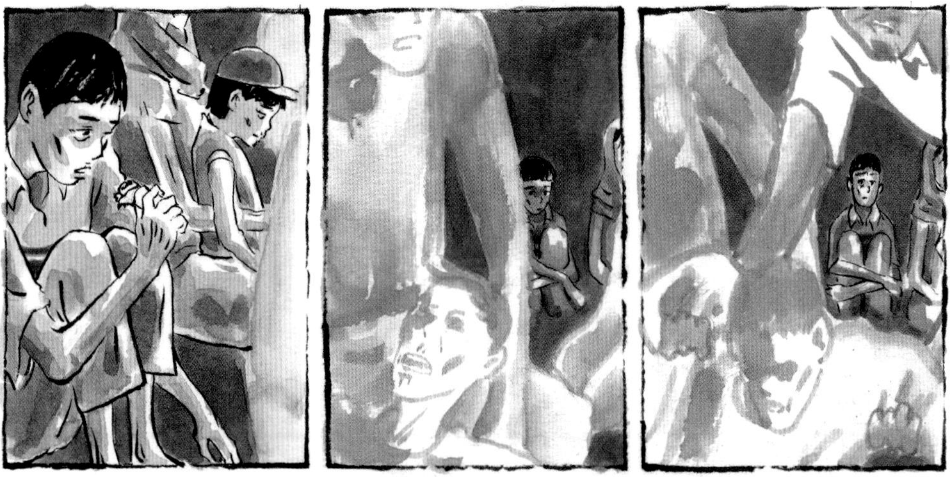

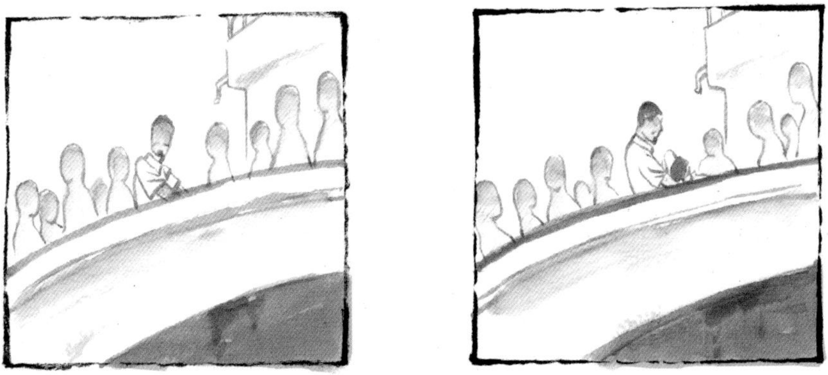

The smuggler threw them in the ocean.

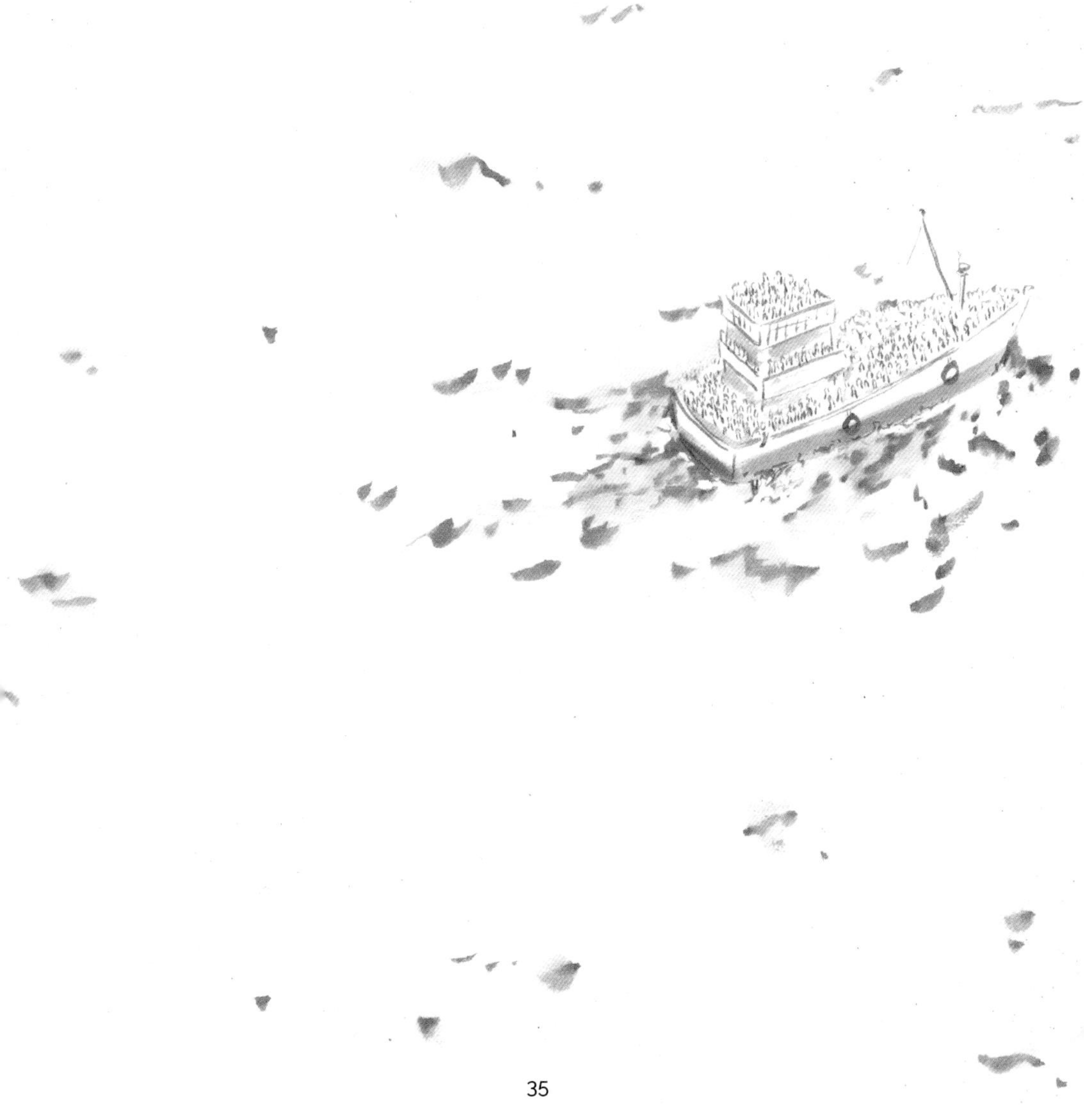

When we got to Malaysia, the smugglers kept us to one room. We could not hear anyone, see anyone, after that.

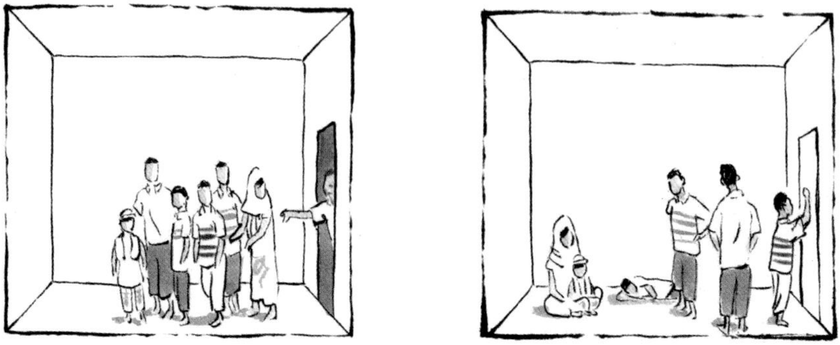

My dad and my two brothers already moved to the United States. The smugglers asked for more money, so my dad contacted them.

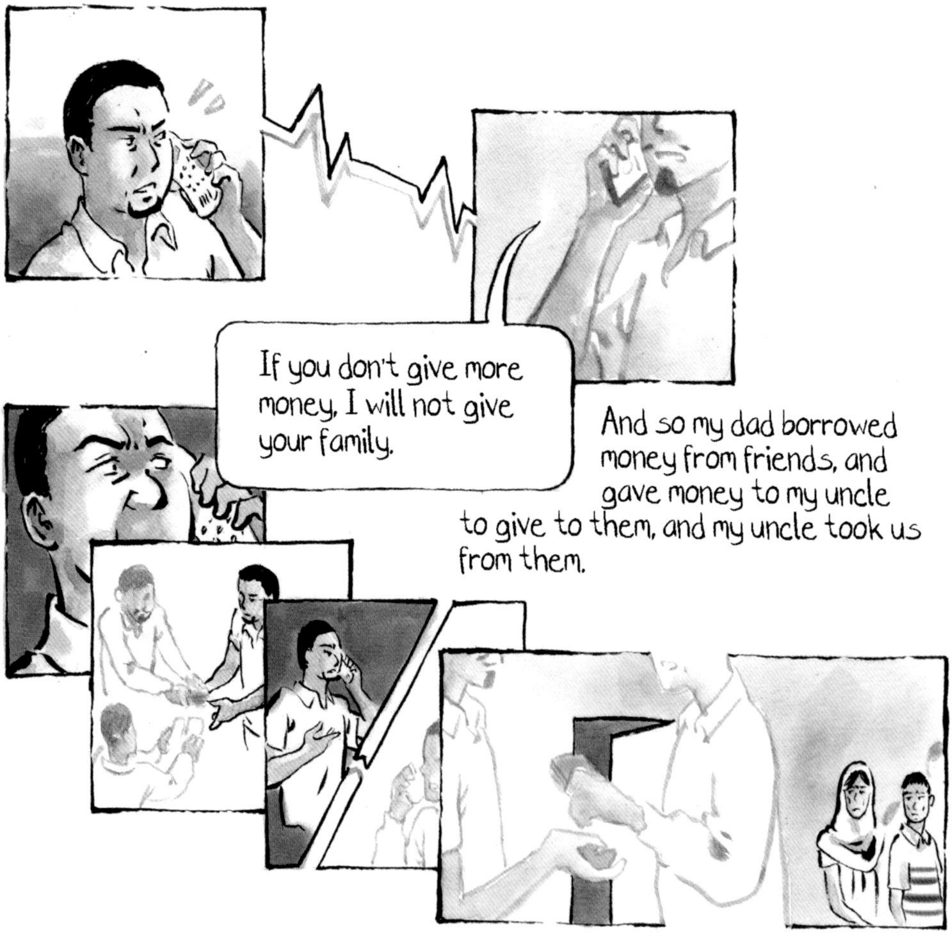
If you don't give more money, I will not give your family.
And so my dad borrowed money from friends, and gave money to my uncle to give to them, and my uncle took us from them.

We were in a lot of trouble in Malaysia, because we did not know anyone and we did not speak the language.

I could not go to school. Refugees could not go to school in Malaysia. We had no documents. We could not be citizens.

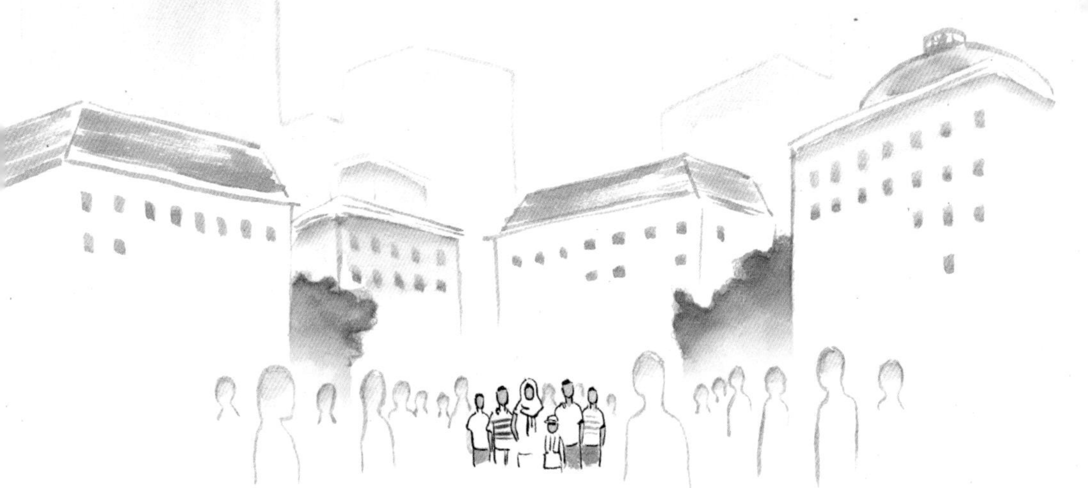

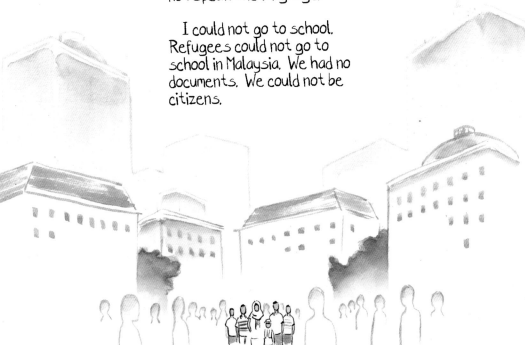

My uncle was working the whole day. He could not help us much. I was trying to work, but there are not many jobs refugees are allowed to work, and they pay us so little, and so I worked hard a lot of the time.

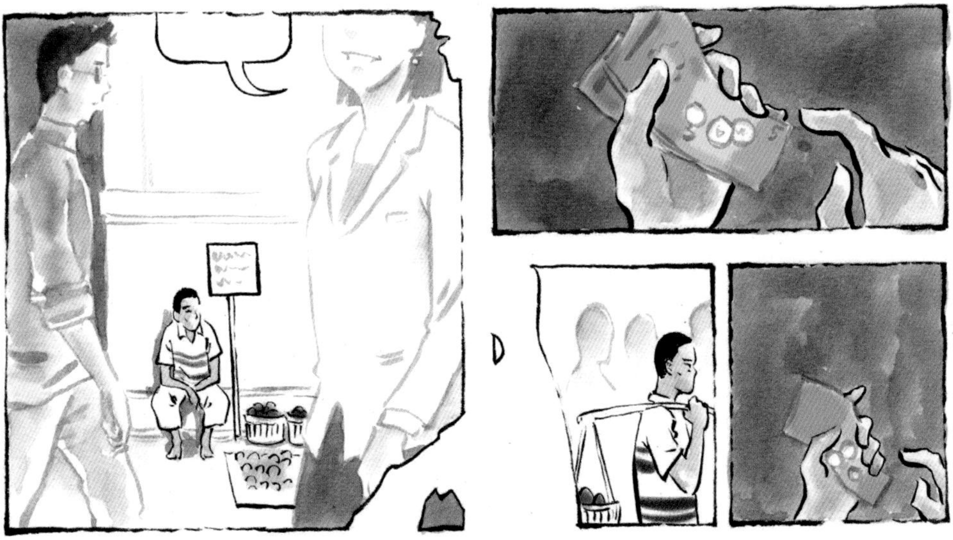

After that, my dad and my brothers were here trying to get us to the United States.

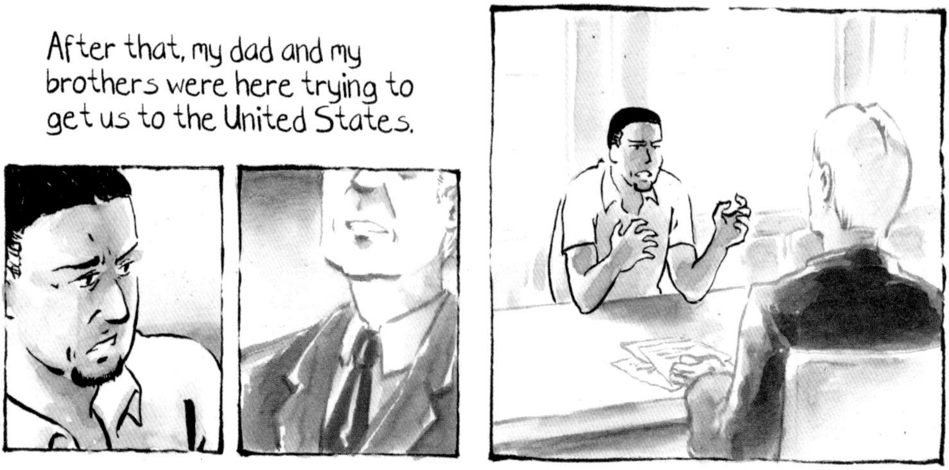

They tried and went to the refugee resettlement office to tell them about us.

We also went as much as we can to the US embassy in Malaysia.

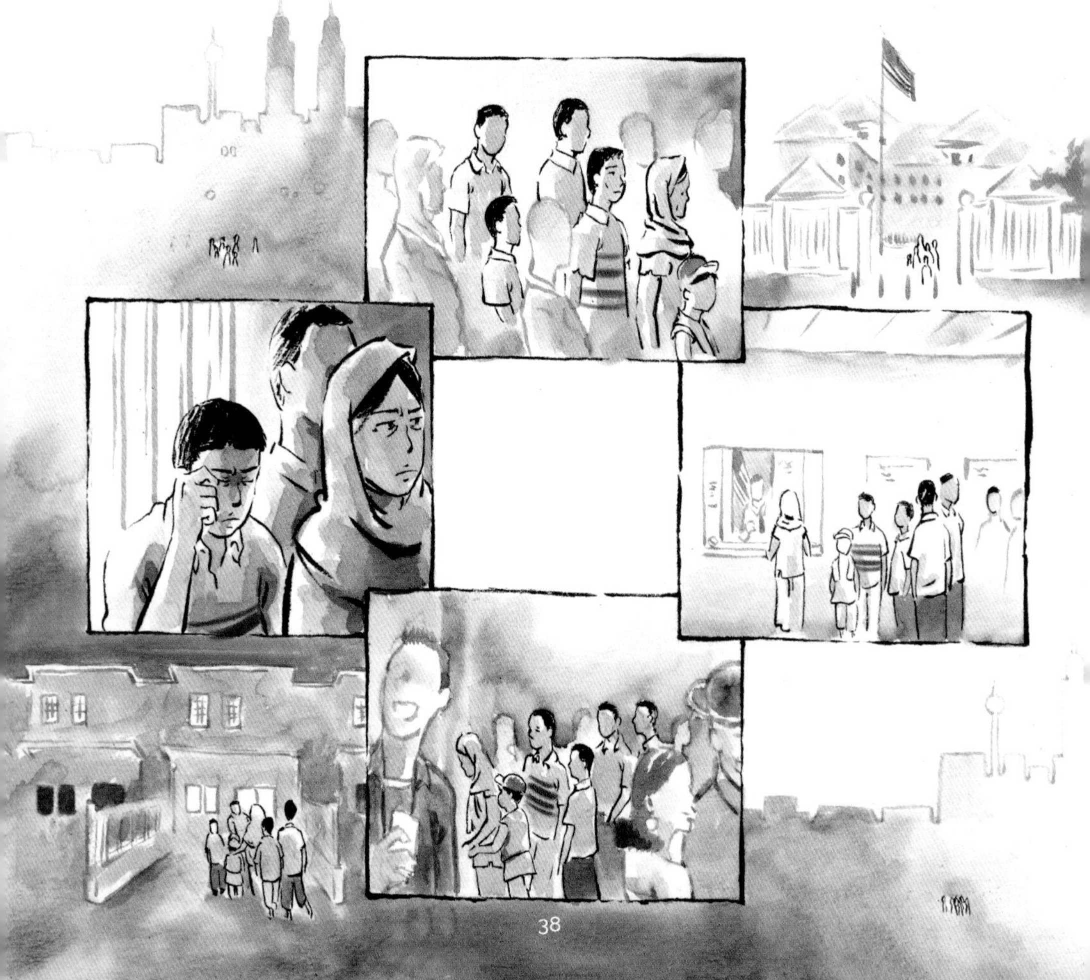

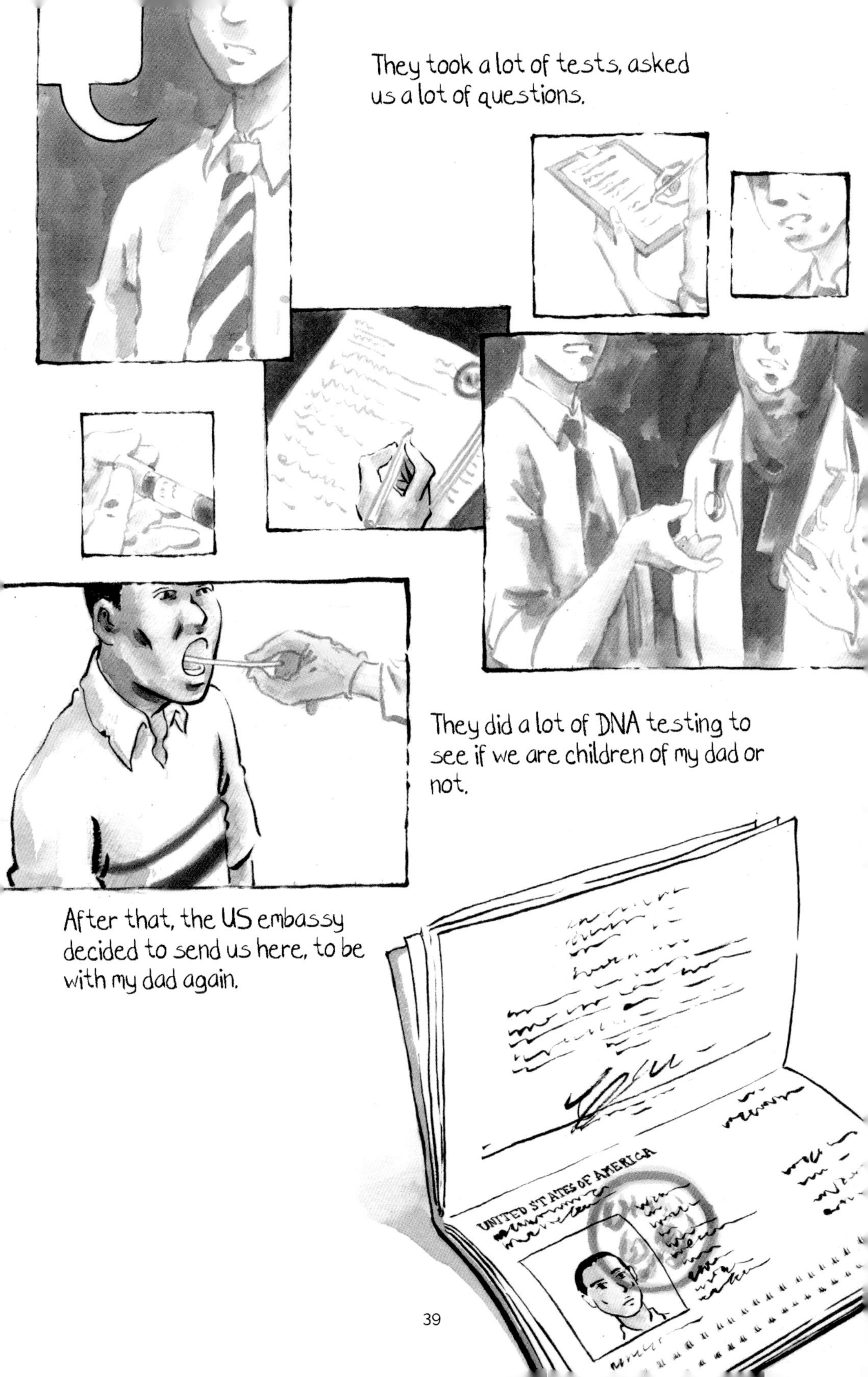
They took a lot of tests, asked us a lot of questions.
They did a lot of DNA testing to see if we are children of my dad or not.
After that, the US embassy decided to send us here, to be with my dad again.
UNITED STATES OF AMERICA

We took a plane from Malaysia to Dubai, and then to Chicago.

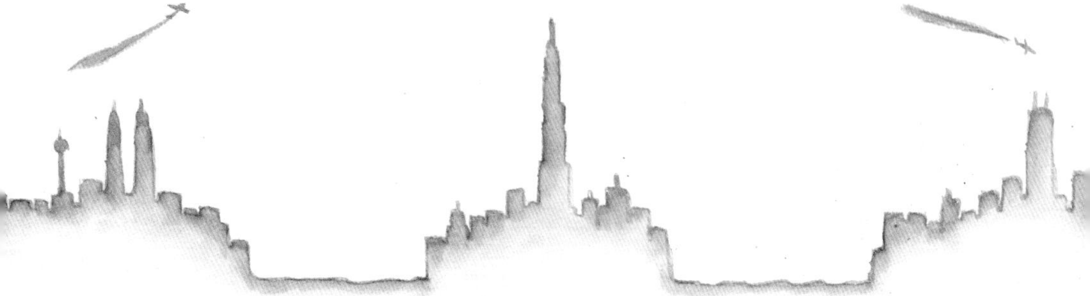

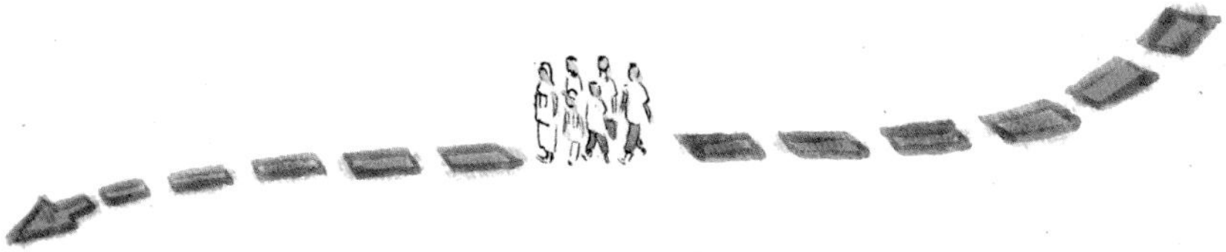

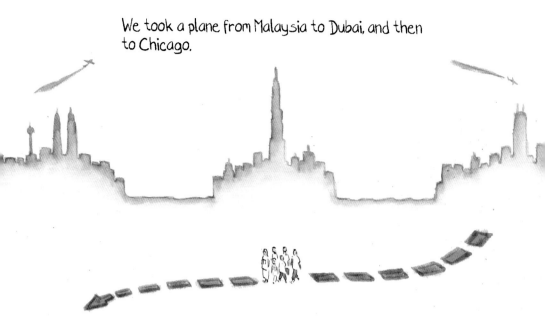

After we landed in Chicago, we got on a bus and we came to Milwaukee.

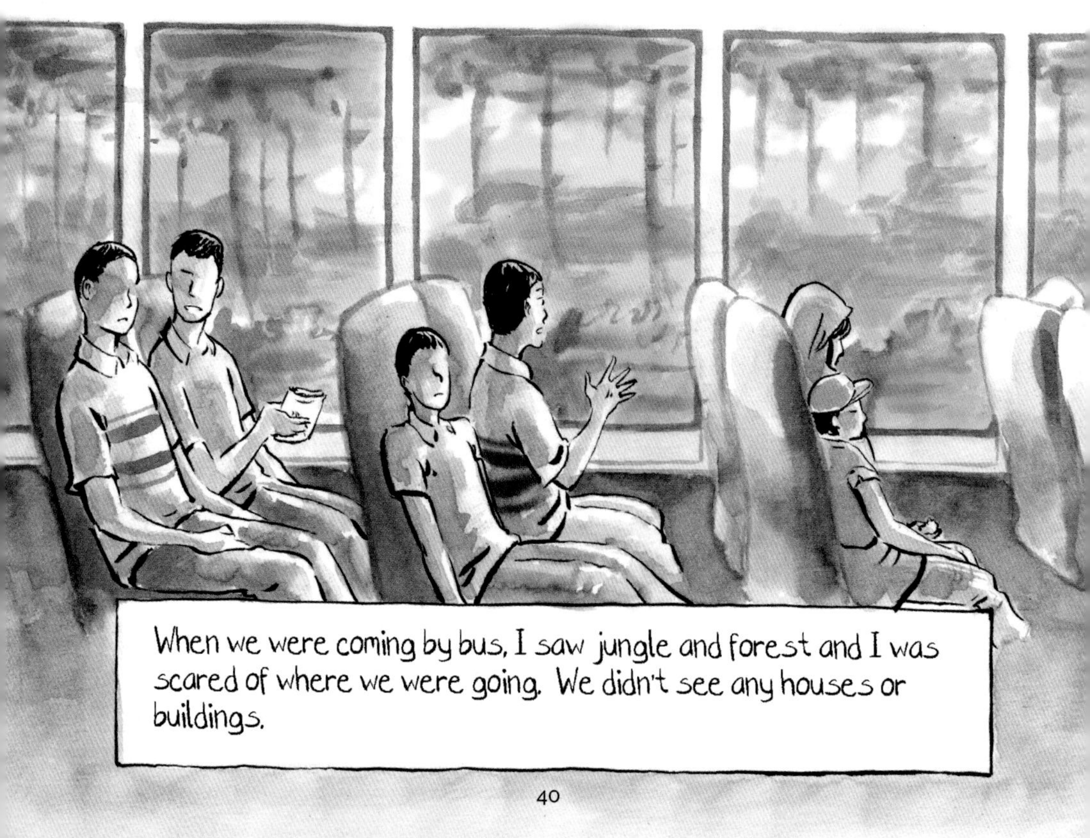
When we were coming by bus, I saw jungle and forest and I was scared of where we were going. We didn't see any houses or buildings.

We got in the Milwaukee airport and my dad and my brothers came to pick us up.

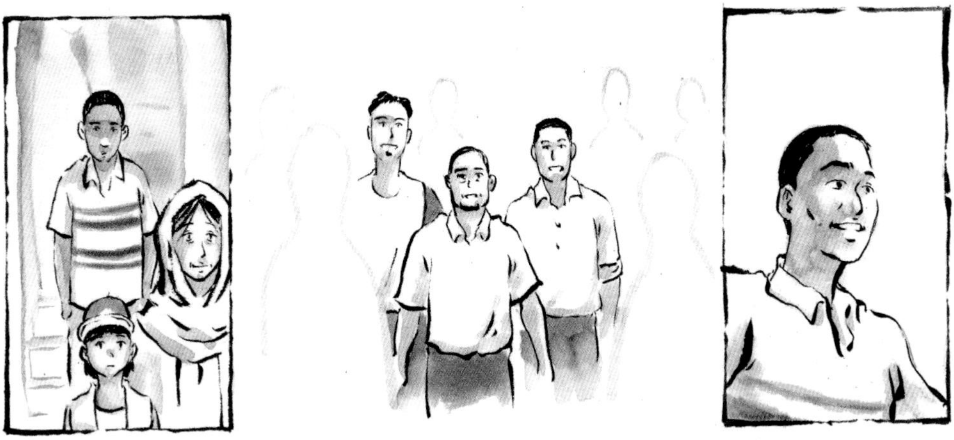

It was summertime in July, and we had no school. My brother took me to a building where they were teaching English for the Burmese community in Milwaukee.

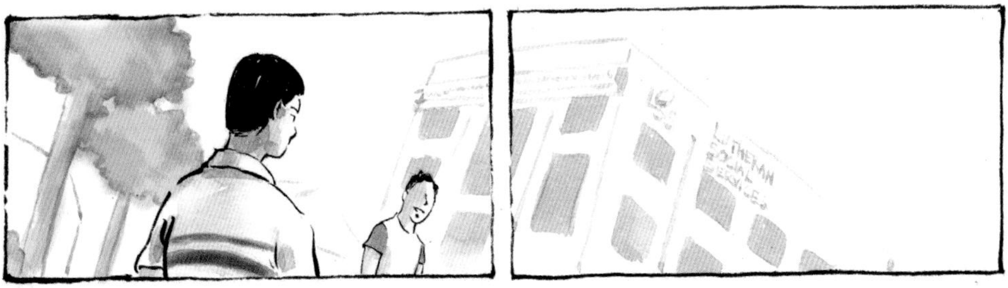

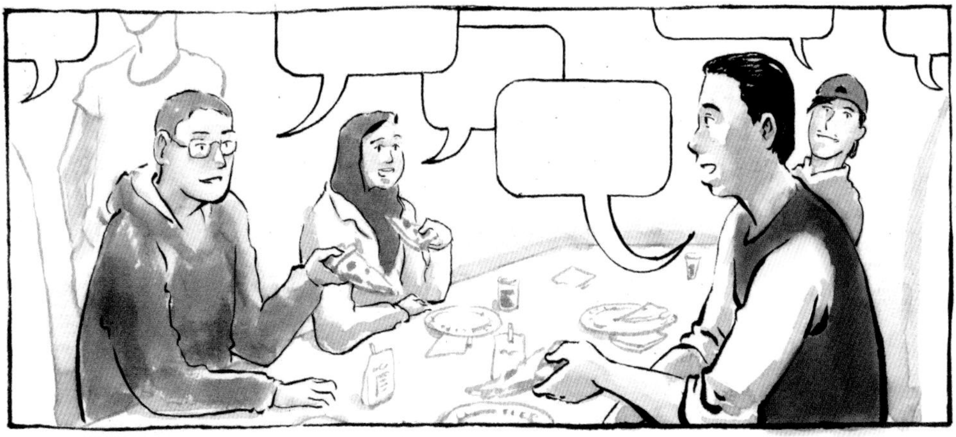

I met a lot of people who speak our language, and I was so happy to talk to them.

After the summer, the caseworker took me to the Milwaukee Public Schools office to apply for school.

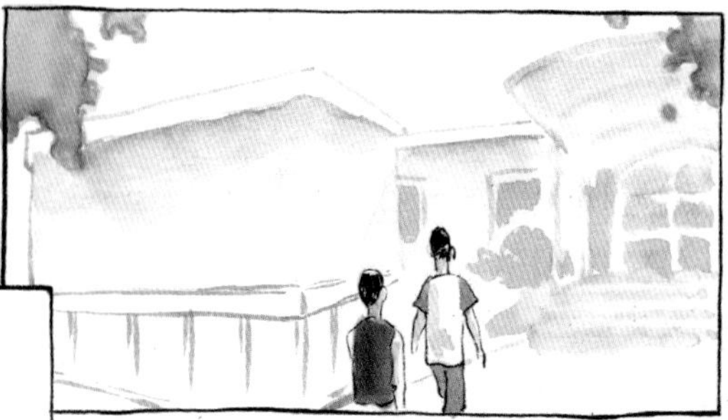

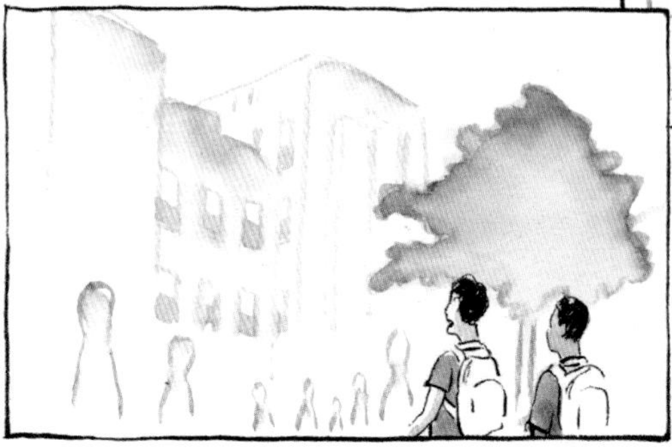

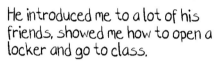

My brother was in 11th or 12th grade, and he said to come to Pulaski High School with him.

He introduced me to a lot of his friends, showed me how to open a locker and go to class.

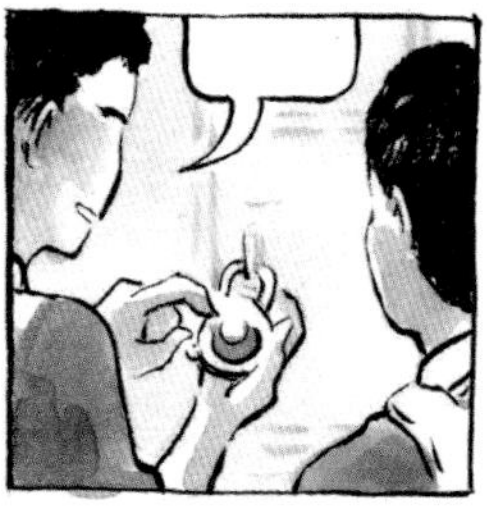

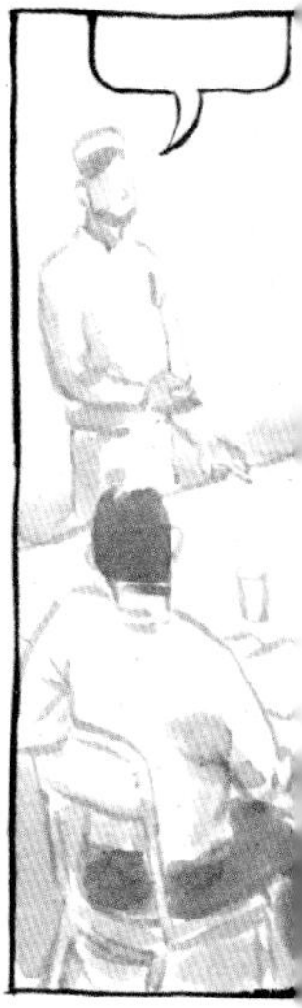

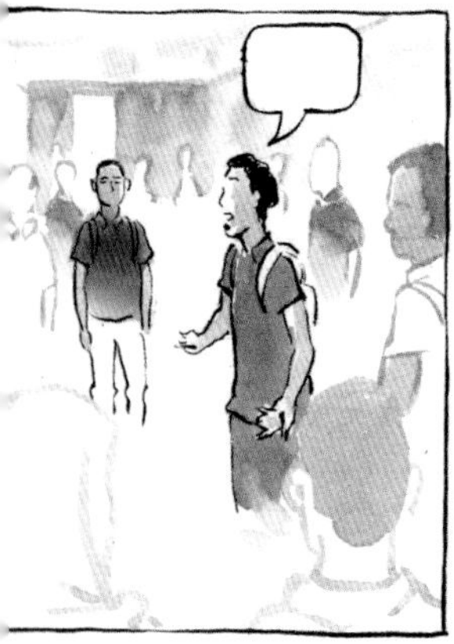

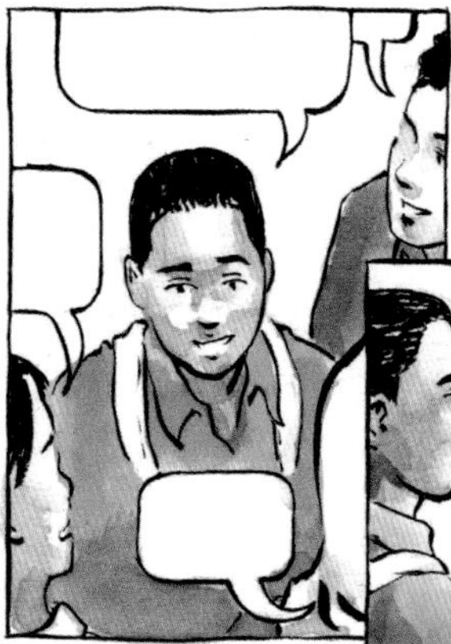

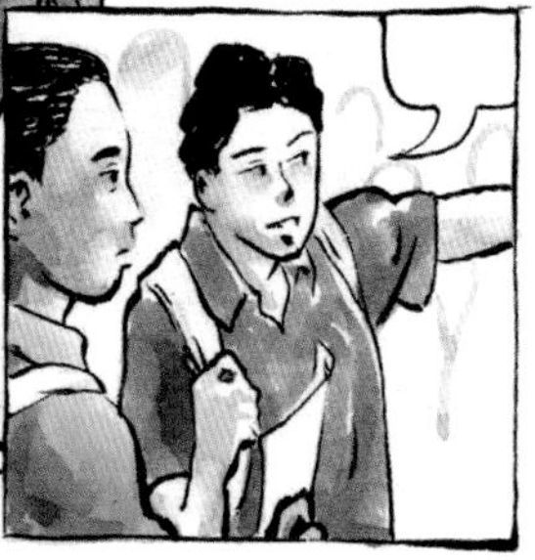

In Milwaukee, there are many Rohingya people.

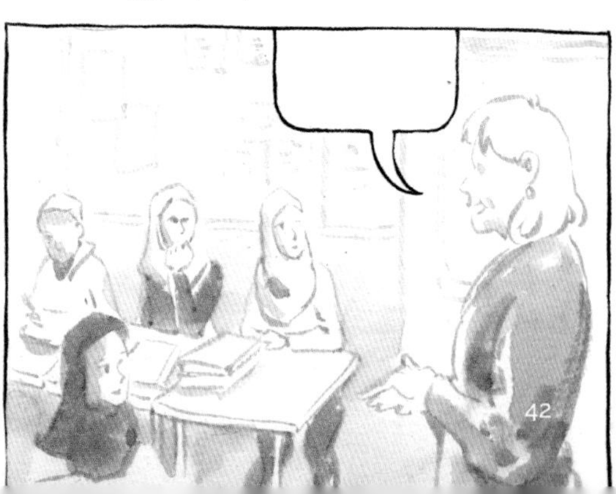

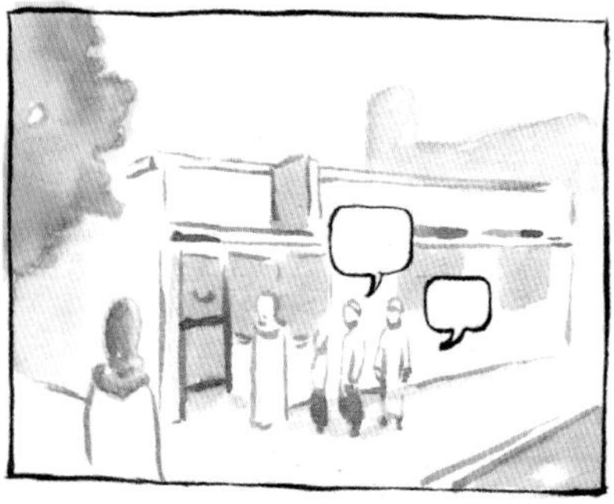

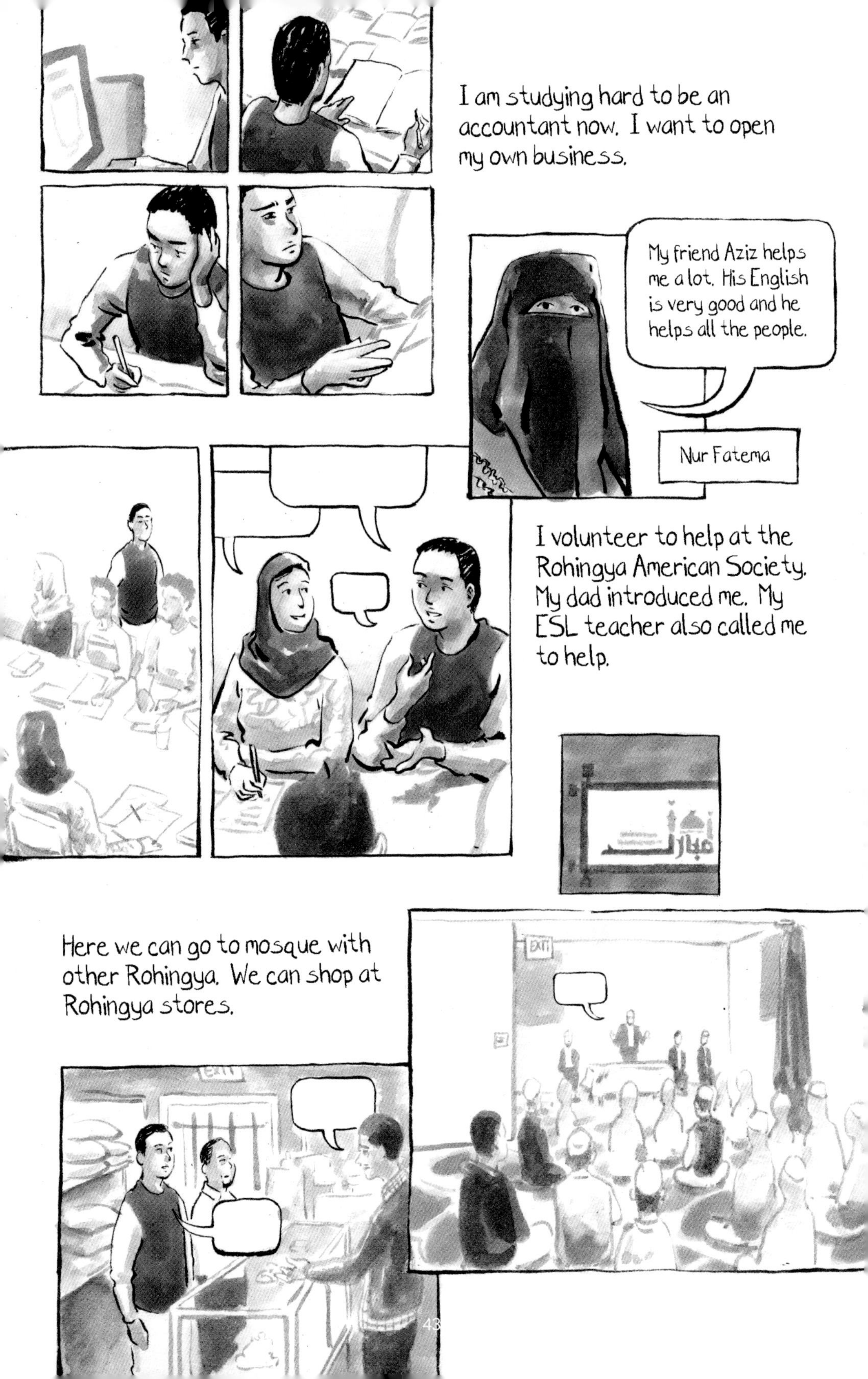
I am studying hard to be an accountant now. I want to open my own business.
My friend Aziz helps me a lot. His English is very good and he helps all the people.
Nur Fatema
I volunteer to help at the Rohingya American Society. My dad introduced me. My ESL teacher also called me to help.
Here we can go to mosque with other Rohingya. We can shop at Rohingya stores.
EXIT
EXIT

We came here to be a full family again, together again.

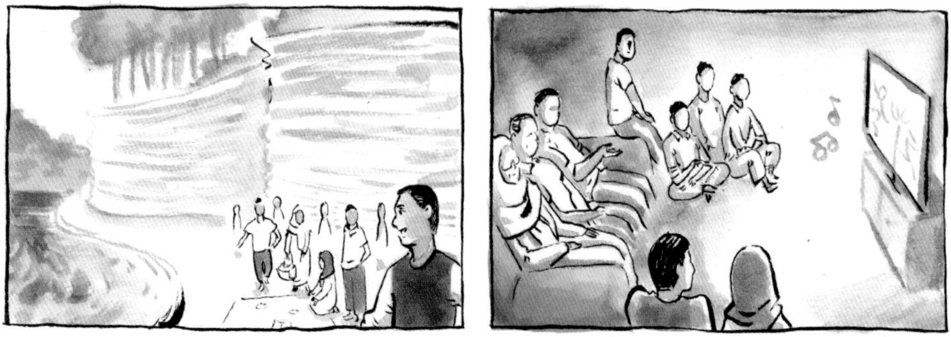

Before, we were separated. Some in Malaysia, some in Myanmar.

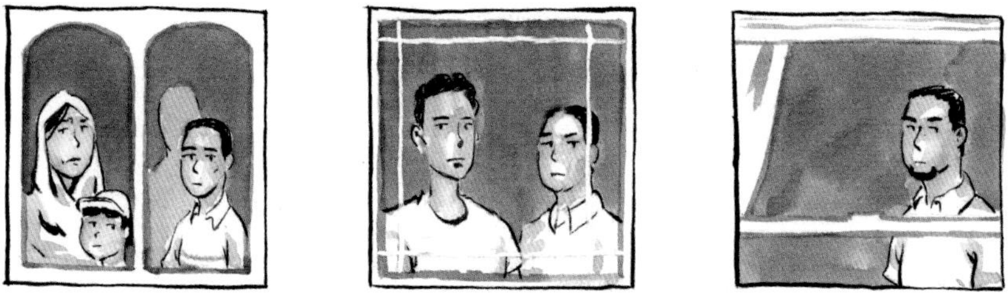

Now we are here. We are a full family, everyone in one house.

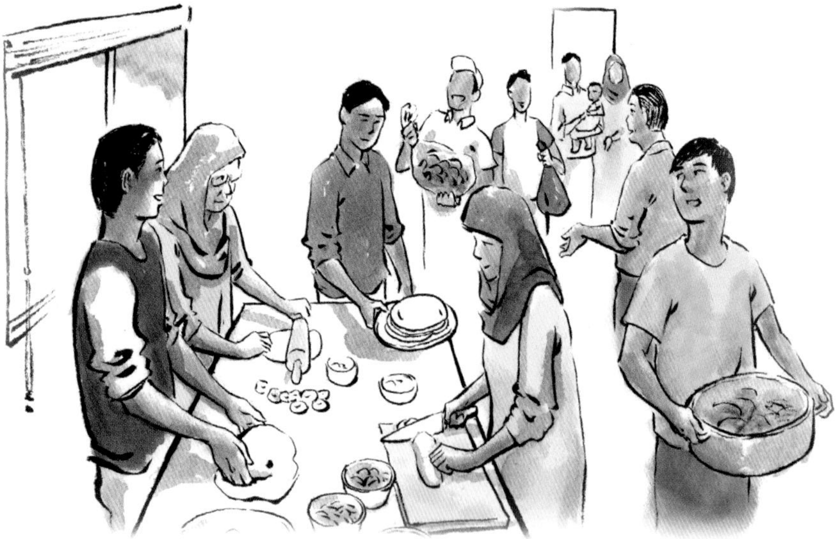

We are so happy.

GLOSSARY

DNA testing (genetic testing): Used to identify changes in DNA sequence or chromosome structure. Genetic testing can also be used to determine biological relatives, such as a child's parentage (genetic mother and father) through DNA paternity testing or be used to broadly determine an individual's ancestry.

ESL teacher: A teacher that educates students whose first language isn't English. They may work with students of all ages and from a variety of backgrounds. ESL, which stands for English as a second language, involves instructing students on reading, writing and how to converse effectively.

Refugee resettlement: A global system of governmental and non-governmental actors that helps resettle refugees to a safe third country. Many refugees cannot go home because of continued conflict, war, and persecution. In such circumstances, they are transferred from one country to another that has agreed to admit them, and ultimately grant them permanent residence. Refugee resettlement to a safe third country is considered for only a small fraction of refugees: those whose conditions are so perilous or whose needs cannot be met in the country where they first sought protection. Only a small number of countries take part in resettlement programs— among them are the United States, Australia, Canada, the Nordic countries, and increasingly some countries in Europe and Latin America.

JAMAICA

CRAIG MOODIE

Born: Kingston, Jamaica
Current: San Francisco, California

Craig Moodie received a 0-1A visa and is a clinical research scientist with over eighteen years of experience in the fields of neuroscience and psychology, with a specialization in functional connectivity magnetic resonance imaging (fcMRI) in clinical populations and behavioral genetics. He is currently researching topics on developing machine learning (ML) and artificial intelligence (AI) tools for neuroimaging-based biomarker identification and application to drug discovery.

www.greencardvoices.org/speakers/craig-moodie

ANA HINOJOSA

Born: Dominican Republic
Current: Atlanta, Georgia

Ana Hinojosa is a Dominican comic artist and illustrator. Most of her work focuses on marginalized voices within the Latinx community such as people who are part of the LGBT community and Afro-Latinos, creating a space within the comics world where people like her can explore, flourish, and possibly fight monsters or the demons within themselves.

www.anahin.com

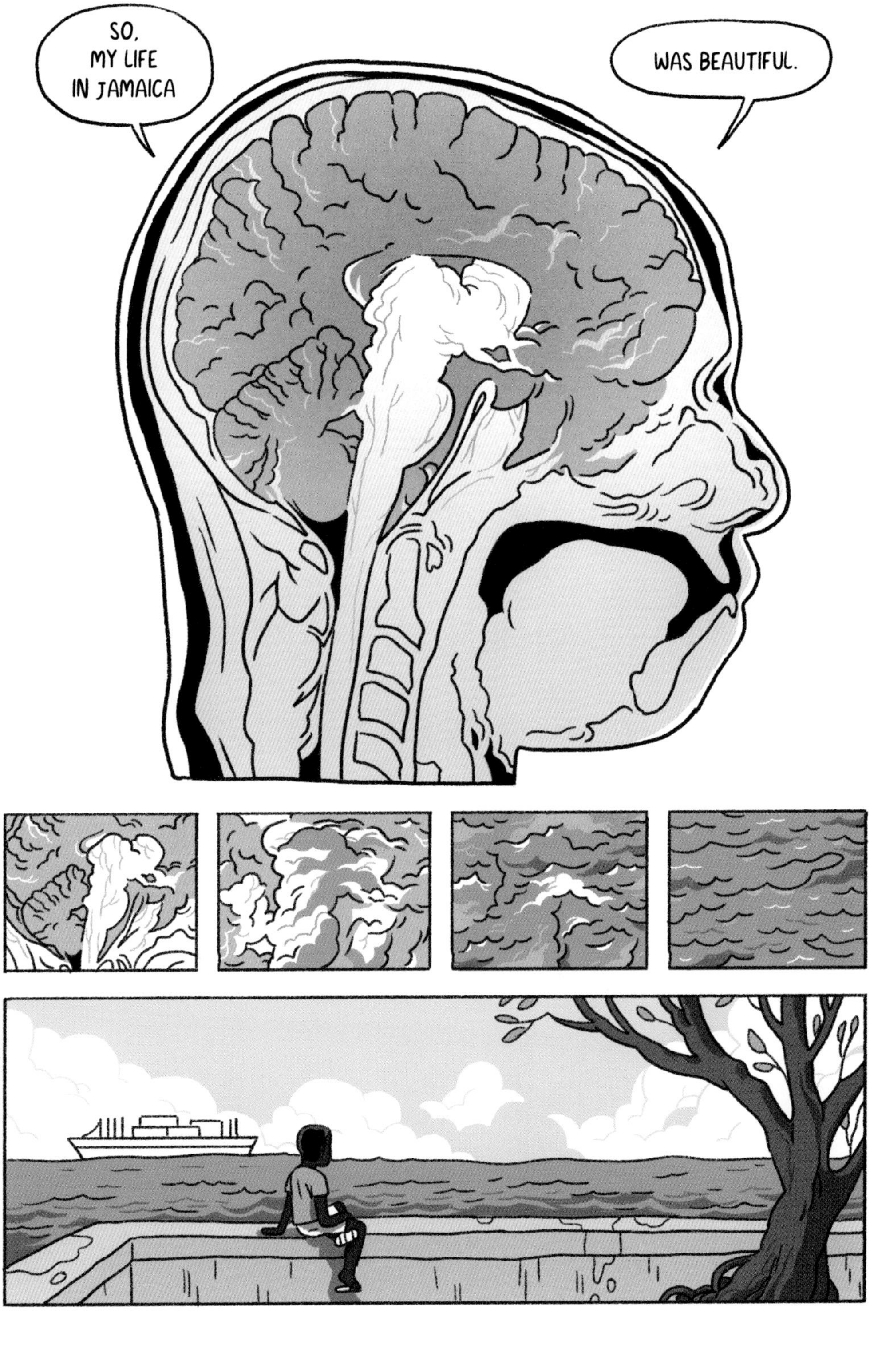
SO, MY LIFE IN JAMAICA
WAS BEAUTIFUL.

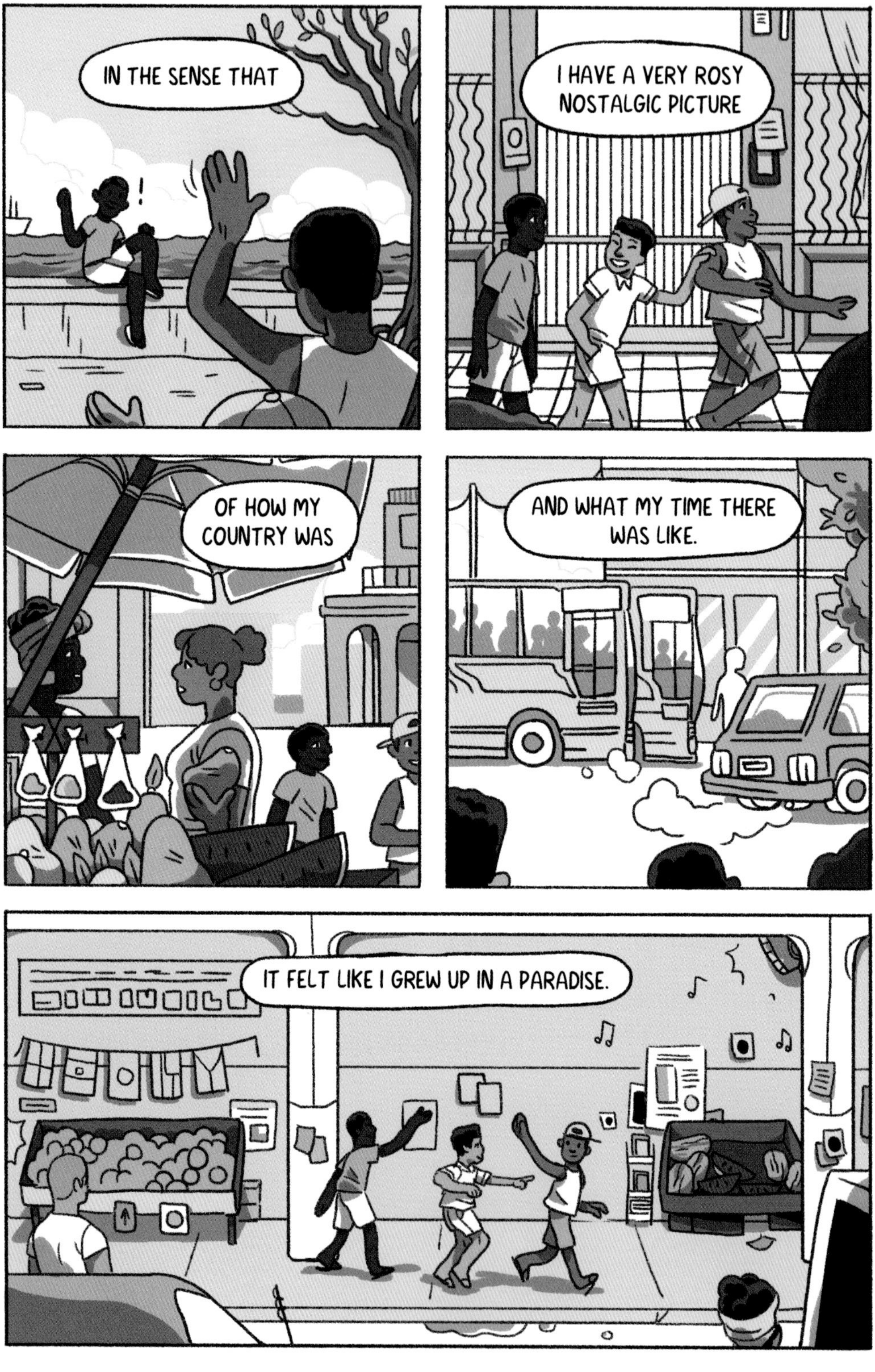
IN THE SENSE THAT
I HAVE A VERY ROSY NOSTALGIC PICTURE
OF HOW MY COUNTRY WAS
AND WHAT MY TIME THERE WAS LIKE.
IT FELT LIKE I GREW UP IN A PARADISE.

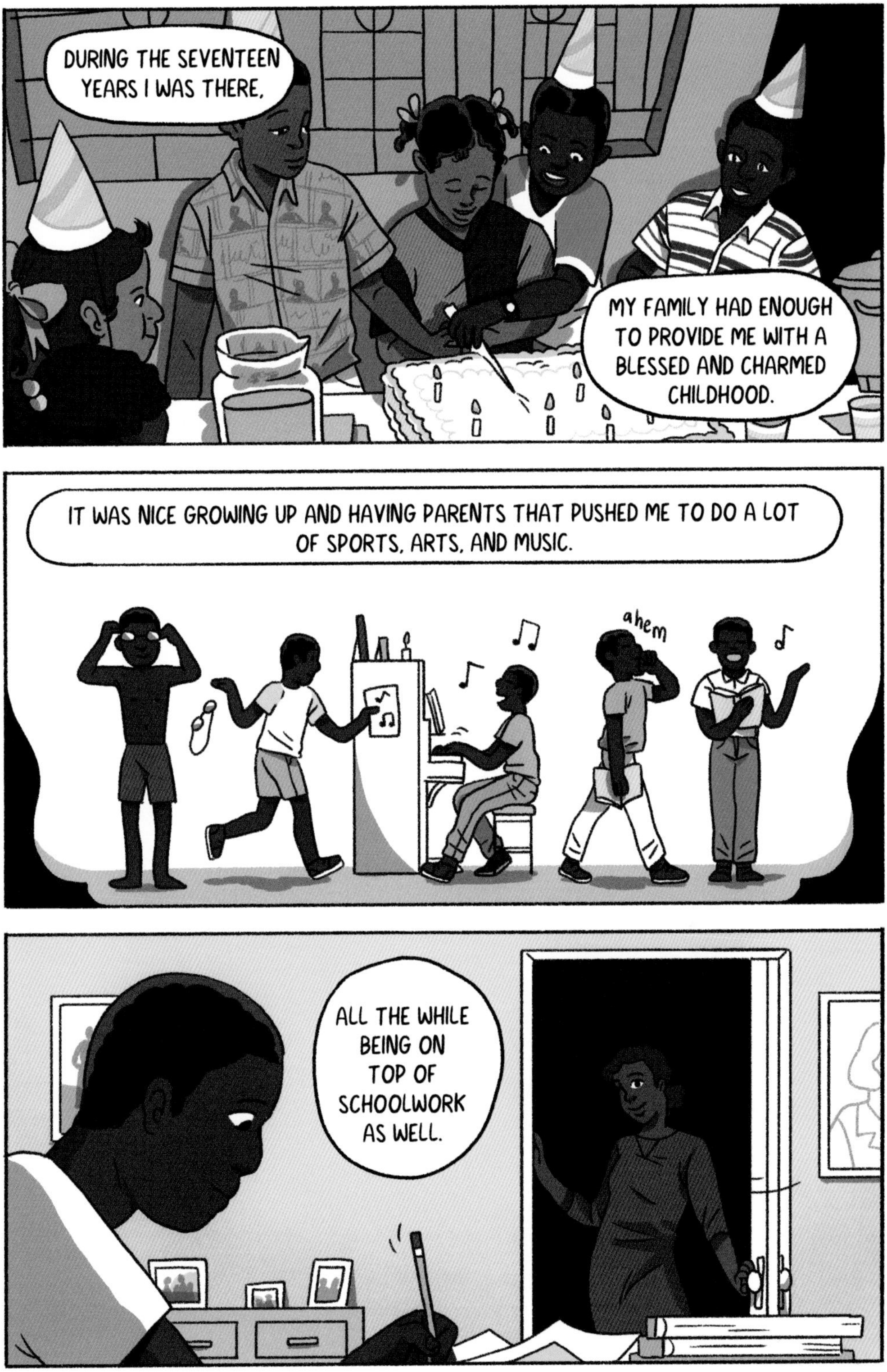
DURING THE SEVENTEEN YEARS I WAS THERE,
MY FAMILY HAD ENOUGH TO PROVIDE ME WITH A BLESSED AND CHARMED CHILDHOOD.
IT WAS NICE GROWING UP AND HAVING PARENTS THAT PUSHED ME TO DO A LOT OF SPORTS, ARTS, AND MUSIC.
ahem
ALL THE WHILE BEING ON TOP OF SCHOOLWORK AS WELL.

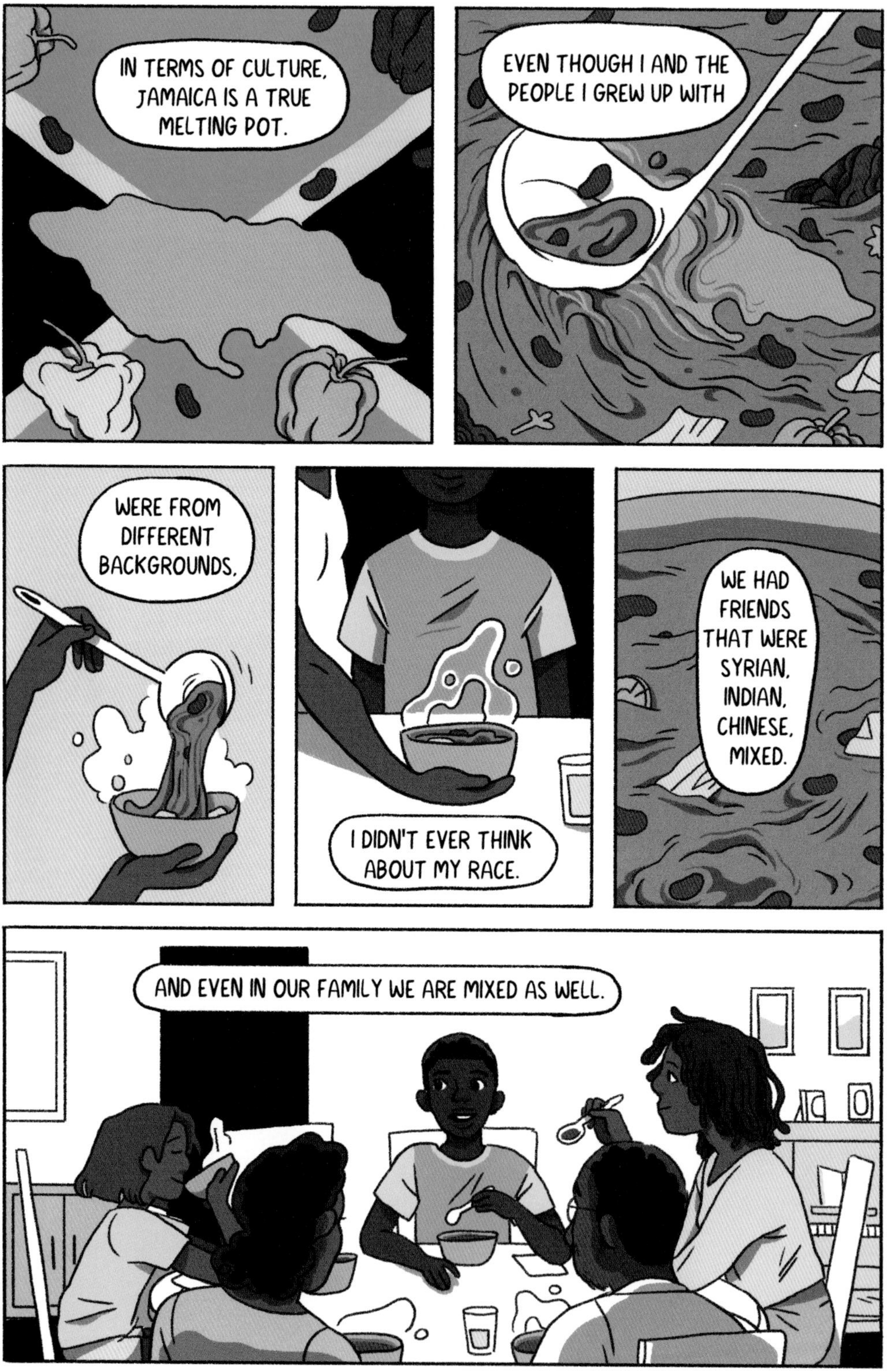
IN TERMS OF CULTURE, JAMAICA IS A TRUE MELTING POT.
EVEN THOUGH I AND THE PEOPLE I GREW UP WITH
WERE FROM DIFFERENT BACKGROUNDS,
I DIDN'T EVER THINK ABOUT MY RACE.
WE HAD FRIENDS THAT WERE SYRIAN, INDIAN, CHINESE, MIXED.
AND EVEN IN OUR FAMILY WE ARE MIXED AS WELL.

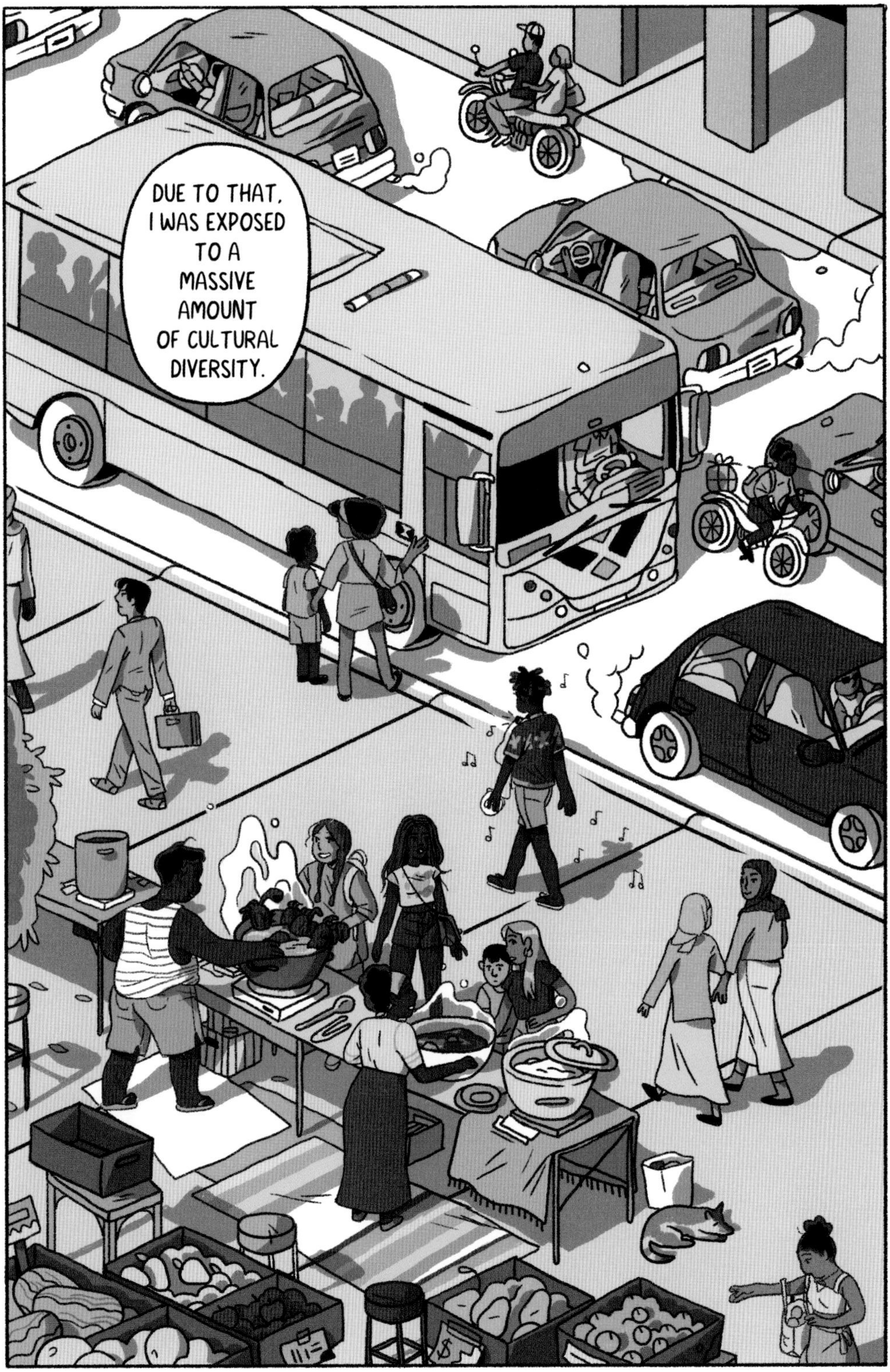
DUE TO THAT, I WAS EXPOSED TO A MASSIVE AMOUNT OF CULTURAL DIVERSITY.

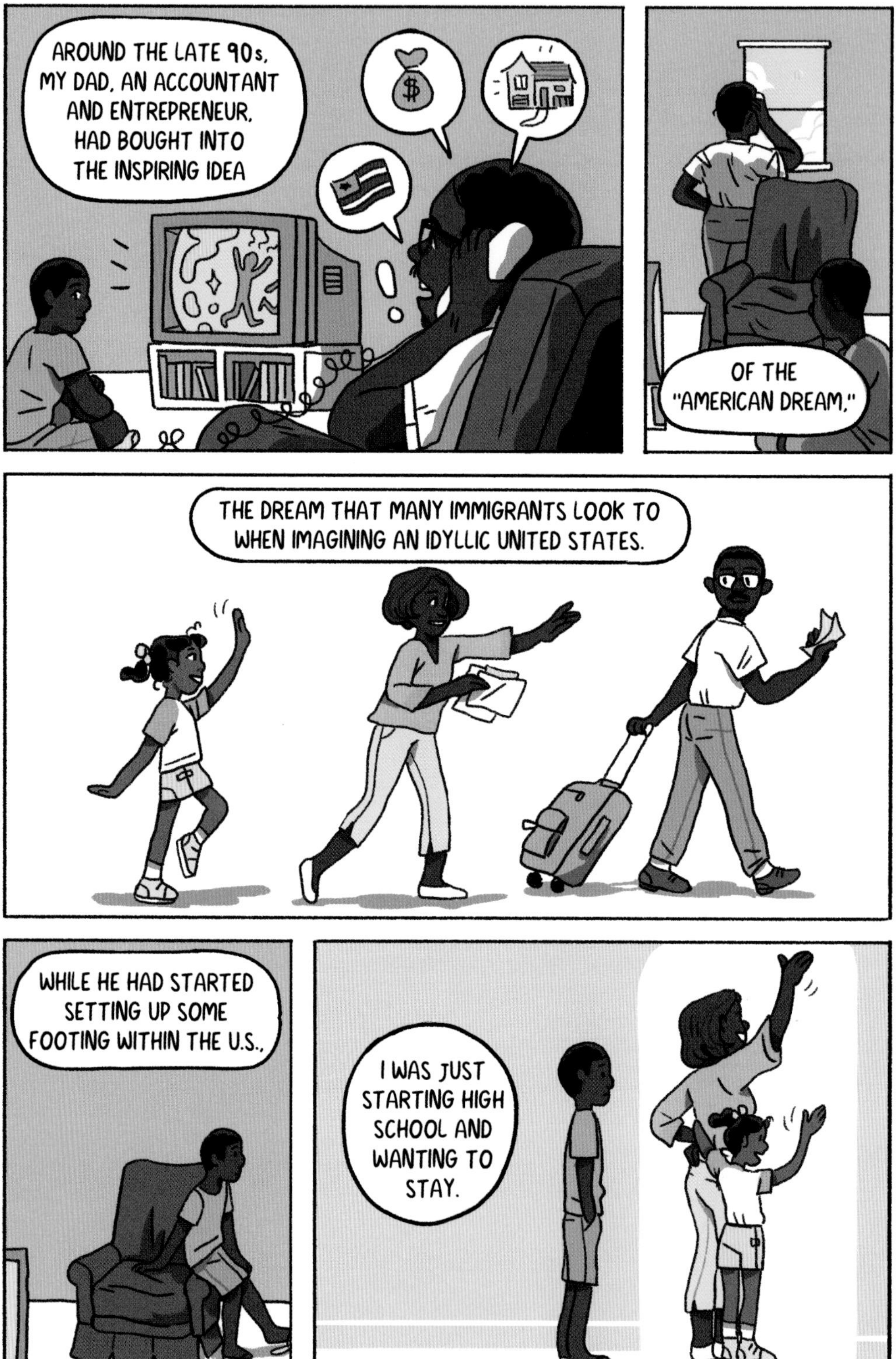
AROUND THE LATE 90s, MY DAD, AN ACCOUNTANT AND ENTREPRENEUR, HAD BOUGHT INTO THE INSPIRING IDEA
OF THE "AMERICAN DREAM,"
THE DREAM THAT MANY IMMIGRANTS LOOK TO WHEN IMAGINING AN IDYLLIC UNITED STATES.
WHILE HE HAD STARTED SETTING UP SOME FOOTING WITHIN THE U.S.,
I WAS JUST STARTING HIGH SCHOOL AND WANTING TO STAY.

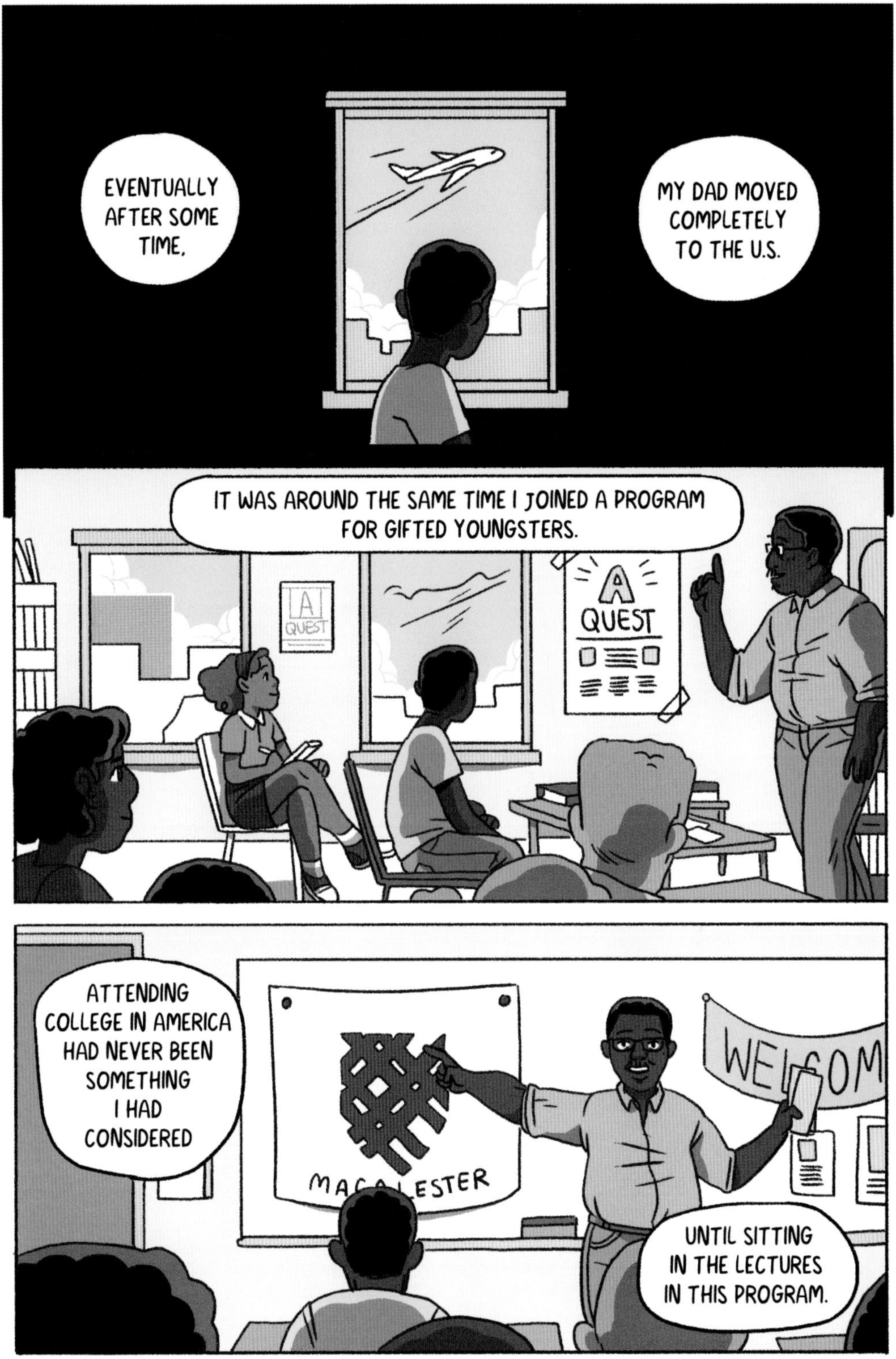
EVENTUALLY AFTER SOME TIME,
MY DAD MOVED COMPLETELY TO THE U.S.
IT WAS AROUND THE SAME TIME I JOINED A PROGRAM FOR GIFTED YOUNGSTERS.
A QUEST
A QUEST
ATTENDING COLLEGE IN AMERICA HAD NEVER BEEN SOMETHING I HAD CONSIDERED
MACALESTER
WELCOM
UNTIL SITTING IN THE LECTURES IN THIS PROGRAM.

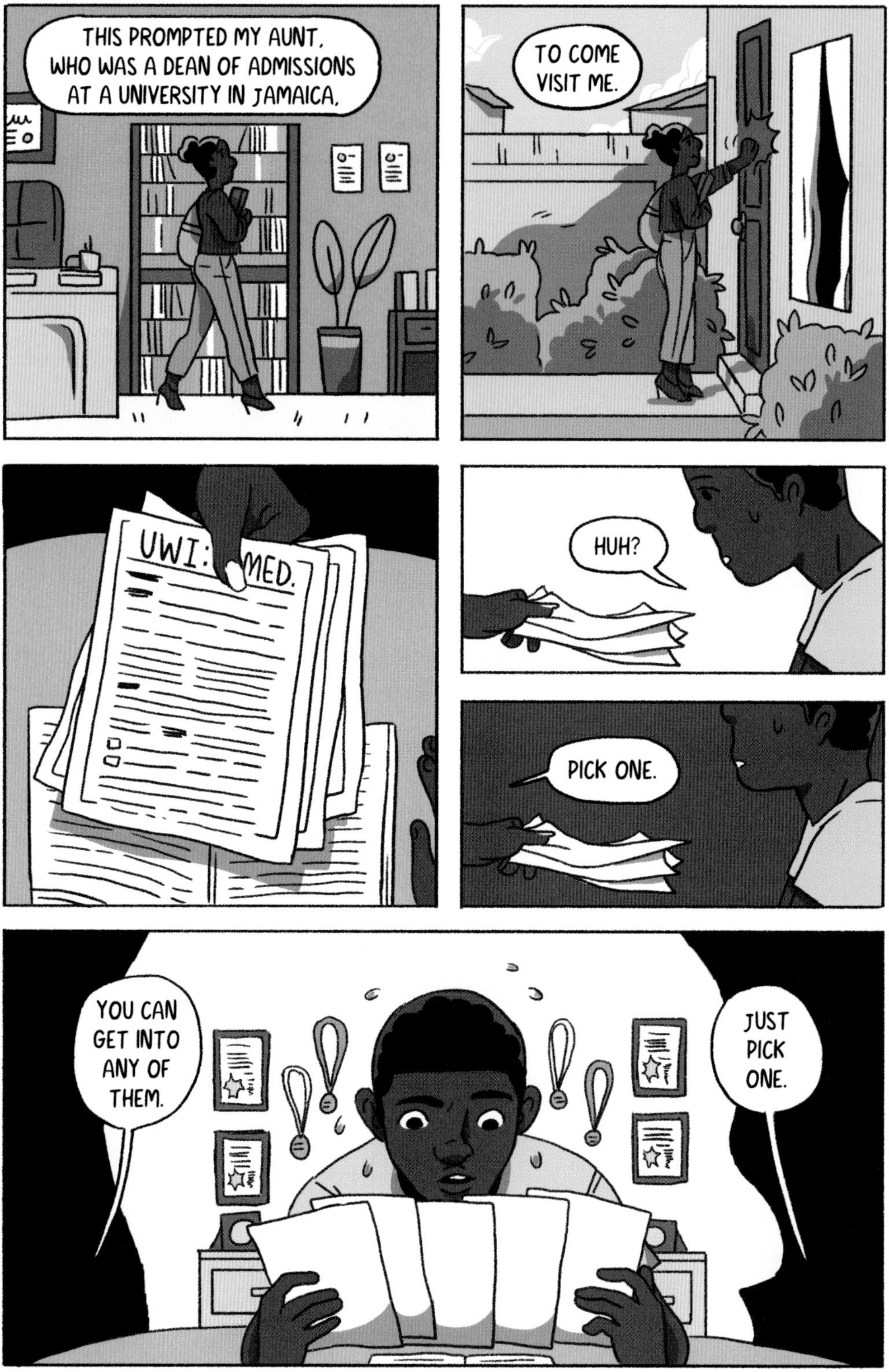
THIS PROMPTED MY AUNT, WHO WAS A DEAN OF ADMISSIONS AT A UNIVERSITY IN JAMAICA,
TO COME VISIT ME.
UWI: MED.
HUH?
PICK ONE.
YOU CAN GET INTO ANY OF THEM.
JUST PICK ONE.

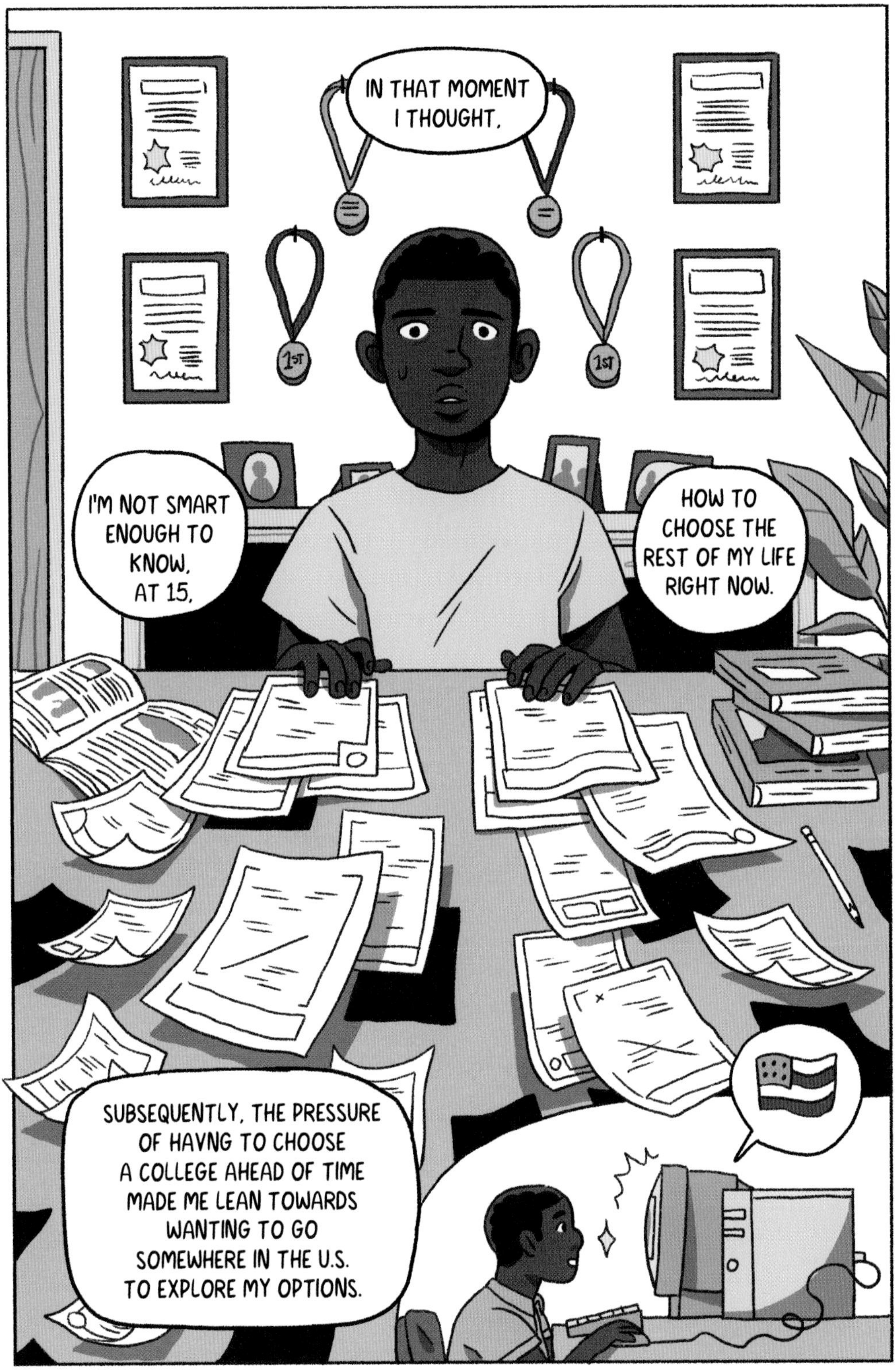
IN THAT MOMENT I THOUGHT,
I'M NOT SMART ENOUGH TO KNOW, AT 15,
HOW TO CHOOSE THE REST OF MY LIFE RIGHT NOW.
SUBSEQUENTLY, THE PRESSURE OF HAVNG TO CHOOSE A COLLEGE AHEAD OF TIME MADE ME LEAN TOWARDS WANTING TO GO SOMEWHERE IN THE U.S. TO EXPLORE MY OPTIONS.

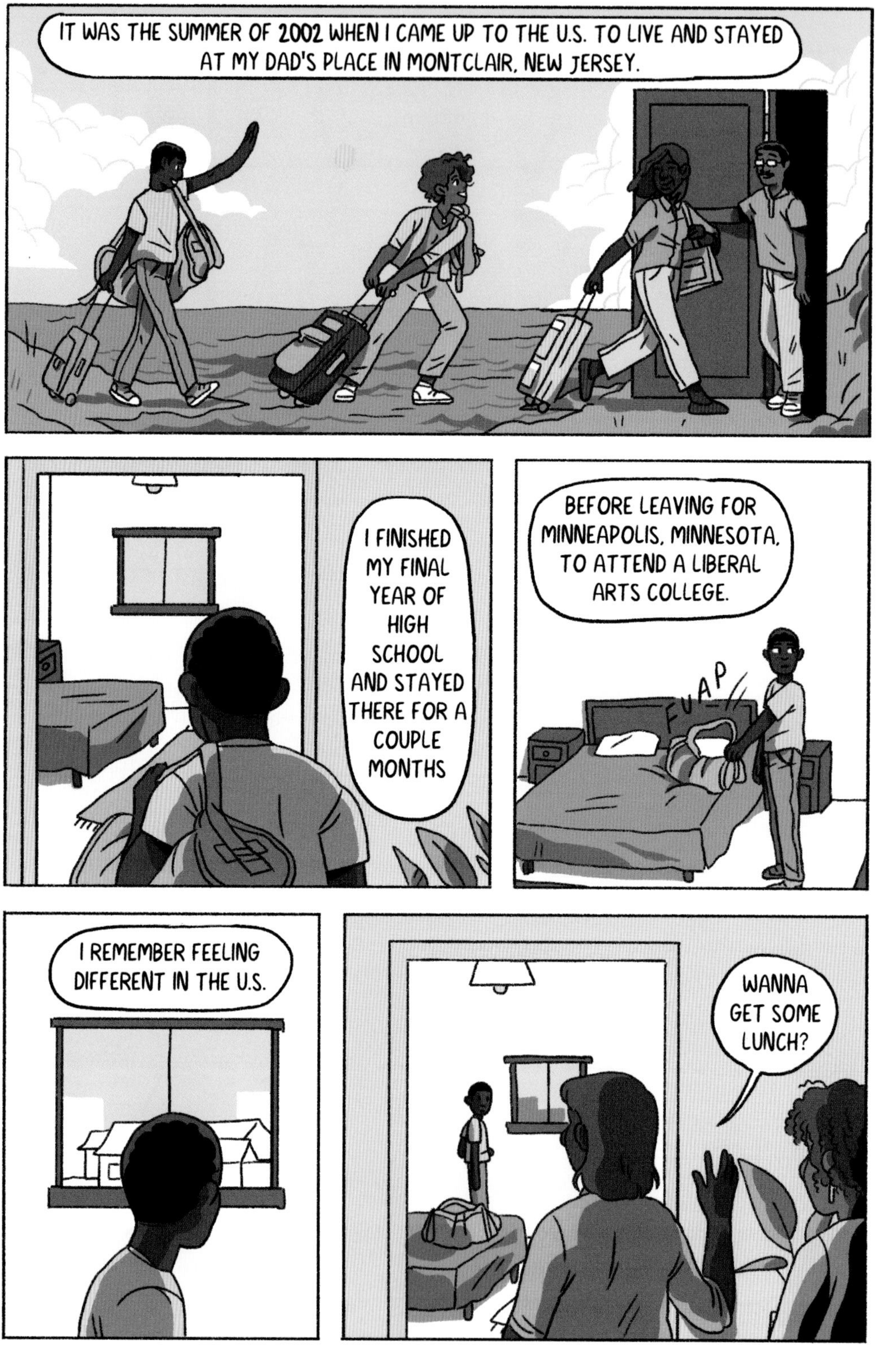
IT WAS THE SUMMER OF 2002 WHEN I CAME UP TO THE U.S. TO LIVE AND STAYED AT MY DAD'S PLACE IN MONTCLAIR, NEW JERSEY.
I FINISHED MY FINAL YEAR OF HIGH SCHOOL AND STAYED THERE FOR A COUPLE MONTHS
BEFORE LEAVING FOR MINNEAPOLIS, MINNESOTA, TO ATTEND A LIBERAL ARTS COLLEGE.
FUAP
I REMEMBER FEELING DIFFERENT IN THE U.S.
WANNA GET SOME LUNCH?

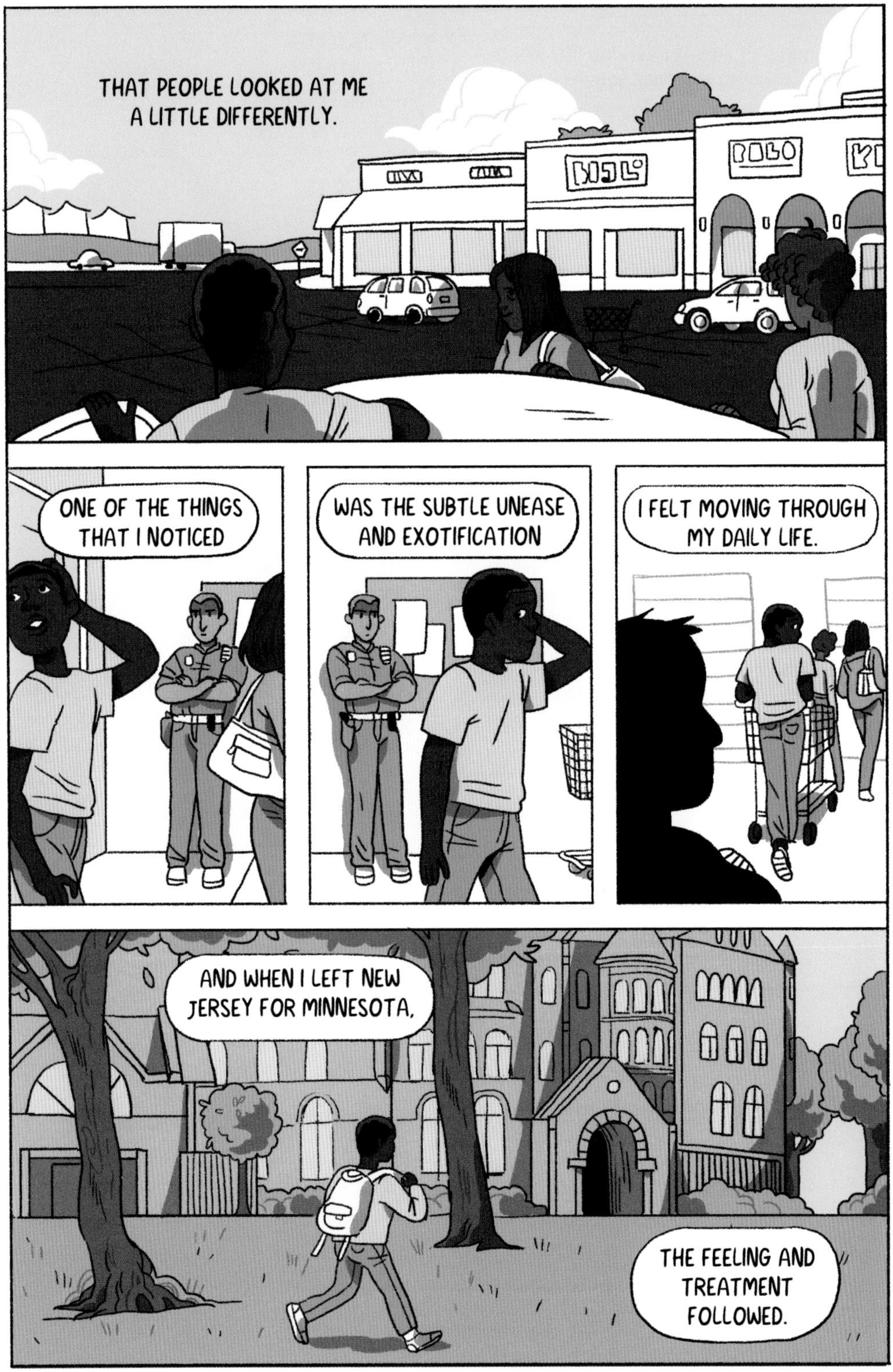
THAT PEOPLE LOOKED AT ME A LITTLE DIFFERENTLY.
ONE OF THE THINGS THAT I NOTICED
WAS THE SUBTLE UNEASE AND EXOTIFICATION
I FELT MOVING THROUGH MY DAILY LIFE.
AND WHEN I LEFT NEW JERSEY FOR MINNESOTA,
THE FEELING AND TREATMENT FOLLOWED.

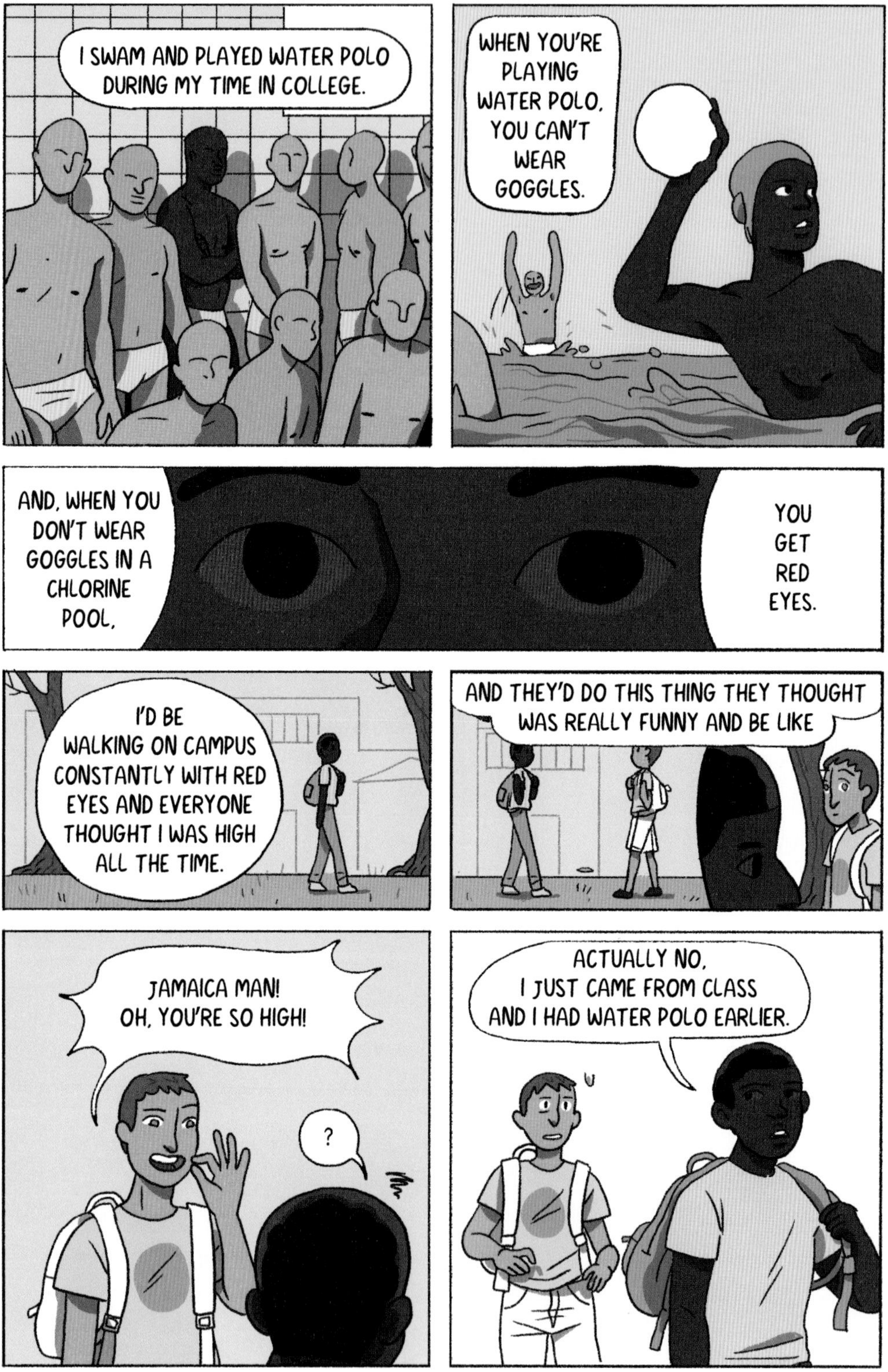
I SWAM AND PLAYED WATER POLO DURING MY TIME IN COLLEGE.
WHEN YOU'RE PLAYING WATER POLO, YOU CAN'T WEAR GOGGLES.
AND, WHEN YOU DON'T WEAR GOGGLES IN A CHLORINE POOL,
YOU GET RED EYES.
I'D BE WALKING ON CAMPUS CONSTANTLY WITH RED EYES AND EVERYONE THOUGHT I WAS HIGH ALL THE TIME.
AND THEY'D DO THIS THING THEY THOUGHT WAS REALLY FUNNY AND BE LIKE
JAMAICA MAN! OH, YOU'RE SO HIGH!
?
ACTUALLY NO, I JUST CAME FROM CLASS AND I HAD WATER POLO EARLIER.

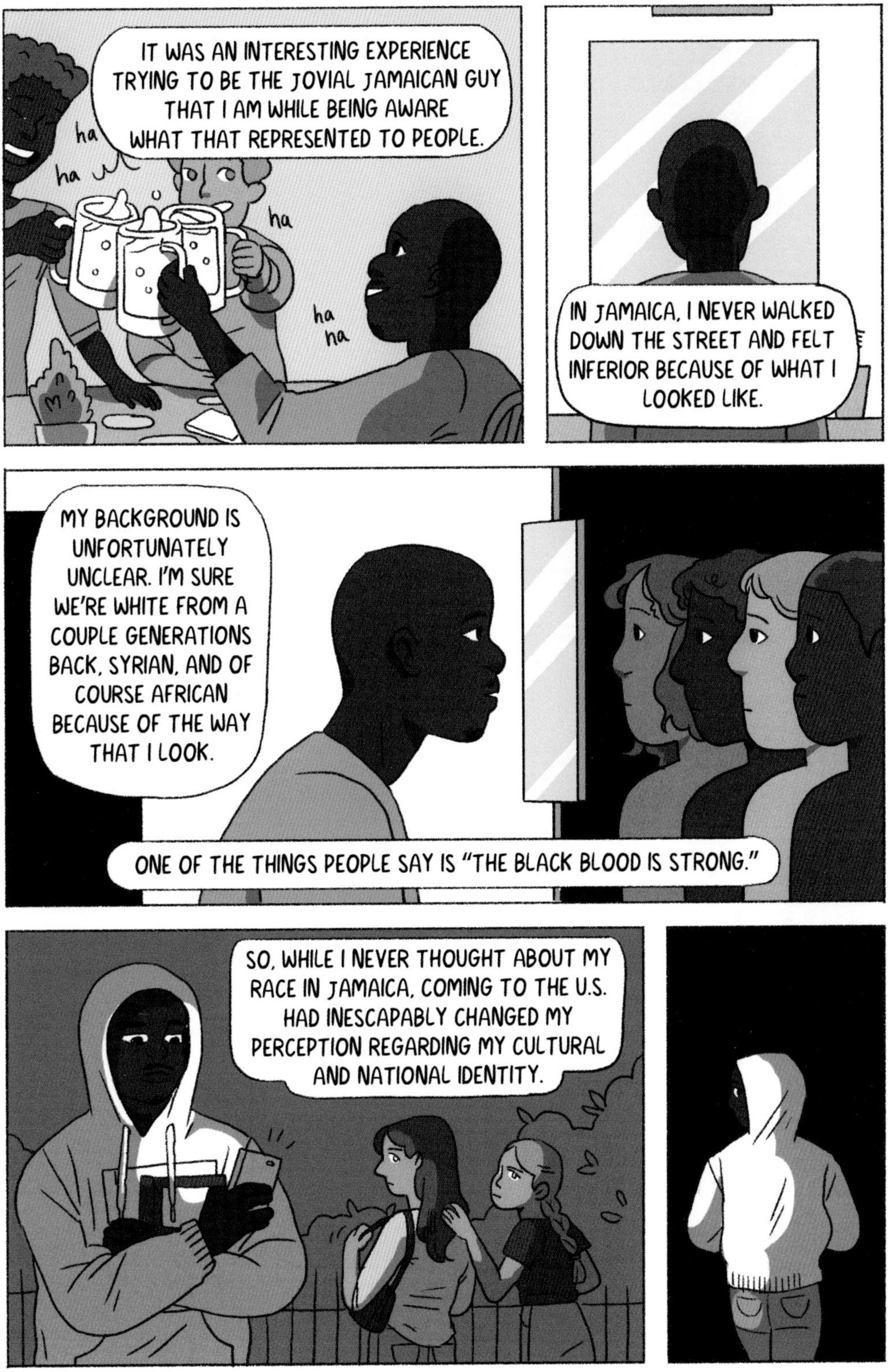
IT WAS AN INTERESTING EXPERIENCE TRYING TO BE THE JOVIAL JAMAICAN GUY THAT I AM WHILE BEING AWARE WHAT THAT REPRESENTED TO PEOPLE.
ha ha ha ha ha
IN JAMAICA, I NEVER WALKED DOWN THE STREET AND FELT INFERIOR BECAUSE OF WHAT I LOOKED LIKE.
MY BACKGROUND IS UNFORTUNATELY UNCLEAR. I'M SURE WE'RE WHITE FROM A COUPLE GENERATIONS BACK, SYRIAN, AND OF COURSE AFRICAN BECAUSE OF THE WAY THAT I LOOK.
ONE OF THE THINGS PEOPLE SAY IS "THE BLACK BLOOD IS STRONG."
SO, WHILE I NEVER THOUGHT ABOUT MY RACE IN JAMAICA, COMING TO THE U.S. HAD INESCAPABLY CHANGED MY PERCEPTION REGARDING MY CULTURAL AND NATIONAL IDENTITY.

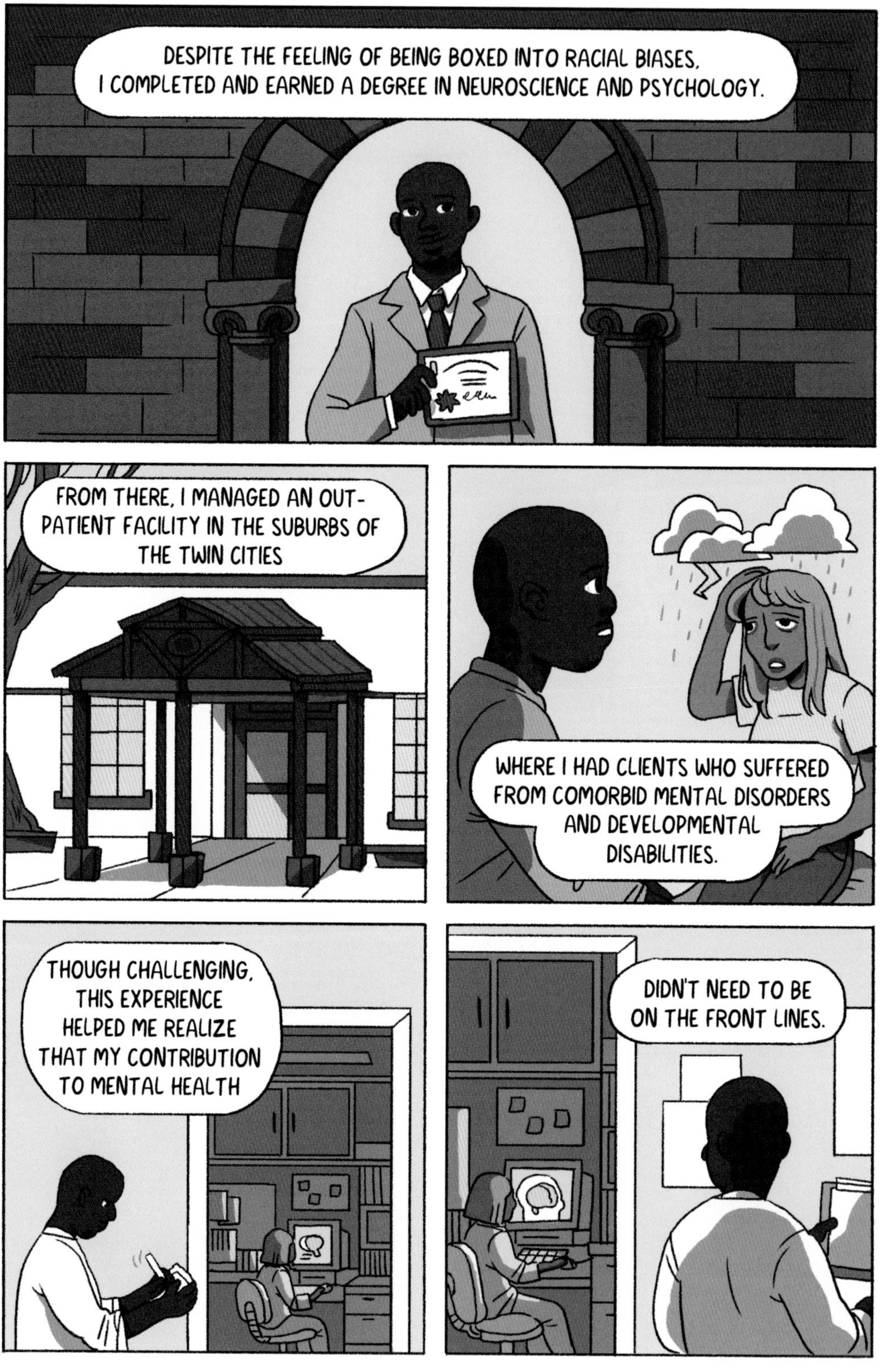
DESPITE THE FEELING OF BEING BOXED INTO RACIAL BIASES, I COMPLETED AND EARNED A DEGREE IN NEUROSCIENCE AND PSYCHOLOGY.
FROM THERE, I MANAGED AN OUT-PATIENT FACILITY IN THE SUBURBS OF THE TWIN CITIES
WHERE I HAD CLIENTS WHO SUFFERED FROM COMORBID MENTAL DISORDERS AND DEVELOPMENTAL DISABILITIES.
THOUGH CHALLENGING, THIS EXPERIENCE HELPED ME REALIZE THAT MY CONTRIBUTION TO MENTAL HEALTH
DIDN'T NEED TO BE ON THE FRONT LINES.

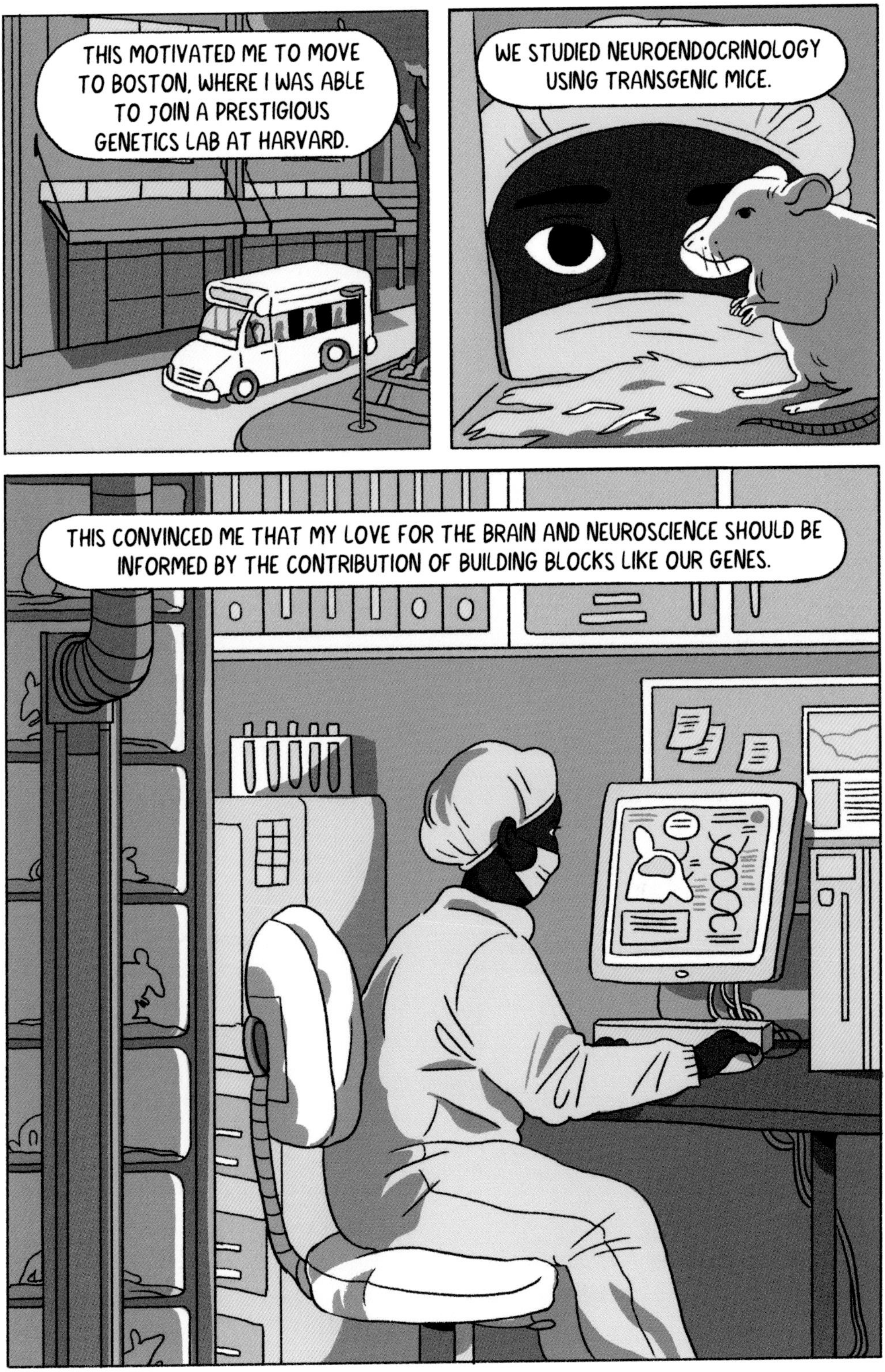
THIS MOTIVATED ME TO MOVE TO BOSTON, WHERE I WAS ABLE TO JOIN A PRESTIGIOUS GENETICS LAB AT HARVARD.
WE STUDIED NEUROENDOCRINOLOGY USING TRANSGENIC MICE.
THIS CONVINCED ME THAT MY LOVE FOR THE BRAIN AND NEUROSCIENCE SHOULD BE INFORMED BY THE CONTRIBUTION OF BUILDING BLOCKS LIKE OUR GENES.

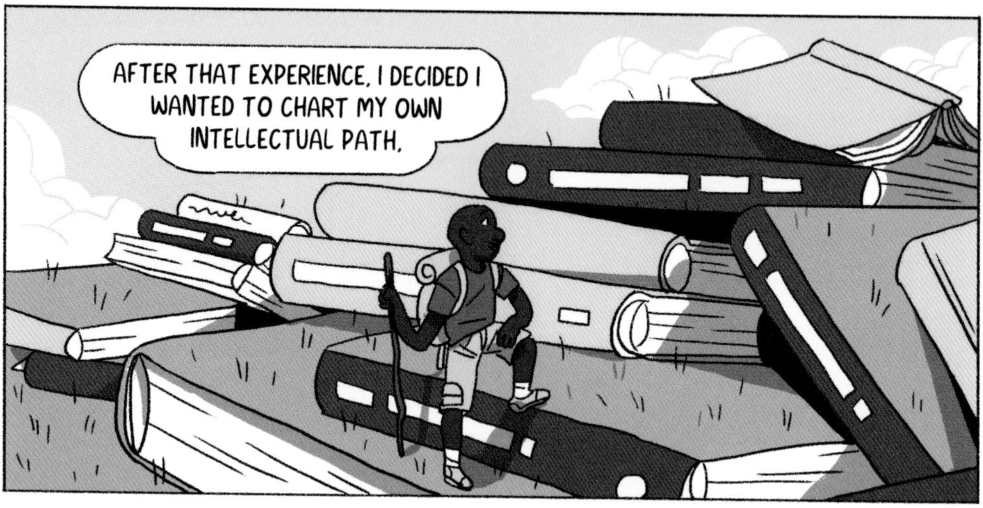
AFTER THAT EXPERIENCE, I DECIDED I WANTED TO CHART MY OWN INTELLECTUAL PATH,

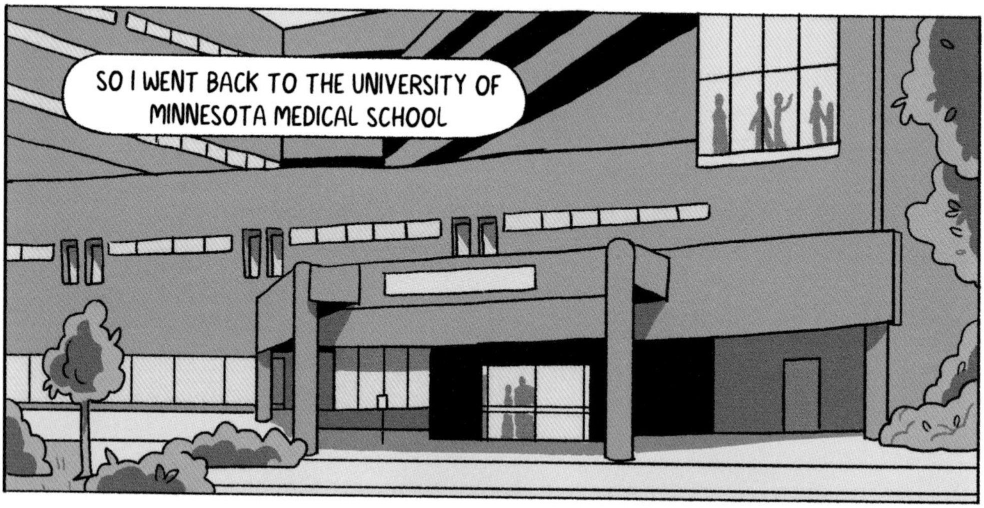
SO I WENT BACK TO THE UNIVERSITY OF MINNESOTA MEDICAL SCHOOL

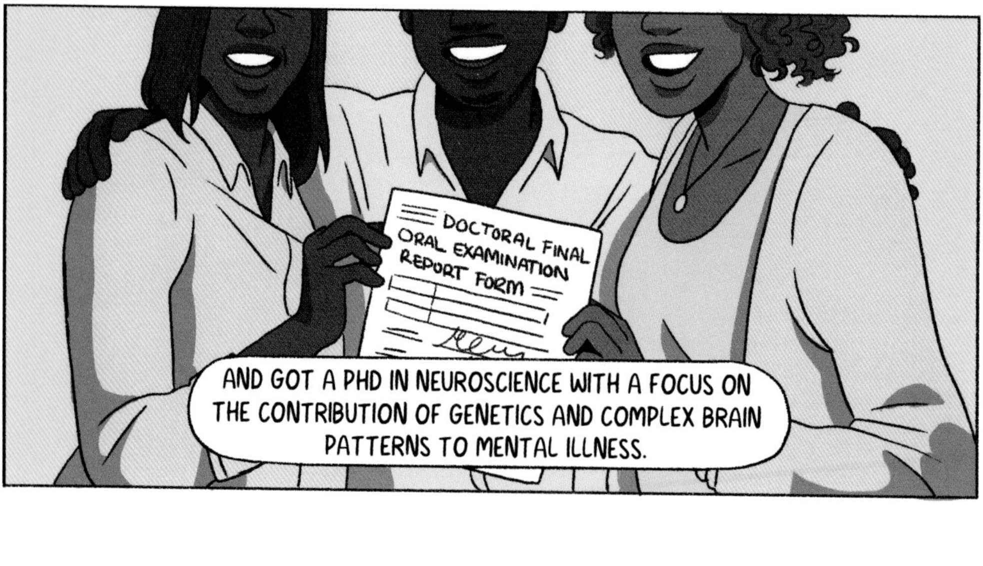
DOCTORAL FINAL ORAL EXAMINATION REPORT FORM
AND GOT A PHD IN NEUROSCIENCE WITH A FOCUS ON THE CONTRIBUTION OF GENETICS AND COMPLEX BRAIN PATTERNS TO MENTAL ILLNESS.

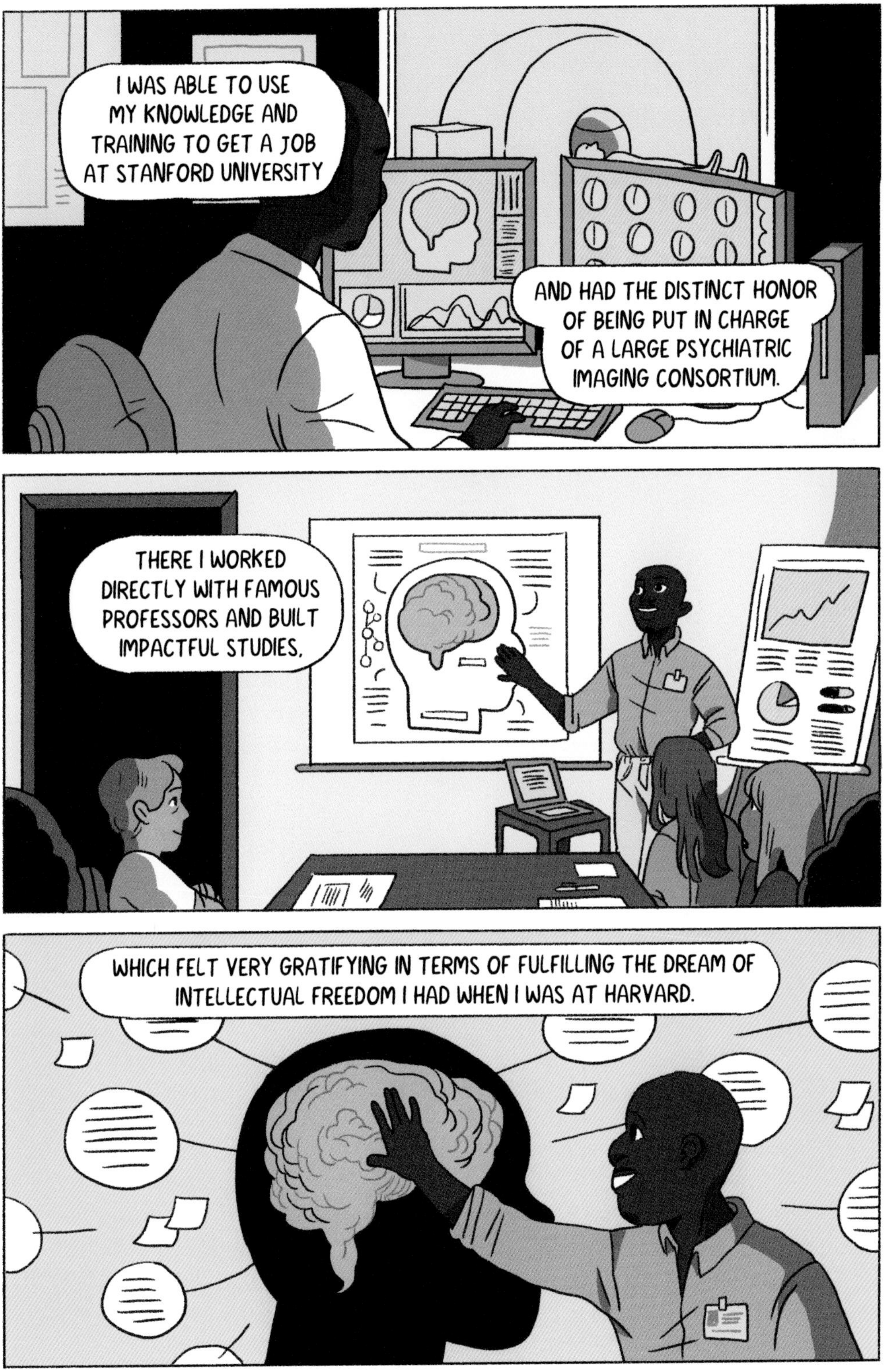
I WAS ABLE TO USE MY KNOWLEDGE AND TRAINING TO GET A JOB AT STANFORD UNIVERSITY
AND HAD THE DISTINCT HONOR OF BEING PUT IN CHARGE OF A LARGE PSYCHIATRIC IMAGING CONSORTIUM.
THERE I WORKED DIRECTLY WITH FAMOUS PROFESSORS AND BUILT IMPACTFUL STUDIES,
WHICH FELT VERY GRATIFYING IN TERMS OF FULFILLING THE DREAM OF INTELLECTUAL FREEDOM I HAD WHEN I WAS AT HARVARD.

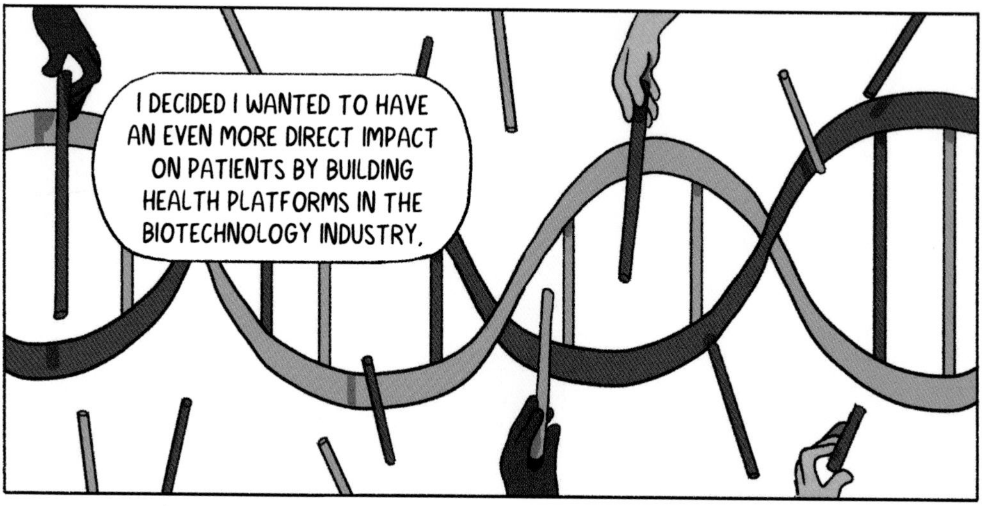
I DECIDED I WANTED TO HAVE AN EVEN MORE DIRECT IMPACT ON PATIENTS BY BUILDING HEALTH PLATFORMS IN THE BIOTECHNOLOGY INDUSTRY,

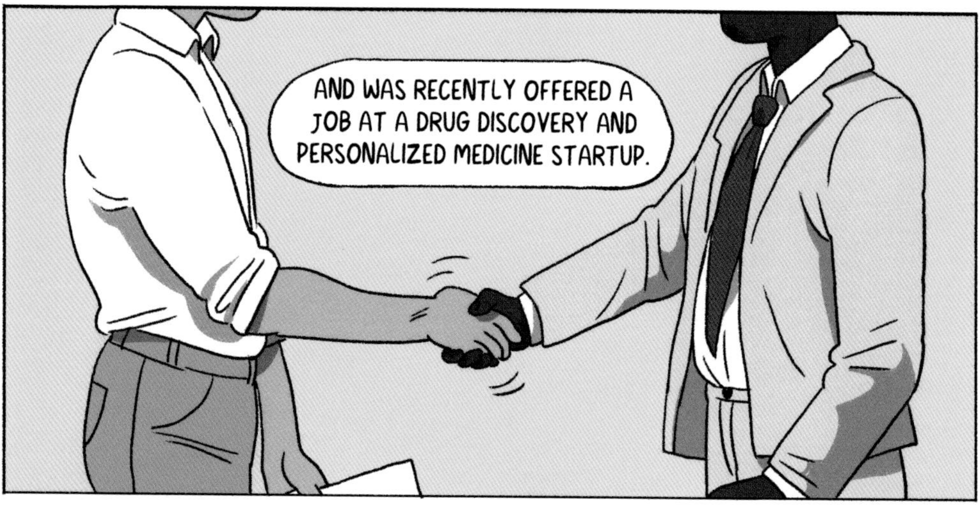
AND WAS RECENTLY OFFERED A JOB AT A DRUG DISCOVERY AND PERSONALIZED MEDICINE STARTUP.

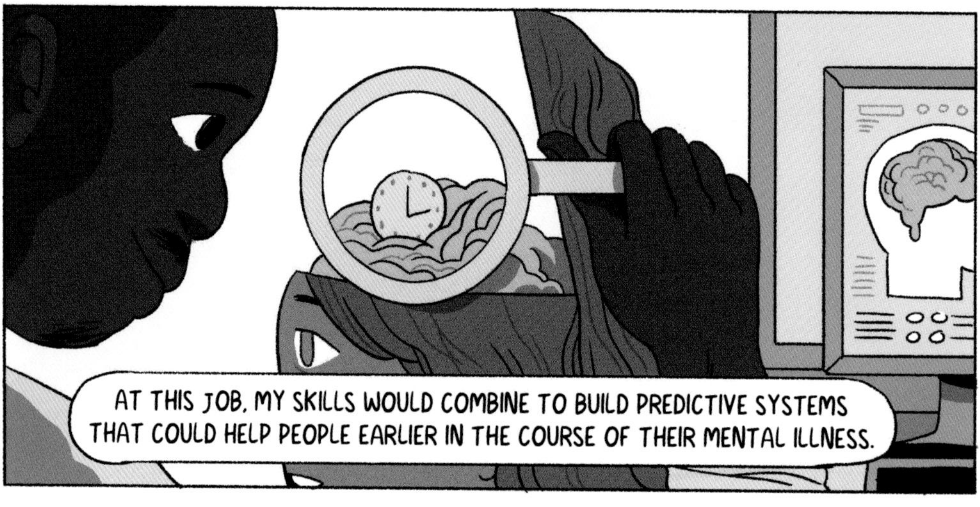
AT THIS JOB, MY SKILLS WOULD COMBINE TO BUILD PREDICTIVE SYSTEMS THAT COULD HELP PEOPLE EARLIER IN THE COURSE OF THEIR MENTAL ILLNESS.

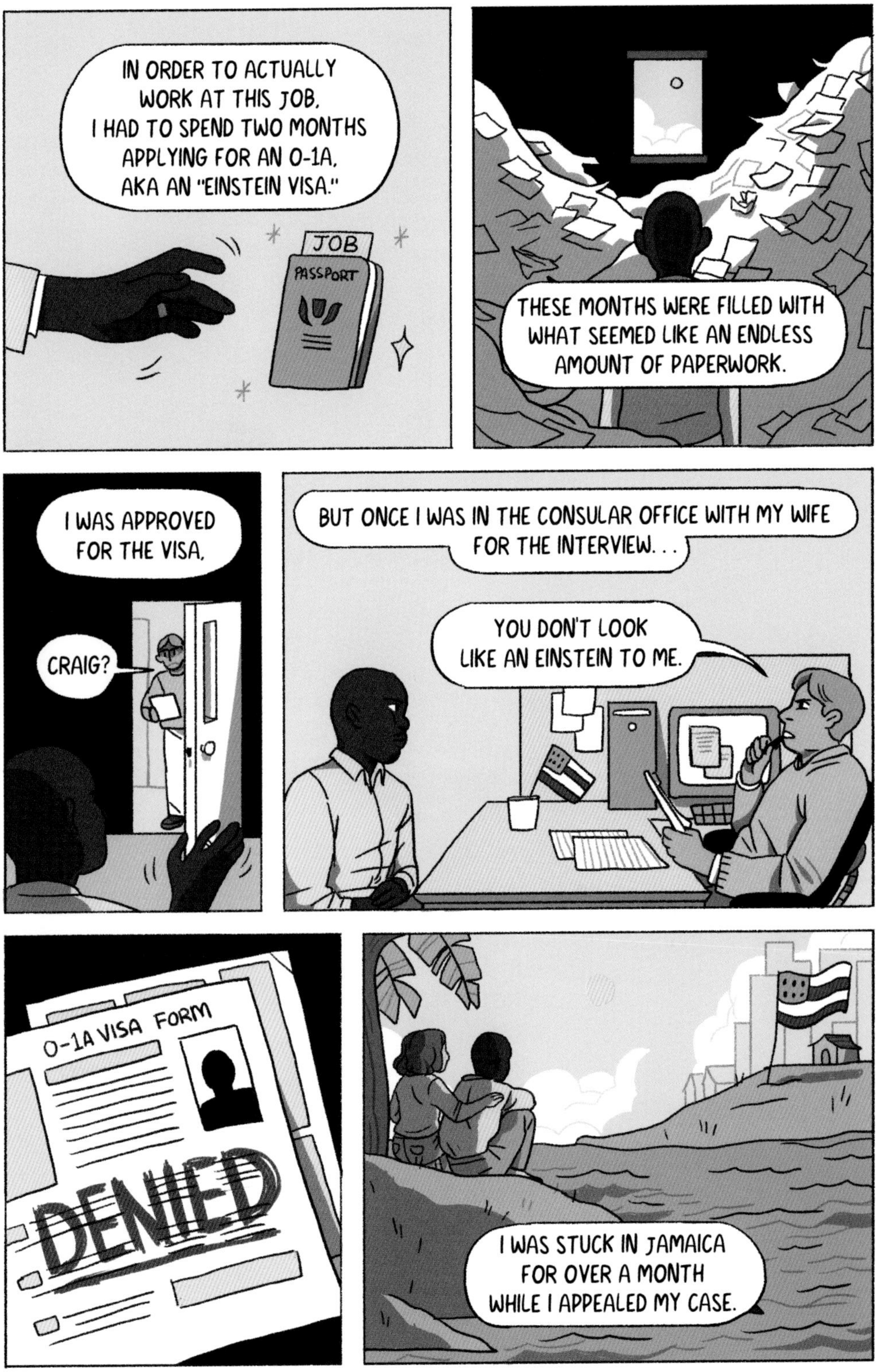
IN ORDER TO ACTUALLY WORK AT THIS JOB, I HAD TO SPEND TWO MONTHS APPLYING FOR AN O-1A, AKA AN "EINSTEIN VISA."
JOB
PASSPORT
THESE MONTHS WERE FILLED WITH WHAT SEEMED LIKE AN ENDLESS AMOUNT OF PAPERWORK.
I WAS APPROVED FOR THE VISA,
CRAIG?
BUT ONCE I WAS IN THE CONSULAR OFFICE WITH MY WIFE FOR THE INTERVIEW. . .
YOU DON'T LOOK LIKE AN EINSTEIN TO ME.
O-1A VISA FORM
DENIED
I WAS STUCK IN JAMAICA FOR OVER A MONTH WHILE I APPEALED MY CASE.

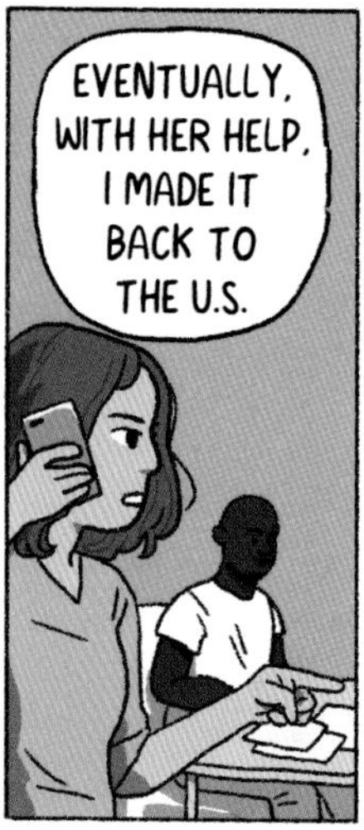
EVENTUALLY, WITH HER HELP, I MADE IT BACK TO THE U.S.

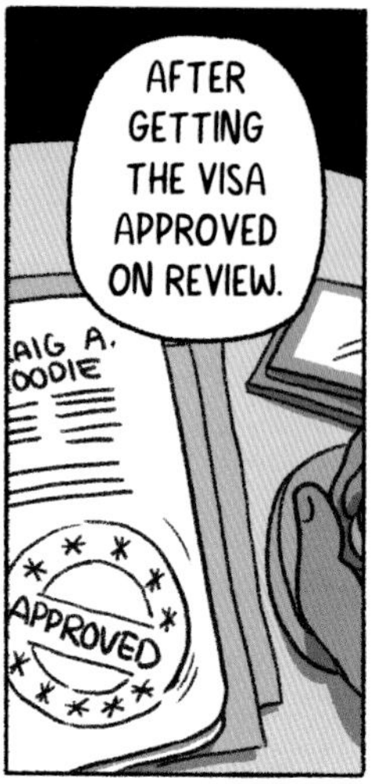
AFTER GETTING THE VISA APPROVED ON REVIEW.
APPROVED

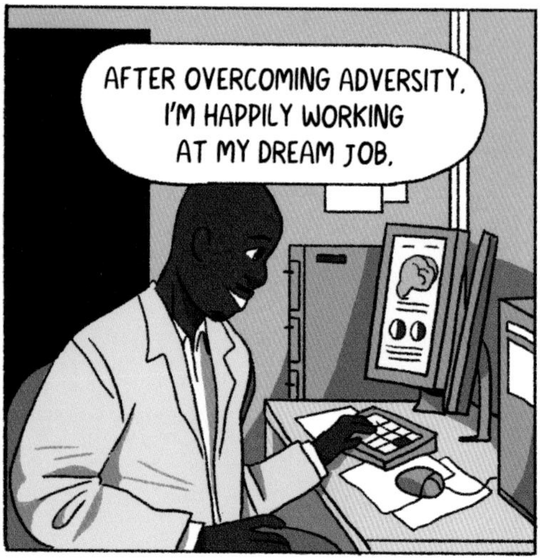
AFTER OVERCOMING ADVERSITY, I'M HAPPILY WORKING AT MY DREAM JOB.

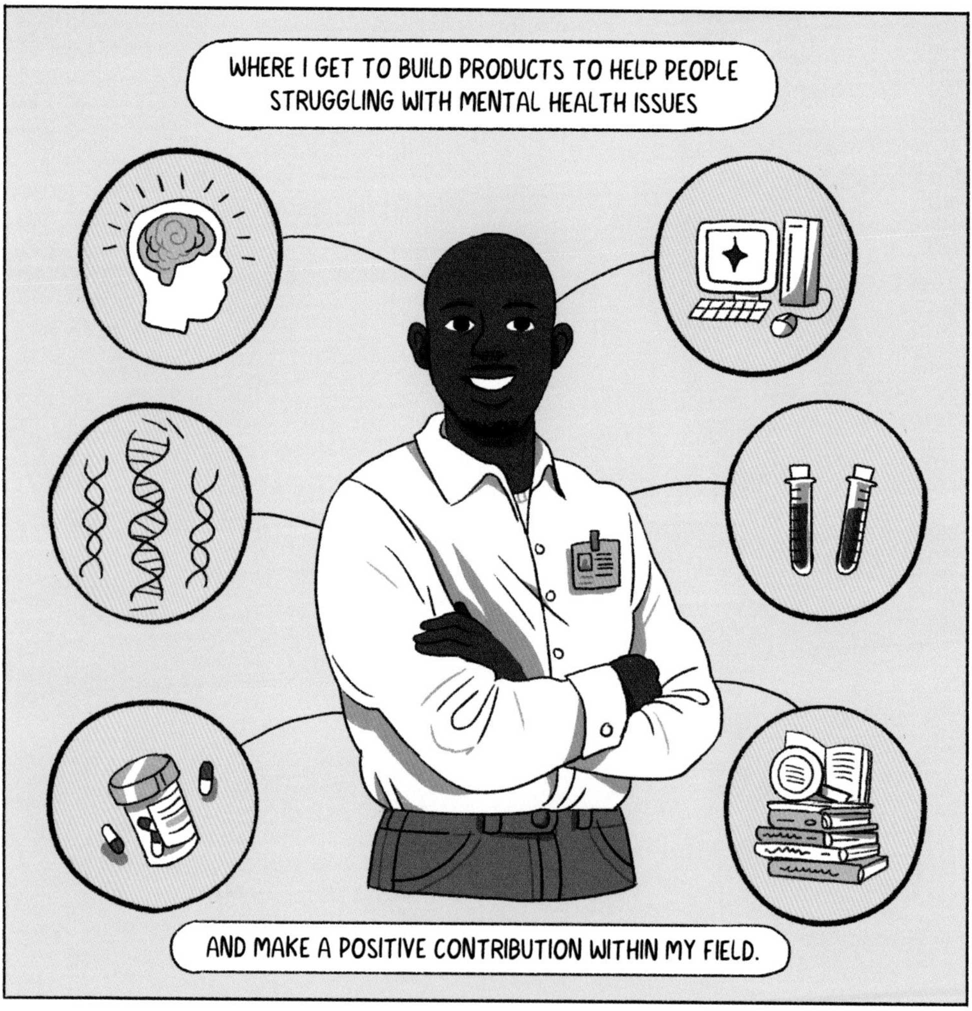
WHERE I GET TO BUILD PRODUCTS TO HELP PEOPLE STRUGGLING WITH MENTAL HEALTH ISSUES
AND MAKE A POSITIVE CONTRIBUTION WITHIN MY FIELD.

GLOSSARY

0-1A visa: A temporary worker visa granted by the United States to an alien "who possesses extraordinary ability in the sciences, arts, education, business, or athletics, or who has a demonstrated record of extraordinary achievement in the motion picture or television industry and has been recognized nationally or internationally for those achievements," and to certain assistants and immediate family members of such aliens.

Comorbid mental disorder: Comorbidity describes two or more disorders or illnesses occurring in the same person. They can occur at the same time or one after the other.

Neuroendocrinology: The branch of biology (specifically of physiology), that studies the interaction between the nervous system and the endocrine system; i.e., how the brain regulates the hormonal activity in the body.

Transgenic mice (genetically modified mouse or genetically engineered mouse): A mouse that has had its genome altered through the use of genetic engineering techniques. Genetically modified mice are commonly used for research or as animal models of human diseases and are also used for research on genes.

Water polo: A competitive team sport played in water between two teams of seven players each. The game consists of four quarters in which the two teams attempt to score goals by throwing the ball into the opposing team's goal. The team with the most goals at the end of the game wins the match.

GUATEMALA

KARELIN

Born: Petén, Guatemala
Current: Atlanta, Georgia

Karelin is a first-generation college student at Emory University studying computer science. She hopes to pursue a career in biology and computer science. In her free time, she enjoys advocating for the Latino community and volunteers with organizations such as the Latin American Association. She is particularly passionate about education for Dreamers, immigrants who were brought to the U.S. as children, like herself, DACA (Deferred Action for Childhood Arrivals) Recipients. She hopes to excel as a professional and give back to her immigrant community.

www.greencardvoices.org/speakers/karelin

MIKE CENTENO

Born: Venezuela
Current: Chicago, Illinois

Mike Centeno is a Venezuelan cartoonist who has been living in the U.S. for almost 10 years. His work has been featured in *The Chicago Reader*, *DigBoston*, *The Nib*, *Southside Weekly*, and he self-publishes his own comics series titled Futile Comics. His stories focus on identity, immigration, and the rise of global populism and authoritarianism which he explores through fiction.

www.mikecenteno.com

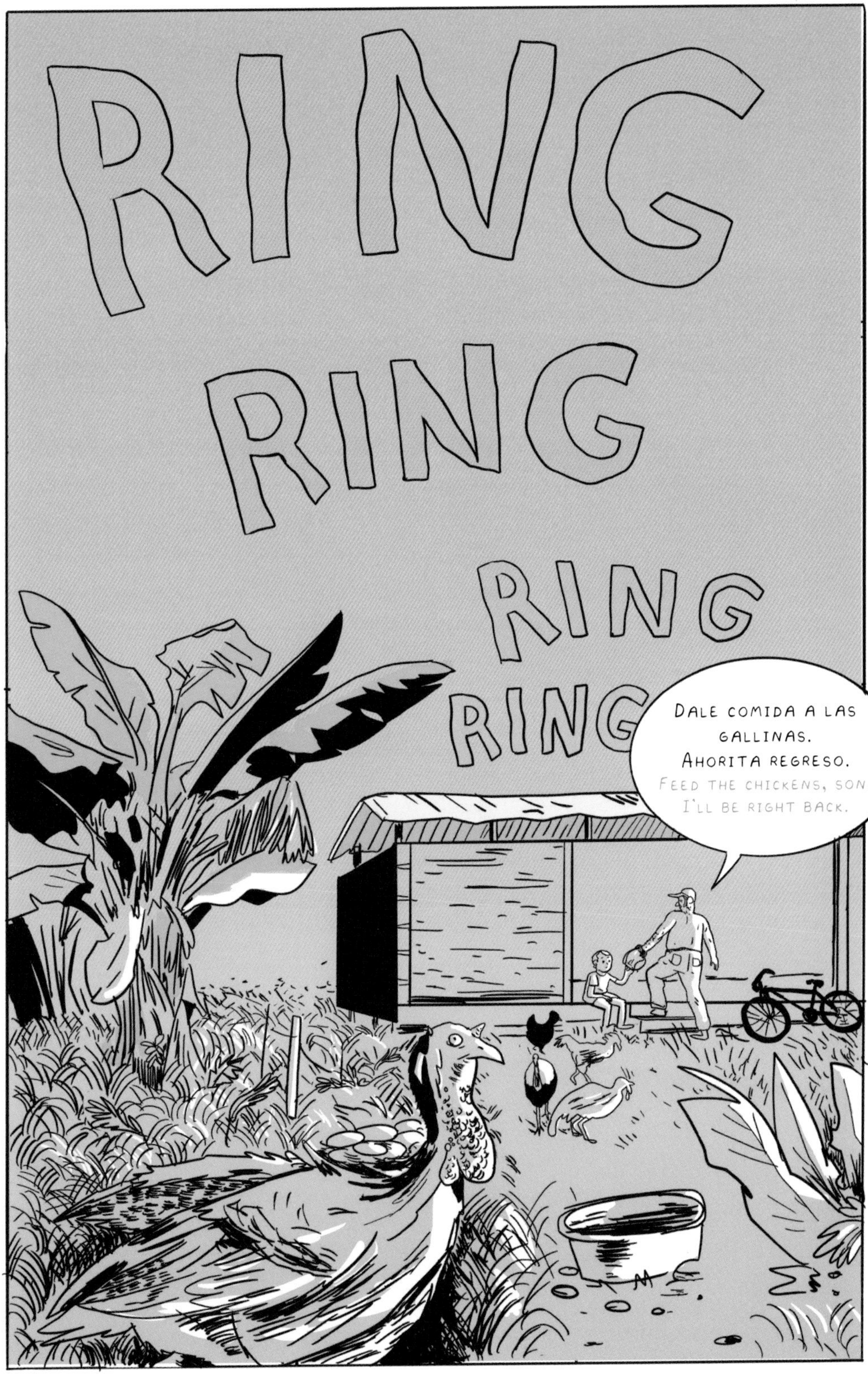
RING
RING
RING
RING
DALE COMIDA A LAS GALLINAS. AHORITA REGRESO.
FEED THE CHICKENS, SON. I'LL BE RIGHT BACK.

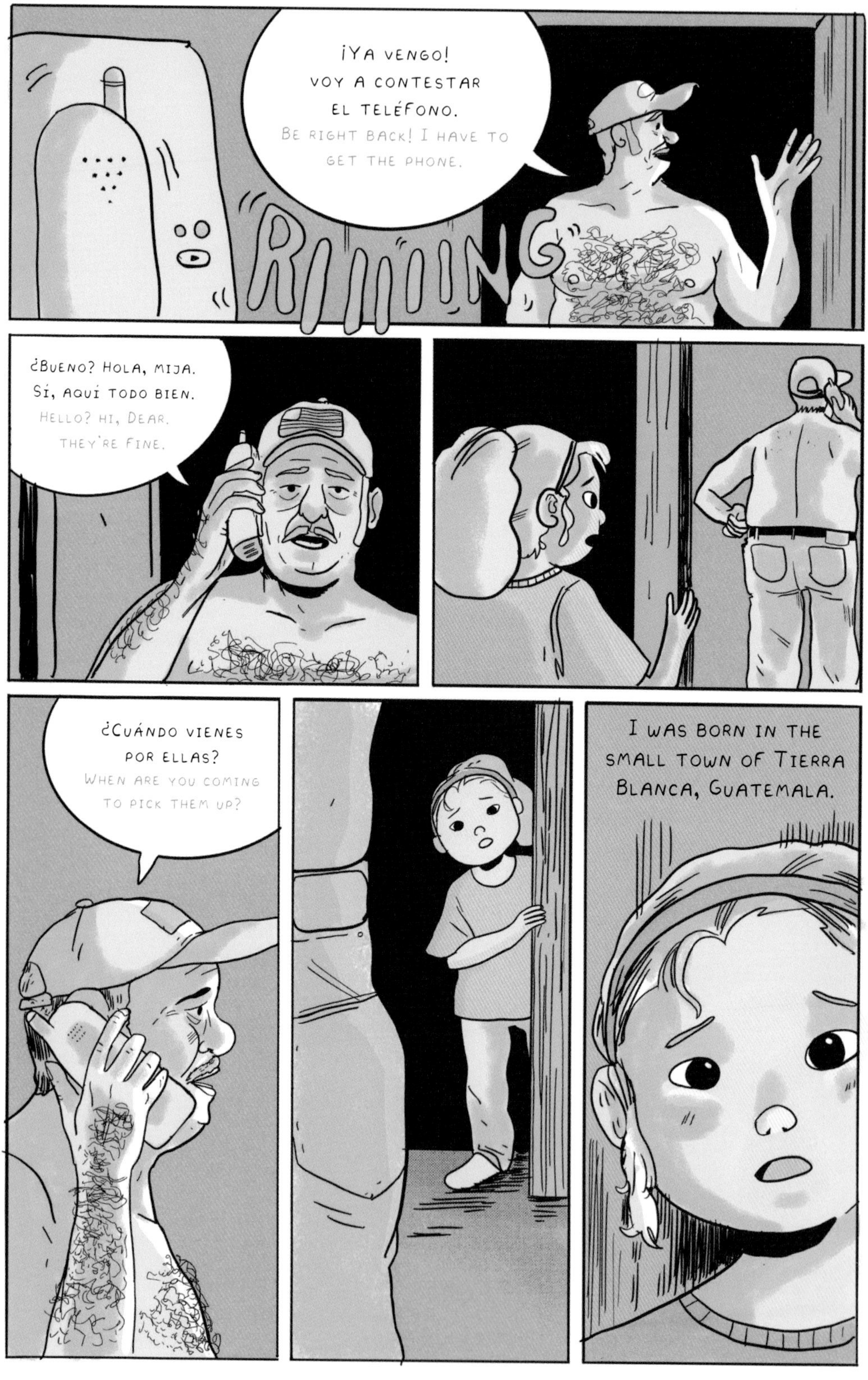
¡YA VENGO! VOY A CONTESTAR EL TELÉFONO.
BE RIGHT BACK! I HAVE TO GET THE PHONE.
RIIIING
¿BUENO? HOLA, MIJA. SÍ, AQUÍ TODO BIEN.
HELLO? HI, DEAR. THEY'RE FINE.
¿CUÁNDO VIENES POR ELLAS?
WHEN ARE YOU COMING TO PICK THEM UP?
I WAS BORN IN THE SMALL TOWN OF TIERRA BLANCA, GUATEMALA.

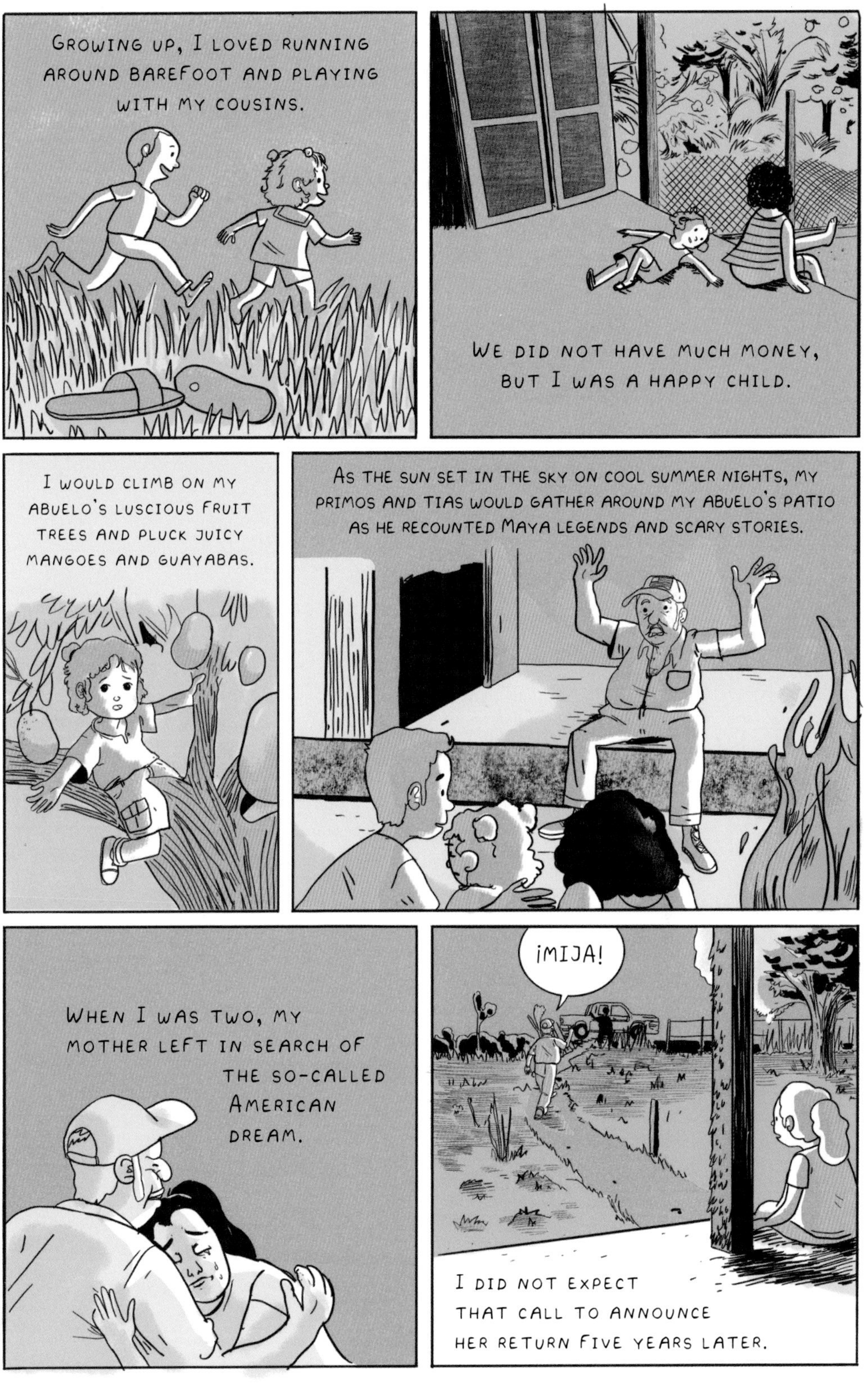
GROWING UP, I LOVED RUNNING AROUND BAREFOOT AND PLAYING WITH MY COUSINS.
WE DID NOT HAVE MUCH MONEY, BUT I WAS A HAPPY CHILD.
I WOULD CLIMB ON MY ABUELO'S LUSCIOUS FRUIT TREES AND PLUCK JUICY MANGOES AND GUAYABAS.
AS THE SUN SET IN THE SKY ON COOL SUMMER NIGHTS, MY PRIMOS AND TIAS WOULD GATHER AROUND MY ABUELO'S PATIO AS HE RECOUNTED MAYA LEGENDS AND SCARY STORIES.
WHEN I WAS TWO, MY MOTHER LEFT IN SEARCH OF THE SO-CALLED AMERICAN DREAM.
¡MIJA!
I DID NOT EXPECT THAT CALL TO ANNOUNCE HER RETURN FIVE YEARS LATER.

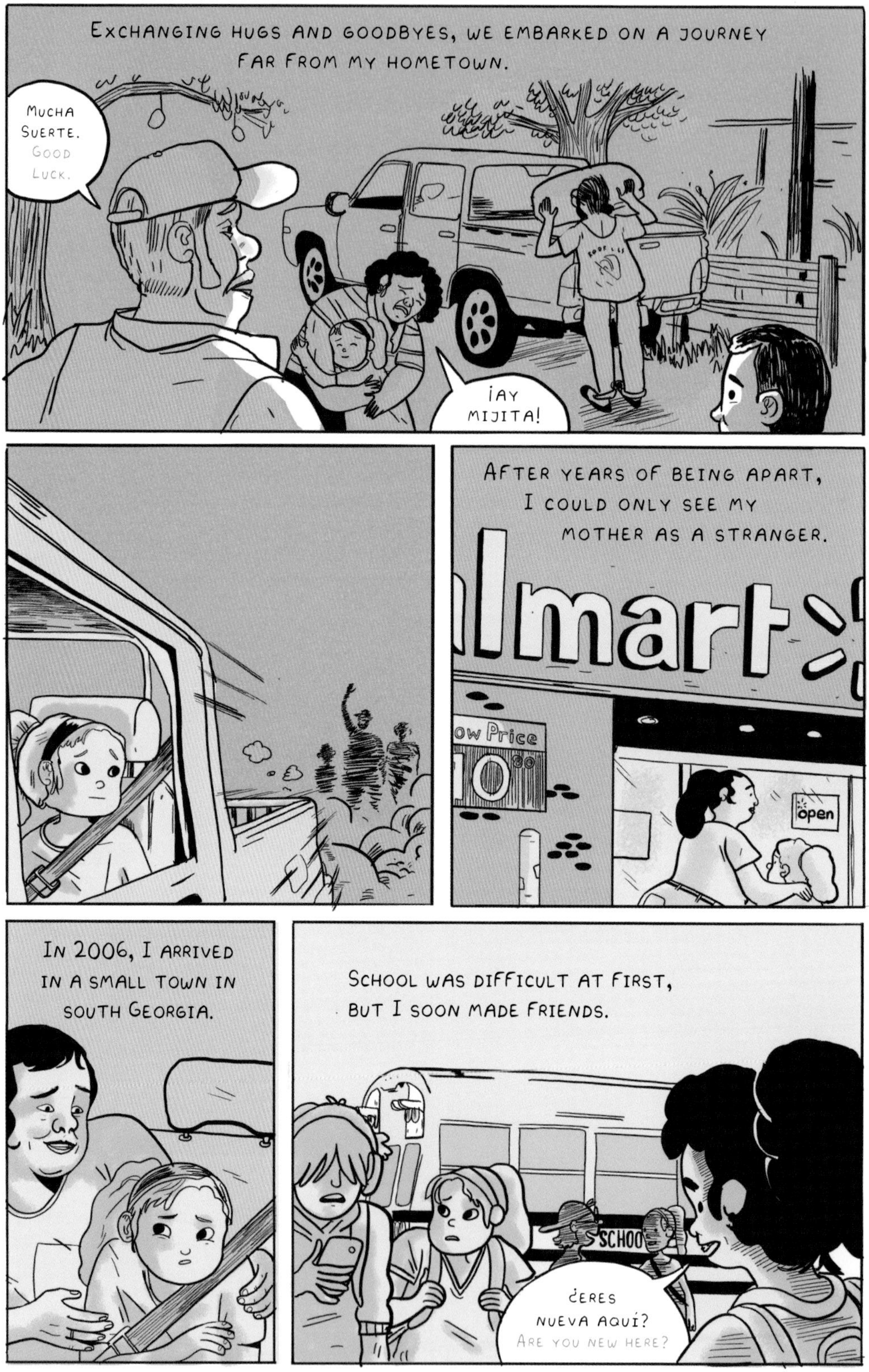
EXCHANGING HUGS AND GOODBYES, WE EMBARKED ON A JOURNEY FAR FROM MY HOMETOWN.
MUCHA SUERTE.
GOOD LUCK.
¡AY MIJITA!
AFTER YEARS OF BEING APART, I COULD ONLY SEE MY MOTHER AS A STRANGER.
open
IN 2006, I ARRIVED IN A SMALL TOWN IN SOUTH GEORGIA.
SCHOOL WAS DIFFICULT AT FIRST, BUT I SOON MADE FRIENDS.
¿ERES NUEVA AQUI?
ARE YOU NEW HERE?

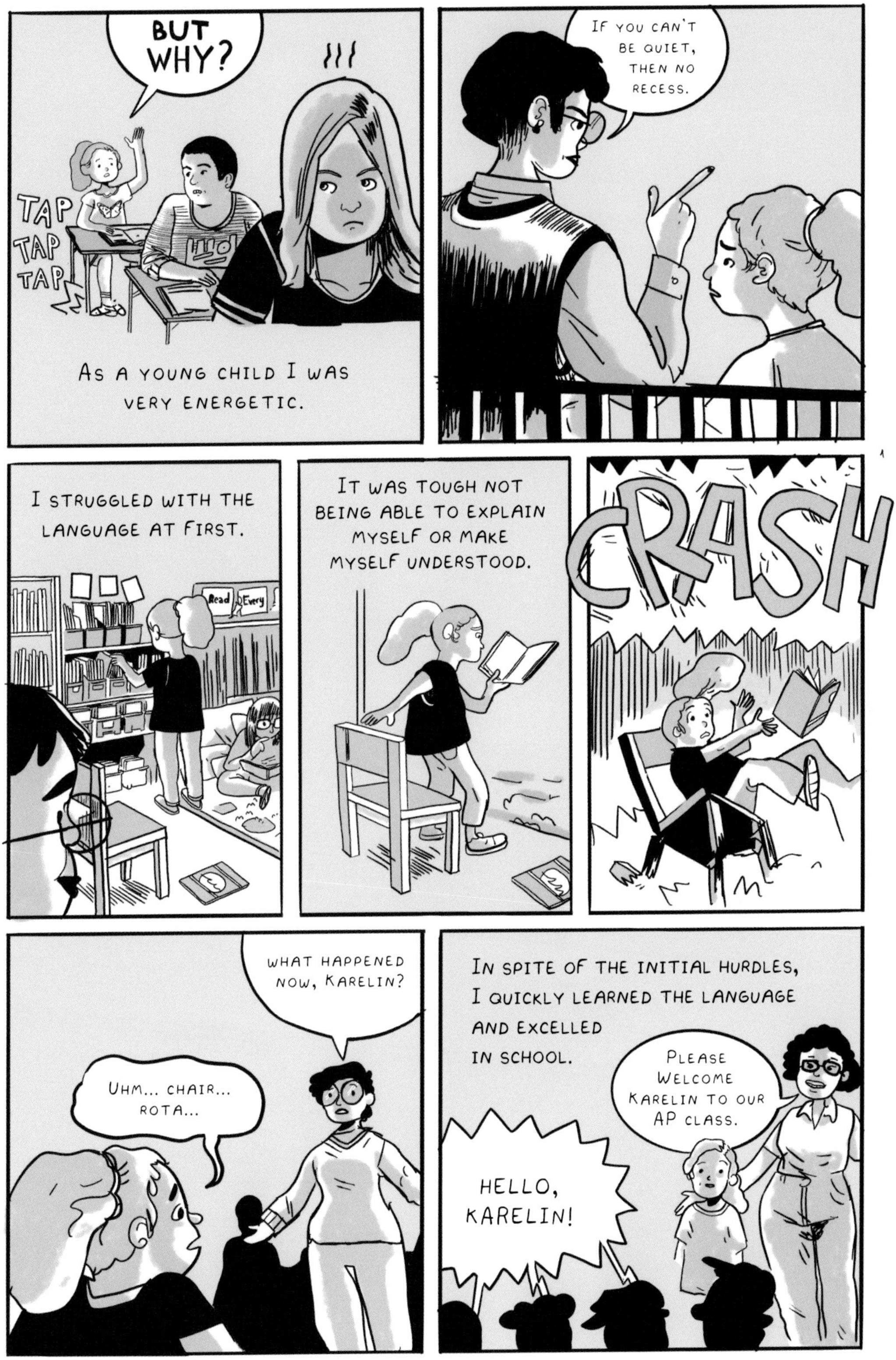
BUT WHY?
TAP TAP TAP
As a young child I was very energetic.
If you can't be quiet, then no recess.
I struggled with the language at first.
Read Every
It was tough not being able to explain myself or make myself understood.
CRASH
What happened now, Karelin?
Uhm... chair... rota...
In spite of the initial hurdles, I quickly learned the language and excelled in school.
Please welcome Karelin to our AP class.
Hello, Karelin!

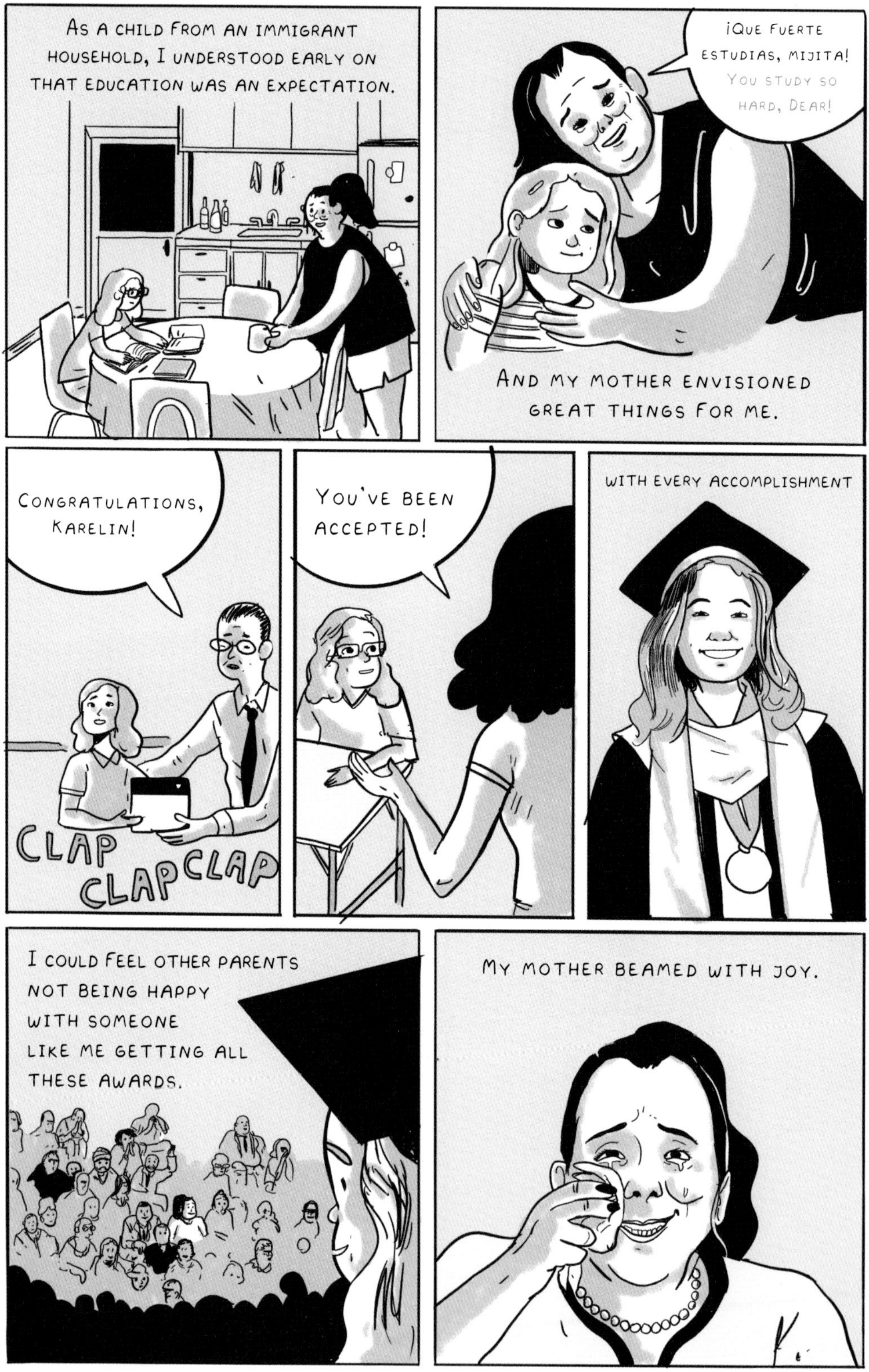

As a child from an immigrant household, I understood early on that education was an expectation.
¡Que fuerte estudias, mijita!
You study so hard, Dear!
And my mother envisioned great things for me.
Congratulations, Karelin!
CLAP CLAP CLAP
You've been accepted!
With every accomplishment
I could feel other parents not being happy with someone like me getting all these awards.
My mother beamed with joy.

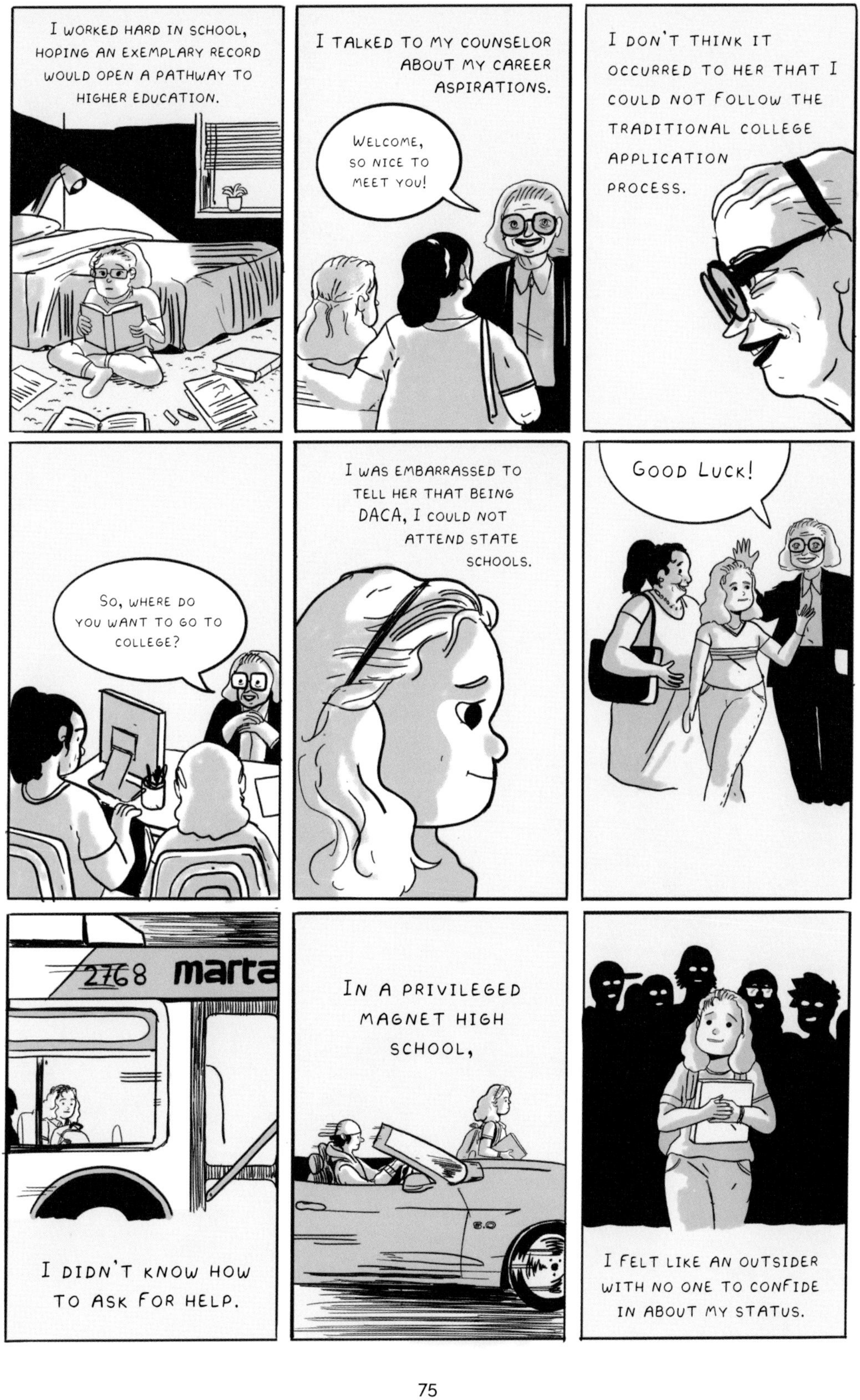
I WORKED HARD IN SCHOOL, HOPING AN EXEMPLARY RECORD WOULD OPEN A PATHWAY TO HIGHER EDUCATION.
I TALKED TO MY COUNSELOR ABOUT MY CAREER ASPIRATIONS.
WELCOME, SO NICE TO MEET YOU!
I DON'T THINK IT OCCURRED TO HER THAT I COULD NOT FOLLOW THE TRADITIONAL COLLEGE APPLICATION PROCESS.
SO, WHERE DO YOU WANT TO GO TO COLLEGE?
I WAS EMBARRASSED TO TELL HER THAT BEING DACA, I COULD NOT ATTEND STATE SCHOOLS.
GOOD LUCK!
2768 marta
I DIDN'T KNOW HOW TO ASK FOR HELP.
IN A PRIVILEGED MAGNET HIGH SCHOOL,
I FELT LIKE AN OUTSIDER WITH NO ONE TO CONFIDE IN ABOUT MY STATUS.

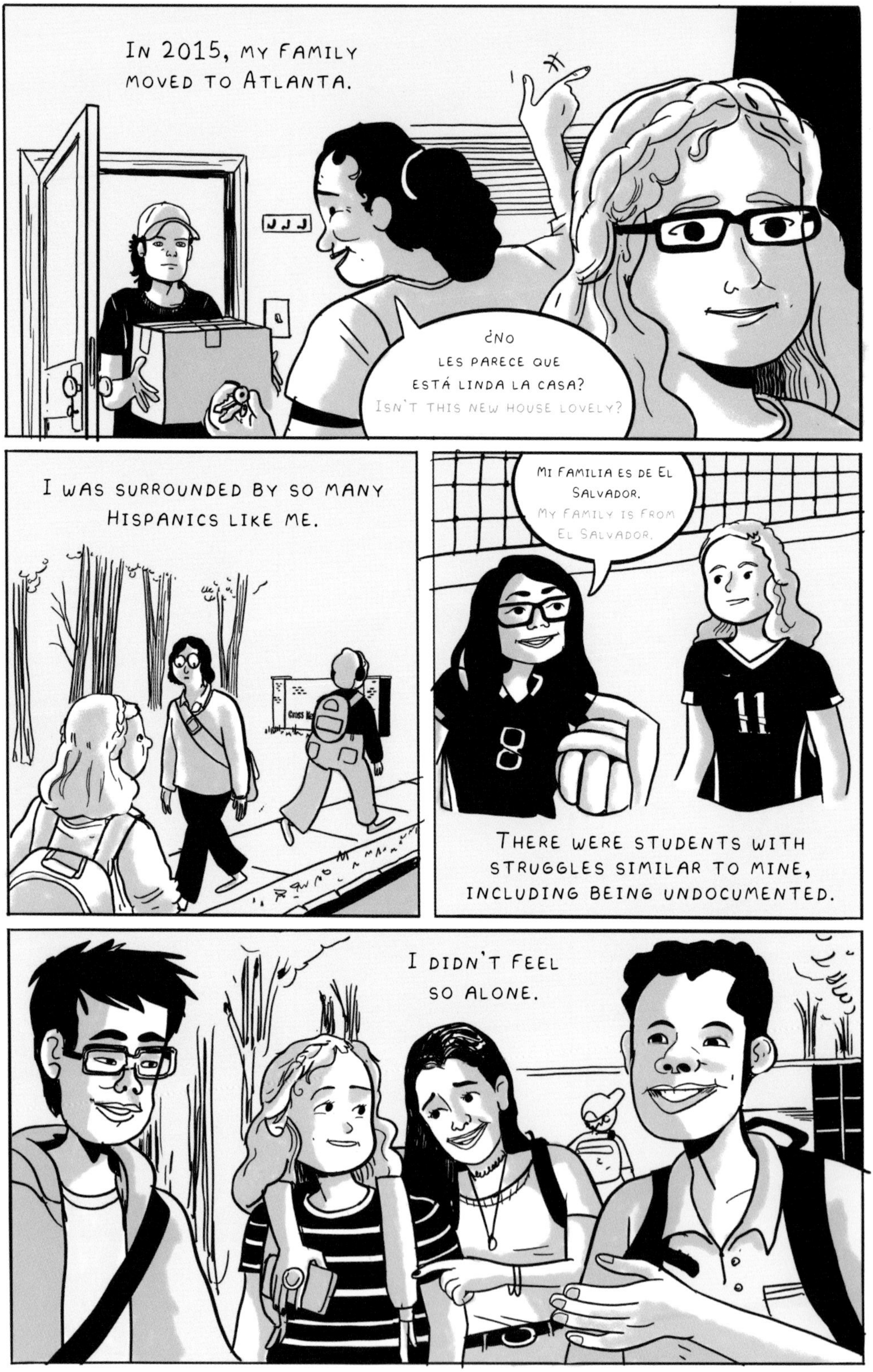

In 2015, my family moved to Atlanta.
¿No les parece que está linda la casa?
Isn't this new house lovely?
I was surrounded by so many Hispanics like me.
Mi familia es de El Salvador.
My family is from El Salvador.
There were students with struggles similar to mine, including being undocumented.
I didn't feel so alone.

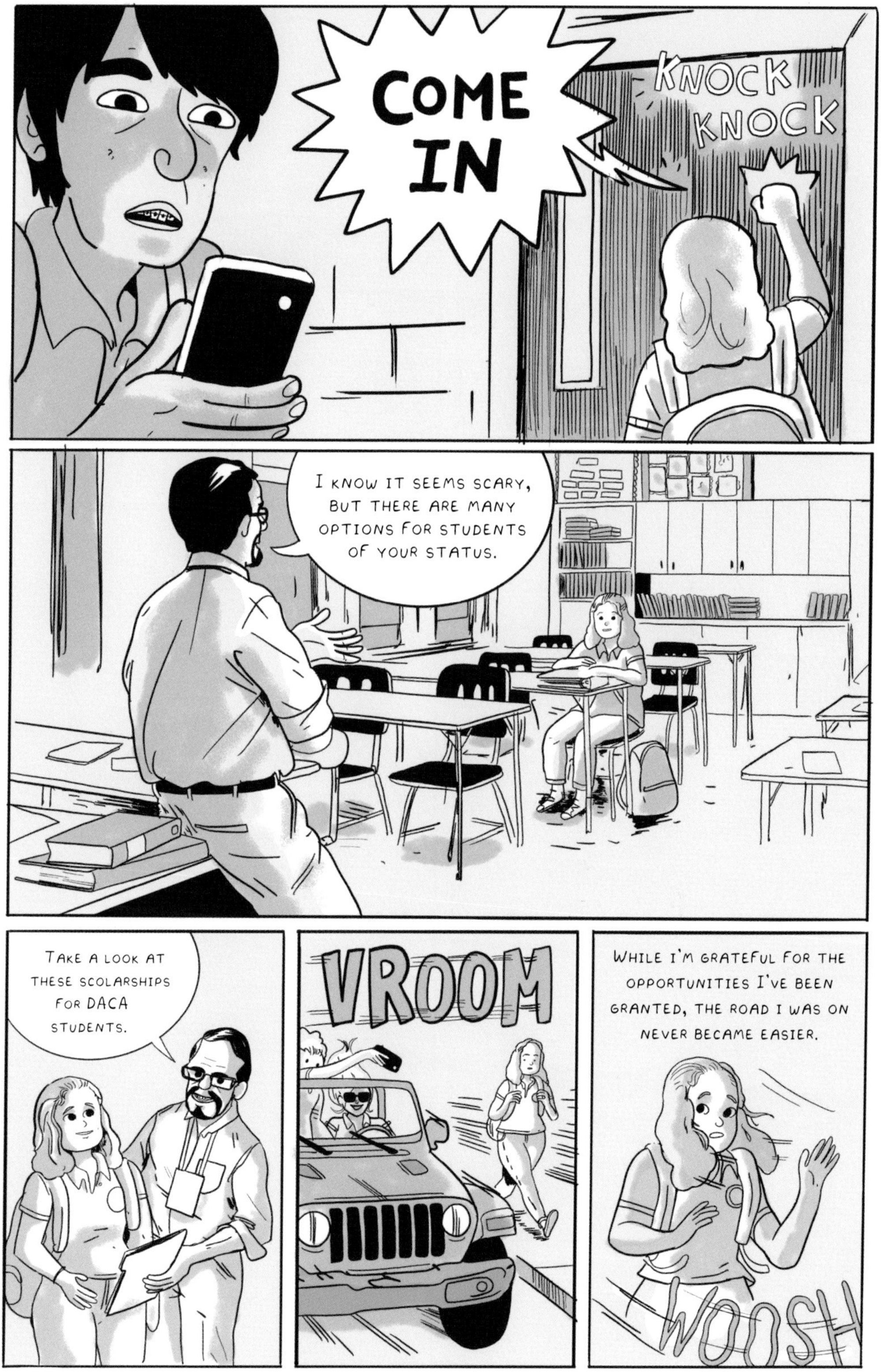
COME IN
KNOCK KNOCK
I KNOW IT SEEMS SCARY, BUT THERE ARE MANY OPTIONS FOR STUDENTS OF YOUR STATUS.
TAKE A LOOK AT THESE SCOLARSHIPS FOR DACA STUDENTS.
VROOM
WHILE I'M GRATEFUL FOR THE OPPORTUNITIES I'VE BEEN GRANTED, THE ROAD I WAS ON NEVER BECAME EASIER.
WOOSH

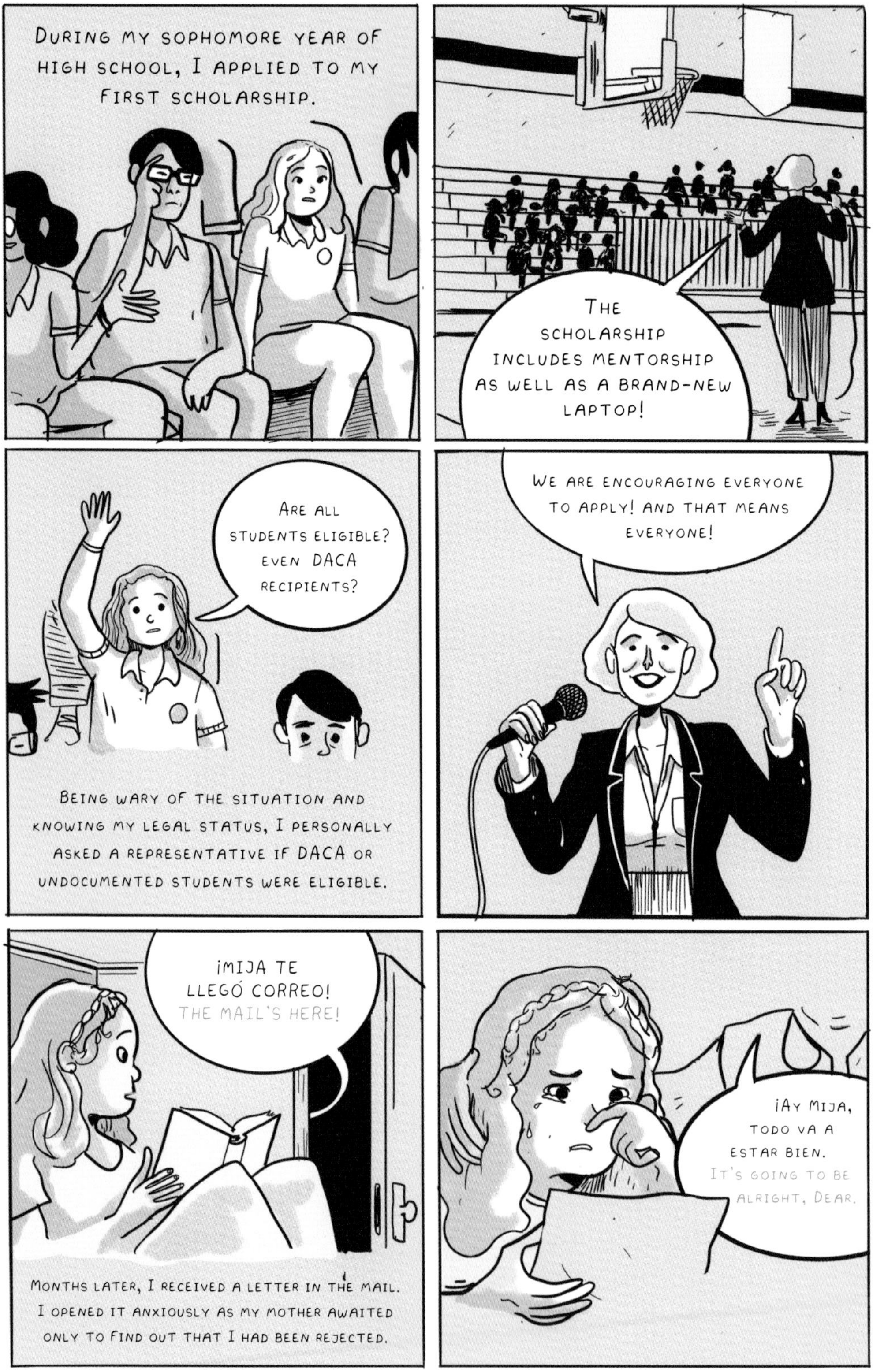
During my sophomore year of high school, I applied to my first scholarship.
The scholarship includes mentorship as well as a brand-new laptop!
Are all students eligible? even DACA recipients?
We are encouraging everyone to apply! And that means everyone!
Being wary of the situation and knowing my legal status, I personally asked a representative if DACA or undocumented students were eligible.
¡Mija te llegó correo!
The mail's here!
Months later, I received a letter in the mail. I opened it anxiously as my mother awaited only to find out that I had been rejected.
¡Ay Mija, todo va a estar bien.
It's going to be alright, Dear.

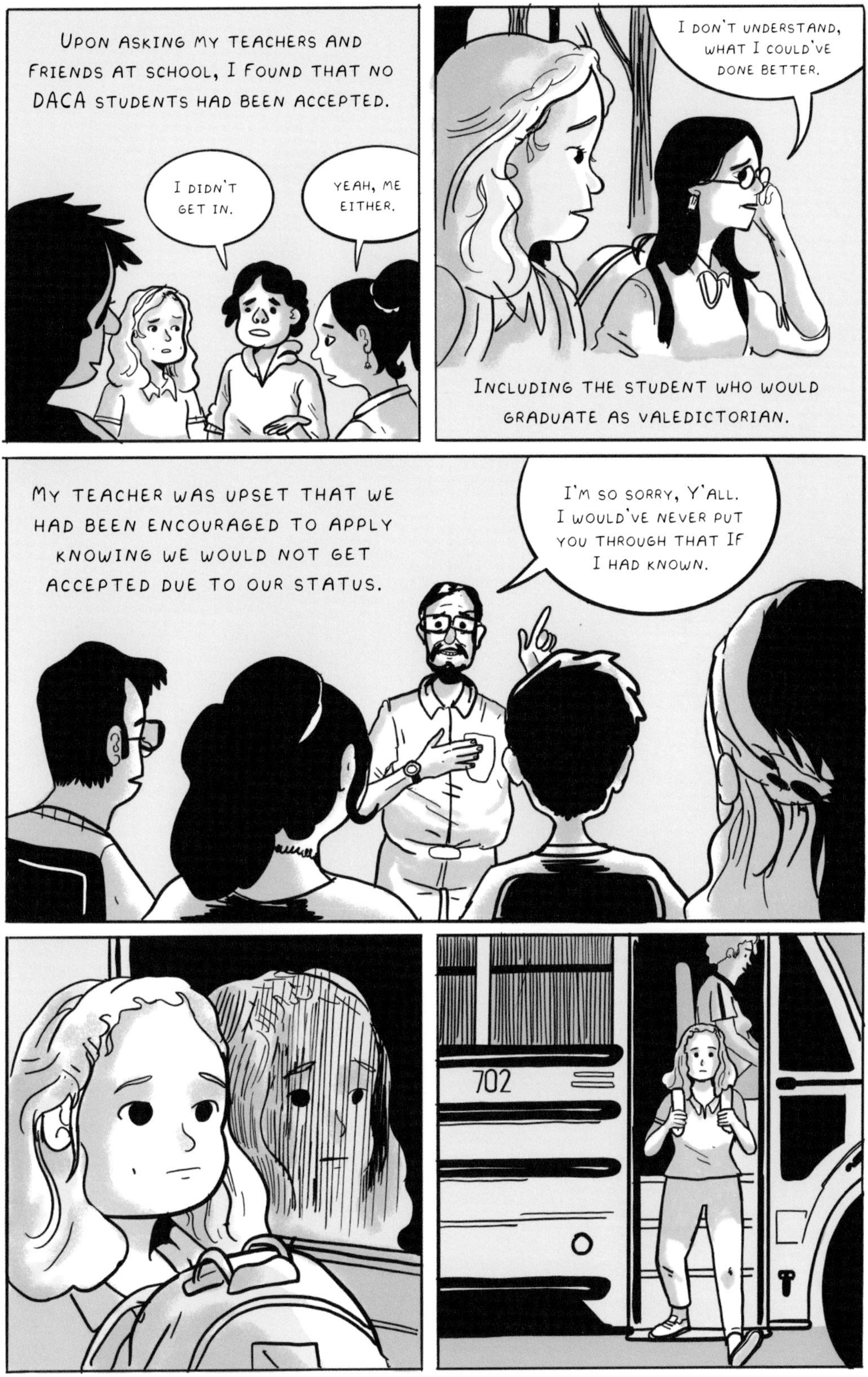
UPON ASKING MY TEACHERS AND FRIENDS AT SCHOOL, I FOUND THAT NO DACA STUDENTS HAD BEEN ACCEPTED.
I DIDN'T GET IN.
YEAH, ME EITHER.
I DON'T UNDERSTAND, WHAT I COULD'VE DONE BETTER.
INCLUDING THE STUDENT WHO WOULD GRADUATE AS VALEDICTORIAN.
MY TEACHER WAS UPSET THAT WE HAD BEEN ENCOURAGED TO APPLY KNOWING WE WOULD NOT GET ACCEPTED DUE TO OUR STATUS.
I'M SO SORRY, Y'ALL. I WOULD'VE NEVER PUT YOU THROUGH THAT IF I HAD KNOWN.
702

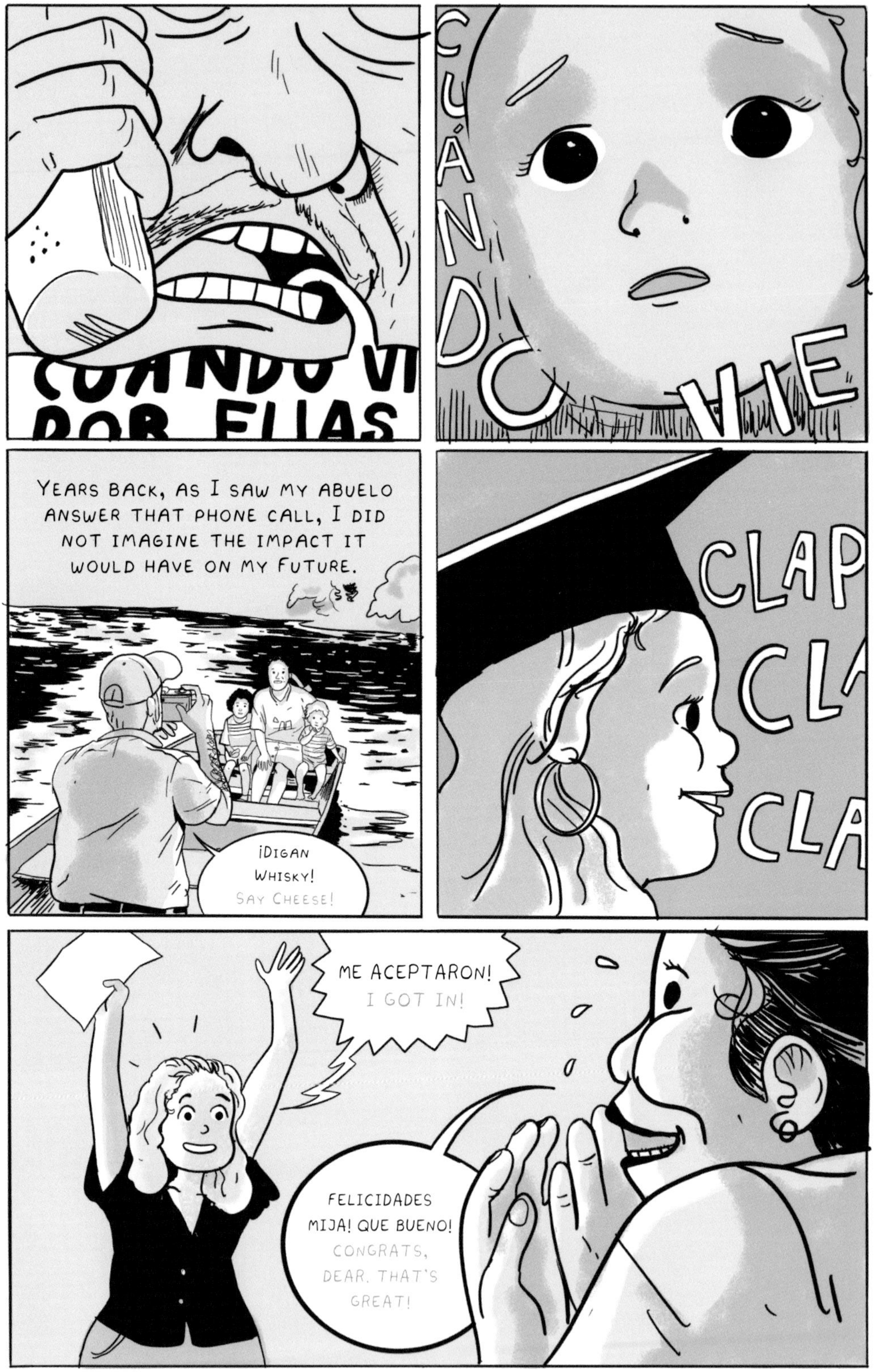
YEARS BACK, AS I SAW MY ABUELO ANSWER THAT PHONE CALL, I DID NOT IMAGINE THE IMPACT IT WOULD HAVE ON MY FUTURE.
¡DIGAN WHISKY!
SAY CHEESE!
CLAP
ME ACEPTARON!
I GOT IN!
FELICIDADES MIJA! QUE BUENO!
CONGRATS, DEAR. THAT'S GREAT!

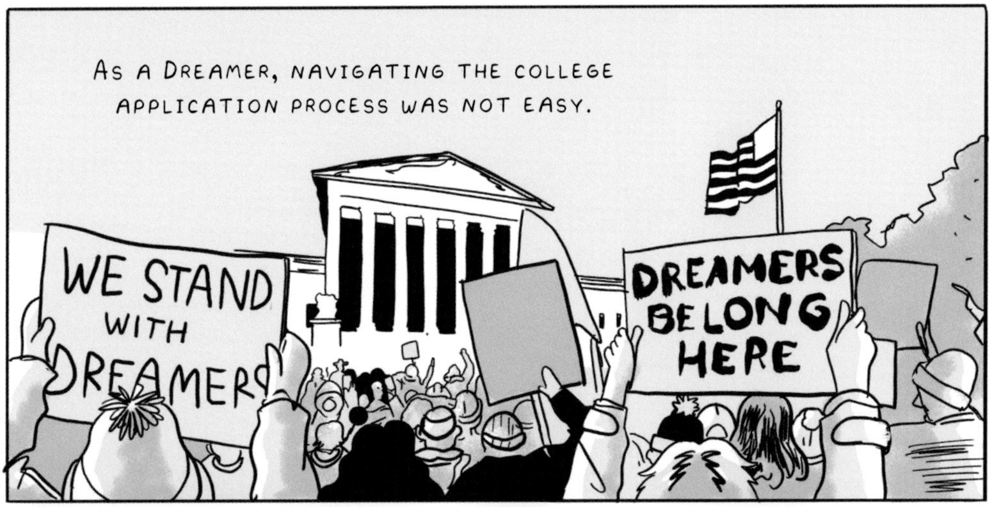
AS A DREAMER, NAVIGATING THE COLLEGE APPLICATION PROCESS WAS NOT EASY.
WE STAND WITH DREAMERS
DREAMERS BELONG HERE

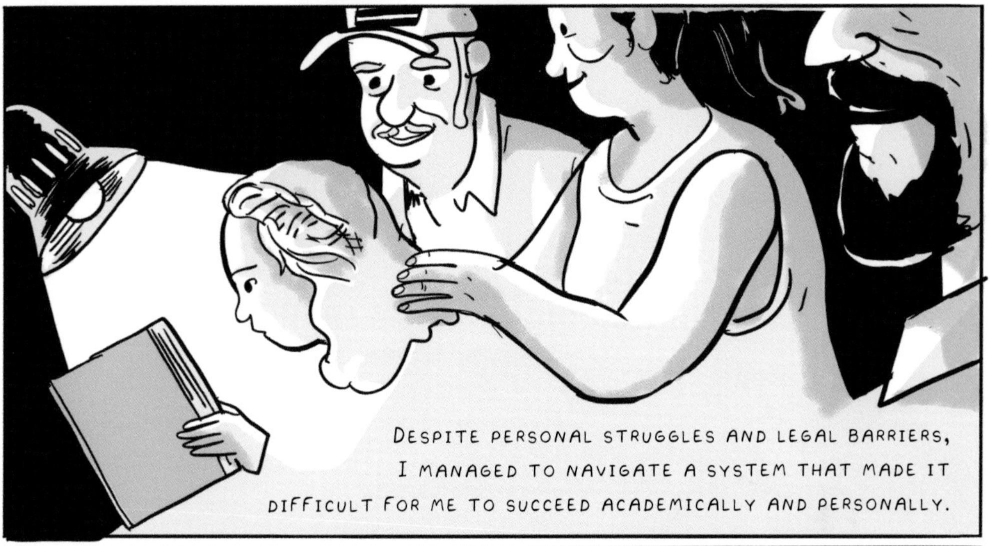
DESPITE PERSONAL STRUGGLES AND LEGAL BARRIERS, I MANAGED TO NAVIGATE A SYSTEM THAT MADE IT DIFFICULT FOR ME TO SUCCEED ACADEMICALLY AND PERSONALLY.

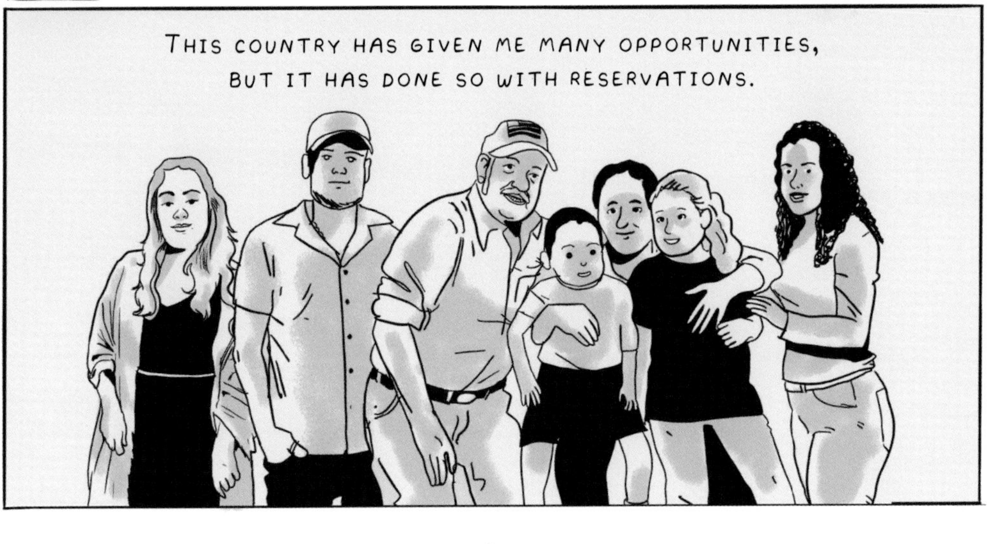
THIS COUNTRY HAS GIVEN ME MANY OPPORTUNITIES, BUT IT HAS DONE SO WITH RESERVATIONS.

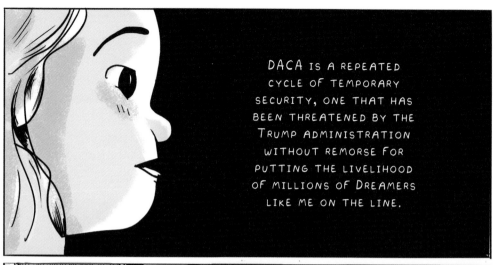

DACA IS A REPEATED CYCLE OF TEMPORARY SECURITY, ONE THAT HAS BEEN THREATENED BY THE *Trump* ADMINISTRATION WITHOUT REMORSE FOR PUTTING THE LIVELIHOOD OF MILLIONS OF *Dreamers* LIKE ME ON THE LINE.

BUT WE ARE STILL HERE...

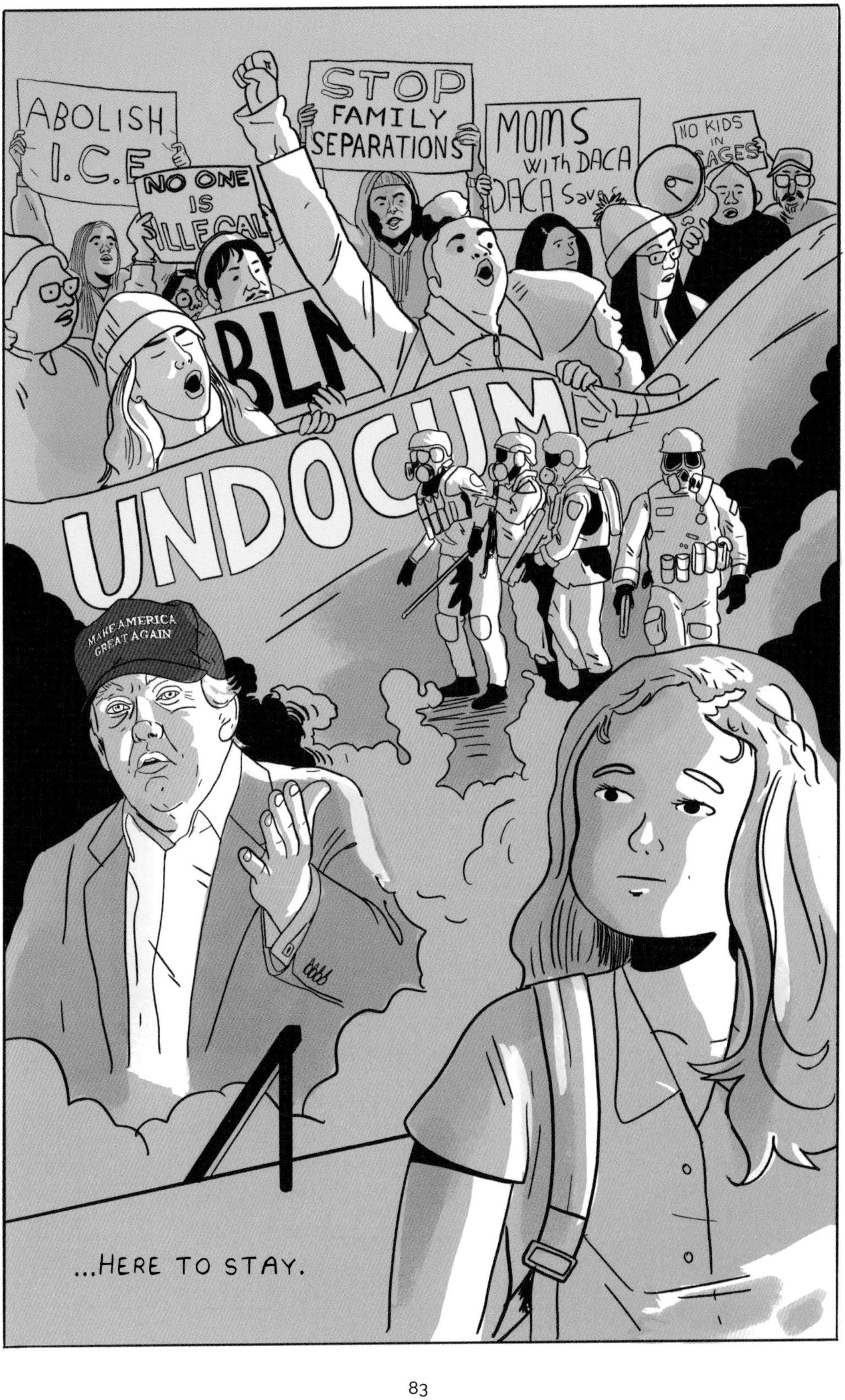
ABOLISH I.C.E
NO ONE IS ILLEGAL
STOP FAMILY SEPARATIONS
MOMS with DACA
DACA Saves
NO KIDS IN CAGES
BLM
UNDOCUM
MAKE AMERICA GREAT AGAIN
...HERE TO STAY.

CHAD AND CAMEROON

RUTH MEKOULOM

Born: N'Djamena, Chad
Current: Fargo, North Dakota

Ruth Mekoulom has lived in Fargo, North Dakota, since the age of thirteen. She attended South Fargo High School and later transferred to Davies High School, where she graduated in 2019. She took classes with other English Language Learner students while also being in the deaf and hard of hearing program. Ruth became a US citizen in October 2020 in the midst of the COVID-19 pandemic. She is a member of the Jehovah's Witnesses and volunteers with organizations in her community. Ruth will start phlebotomy studies in the summer of 2021 and hopes to work with elders as a certified nurse assistant.

www.greencardvoices.org/speakers/ruth-mekoulom

HOP

Hop is the Cameroonian-U.S. researcher artist collective creating graphic novels at the intersection of language, culture, and oral traditions; team members include:

Guy Bertin "BG" Beyem Gouong is a Cameroonian illustrator. As a multitalented artist, Guy Bertin is a master dancer and painter and plays the violin as well as the piano. Guy Bertin holds an MA in visual arts from the University of Yaoundé I. His research focuses on defining an African artistic canon contrary to the Greek canon. **Sandjock Likinè** is an Indigenous African researcher artist. She reclaims, documents and revitalizes (through various artforms) the oral stories and life histories of her people, the Bàsàa people of Cameroon. Sandjock is a Bàsàa Cameroonian, born American. She received her PhD from the University of Minnesota. **Gérard Nyunai Ngan** is a PhD candidate at the University of Yaoundé I. His research focuses on artistic creation as a tool for urban planning. Gérard is a Cameroonian curator, founder and promoter of Pousse-pions, the only international festival of board games in sub-Saharan Africa. Gérard is also a photographer and cartoonist.

Az Sperry is a Minneapolis-based cartoonist making comix about anger, loss, grief, and hope. Some of her stories are real, some are made up, but she can no longer tell the difference. www.azsperry.com

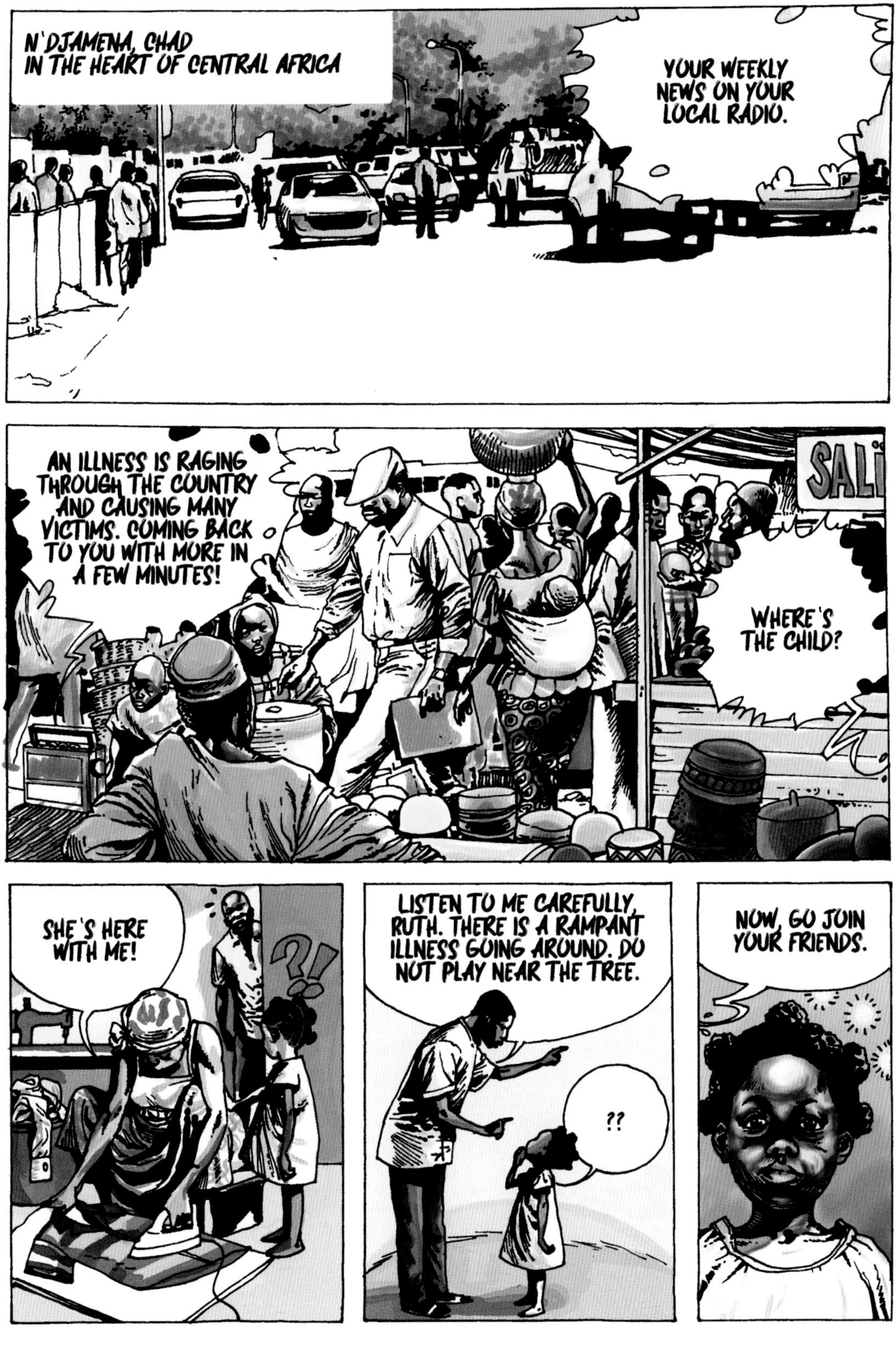
N'DJAMENA, CHAD
IN THE HEART OF CENTRAL AFRICA
YOUR WEEKLY NEWS ON YOUR LOCAL RADIO.
AN ILLNESS IS RAGING THROUGH THE COUNTRY AND CAUSING MANY VICTIMS. COMING BACK TO YOU WITH MORE IN A FEW MINUTES!
WHERE'S THE CHILD?
SHE'S HERE WITH ME!
?!
LISTEN TO ME CAREFULLY, RUTH. THERE IS A RAMPANT ILLNESS GOING AROUND. DO NOT PLAY NEAR THE TREE.
??
NOW, GO JOIN YOUR FRIENDS.

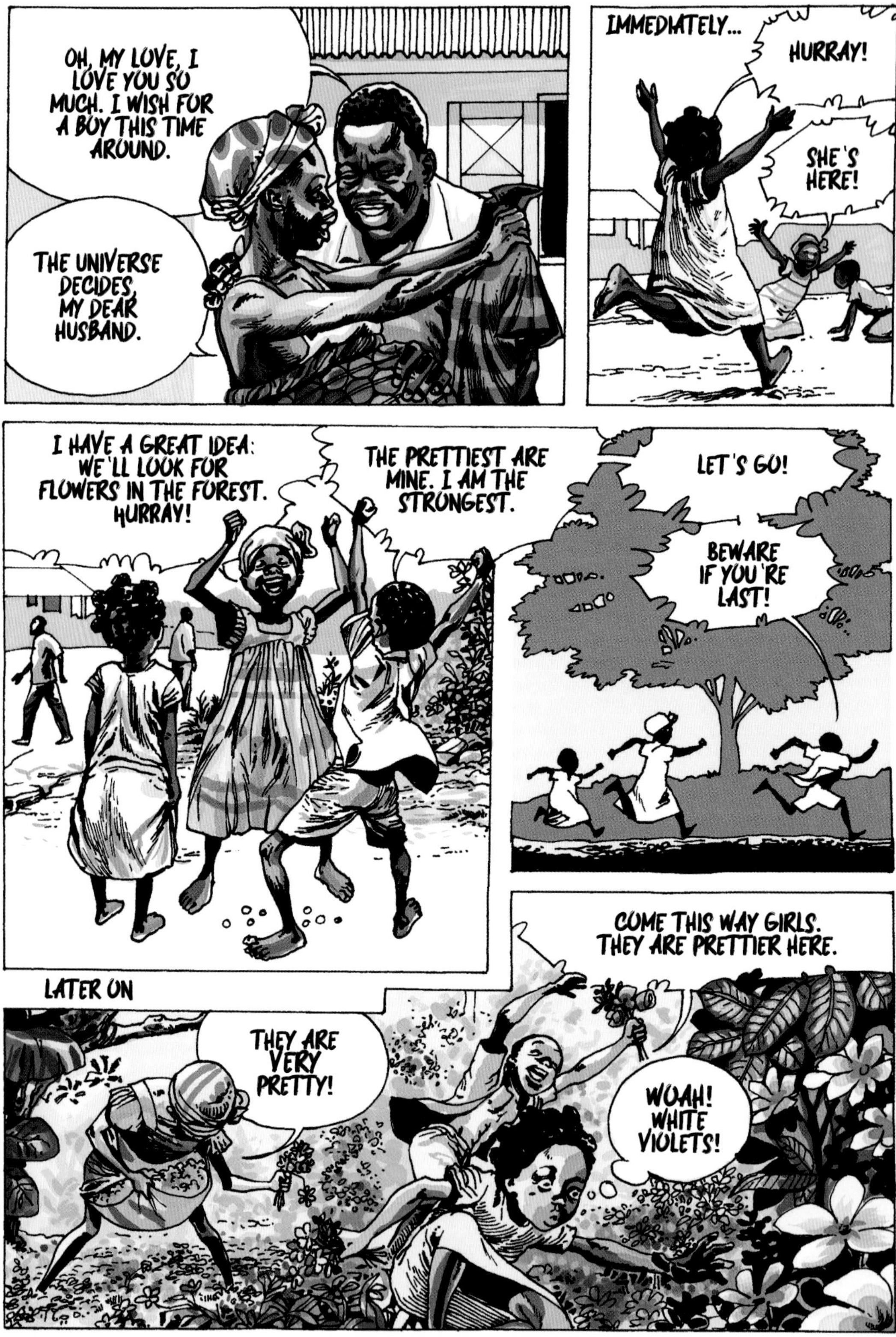
OH, MY LOVE, I LOVE YOU SO MUCH. I WISH FOR A BOY THIS TIME AROUND.
THE UNIVERSE DECIDES, MY DEAR HUSBAND.
IMMEDIATELY...
HURRAY!
SHE'S HERE!
I HAVE A GREAT IDEA: WE'LL LOOK FOR FLOWERS IN THE FOREST. HURRAY!
THE PRETTIEST ARE MINE. I AM THE STRONGEST.
LET'S GO!
BEWARE IF YOU'RE LAST!
COME THIS WAY GIRLS. THEY ARE PRETTIER HERE.
LATER ON
THEY ARE VERY PRETTY!
WOAH! WHITE VIOLETS!

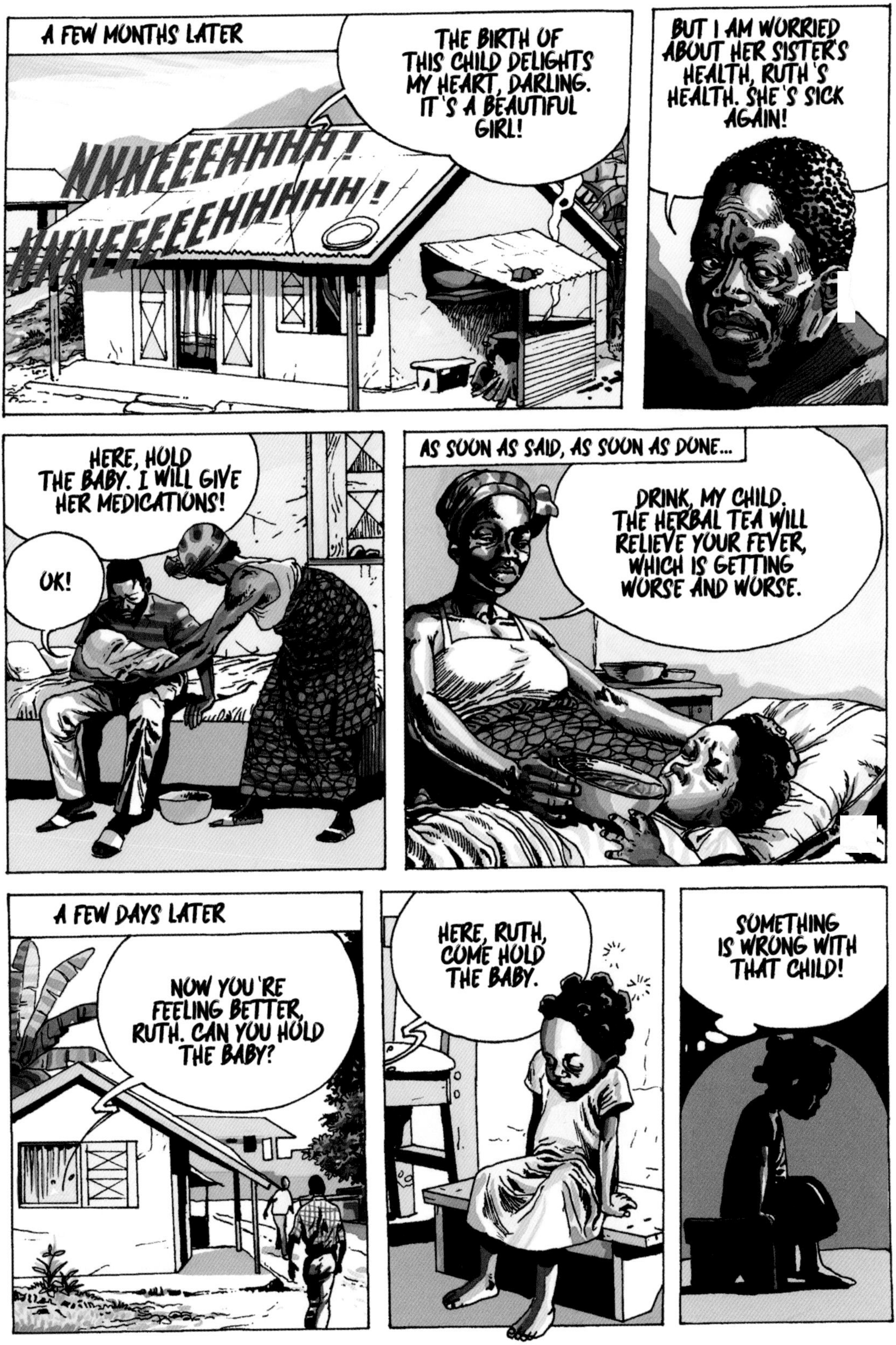
A FEW MONTHS LATER
THE BIRTH OF THIS CHILD DELIGHTS MY HEART, DARLING. IT'S A BEAUTIFUL GIRL!
NNNEEEHHHHH!
NNNEEEEEHHHHHH!
BUT I AM WORRIED ABOUT HER SISTER'S HEALTH, RUTH'S HEALTH. SHE'S SICK AGAIN!
HERE, HOLD THE BABY. I WILL GIVE HER MEDICATIONS!
OK!
AS SOON AS SAID, AS SOON AS DONE...
DRINK, MY CHILD. THE HERBAL TEA WILL RELIEVE YOUR FEVER, WHICH IS GETTING WORSE AND WORSE.
A FEW DAYS LATER
NOW YOU'RE FEELING BETTER, RUTH. CAN YOU HOLD THE BABY?
HERE, RUTH, COME HOLD THE BABY.
SOMETHING IS WRONG WITH THAT CHILD!

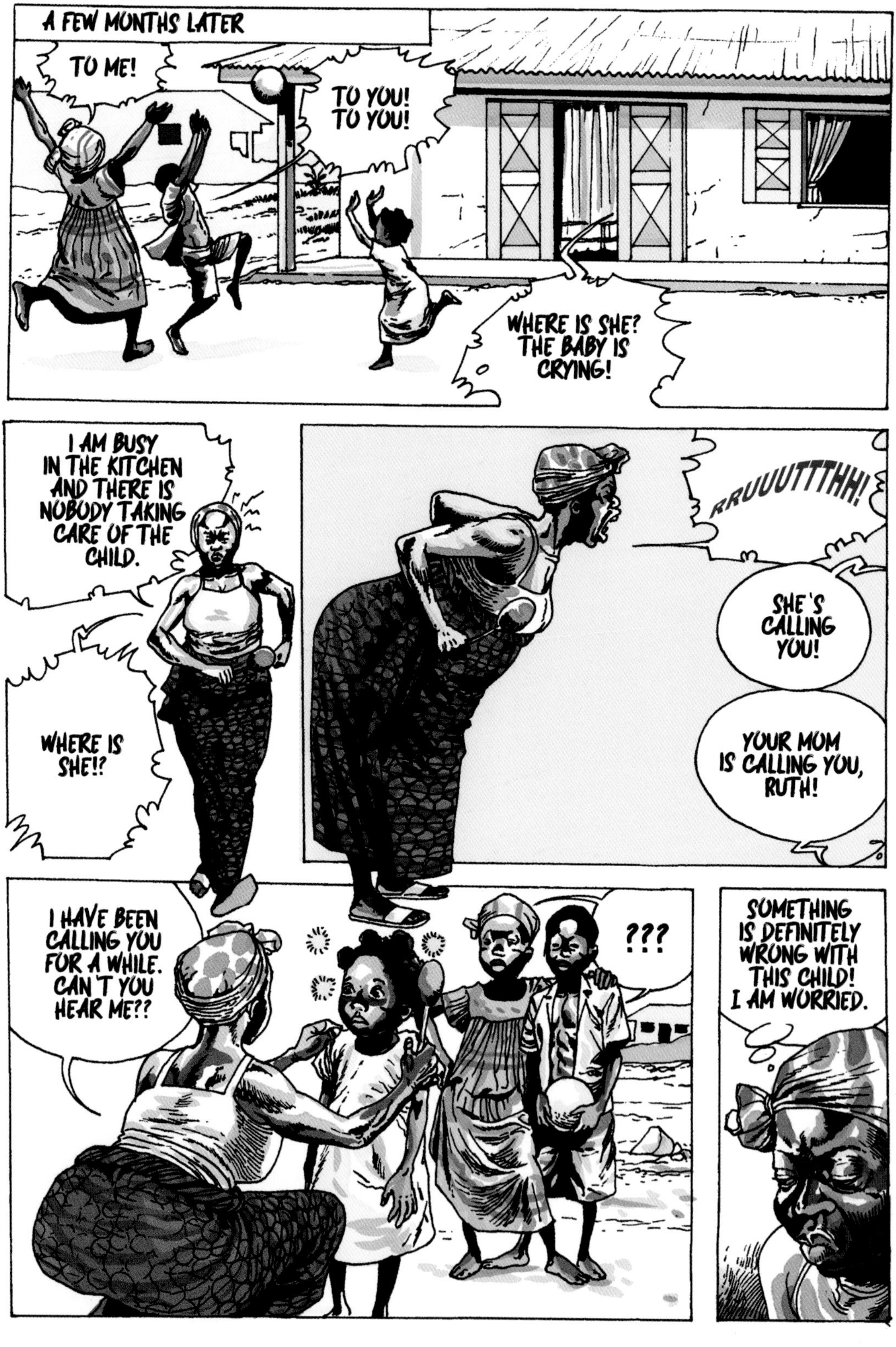
A FEW MONTHS LATER
TO ME!
TO YOU! TO YOU!
WHERE IS SHE? THE BABY IS CRYING!
I AM BUSY IN THE KITCHEN AND THERE IS NOBODY TAKING CARE OF THE CHILD.
WHERE IS SHE!?
RRUUUTTTHH!
SHE'S CALLING YOU!
YOUR MOM IS CALLING YOU, RUTH!
I HAVE BEEN CALLING YOU FOR A WHILE. CAN'T YOU HEAR ME??
???
SOMETHING IS DEFINITELY WRONG WITH THIS CHILD! I AM WORRIED.

AN EVENING, A FEW MONTHS LATER

THE REASON WE GATHER ALL TONIGHT IS TO DISCUSS ESCALATING VIOLENCE IN OUR AREA. IT IS NOT SAFE HERE ANYMORE.

AS HER GRANDPARENTS, WE ARE ALSO WORRIED ABOUT RUTH'S HEALTH.

ONCE WE GET TO CAMEROON, WE WILL KNOW WHAT TO DO, NANA AND PAPA.

YOU MUST...

AND IN THE FOLLOWING WEEKS, THE FAMILY FLED TO CAMEROON, A COUNTRY NEIGHBORING CHAD, TO ESCAPE VIOLENCE.

N'DJAMENA

YAOUNDE

ONCE IN CAMEROON, RUTH'S MOM BROUGHT HER TO THE HOSPITAL...

HÔPITAL GÈRE

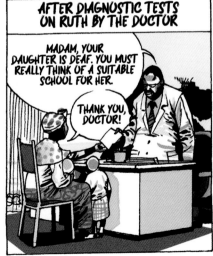

AFTER DIAGNOSTIC TESTS ON RUTH BY THE DOCTOR

MADAM, YOUR DAUGHTER IS DEAF. YOU MUST REALLY THINK OF A SUITABLE SCHOOL FOR HER.

THANK YOU, DOCTOR!

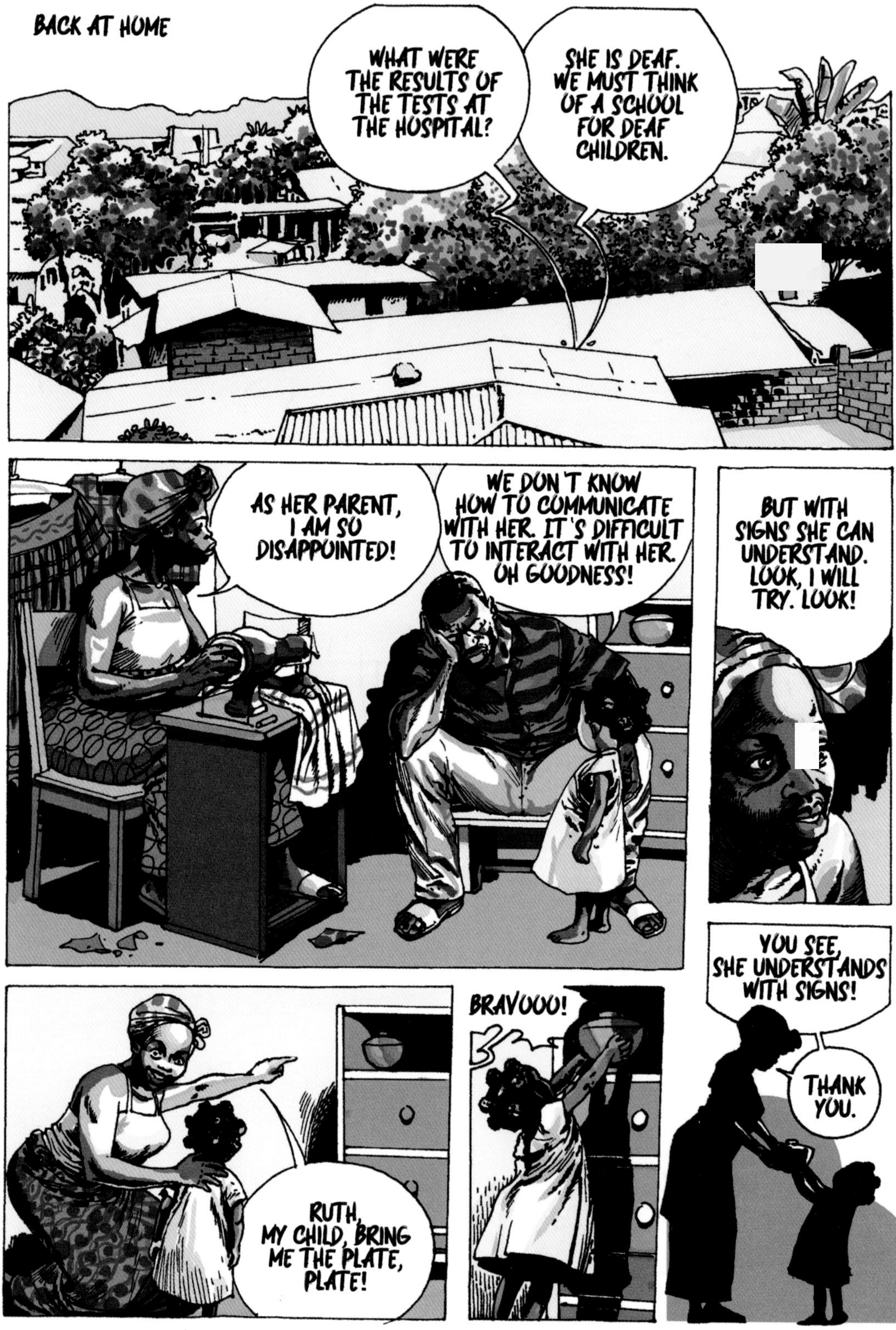
BACK AT HOME
WHAT WERE THE RESULTS OF THE TESTS AT THE HOSPITAL?
SHE IS DEAF. WE MUST THINK OF A SCHOOL FOR DEAF CHILDREN.
AS HER PARENT, I AM SO DISAPPOINTED!
WE DON'T KNOW HOW TO COMMUNICATE WITH HER. IT'S DIFFICULT TO INTERACT WITH HER. OH GOODNESS!
BUT WITH SIGNS SHE CAN UNDERSTAND. LOOK, I WILL TRY. LOOK!
RUTH, MY CHILD, BRING ME THE PLATE, PLATE!
BRAVOOO!
YOU SEE, SHE UNDERSTANDS WITH SIGNS!
THANK YOU.

SEVERAL MONTHS LATER

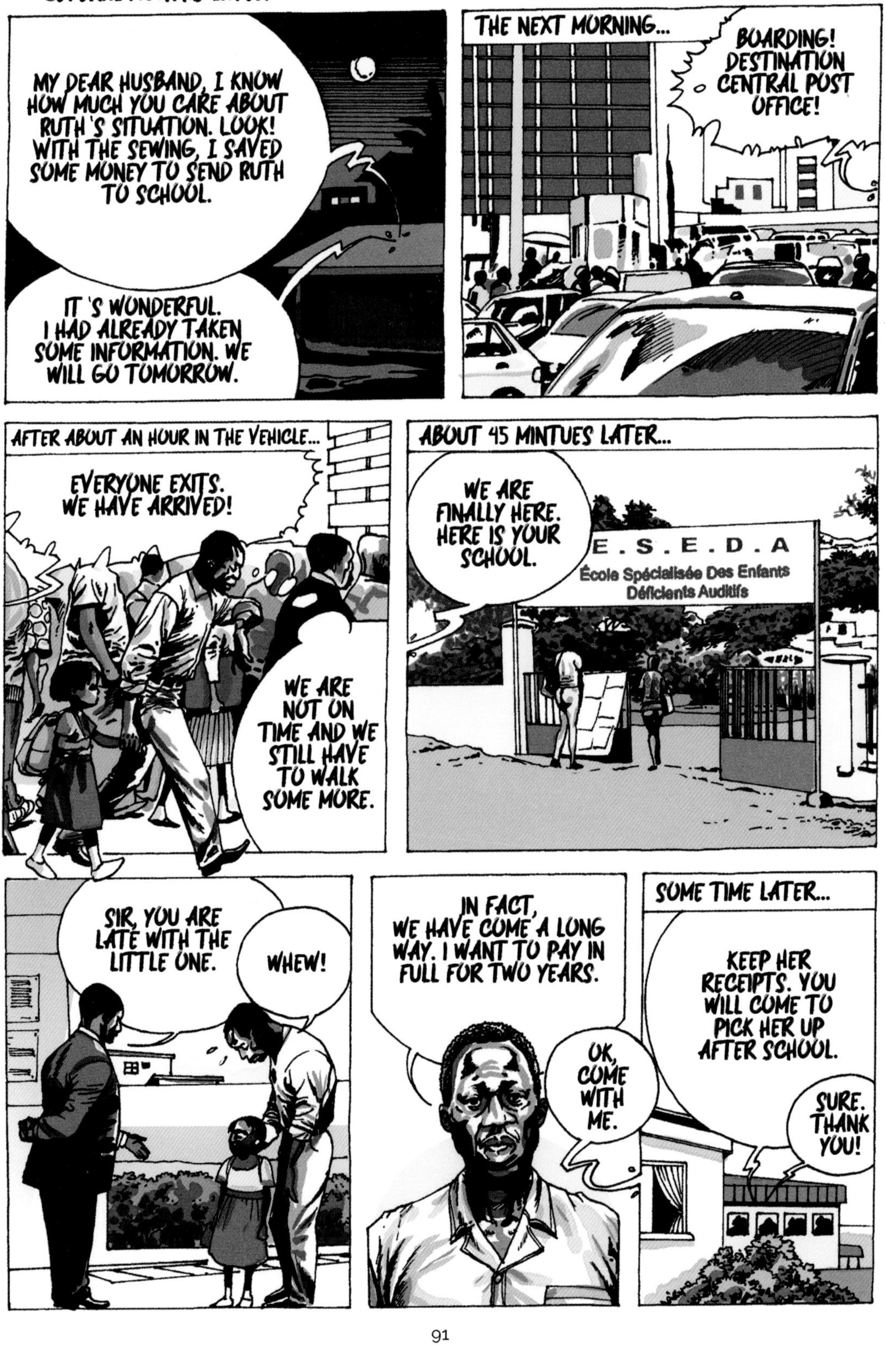
MY DEAR HUSBAND, I KNOW HOW MUCH YOU CARE ABOUT RUTH'S SITUATION. LOOK! WITH THE SEWING, I SAVED SOME MONEY TO SEND RUTH TO SCHOOL.
IT'S WONDERFUL. I HAD ALREADY TAKEN SOME INFORMATION. WE WILL GO TOMORROW.
THE NEXT MORNING...
BOARDING! DESTINATION CENTRAL POST OFFICE!
AFTER ABOUT AN HOUR IN THE VEHICLE...
EVERYONE EXITS. WE HAVE ARRIVED!
WE ARE NOT ON TIME AND WE STILL HAVE TO WALK SOME MORE.
ABOUT 45 MINTUES LATER...
WE ARE FINALLY HERE. HERE IS YOUR SCHOOL.
E.S.E.D.A
École Spécialisée Des Enfants Déficients Auditifs
SIR, YOU ARE LATE WITH THE LITTLE ONE.
WHEW!
IN FACT, WE HAVE COME A LONG WAY. I WANT TO PAY IN FULL FOR TWO YEARS.
OK, COME WITH ME.
SOME TIME LATER...
KEEP HER RECEIPTS. YOU WILL COME TO PICK HER UP AFTER SCHOOL.
SURE. THANK YOU!

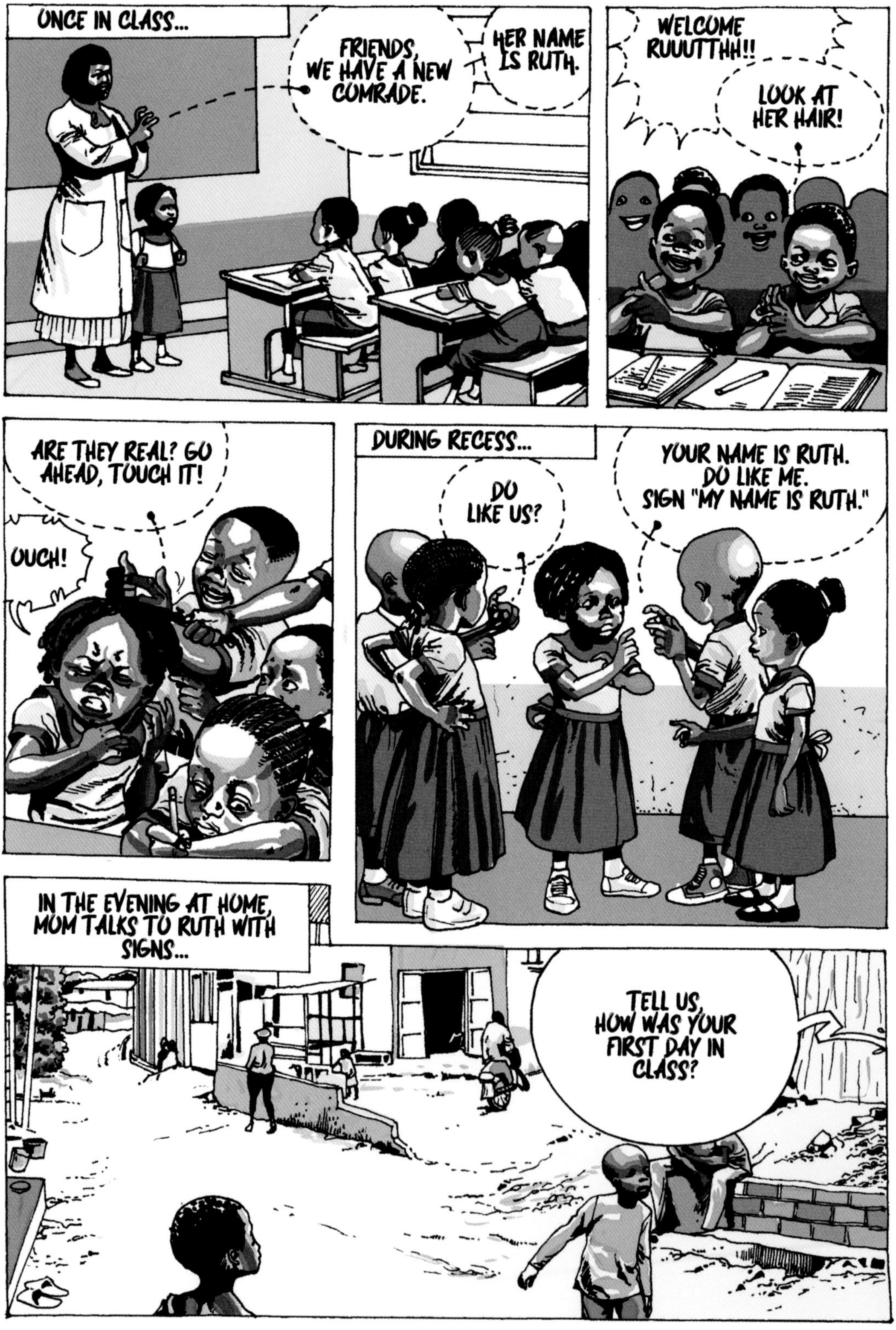

ONCE IN CLASS...
FRIENDS, WE HAVE A NEW COMRADE.
HER NAME IS RUTH.
WELCOME RUUUTTHH!!
LOOK AT HER HAIR!
ARE THEY REAL? GO AHEAD, TOUCH IT!
OUCH!
DURING RECESS...
DO LIKE US?
YOUR NAME IS RUTH. DO LIKE ME. SIGN "MY NAME IS RUTH."
IN THE EVENING AT HOME, MOM TALKS TO RUTH WITH SIGNS...
TELL US, HOW WAS YOUR FIRST DAY IN CLASS?

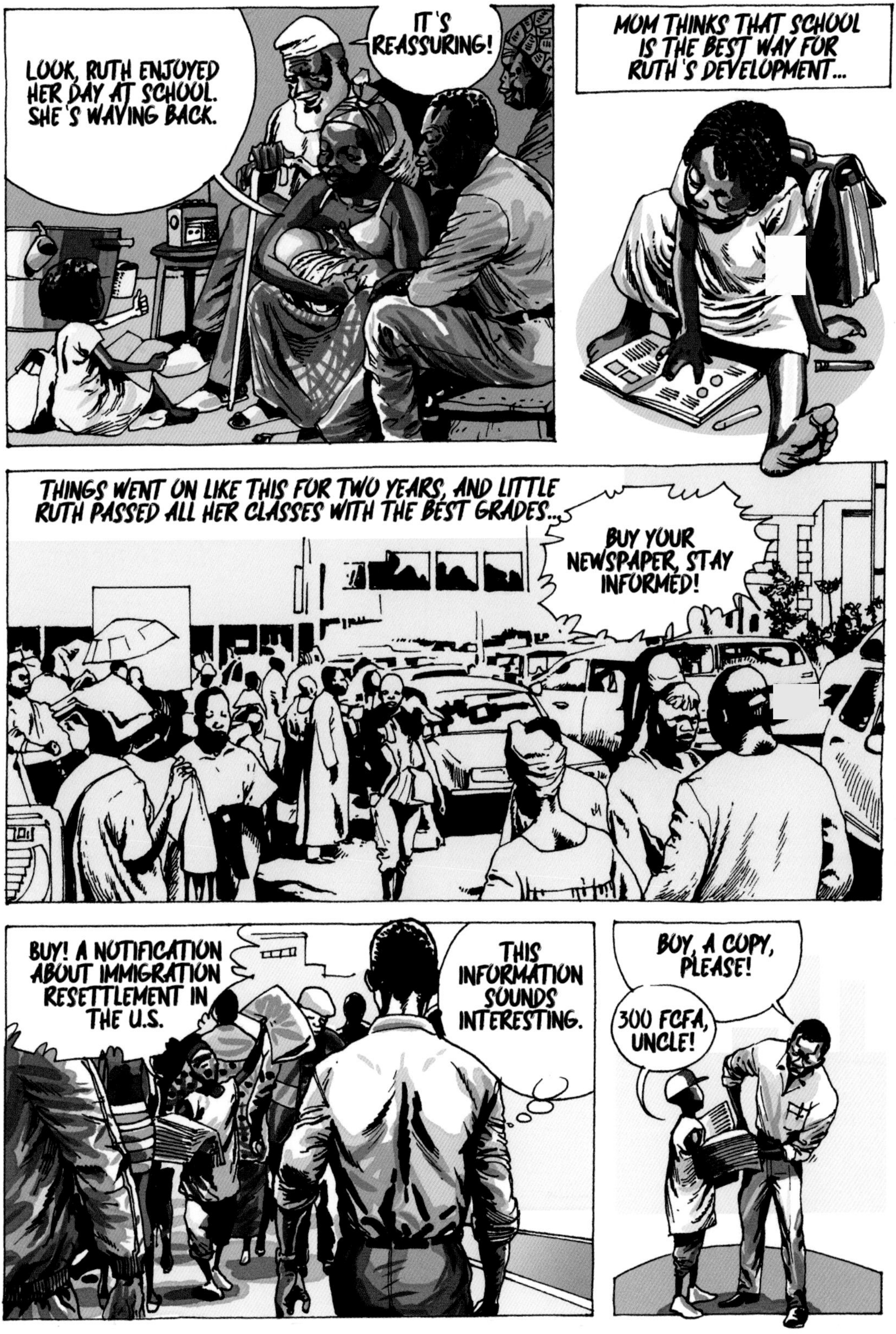
LOOK, RUTH ENJOYED HER DAY AT SCHOOL. SHE'S WAVING BACK.
IT'S REASSURING!
MOM THINKS THAT SCHOOL IS THE BEST WAY FOR RUTH'S DEVELOPMENT...
THINGS WENT ON LIKE THIS FOR TWO YEARS, AND LITTLE RUTH PASSED ALL HER CLASSES WITH THE BEST GRADES...
BUY YOUR NEWSPAPER, STAY INFORMED!
BUY! A NOTIFICATION ABOUT IMMIGRATION RESETTLEMENT IN THE U.S.
THIS INFORMATION SOUNDS INTERESTING.
BUY, A COPY, PLEASE!
300 FCFA, UNCLE!

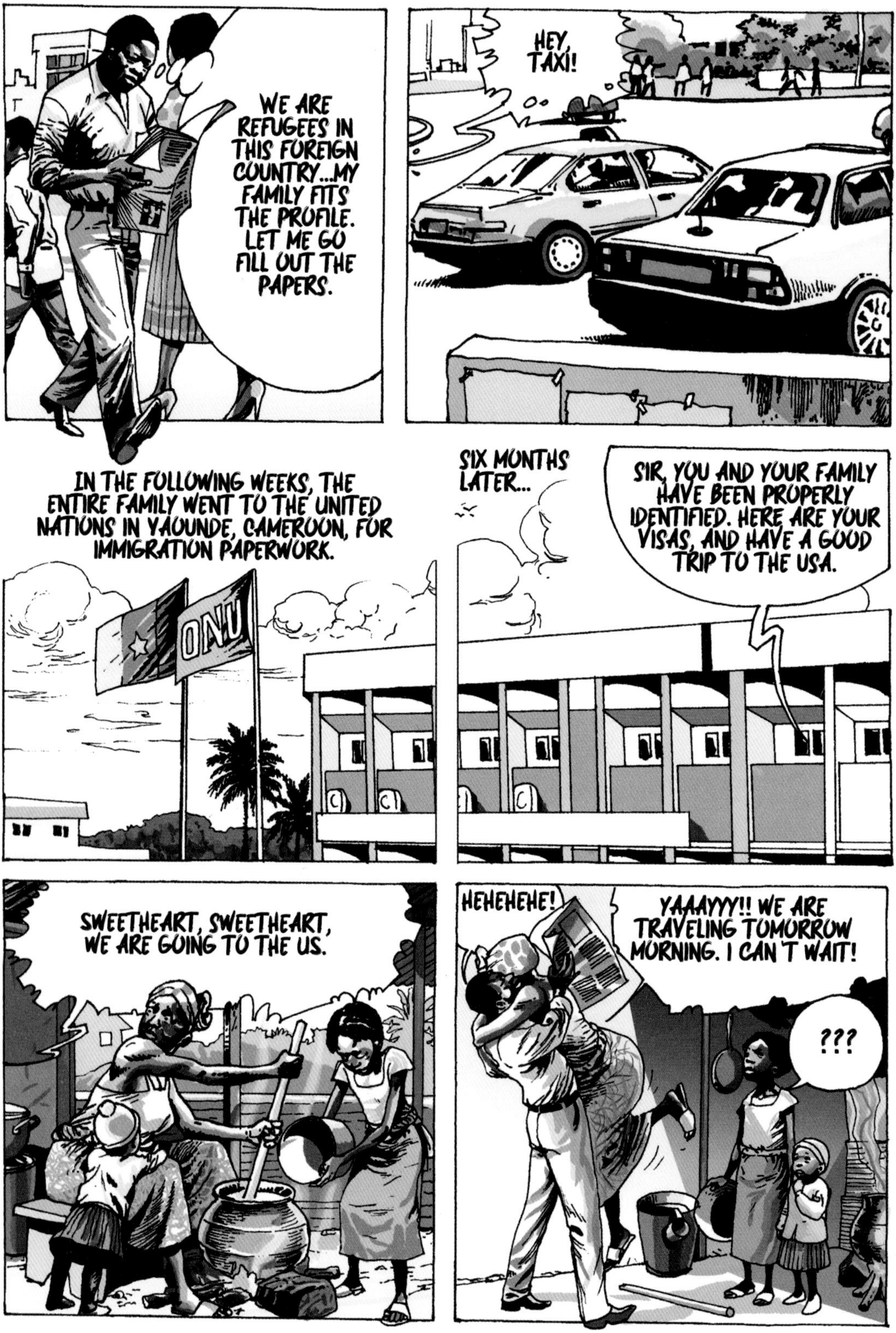
WE ARE REFUGEES IN THIS FOREIGN COUNTRY...MY FAMILY FITS THE PROFILE. LET ME GO FILL OUT THE PAPERS.
HEY, TAXI!
IN THE FOLLOWING WEEKS, THE ENTIRE FAMILY WENT TO THE UNITED NATIONS IN YAOUNDE, CAMEROON, FOR IMMIGRATION PAPERWORK.
ONU
SIX MONTHS LATER...
SIR, YOU AND YOUR FAMILY HAVE BEEN PROPERLY IDENTIFIED. HERE ARE YOUR VISAS, AND HAVE A GOOD TRIP TO THE USA.
SWEETHEART, SWEETHEART, WE ARE GOING TO THE US.
HEHEHEHE!
YAAAYYY!! WE ARE TRAVELING TOMORROW MORNING. I CAN'T WAIT!
???

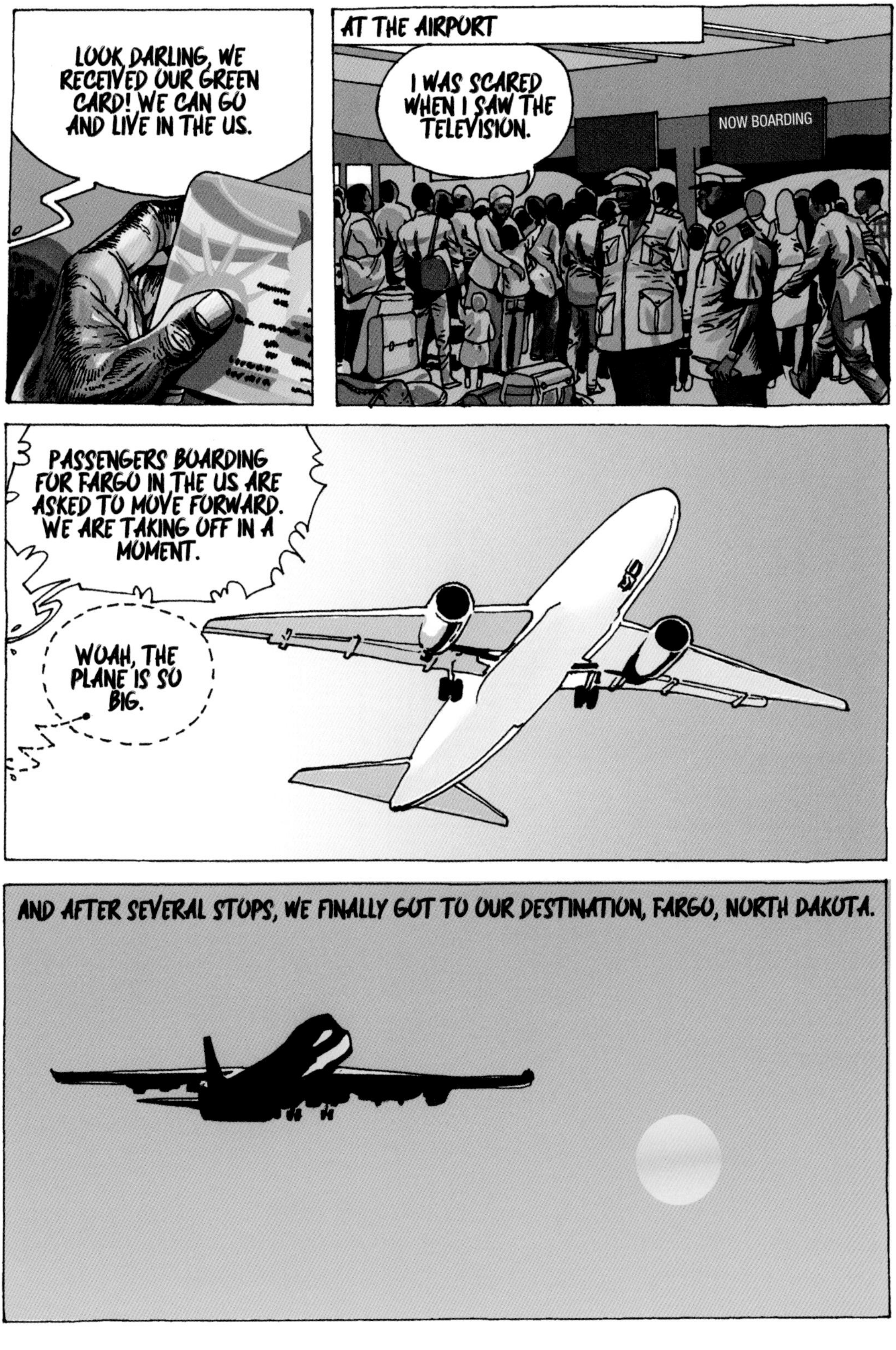
LOOK DARLING, WE RECEIVED OUR GREEN CARD! WE CAN GO AND LIVE IN THE US.
AT THE AIRPORT
I WAS SCARED WHEN I SAW THE TELEVISION.
NOW BOARDING
PASSENGERS BOARDING FOR FARGO IN THE US ARE ASKED TO MOVE FORWARD. WE ARE TAKING OFF IN A MOMENT.
WOAH, THE PLANE IS SO BIG.
AND AFTER SEVERAL STOPS, WE FINALLY GOT TO OUR DESTINATION, FARGO, NORTH DAKOTA.

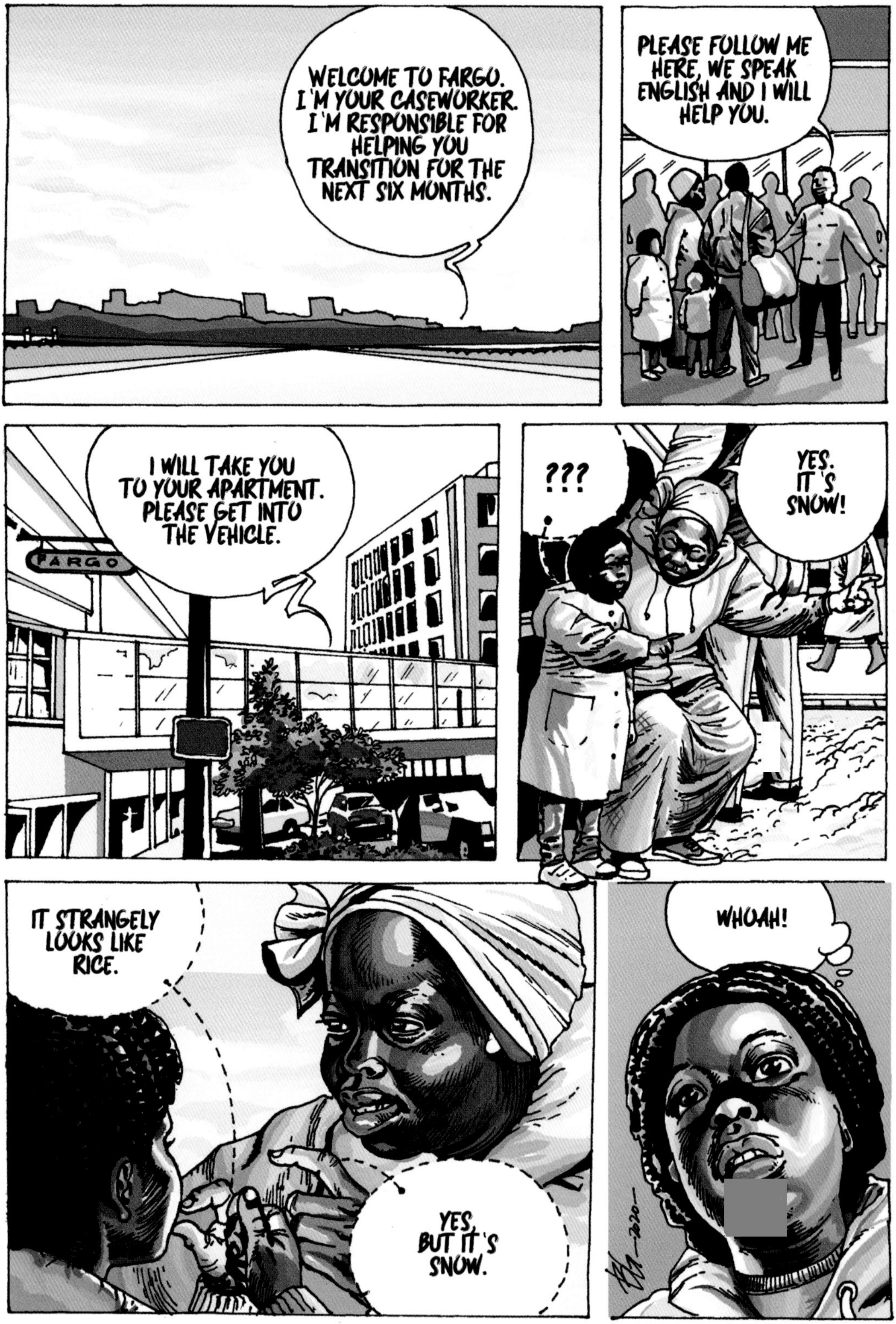
WELCOME TO FARGO. I'M YOUR CASEWORKER. I'M RESPONSIBLE FOR HELPING YOU TRANSITION FOR THE NEXT SIX MONTHS.
PLEASE FOLLOW ME HERE, WE SPEAK ENGLISH AND I WILL HELP YOU.
I WILL TAKE YOU TO YOUR APARTMENT. PLEASE GET INTO THE VEHICLE.
FARGO
???
YES. IT'S SNOW!
IT STRANGELY LOOKS LIKE RICE.
YES, BUT IT'S SNOW.
WHOAH!

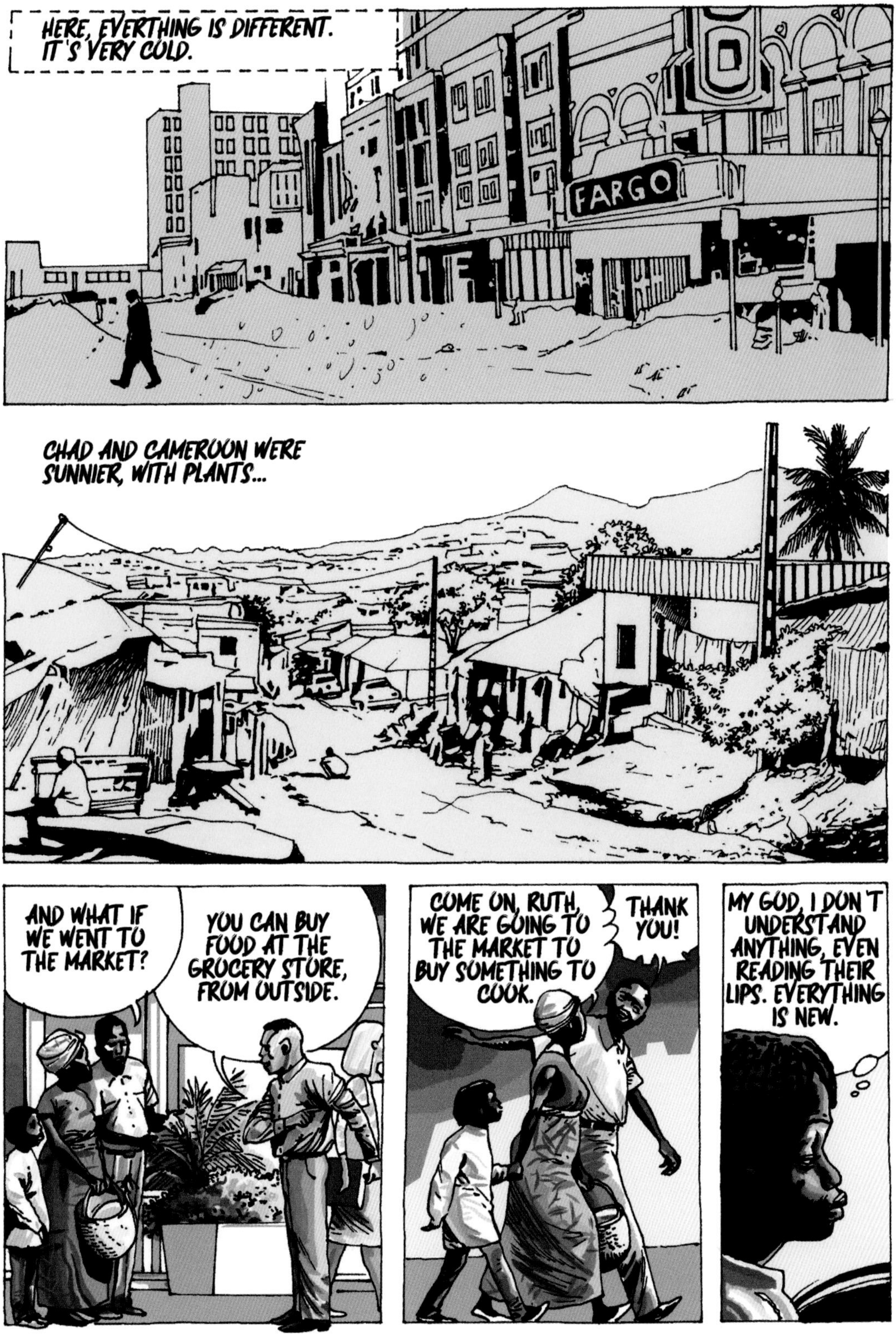
HERE, EVERTHING IS DIFFERENT. IT'S VERY COLD.
FARGO
CHAD AND CAMEROON WERE SUNNIER, WITH PLANTS...
AND WHAT IF WE WENT TO THE MARKET?
YOU CAN BUY FOOD AT THE GROCERY STORE, FROM OUTSIDE.
COME ON, RUTH, WE ARE GOING TO THE MARKET TO BUY SOMETHING TO COOK.
THANK YOU!
MY GOD, I DON'T UNDERSTAND ANYTHING, EVEN READING THEIR LIPS. EVERYTHING IS NEW.

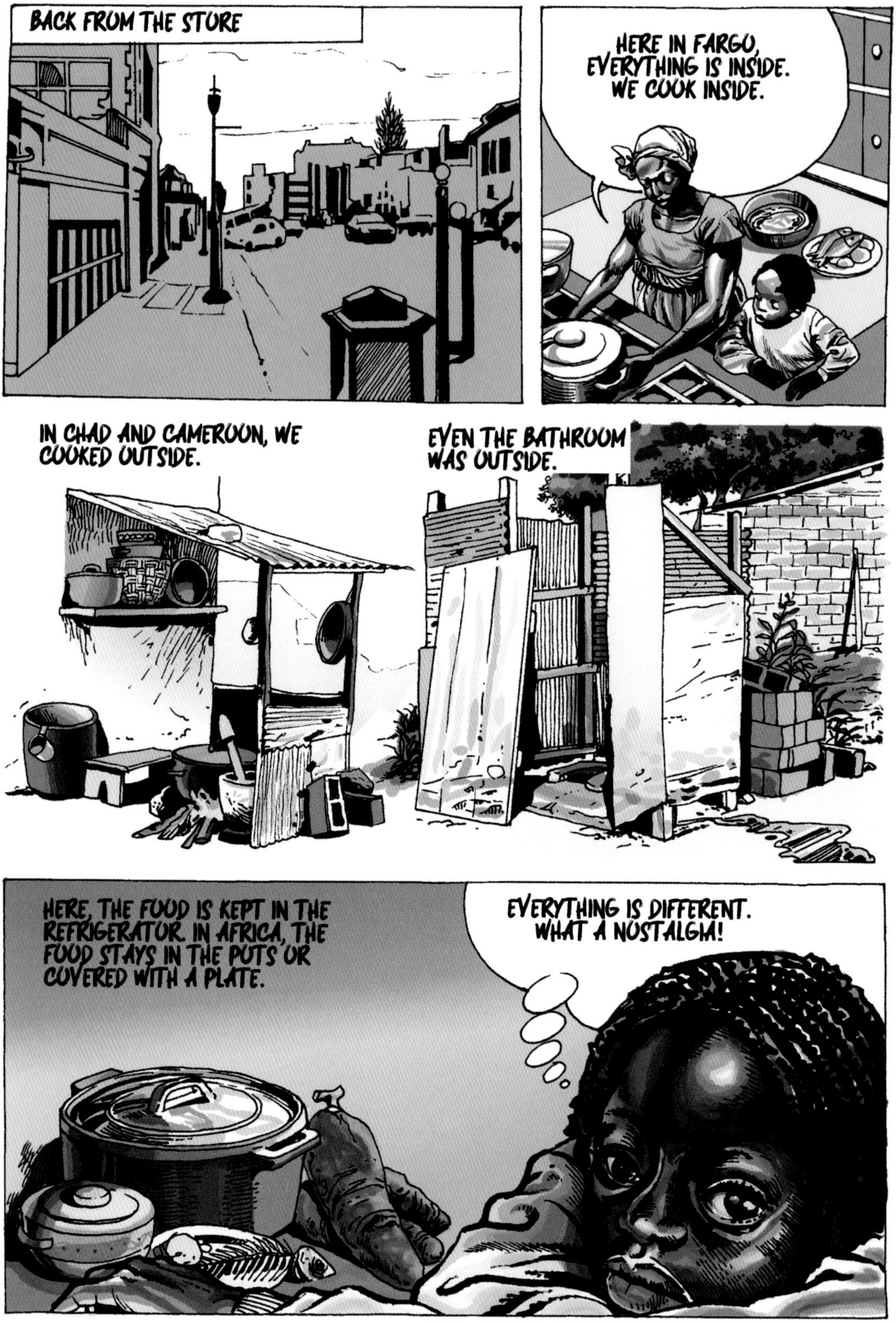
BACK FROM THE STORE
HERE IN FARGO, EVERYTHING IS INSIDE. WE COOK INSIDE.
IN CHAD AND CAMEROON, WE COOKED OUTSIDE.
EVEN THE BATHROOM WAS OUTSIDE.
HERE, THE FOOD IS KEPT IN THE REFRIGERATOR. IN AFRICA, THE FOOD STAYS IN THE POTS OR COVERED WITH A PLATE.
EVERYTHING IS DIFFERENT. WHAT A NOSTALGIA!

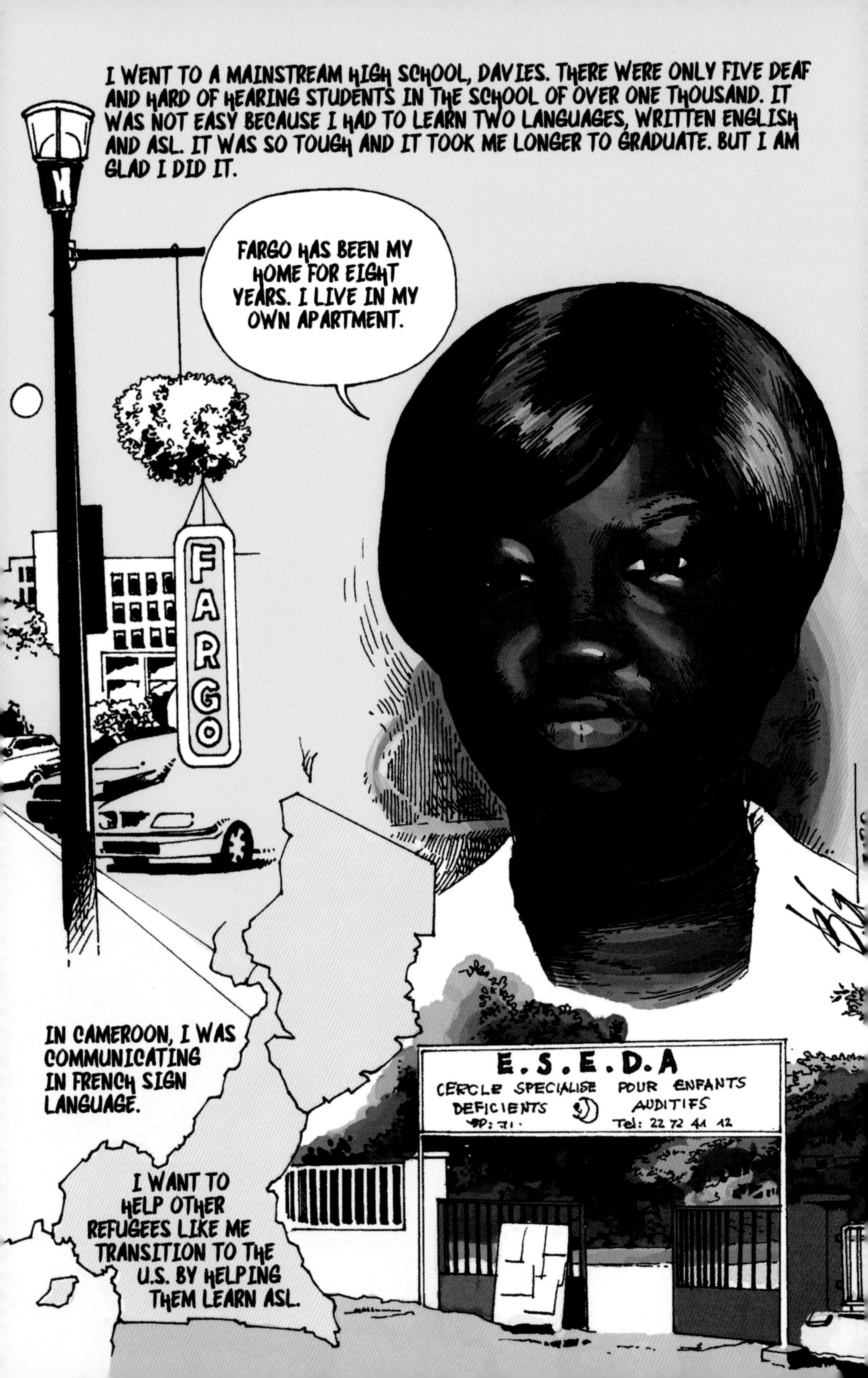
I WENT TO A MAINSTREAM HIGH SCHOOL, DAVIES. THERE WERE ONLY FIVE DEAF AND HARD OF HEARING STUDENTS IN THE SCHOOL OF OVER ONE THOUSAND. IT WAS NOT EASY BECAUSE I HAD TO LEARN TWO LANGUAGES, WRITTEN ENGLISH AND ASL. IT WAS SO TOUGH AND IT TOOK ME LONGER TO GRADUATE. BUT I AM GLAD I DID IT.
FARGO HAS BEEN MY HOME FOR EIGHT YEARS. I LIVE IN MY OWN APARTMENT.
FARGO
IN CAMEROON, I WAS COMMUNICATING IN FRENCH SIGN LANGUAGE.
E.S.E.D.A
CERCLE SPECIALISE POUR ENFANTS DEFICIENTS AUDITIFS
Tel: 22 72 41 12
I WANT TO HELP OTHER REFUGEES LIKE ME TRANSITION TO THE U.S. BY HELPING THEM LEARN ASL.

KAZAKHSTAN

ALEX TSIPENYUK

Born: Almaty, Kazakhstan
Current: Rochester, New York

Alex Tsipenyuk is Russian and is the youngest in his family with one older brother. Alex is currently a junior at Brighton High School in Rochester, New York. Alex's long-term goal is to either major in chemistry and/or biology. In his free time, Alex enjoys playing soccer with his friends outside and playing video games. Alex is happy to live in the U.S. because it's a country of opportunities, unlike his homeland.

www.greencardvoices.org/speakers/alex-tsipenyuk

TOM KACZYNSKI

Born: Poland
Current: Minneapolis, Minnesota

Tom Kaczynski is a cartoonist, writer, publisher, and teacher. He is the author of the Eisner Award nominated graphic novel *Beta Testing the Ongoing Apocalypse* (Fantagraphics), *Cartoon Dialectics* series, and the forthcoming *Trans Terra* graphic novel. His comics have appeared in countless anthologies, including *The Nib*, *Mome*, and many more. Tom is the founder of multiple award-winning Uncivilized Books, a boutique graphic novel publishing house. Since its inception, Uncivilized Books has published acclaimed and award nominated graphic novels by Gabrielle Bell, Noah Van Sciver, David B., Joann Sfar, Sophie Yanow, Craig Thompson, and many others. He also teaches comics at Minneapolis College of Art & Design and the University of Minnesota. He lives in Minneapolis with his partner Nikki, a cat, and a dog.

www.tomkaczynski.com

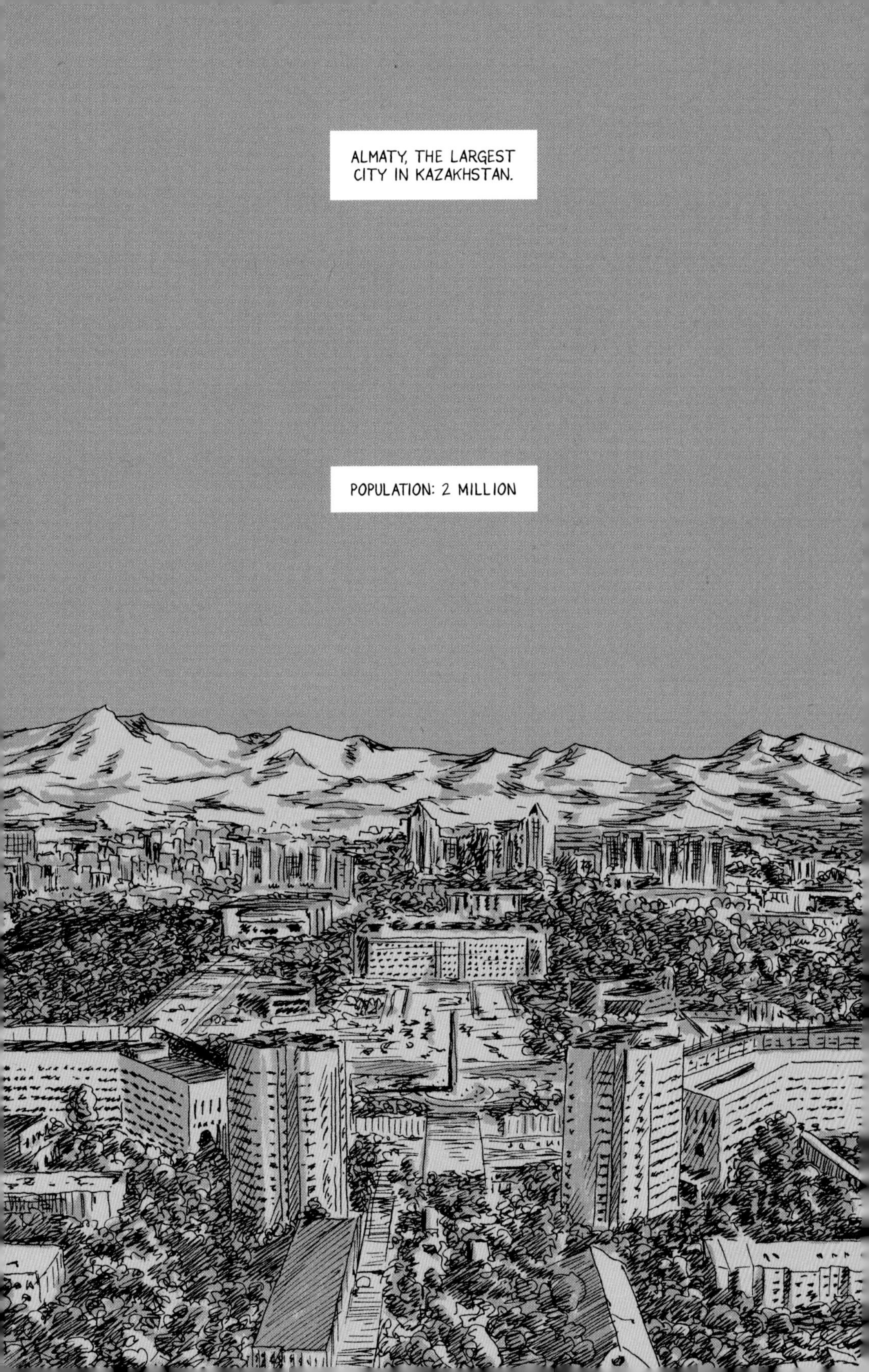
ALMATY, THE LARGEST CITY IN KAZAKHSTAN.
POPULATION: 2 MILLION

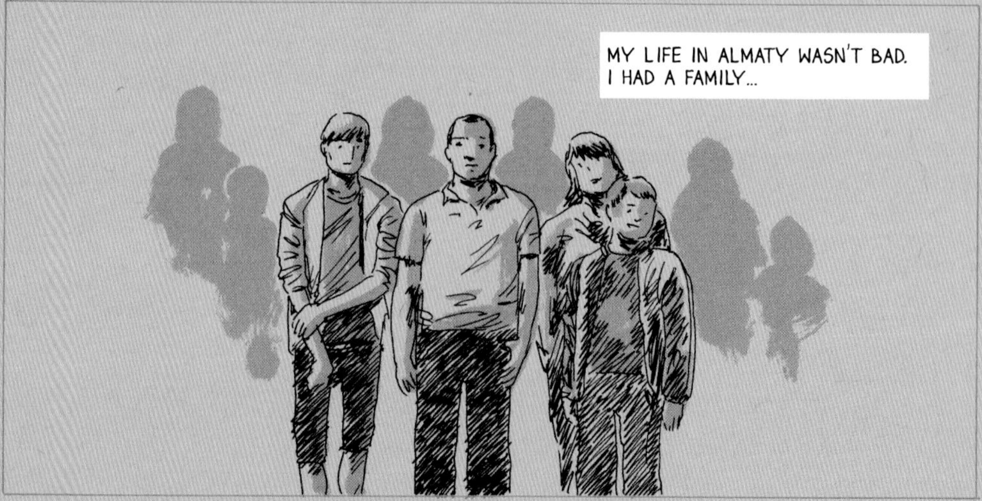
MY LIFE IN ALMATY WASN'T BAD.
I HAD A FAMILY...

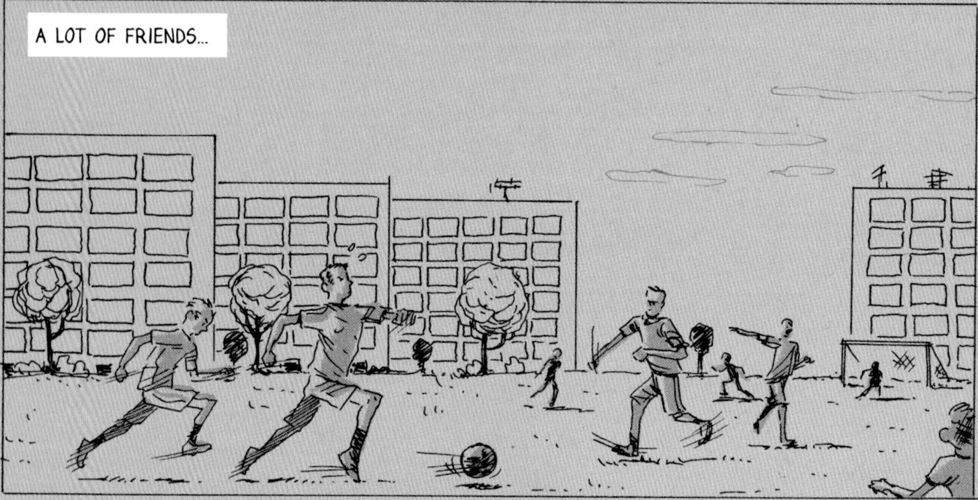
A LOT OF FRIENDS...

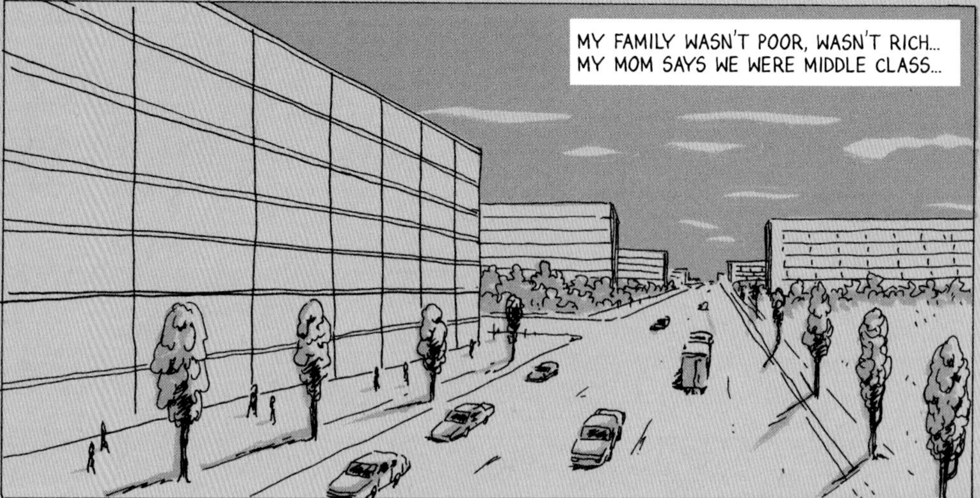
MY FAMILY WASN'T POOR, WASN'T RICH...
MY MOM SAYS WE WERE MIDDLE CLASS...

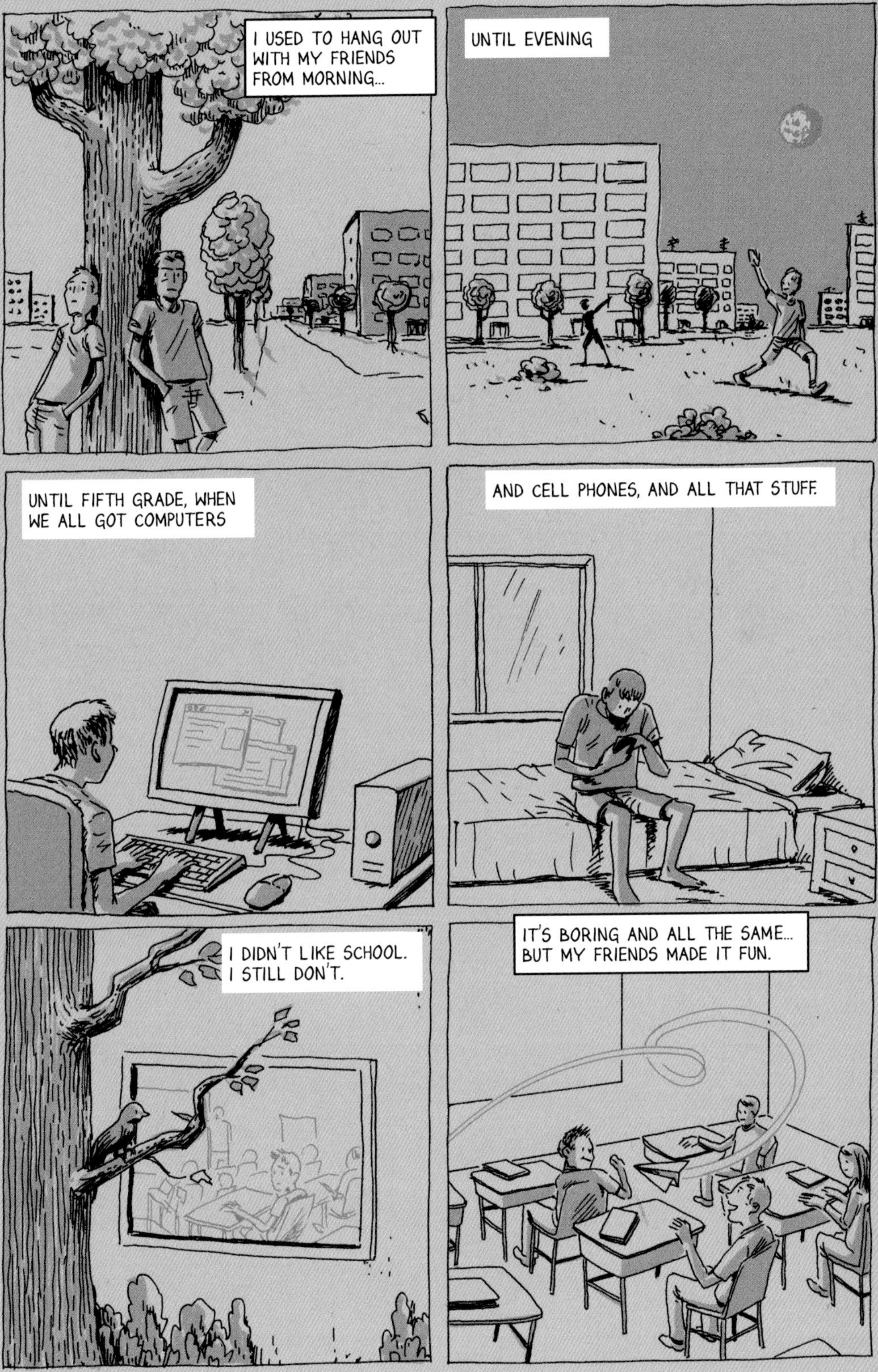
I USED TO HANG OUT WITH MY FRIENDS FROM MORNING...
UNTIL EVENING
UNTIL FIFTH GRADE, WHEN WE ALL GOT COMPUTERS
AND CELL PHONES, AND ALL THAT STUFF.
I DIDN'T LIKE SCHOOL. I STILL DON'T.
IT'S BORING AND ALL THE SAME... BUT MY FRIENDS MADE IT FUN.

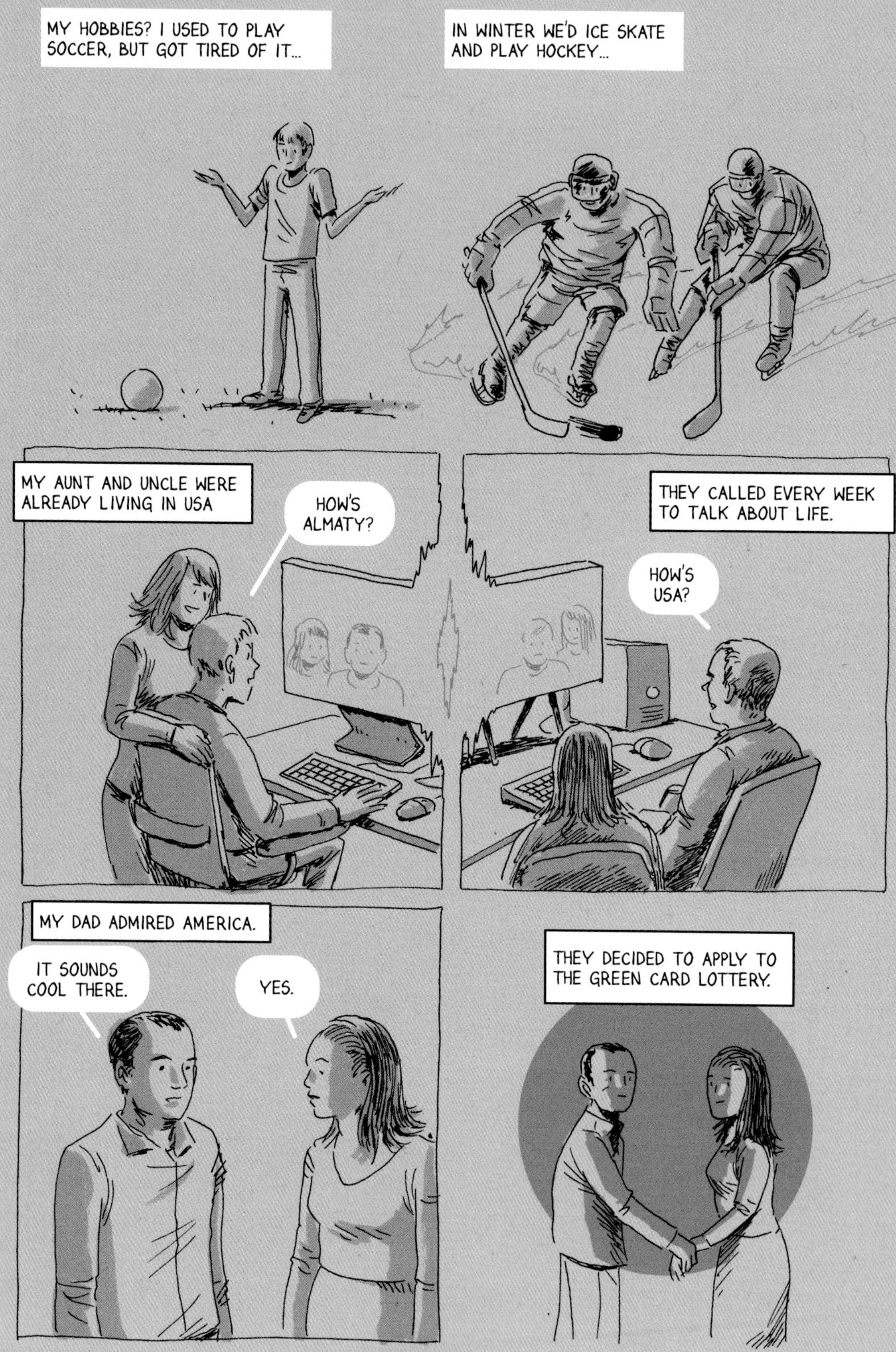
MY HOBBIES? I USED TO PLAY SOCCER, BUT GOT TIRED OF IT...
IN WINTER WE'D ICE SKATE AND PLAY HOCKEY...
MY AUNT AND UNCLE WERE ALREADY LIVING IN USA
HOW'S ALMATY?
THEY CALLED EVERY WEEK TO TALK ABOUT LIFE.
HOW'S USA?
MY DAD ADMIRED AMERICA.
IT SOUNDS COOL THERE.
YES.
THEY DECIDED TO APPLY TO THE GREEN CARD LOTTERY.

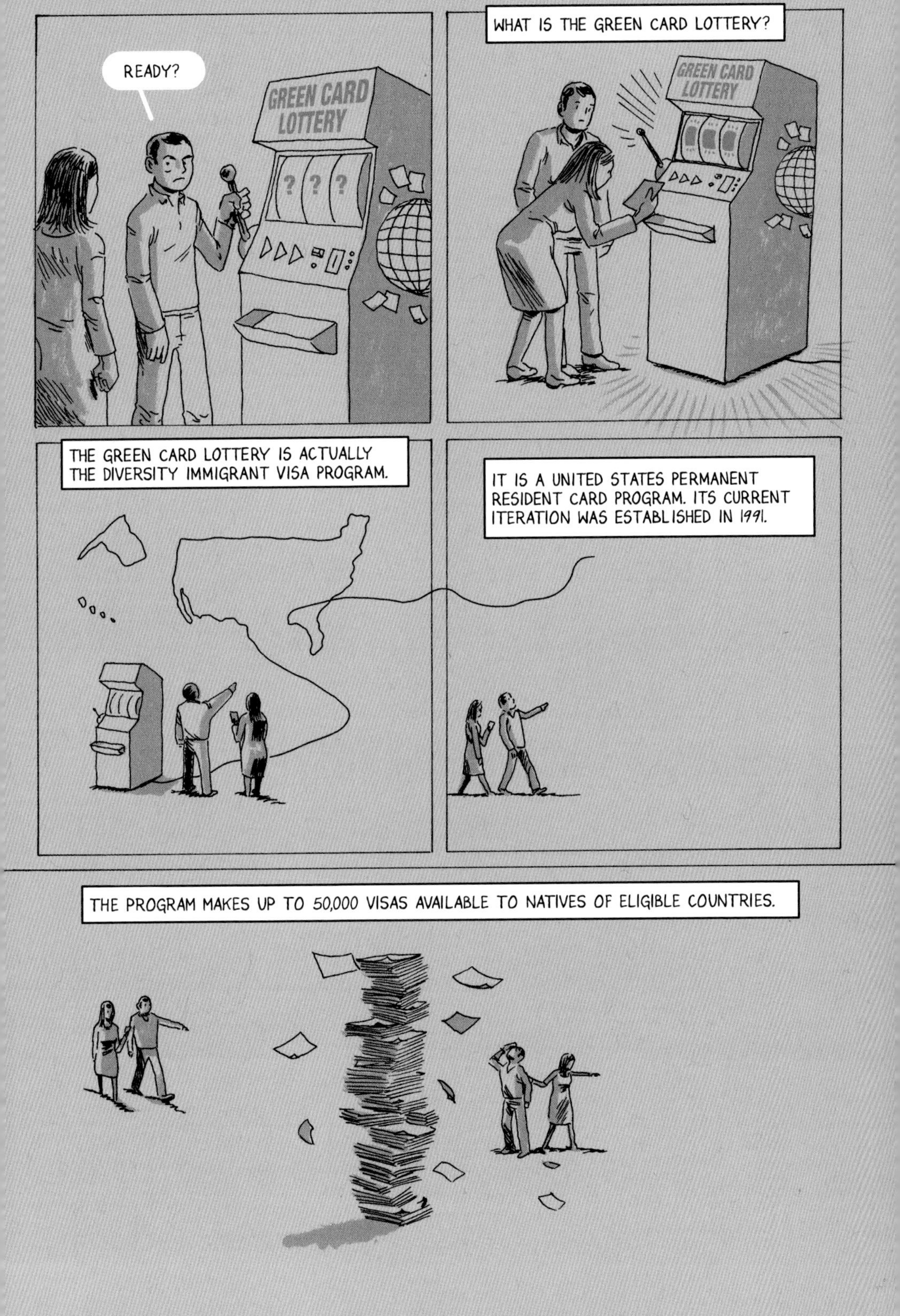
READY?
WHAT IS THE GREEN CARD LOTTERY?
GREEN CARD LOTTERY
THE GREEN CARD LOTTERY IS ACTUALLY THE DIVERSITY IMMIGRANT VISA PROGRAM.
IT IS A UNITED STATES PERMANENT RESIDENT CARD PROGRAM. ITS CURRENT ITERATION WAS ESTABLISHED IN 1991.
THE PROGRAM MAKES UP TO 50,000 VISAS AVAILABLE TO NATIVES OF ELIGIBLE COUNTRIES.

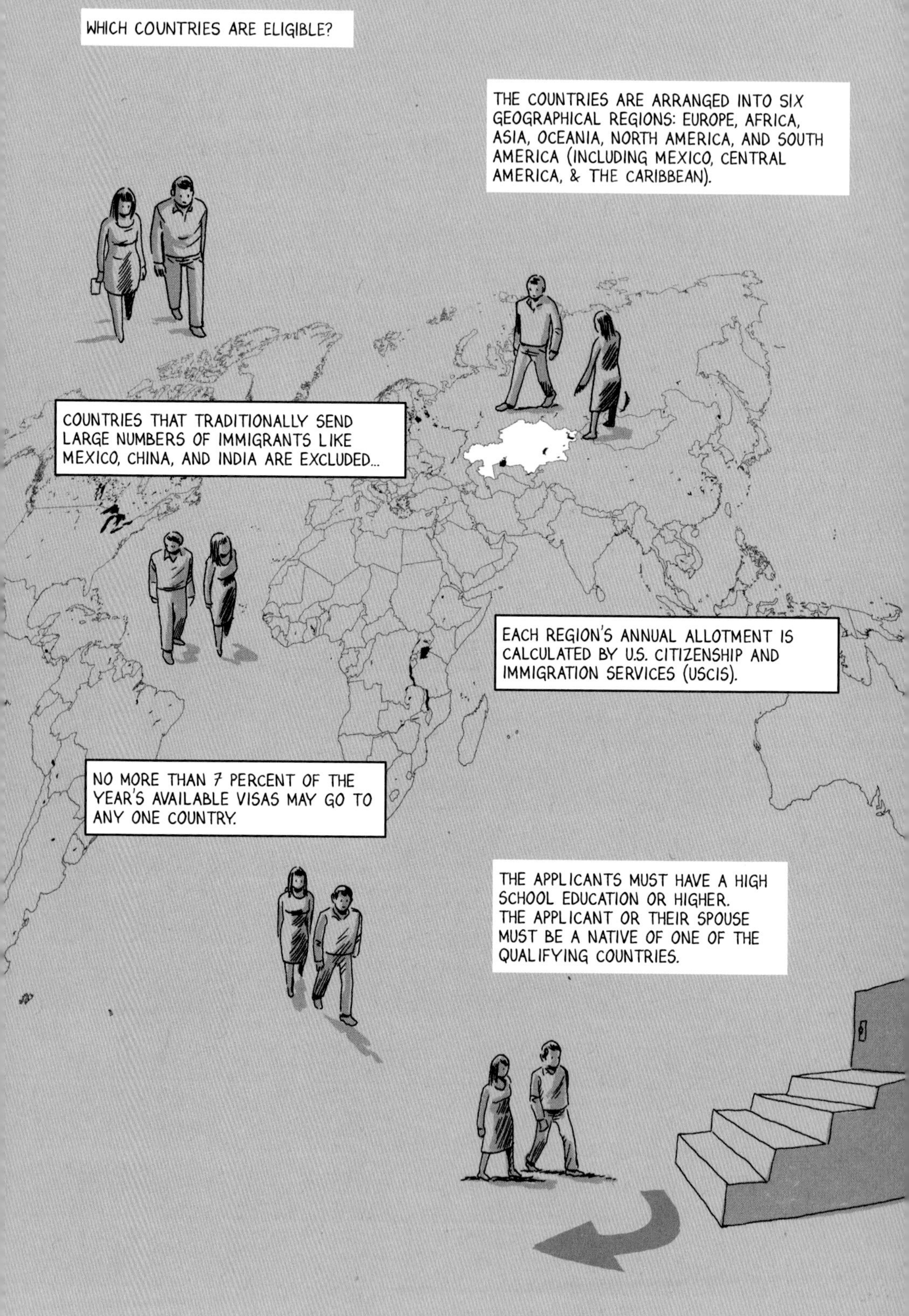
WHICH COUNTRIES ARE ELIGIBLE?
THE COUNTRIES ARE ARRANGED INTO SIX GEOGRAPHICAL REGIONS: EUROPE, AFRICA, ASIA, OCEANIA, NORTH AMERICA, AND SOUTH AMERICA (INCLUDING MEXICO, CENTRAL AMERICA, & THE CARIBBEAN).
COUNTRIES THAT TRADITIONALLY SEND LARGE NUMBERS OF IMMIGRANTS LIKE MEXICO, CHINA, AND INDIA ARE EXCLUDED...
EACH REGION'S ANNUAL ALLOTMENT IS CALCULATED BY U.S. CITIZENSHIP AND IMMIGRATION SERVICES (USCIS).
NO MORE THAN 7 PERCENT OF THE YEAR'S AVAILABLE VISAS MAY GO TO ANY ONE COUNTRY.
THE APPLICANTS MUST HAVE A HIGH SCHOOL EDUCATION OR HIGHER.
THE APPLICANT OR THEIR SPOUSE MUST BE A NATIVE OF ONE OF THE QUALIFYING COUNTRIES.

THE PROGRAM IS KNOWN AS THE "DIVERSITY LOTTERY" SINCE POTENTIAL VISA RECIPIENTS ARE RANDOMLY SELECTED FROM A LARGE POOL OF QUALIFIED ENTRIES.

THE ODDS OF BEING SELECTED ARE VERY SMALL. EACH YEAR AN AVERAGE OF 13.5 MILLION PEOPLE APPLY.

2009	2010	2011	2012	2013	2014	2015	2016	2017
16.5 MILLION	19.7 MILLION	12.6 MILLION	14.6 MILLION	14.3 MILLION	17.6 MILLION	19.3 MILLION	23.1 MILLION	22.4 MILLION

"WINNING" THE LOTTERY DOES NOT GUARANTEE ADMISSION TO THE U.S.—

CONGRATULATIONS, YOU WON—

THE OPPORTUNITY TO APPLY!

LOTTERY WINNERS HAVE A SHORT TIME TO FILE PAPERWORK AND UNDERGO SCREENINGS—

THE CLOCK STARTS NOW.

!

ELECTRONIC SCREENINGS

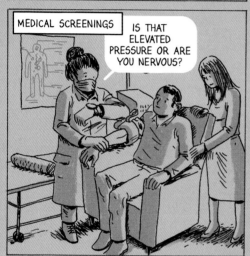

MEDICAL SCREENINGS

IS THAT ELEVATED PRESSURE OR ARE YOU NERVOUS?

PERSONAL SCREENINGS

TELL ME ABOUT EVERY JOB YOU EVER HAD—

AFTER ALL SCREENINGS ARE COMPLETE... THEN MAYBE THE APPLICANTS ARE GRANTED PERMISSION TO ENTER THE U.S.

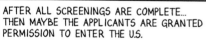

CONGRATS.

EVEN AFTER ALL THAT, UPON ARRIVAL, THE APPLICANTS ARE SET IN A SMALL ROOM AT THE AIRPORT—

WAIT HERE.

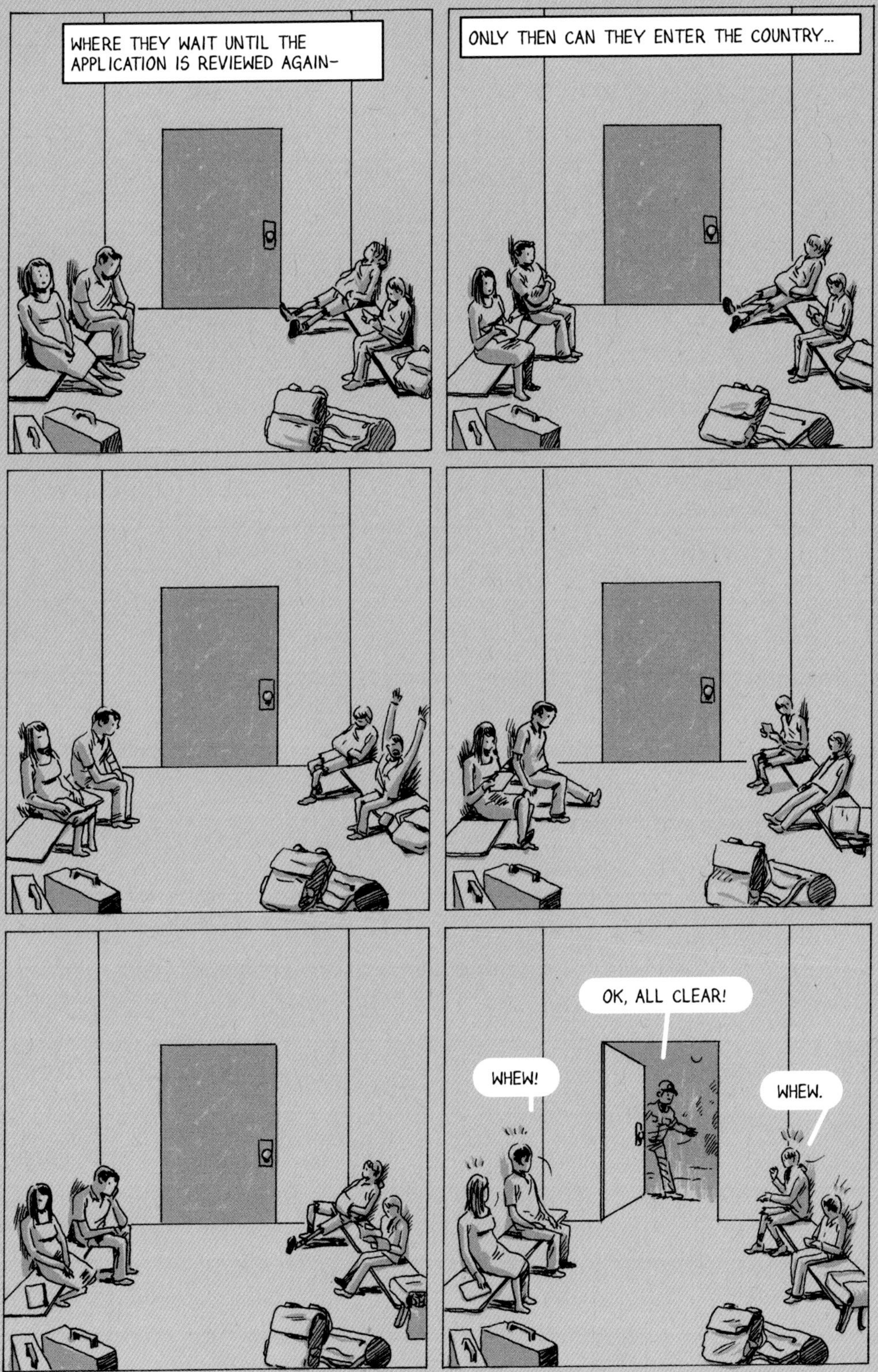
WHERE THEY WAIT UNTIL THE APPLICATION IS REVIEWED AGAIN-
ONLY THEN CAN THEY ENTER THE COUNTRY...
OK, ALL CLEAR!
WHEW!
WHEW.

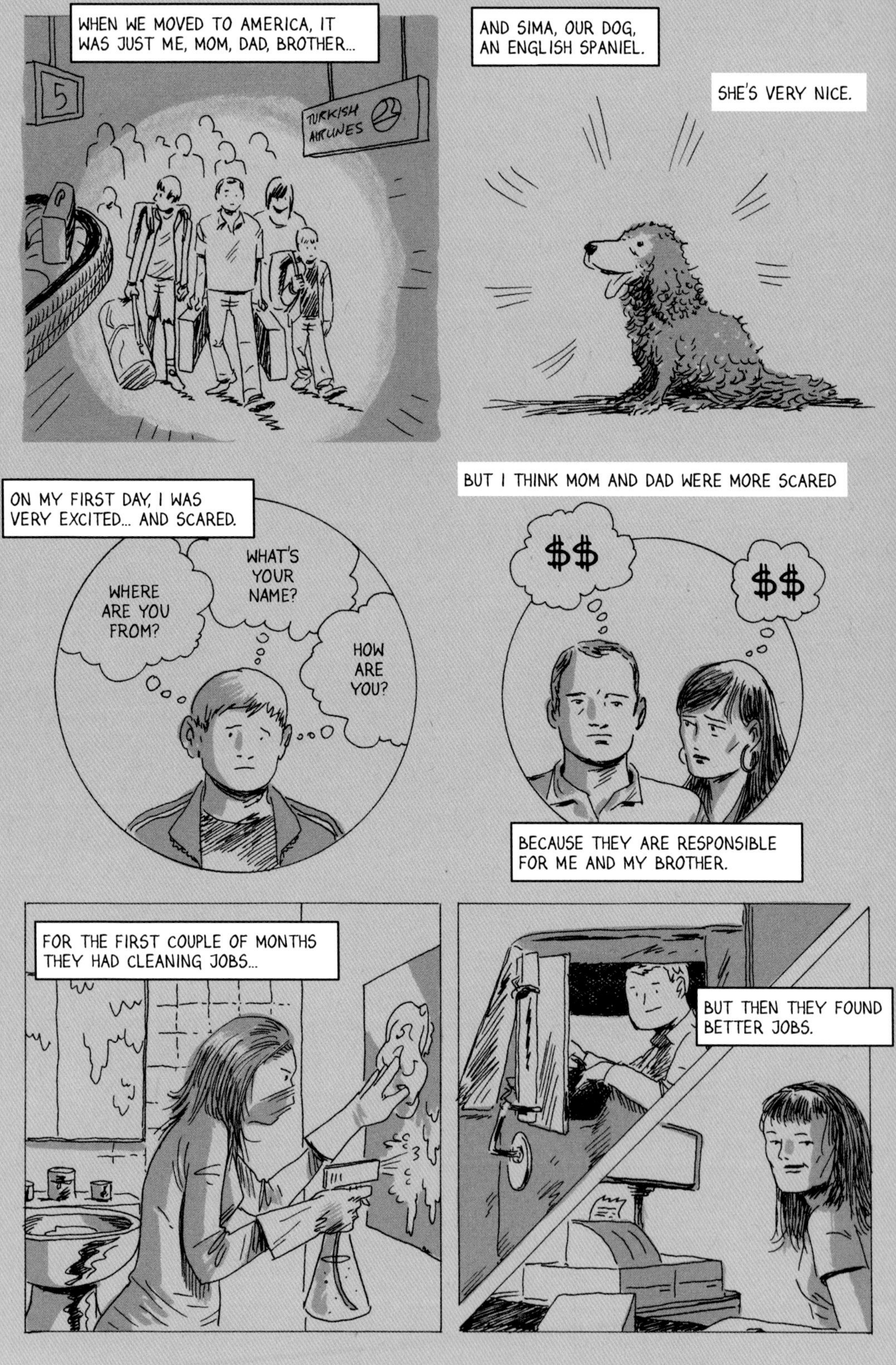
WHEN WE MOVED TO AMERICA, IT WAS JUST ME, MOM, DAD, BROTHER...
TURKISH AIRLINES
AND SIMA, OUR DOG, AN ENGLISH SPANIEL.
SHE'S VERY NICE.
ON MY FIRST DAY, I WAS VERY EXCITED... AND SCARED.
WHERE ARE YOU FROM?
WHAT'S YOUR NAME?
HOW ARE YOU?
BUT I THINK MOM AND DAD WERE MORE SCARED
$$
$$
BECAUSE THEY ARE RESPONSIBLE FOR ME AND MY BROTHER.
FOR THE FIRST COUPLE OF MONTHS THEY HAD CLEANING JOBS...
BUT THEN THEY FOUND BETTER JOBS.

ROCHESTER, NY

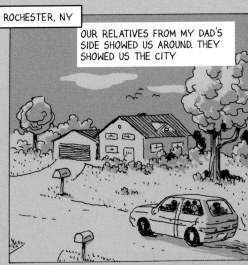

OUR RELATIVES FROM MY DAD'S SIDE SHOWED US AROUND. THEY SHOWED US THE CITY

AND MY SCHOOL.

WHEN SCHOOL STARTED, IT WAS THE WORST

THIS IS ALEX FROM KAZAKHSTAN

I DIDN'T KNOW THE LANGUAGE.

BLAH, BLAH, BLAH, HELLO, BLAH, AND BLAH, BLAH

I COULDN'T SPEAK IT

ALEX?

UH... SORRY.

WHAT'S KAZAKHSTAN LIKE?

AND THAT MADE IT DIFFICULT TO MAKE FRIENDS.

UH... NICE?

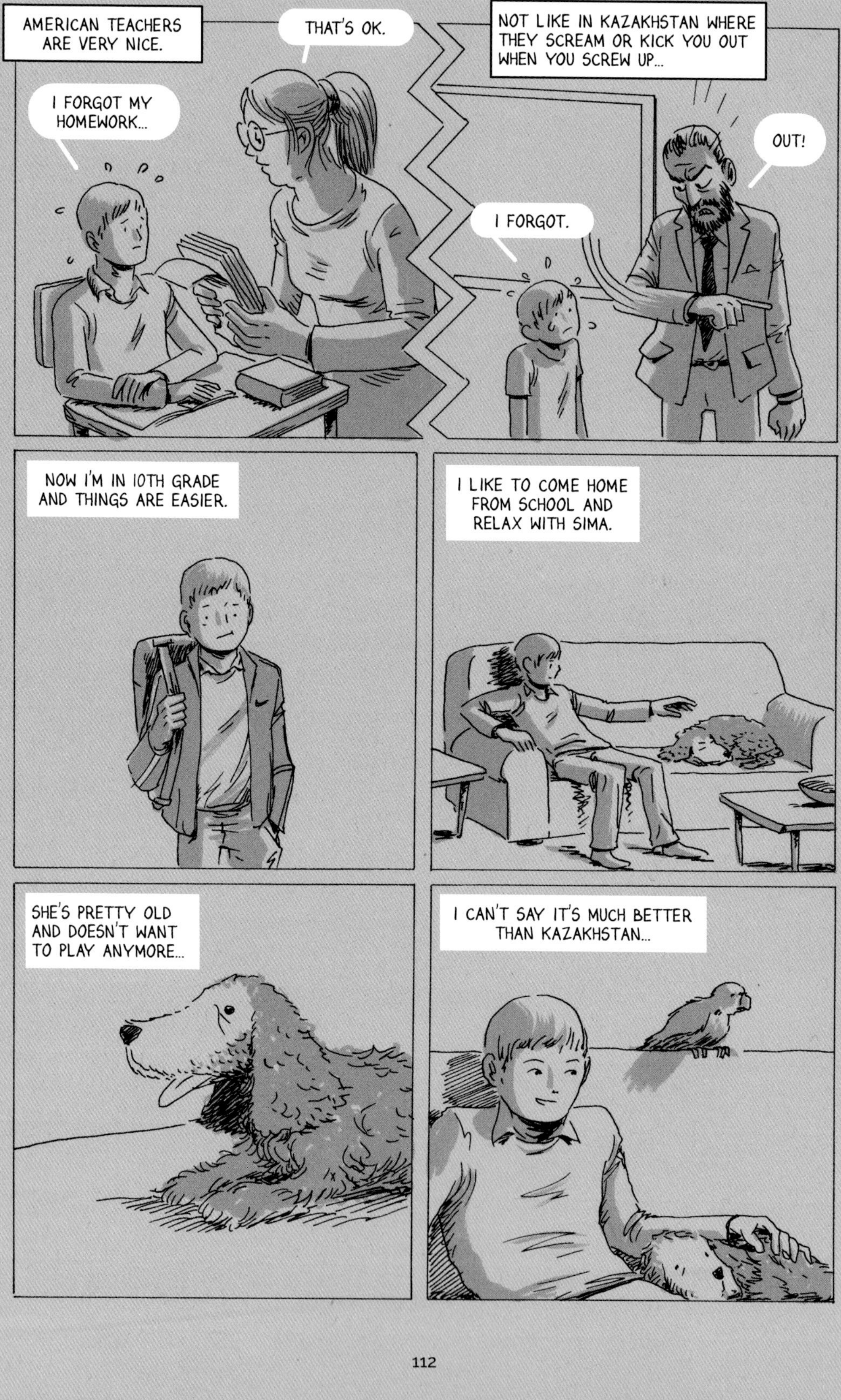
AMERICAN TEACHERS ARE VERY NICE.
I FORGOT MY HOMEWORK...
THAT'S OK.
NOT LIKE IN KAZAKHSTAN WHERE THEY SCREAM OR KICK YOU OUT WHEN YOU SCREW UP...
I FORGOT.
OUT!
NOW I'M IN 10TH GRADE AND THINGS ARE EASIER.
I LIKE TO COME HOME FROM SCHOOL AND RELAX WITH SIMA.
SHE'S PRETTY OLD AND DOESN'T WANT TO PLAY ANYMORE...
I CAN'T SAY IT'S MUCH BETTER THAN KAZAKHSTAN...

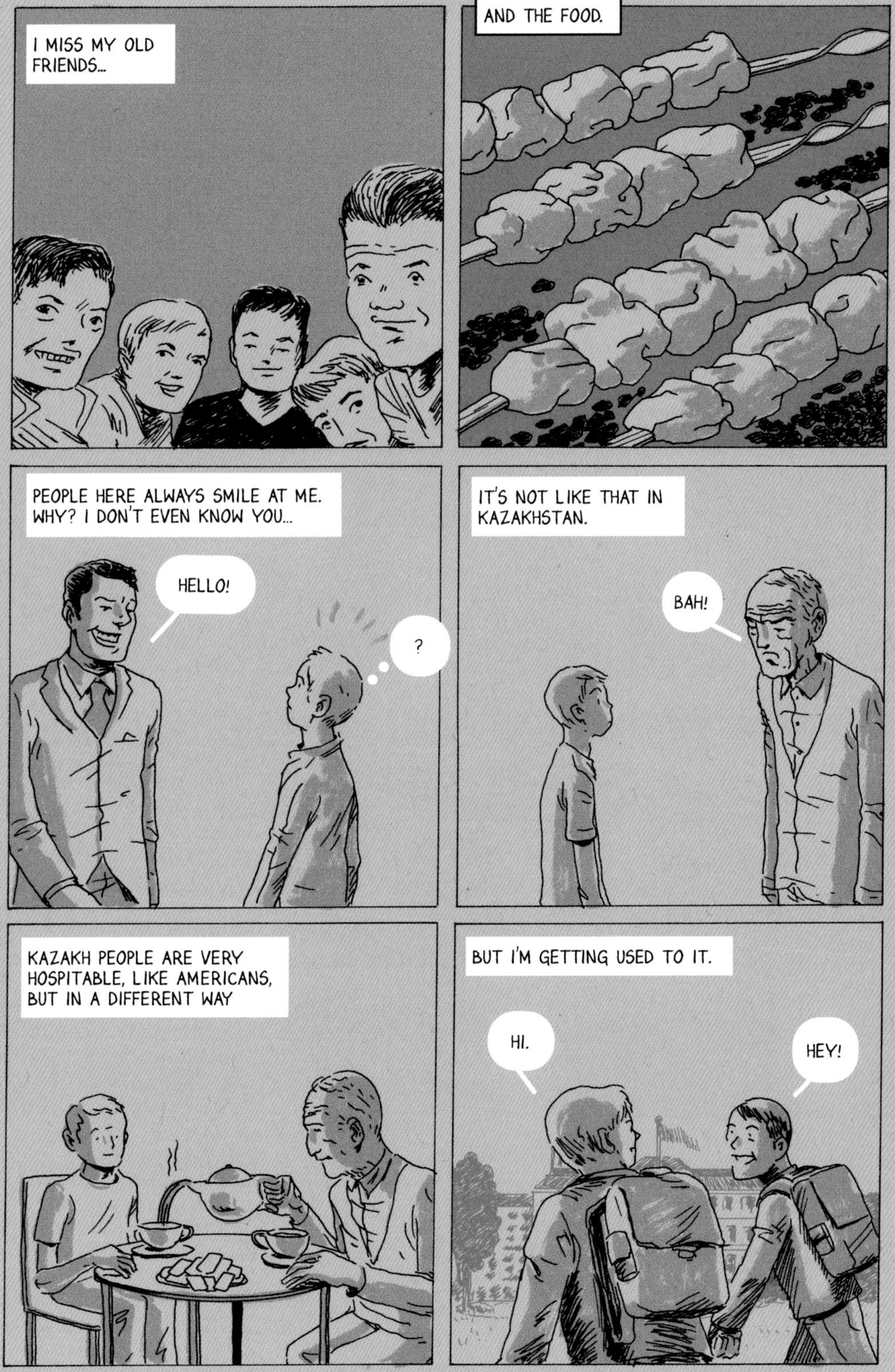
I MISS MY OLD FRIENDS...
AND THE FOOD.
PEOPLE HERE ALWAYS SMILE AT ME. WHY? I DON'T EVEN KNOW YOU...
HELLO!
?
IT'S NOT LIKE THAT IN KAZAKHSTAN.
BAH!
KAZAKH PEOPLE ARE VERY HOSPITABLE, LIKE AMERICANS, BUT IN A DIFFERENT WAY
BUT I'M GETTING USED TO IT.
HI.
HEY!

MY FAVORITE SUBJECTS ARE THE SCIENCES.

I DON'T LIKE MATH, ESPECIALLY GEOMETRY.

IS THIS SQUARE A RHOMBUS?

IT'S KIND OF SILLY.

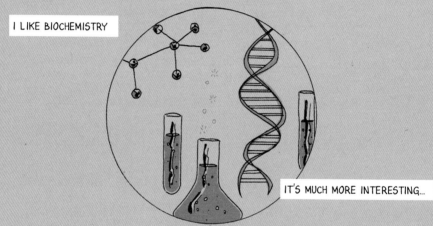

I LIKE BIOCHEMISTRY

IT'S MUCH MORE INTERESTING...

IN THE FUTURE I HOPE TO CONTRIBUTE TO THE U.S. IN A SCIENTIFIC WAY.

MAYBE A CURE FOR CANCER?

WHO KNOWS WHAT THE FUTURE WILL BRING?

PAKISTAN

ZURYA ANJUM

Born: Quetta, Pakistan
Current: St. Cloud, Minnesota

Zurya Anjum is a proud Muslim American and psychiatrist. She immigrated to the U.S. in 1999. Her career was built around helping people deal with their mental health issues. She has lived in Minnesota for 21 years with her husband, two kids, cat, and two parakeets. Zurya and her family love to travel to different parts of the world to learn about different cultures and religions and try new food. In her free time, Zurya enjoys volunteering and working with organizations to promote awareness of inequality and provide opportunities for people to grow their understanding of diversity.

www.greencardvoices.org/speakers/zurya-anjum

TOUFIC EL RASSI

Born: Lebanon
Current: Chicago, Illinois

Toufic El Rassi is an artist and professor based in Chicago. He was born in Lebanon and immigrated to the U.S. as a child. He is a commentator on the Middle East and the artist/author of *Arab in America* and *Babylon Burning*, published by Last Gasp San Francisco.

www.instagram.com/toufic_el_rassi

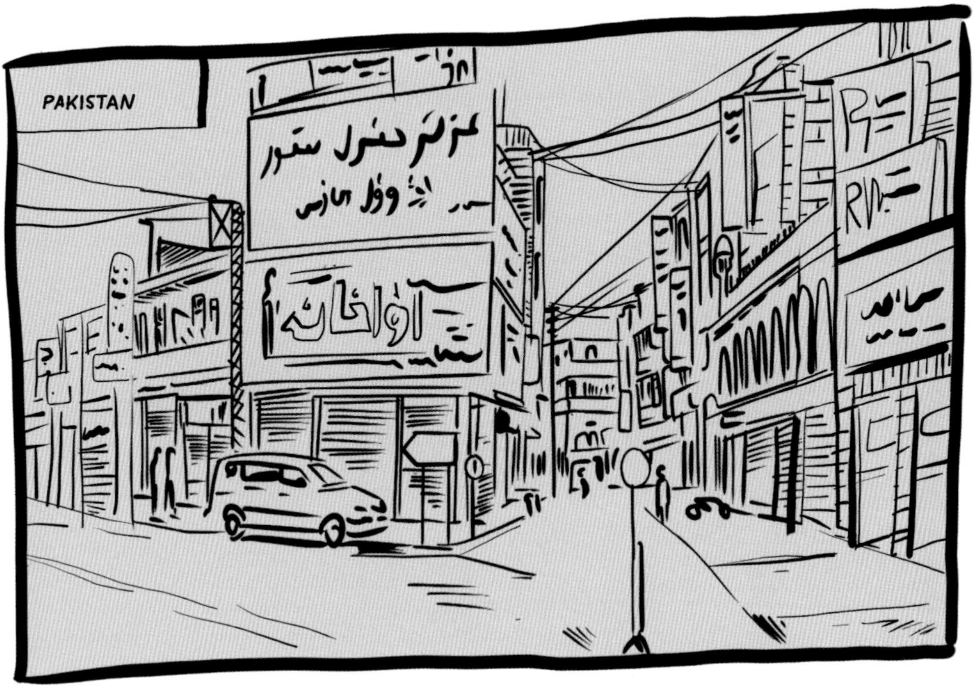
PAKISTAN

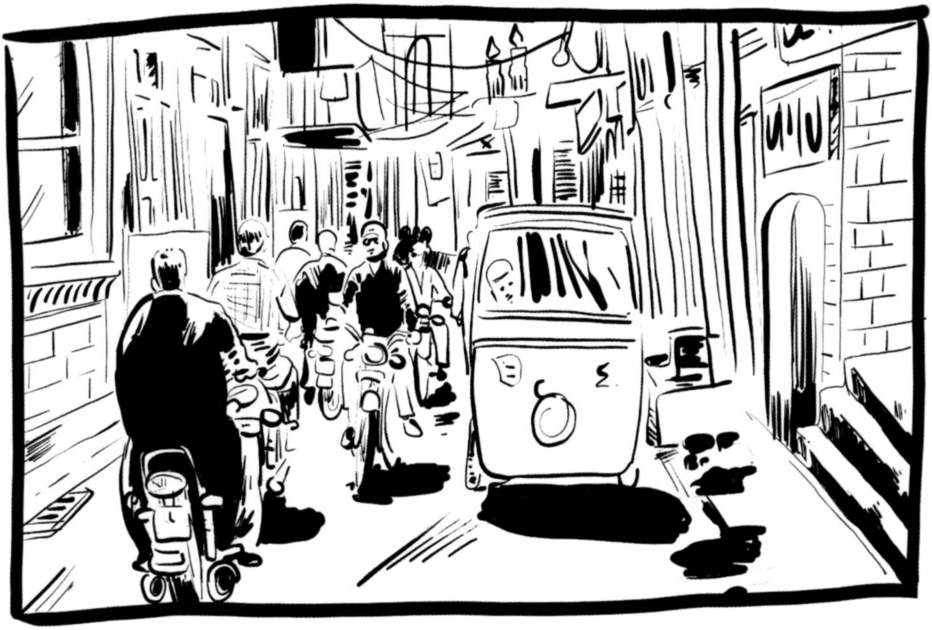

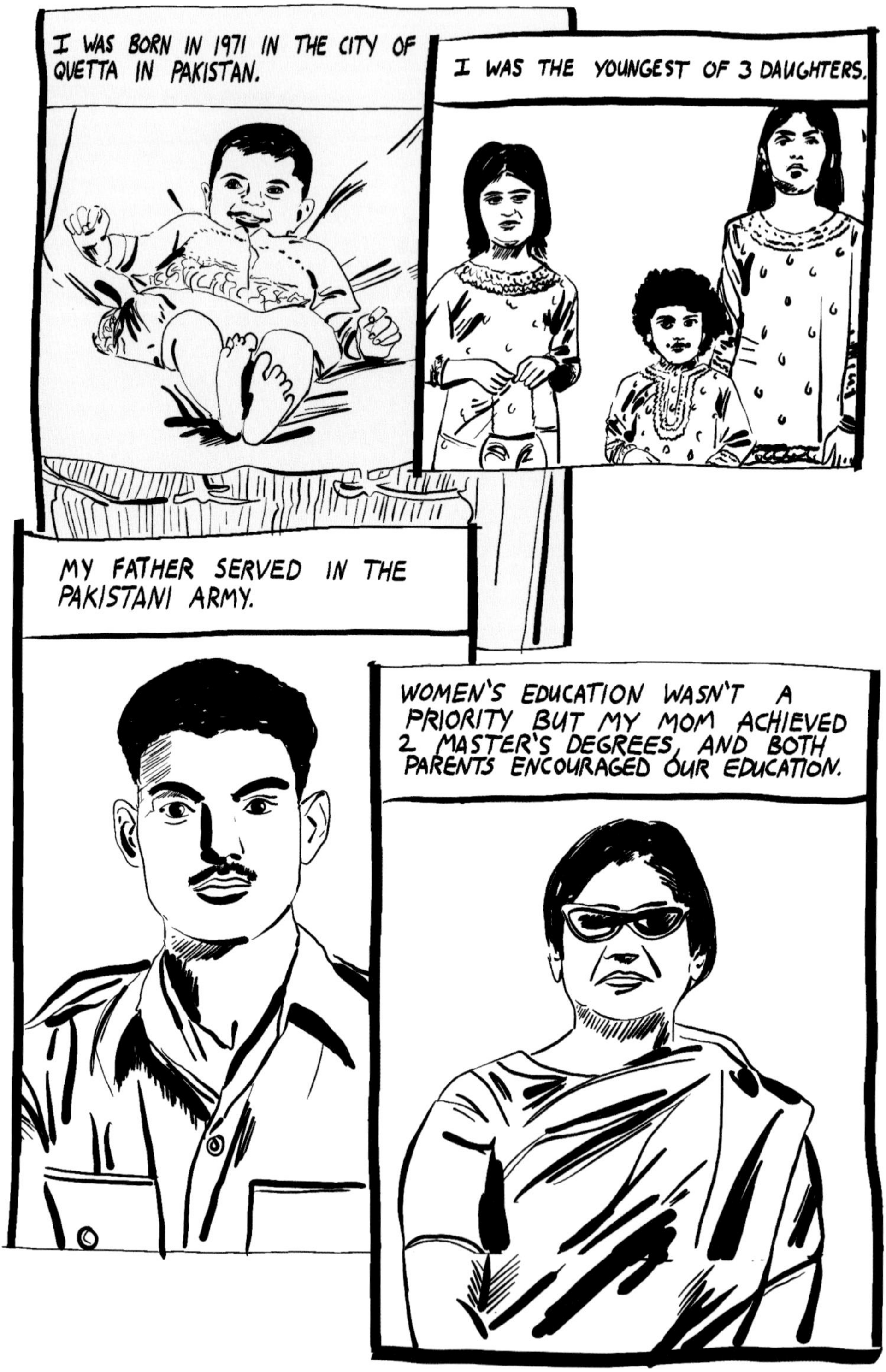
I WAS BORN IN 1971 IN THE CITY OF QUETTA IN PAKISTAN.
I WAS THE YOUNGEST OF 3 DAUGHTERS.
MY FATHER SERVED IN THE PAKISTANI ARMY.
WOMEN'S EDUCATION WASN'T A PRIORITY BUT MY MOM ACHIEVED 2 MASTER'S DEGREES, AND BOTH PARENTS ENCOURAGED OUR EDUCATION.

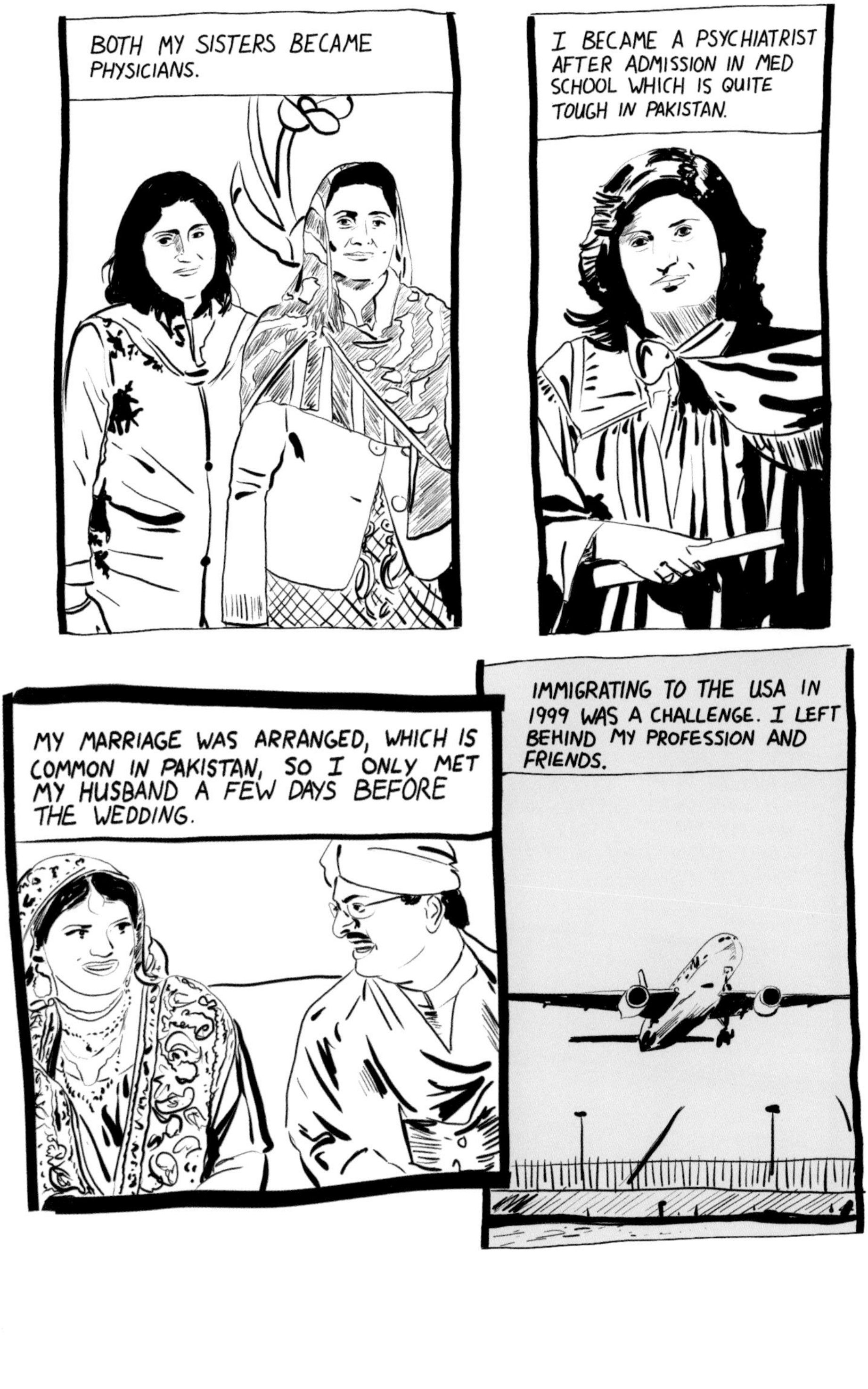
BOTH MY SISTERS BECAME PHYSICIANS.
I BECAME A PSYCHIATRIST AFTER ADMISSION IN MED SCHOOL WHICH IS QUITE TOUGH IN PAKISTAN.
MY MARRIAGE WAS ARRANGED, WHICH IS COMMON IN PAKISTAN, SO I ONLY MET MY HUSBAND A FEW DAYS BEFORE THE WEDDING.
IMMIGRATING TO THE USA IN 1999 WAS A CHALLENGE. I LEFT BEHIND MY PROFESSION AND FRIENDS.

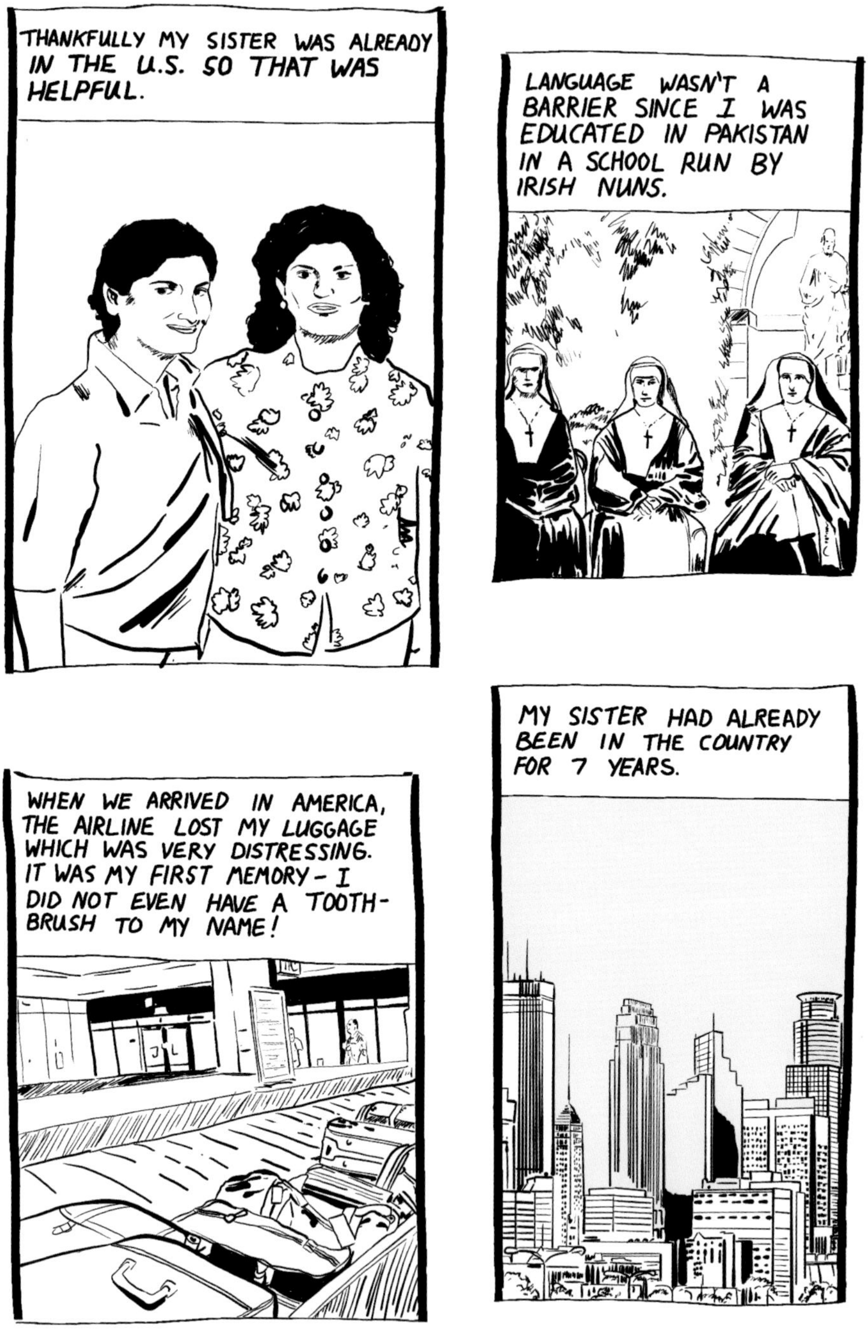
THANKFULLY MY SISTER WAS ALREADY IN THE U.S. SO THAT WAS HELPFUL.
LANGUAGE WASN'T A BARRIER SINCE I WAS EDUCATED IN PAKISTAN IN A SCHOOL RUN BY IRISH NUNS.
WHEN WE ARRIVED IN AMERICA, THE AIRLINE LOST MY LUGGAGE WHICH WAS VERY DISTRESSING. IT WAS MY FIRST MEMORY - I DID NOT EVEN HAVE A TOOTH-BRUSH TO MY NAME!
MY SISTER HAD ALREADY BEEN IN THE COUNTRY FOR 7 YEARS.

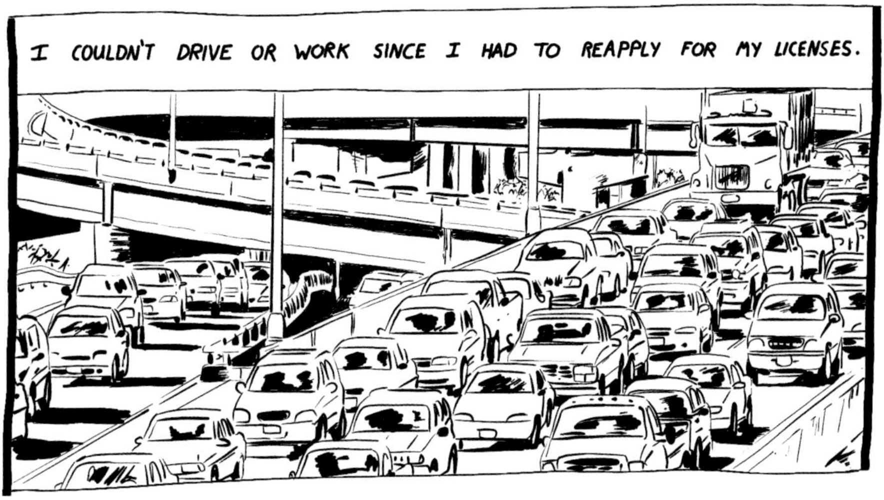
I COULDN'T DRIVE OR WORK SINCE I HAD TO REAPPLY FOR MY LICENSES.

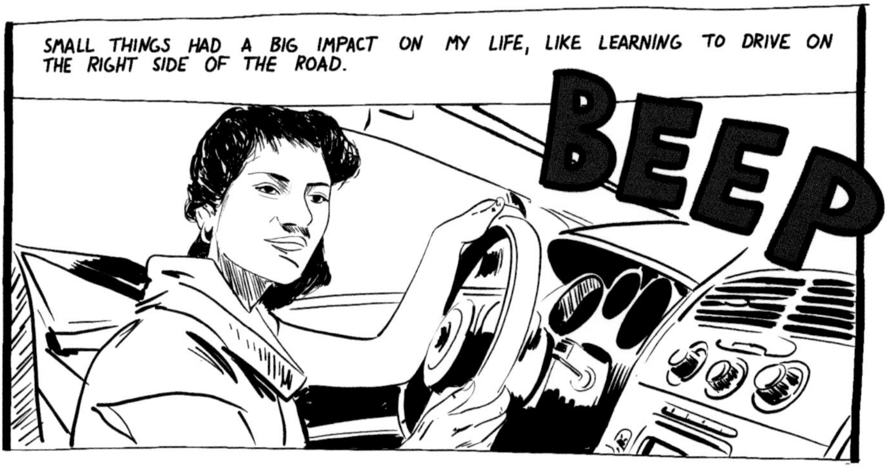
SMALL THINGS HAD A BIG IMPACT ON MY LIFE, LIKE LEARNING TO DRIVE ON THE RIGHT SIDE OF THE ROAD.
BEEP

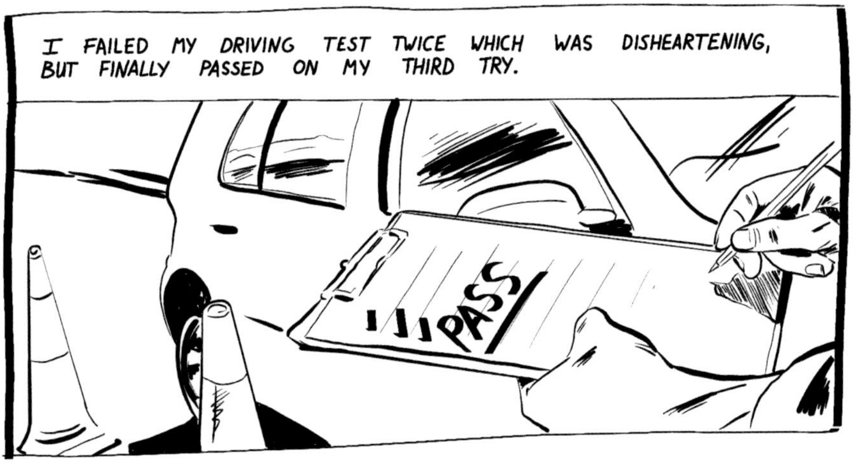
I FAILED MY DRIVING TEST TWICE WHICH WAS DISHEARTENING, BUT FINALLY PASSED ON MY THIRD TRY.
PASS

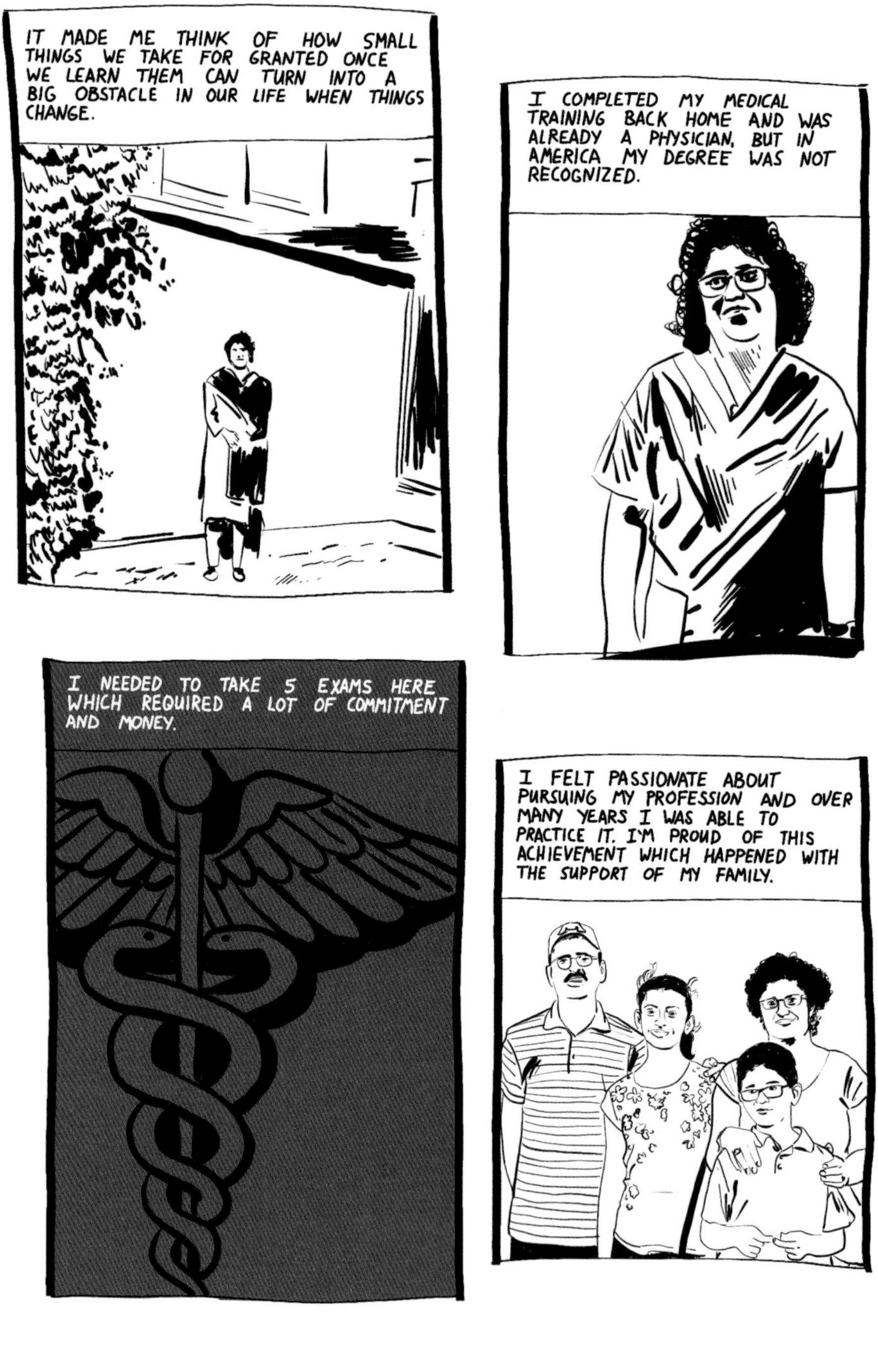
IT MADE ME THINK OF HOW SMALL THINGS WE TAKE FOR GRANTED ONCE WE LEARN THEM CAN TURN INTO A BIG OBSTACLE IN OUR LIFE WHEN THINGS CHANGE.
I COMPLETED MY MEDICAL TRAINING BACK HOME AND WAS ALREADY A PHYSICIAN, BUT IN AMERICA MY DEGREE WAS NOT RECOGNIZED.
I NEEDED TO TAKE 5 EXAMS HERE WHICH REQUIRED A LOT OF COMMITMENT AND MONEY.
I FELT PASSIONATE ABOUT PURSUING MY PROFESSION AND OVER MANY YEARS I WAS ABLE TO PRACTICE IT. I'M PROUD OF THIS ACHIEVEMENT WHICH HAPPENED WITH THE SUPPORT OF MY FAMILY.

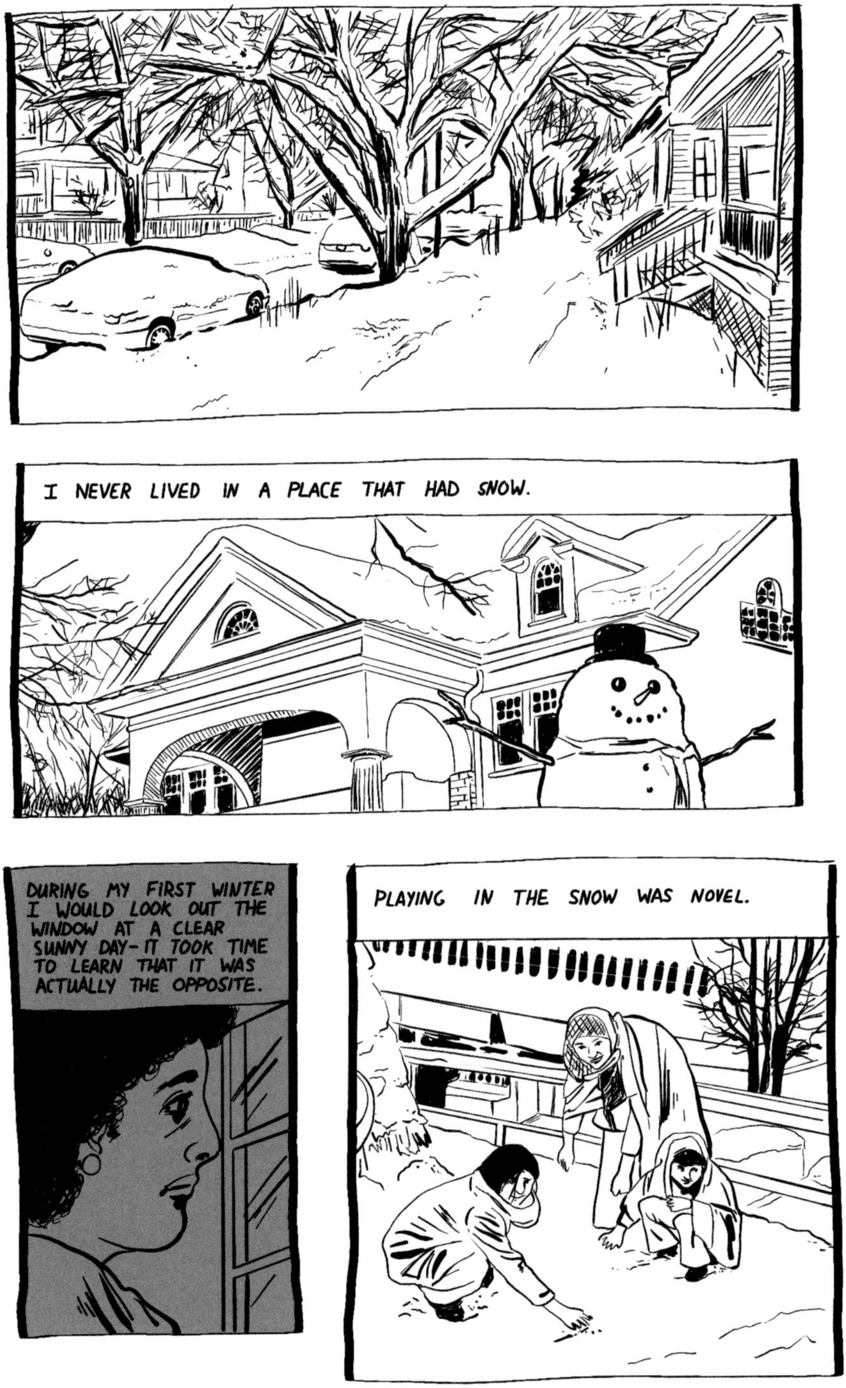
I NEVER LIVED IN A PLACE THAT HAD SNOW.
DURING MY FIRST WINTER I WOULD LOOK OUT THE WINDOW AT A CLEAR SUNNY DAY- IT TOOK TIME TO LEARN THAT IT WAS ACTUALLY THE OPPOSITE.
PLAYING IN THE SNOW WAS NOVEL.

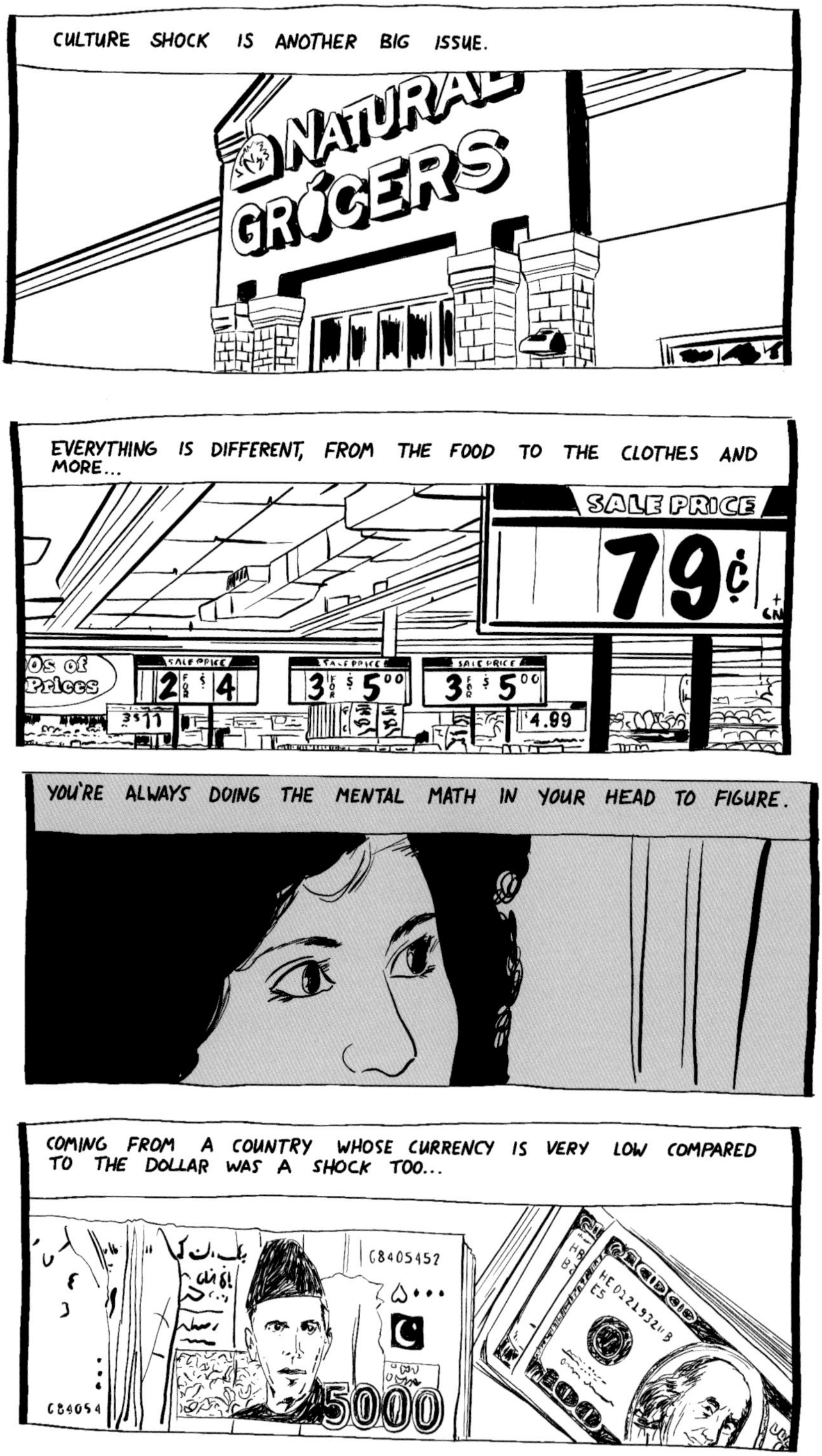

CULTURE SHOCK IS ANOTHER BIG ISSUE.
NATURAL GROCERS
EVERYTHING IS DIFFERENT, FROM THE FOOD TO THE CLOTHES AND MORE...
SALE PRICE
79¢
YOU'RE ALWAYS DOING THE MENTAL MATH IN YOUR HEAD TO FIGURE.
COMING FROM A COUNTRY WHOSE CURRENCY IS VERY LOW COMPARED TO THE DOLLAR WAS A SHOCK TOO...
5000

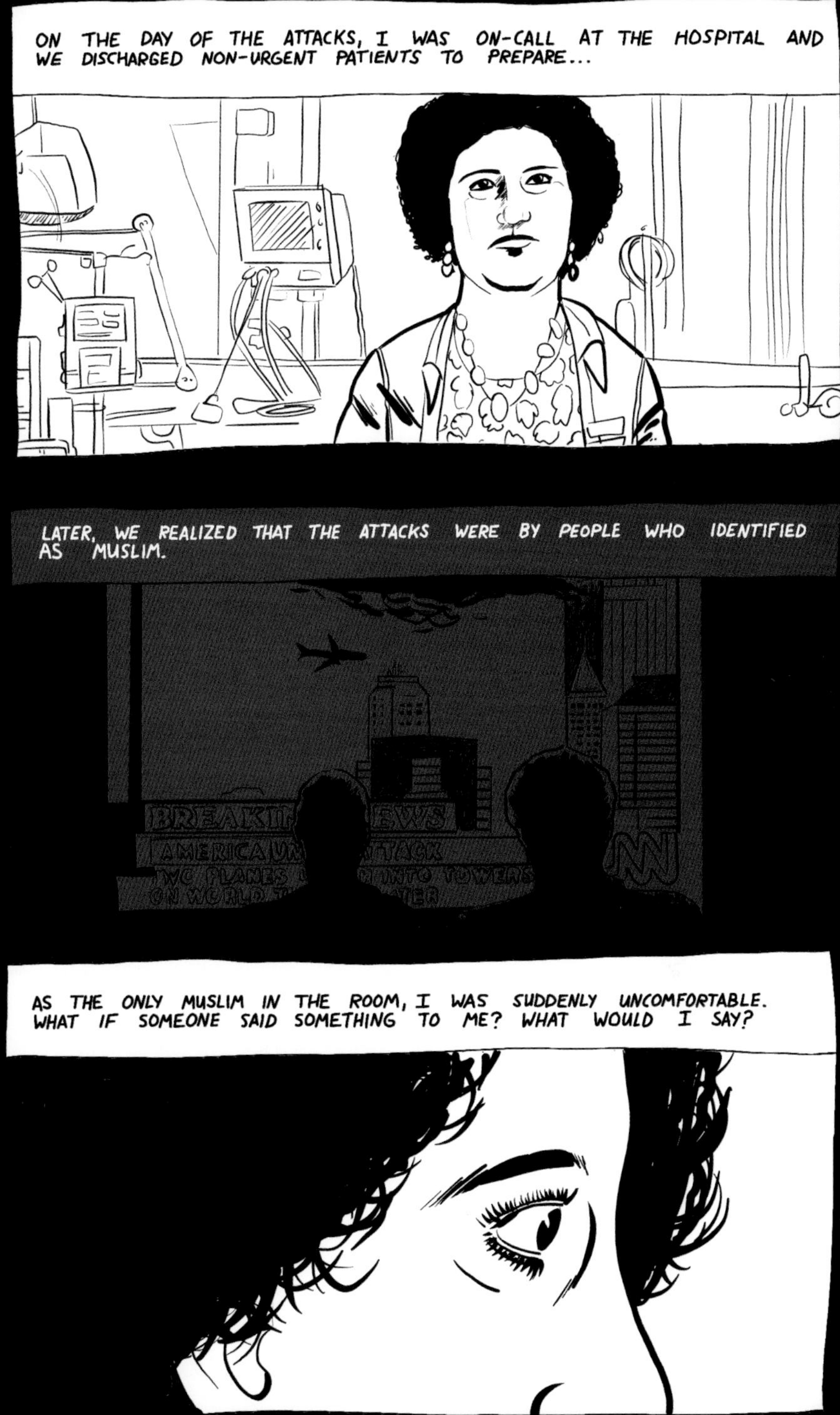
ON THE DAY OF THE ATTACKS, I WAS ON-CALL AT THE HOSPITAL AND WE DISCHARGED NON-URGENT PATIENTS TO PREPARE...
LATER, WE REALIZED THAT THE ATTACKS WERE BY PEOPLE WHO IDENTIFIED AS MUSLIM.
AS THE ONLY MUSLIM IN THE ROOM, I WAS SUDDENLY UNCOMFORTABLE. WHAT IF SOMEONE SAID SOMETHING TO ME? WHAT WOULD I SAY?

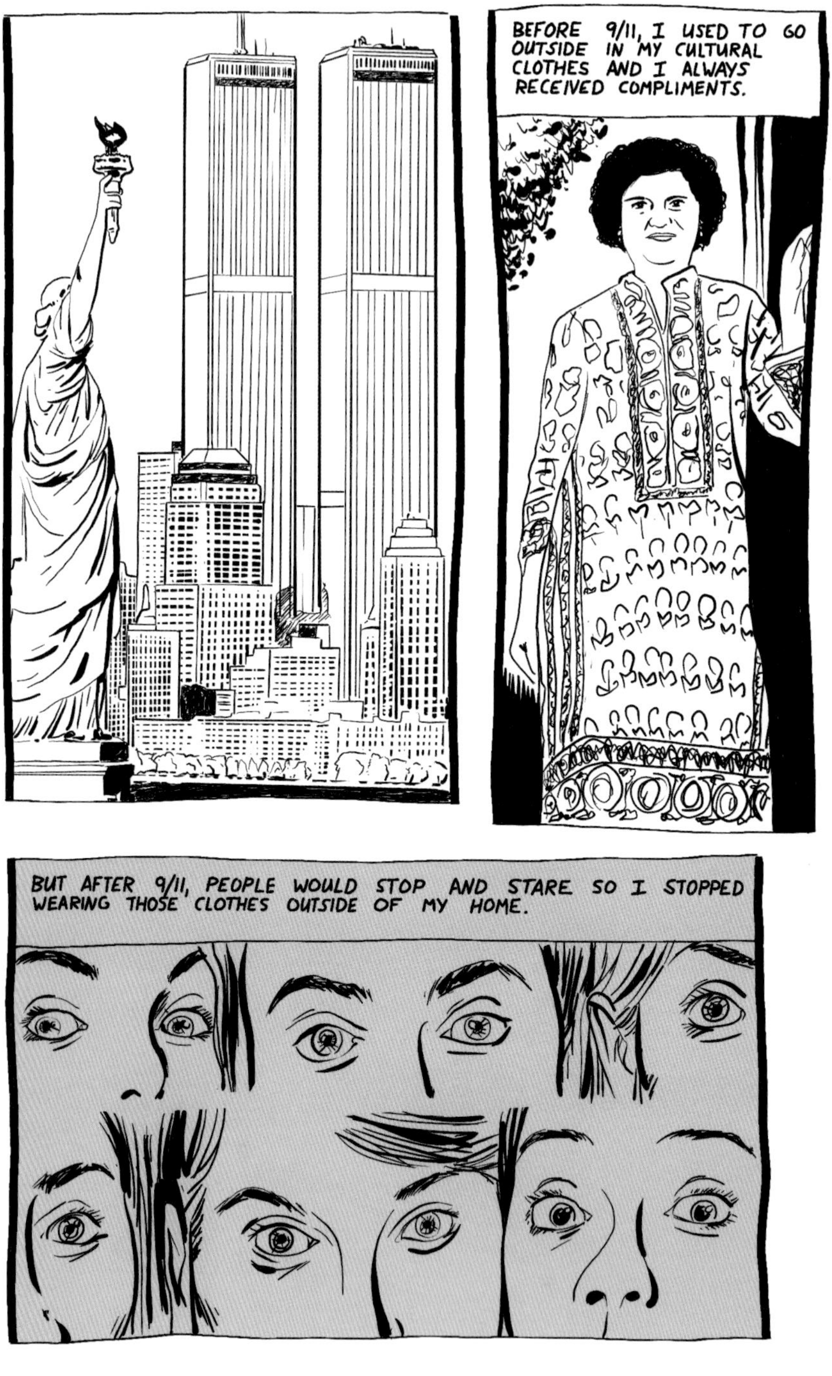
BEFORE 9/11, I USED TO GO OUTSIDE IN MY CULTURAL CLOTHES AND I ALWAYS RECEIVED COMPLIMENTS.
BUT AFTER 9/11, PEOPLE WOULD STOP AND STARE SO I STOPPED WEARING THOSE CLOTHES OUTSIDE OF MY HOME.

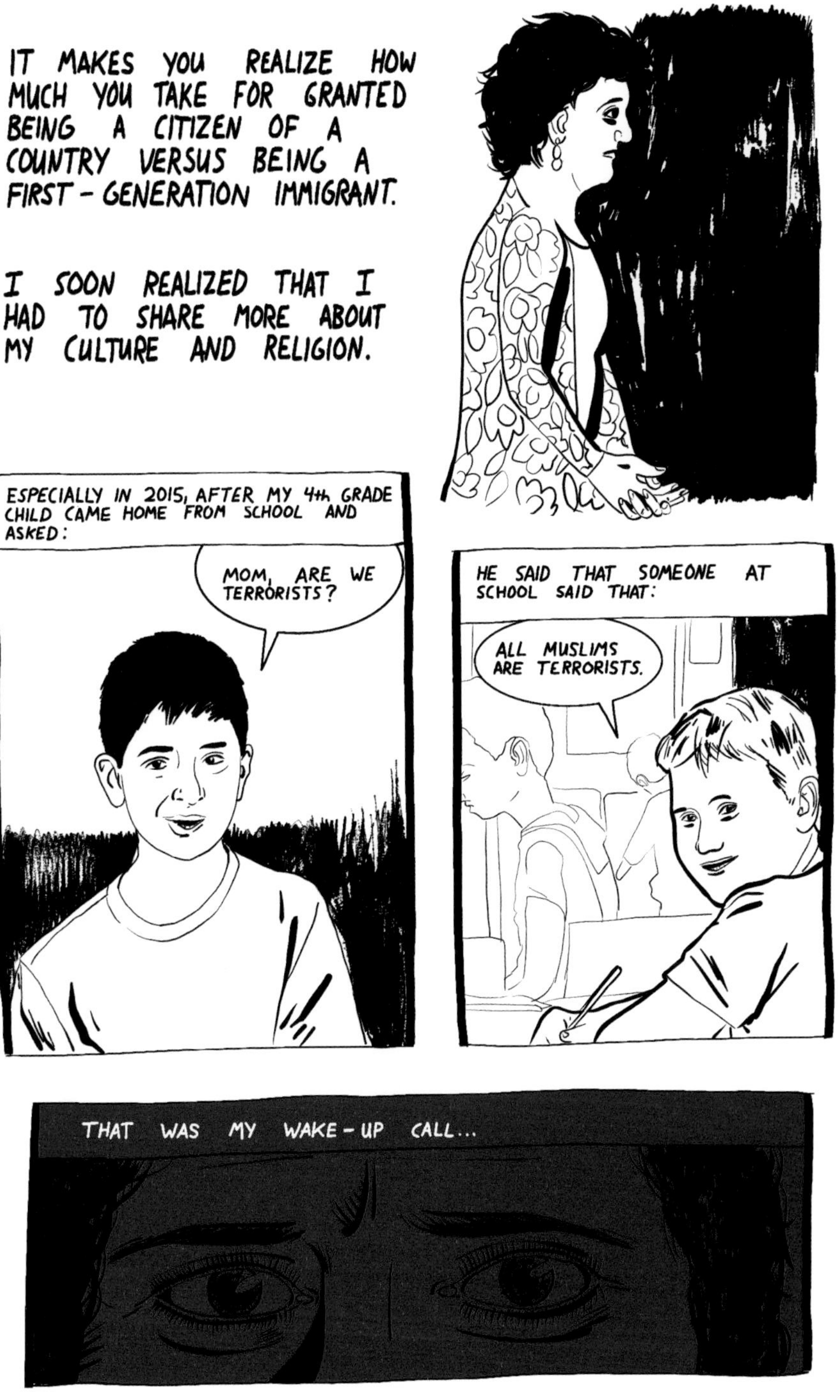
IT MAKES YOU REALIZE HOW MUCH YOU TAKE FOR GRANTED BEING A CITIZEN OF A COUNTRY VERSUS BEING A FIRST-GENERATION IMMIGRANT.
I SOON REALIZED THAT I HAD TO SHARE MORE ABOUT MY CULTURE AND RELIGION.
ESPECIALLY IN 2015, AFTER MY 4th GRADE CHILD CAME HOME FROM SCHOOL AND ASKED:
MOM, ARE WE TERRORISTS?
HE SAID THAT SOMEONE AT SCHOOL SAID THAT:
ALL MUSLIMS ARE TERRORISTS.
THAT WAS MY WAKE-UP CALL...

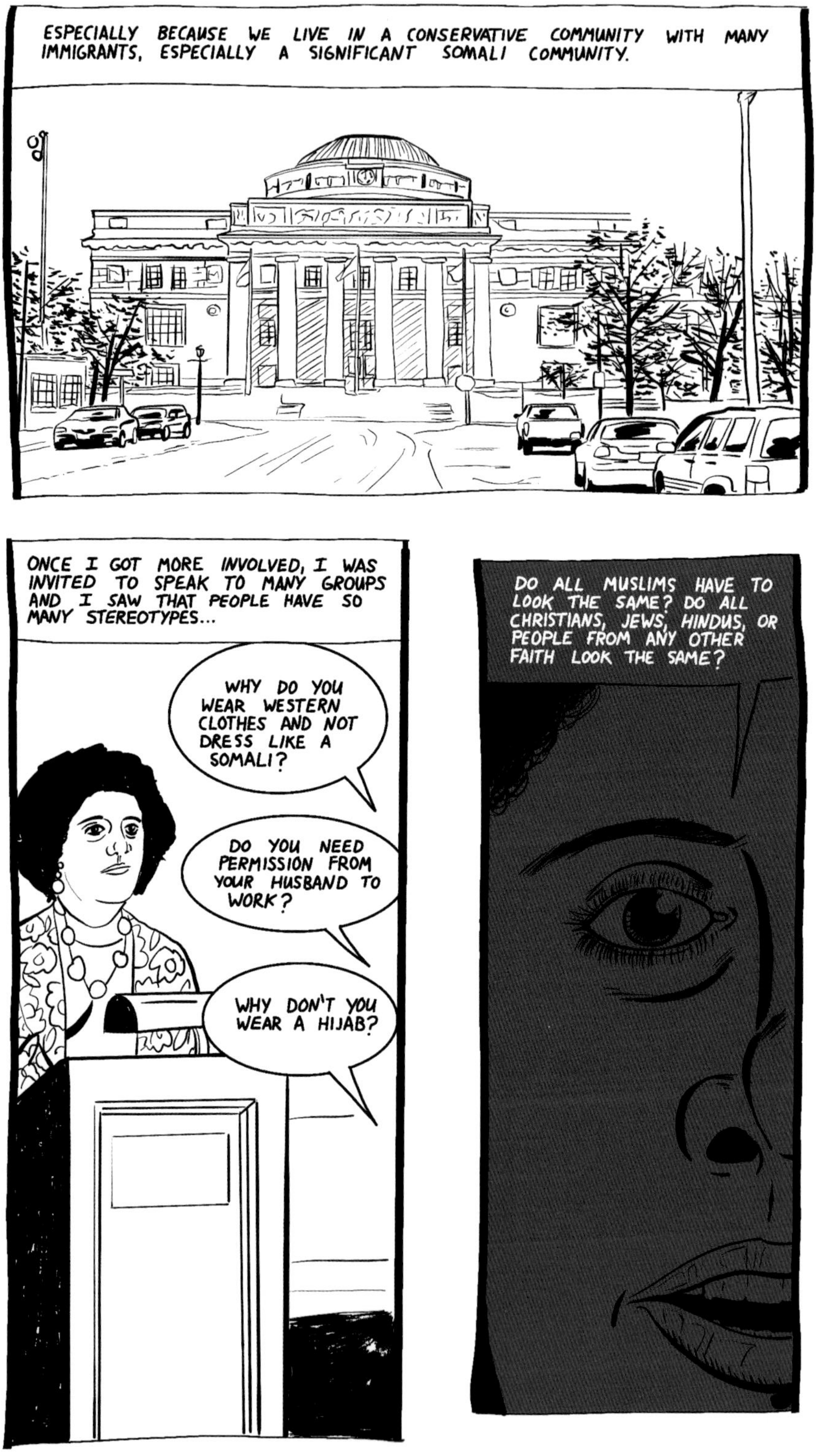
ESPECIALLY BECAUSE WE LIVE IN A CONSERVATIVE COMMUNITY WITH MANY IMMIGRANTS, ESPECIALLY A SIGNIFICANT SOMALI COMMUNITY.
ONCE I GOT MORE INVOLVED, I WAS INVITED TO SPEAK TO MANY GROUPS AND I SAW THAT PEOPLE HAVE SO MANY STEREOTYPES...
WHY DO YOU WEAR WESTERN CLOTHES AND NOT DRESS LIKE A SOMALI?
DO YOU NEED PERMISSION FROM YOUR HUSBAND TO WORK?
WHY DON'T YOU WEAR A HIJAB?
DO ALL MUSLIMS HAVE TO LOOK THE SAME? DO ALL CHRISTIANS, JEWS, HINDUS, OR PEOPLE FROM ANY OTHER FAITH LOOK THE SAME?

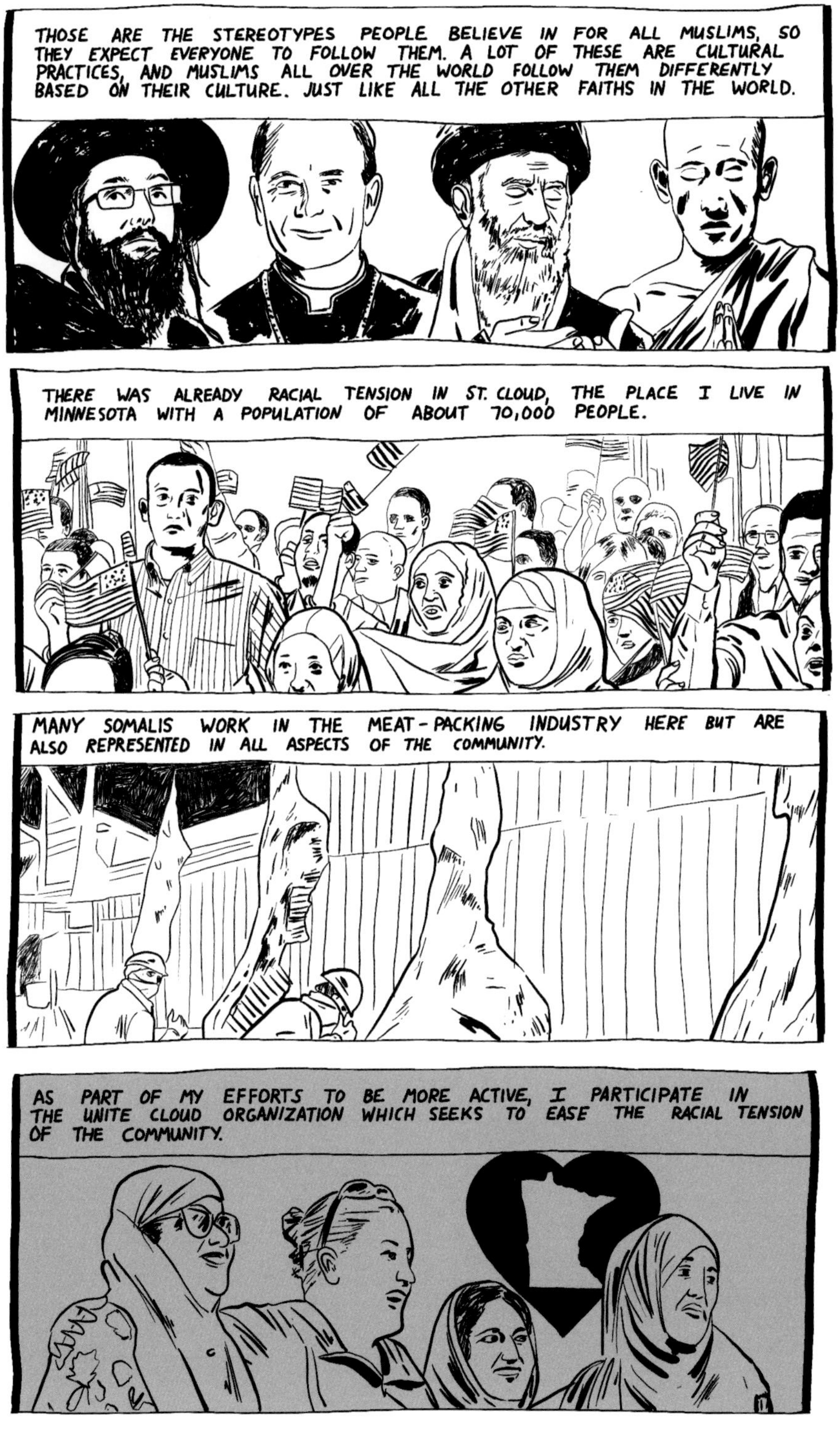
THOSE ARE THE STEREOTYPES PEOPLE BELIEVE IN FOR ALL MUSLIMS, SO THEY EXPECT EVERYONE TO FOLLOW THEM. A LOT OF THESE ARE CULTURAL PRACTICES, AND MUSLIMS ALL OVER THE WORLD FOLLOW THEM DIFFERENTLY BASED ON THEIR CULTURE. JUST LIKE ALL THE OTHER FAITHS IN THE WORLD.
THERE WAS ALREADY RACIAL TENSION IN ST. CLOUD, THE PLACE I LIVE IN MINNESOTA WITH A POPULATION OF ABOUT 70,000 PEOPLE.
MANY SOMALIS WORK IN THE MEAT-PACKING INDUSTRY HERE BUT ARE ALSO REPRESENTED IN ALL ASPECTS OF THE COMMUNITY.
AS PART OF MY EFFORTS TO BE MORE ACTIVE, I PARTICIPATE IN THE UNITE CLOUD ORGANIZATION WHICH SEEKS TO EASE THE RACIAL TENSION OF THE COMMUNITY.

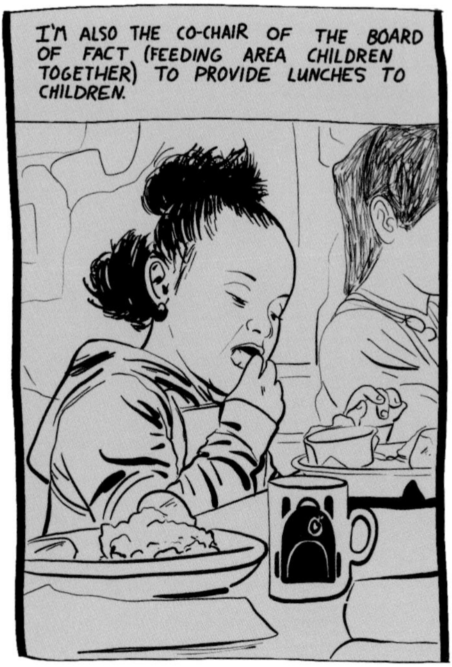
I'M ALSO THE CO-CHAIR OF THE BOARD OF FACT (FEEDING AREA CHILDREN TOGETHER) TO PROVIDE LUNCHES TO CHILDREN.

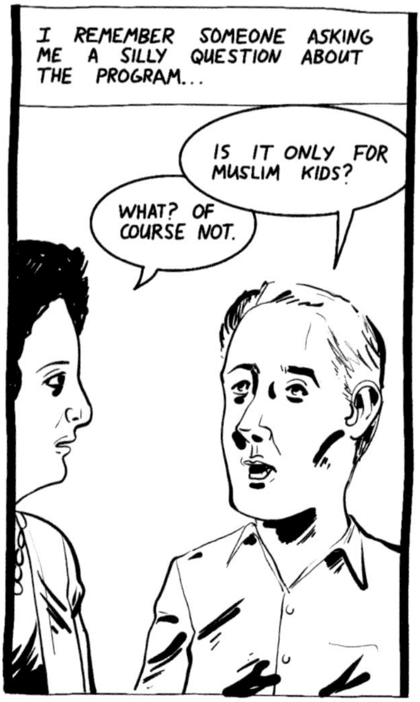
I REMEMBER SOMEONE ASKING ME A SILLY QUESTION ABOUT THE PROGRAM...
IS IT ONLY FOR MUSLIM KIDS?
WHAT? OF COURSE NOT.

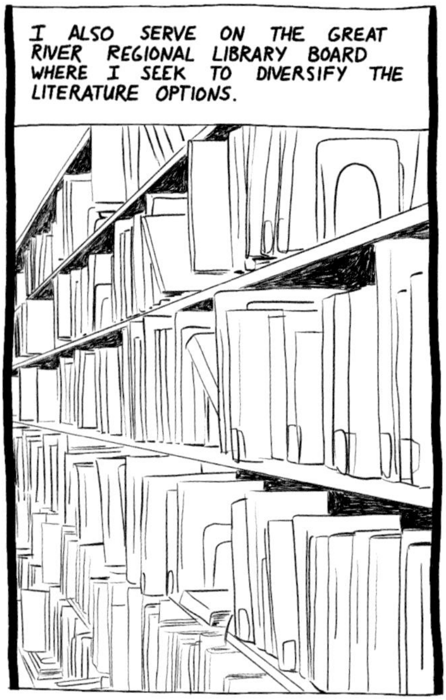
I ALSO SERVE ON THE GREAT RIVER REGIONAL LIBRARY BOARD WHERE I SEEK TO DIVERSIFY THE LITERATURE OPTIONS.

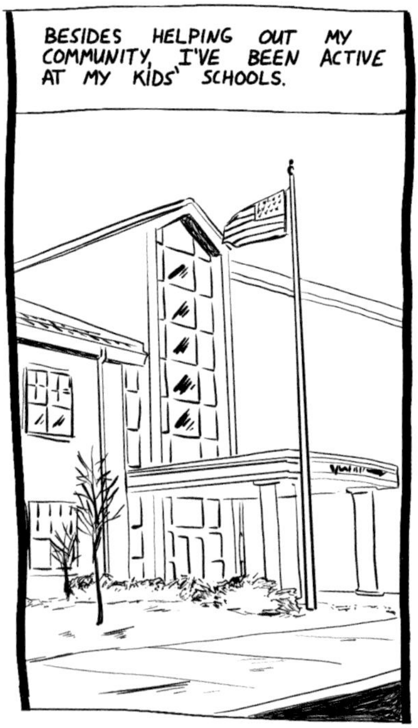
BESIDES HELPING OUT MY COMMUNITY, I'VE BEEN ACTIVE AT MY KIDS' SCHOOLS.

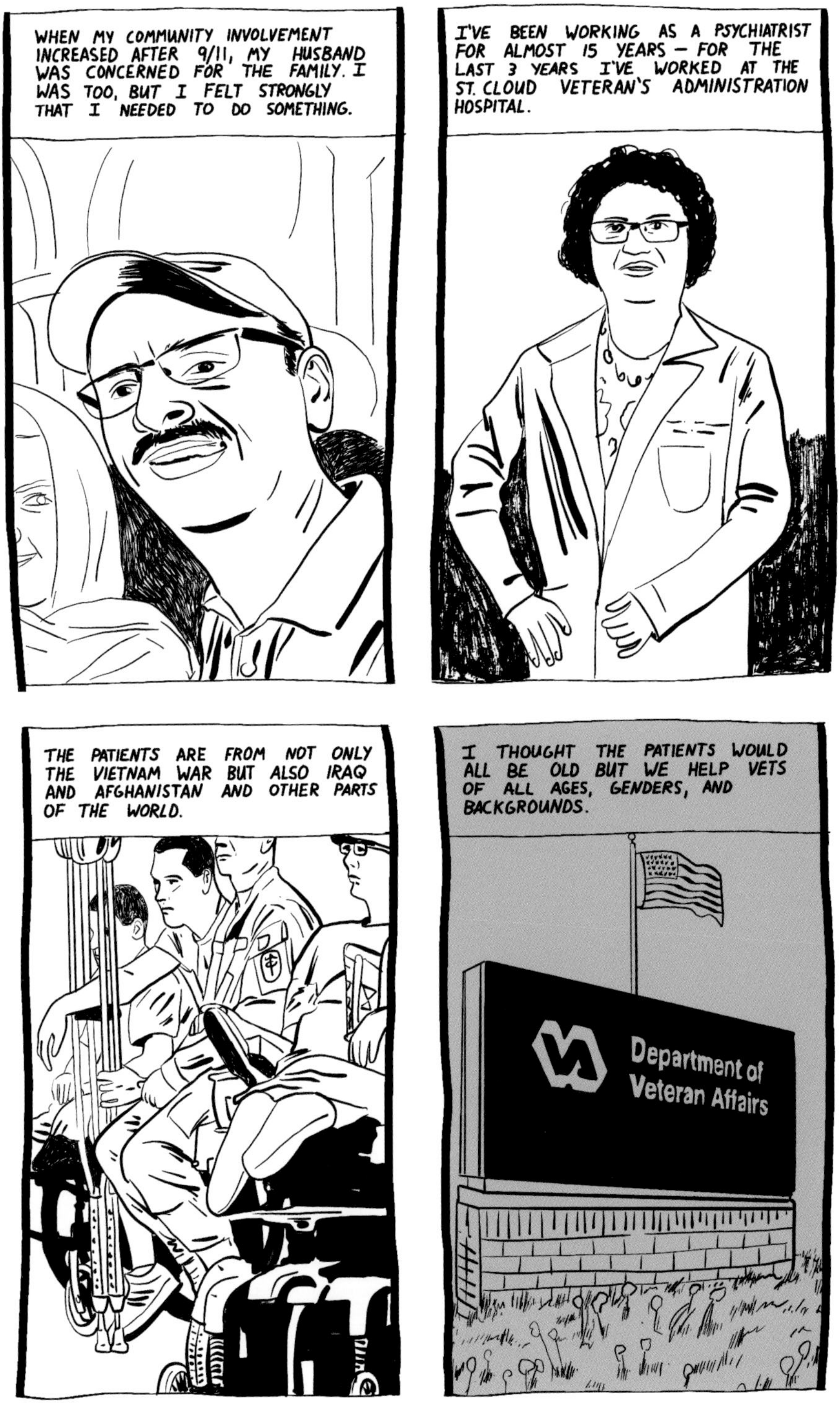
WHEN MY COMMUNITY INVOLVEMENT INCREASED AFTER 9/11, MY HUSBAND WAS CONCERNED FOR THE FAMILY. I WAS TOO, BUT I FELT STRONGLY THAT I NEEDED TO DO SOMETHING.
I'VE BEEN WORKING AS A PSYCHIATRIST FOR ALMOST 15 YEARS – FOR THE LAST 3 YEARS I'VE WORKED AT THE ST. CLOUD VETERAN'S ADMINISTRATION HOSPITAL.
THE PATIENTS ARE FROM NOT ONLY THE VIETNAM WAR BUT ALSO IRAQ AND AFGHANISTAN AND OTHER PARTS OF THE WORLD.
I THOUGHT THE PATIENTS WOULD ALL BE OLD BUT WE HELP VETS OF ALL AGES, GENDERS, AND BACKGROUNDS.
Department of
Veteran Affairs

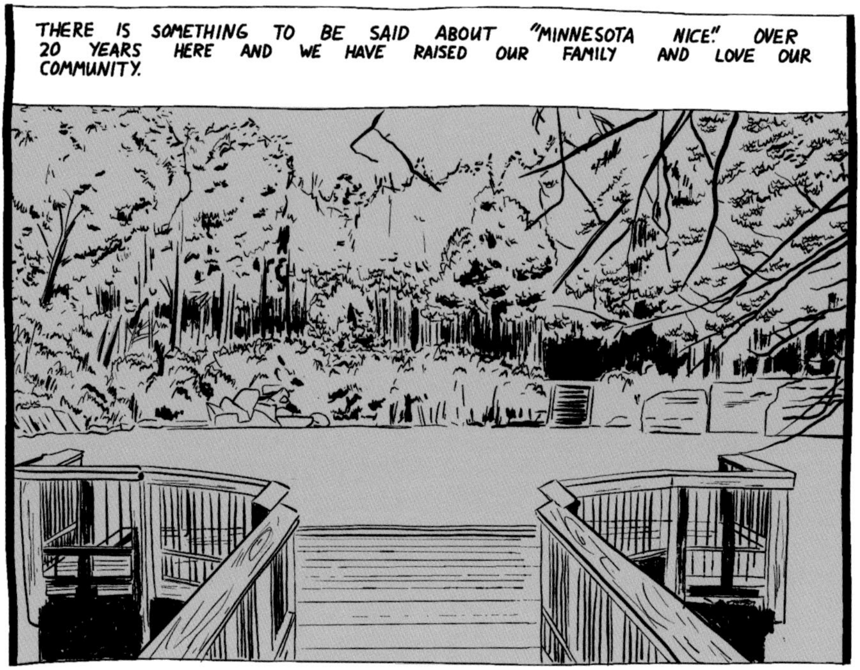
THERE IS SOMETHING TO BE SAID ABOUT "MINNESOTA NICE." OVER 20 YEARS HERE AND WE HAVE RAISED OUR FAMILY AND LOVE OUR COMMUNITY.

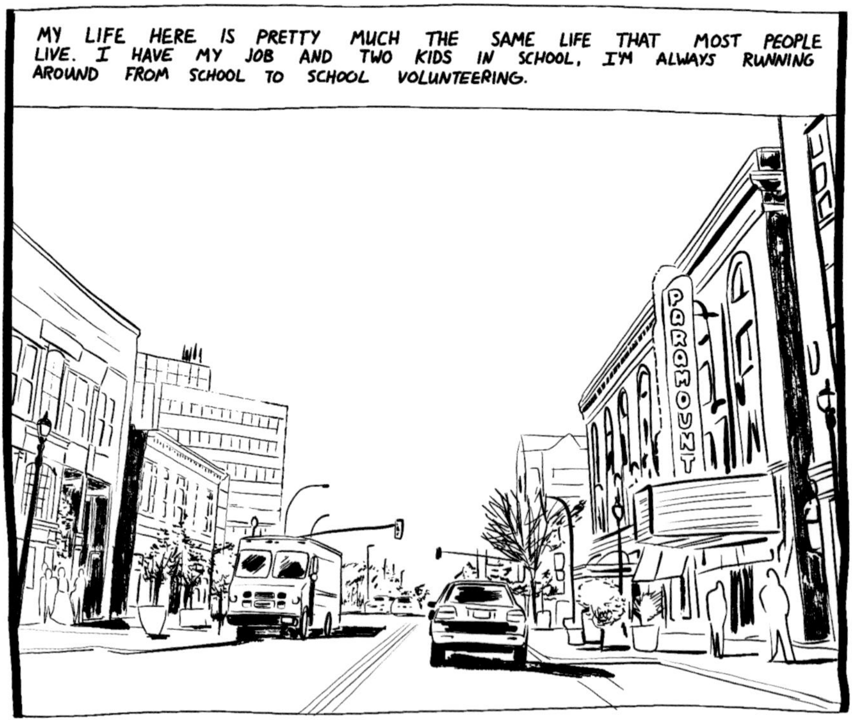
MY LIFE HERE IS PRETTY MUCH THE SAME LIFE THAT MOST PEOPLE LIVE. I HAVE MY JOB AND TWO KIDS IN SCHOOL, I'M ALWAYS RUNNING AROUND FROM SCHOOL TO SCHOOL VOLUNTEERING.
PARAMOUNT

EVERY YEAR AROUND EID CELEBRATION, I TALK TO MY KIDS' CLASSMATES AND ANSWER QUESTIONS ABOUT OUR FAITH AND ENCOURAGING THEM TO VOLUNTEER.

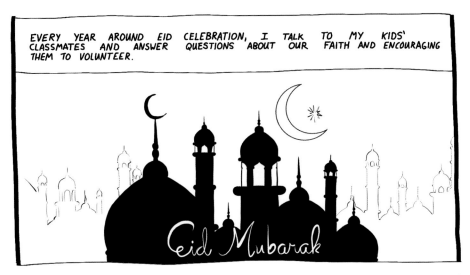

KIDS ARE SO INNOCENT AND ASK QUESTIONS WITHOUT ANY FEAR OR PREJUDICE.

I BELIEVE THIS IS ONE OF THE MOST IMPORTANT THINGS WE CAN DO TO HELP EACH OTHER RECOGNIZE THAT WE ALL PRETTY MUCH HAVE THE SAME LIFE.

MEXICO AND PHILIPPINES

SERGIO CENOCH & MARY ANNE QUIROZ

Born: Mexico and Philippines
Current: St. Paul, Minnesota

Together with their five children, Sergio Cenoch and Mary Anne Quiroz, have been practicing and promoting traditional Mexica Nahua culture for over two decades. They have led, taught, and organized community events, festivals, conferences, and artist residencies throughout the state of Minnesota as well as nationally and internationally. In 2015, they co-founded Indigenous Roots, an arts organization that provides space and opportunities for Native, Black, Brown, and Indigenous artists and organizers rooted in arts, culture, and activism. Then in May 2017, Indigenous Roots opened its cultural arts center on the East Side of Saint Paul in partnership with a collective of artists, cultural groups, and organizations.

www.greencardvoices.org/speakers/mary-anne-sergio-quiroz

CAMILO AGUIRRE

Born: Colombia
Current: Minneapolis, Minnesota

Camilo Aguirre is a Colombian artist and has graduated from the MFA program at the Minneapolis College of Arts and Design and the Instituto Departamental de Bellas Artes de Cali. Camilo's artistic practices vary between fine arts and comics. Camilo has published multiple graphic novels in Colombia, focusing on the genre of documentary comics and historical memory, addressing issues such as forced dispossession, union movements, and the role of testimony and anecdote in comics.

https://linktr.ee/camiloaguirre

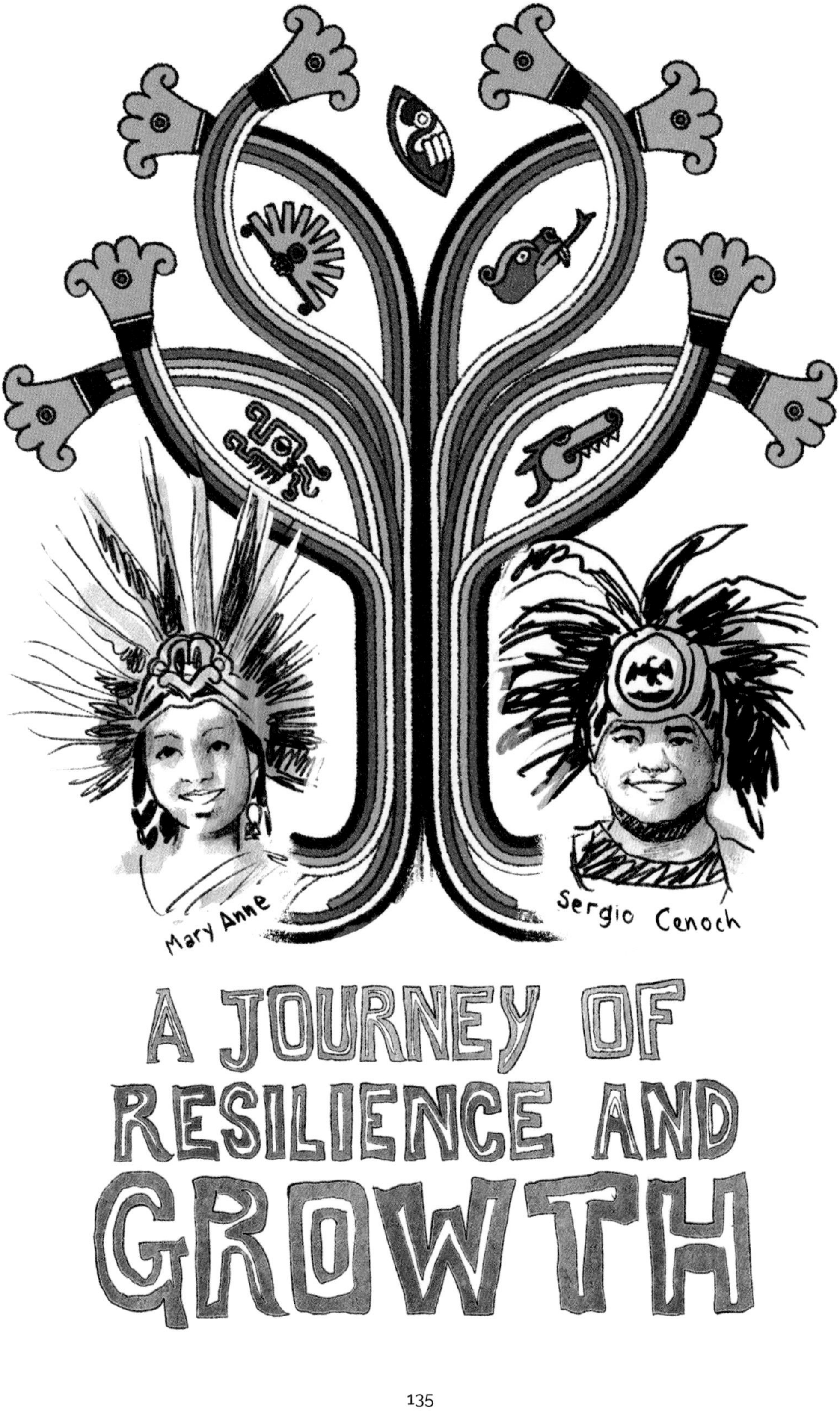
Mary Anne
Sergio Cenoch

A JOURNEY OF RESILIENCE AND GROWTH

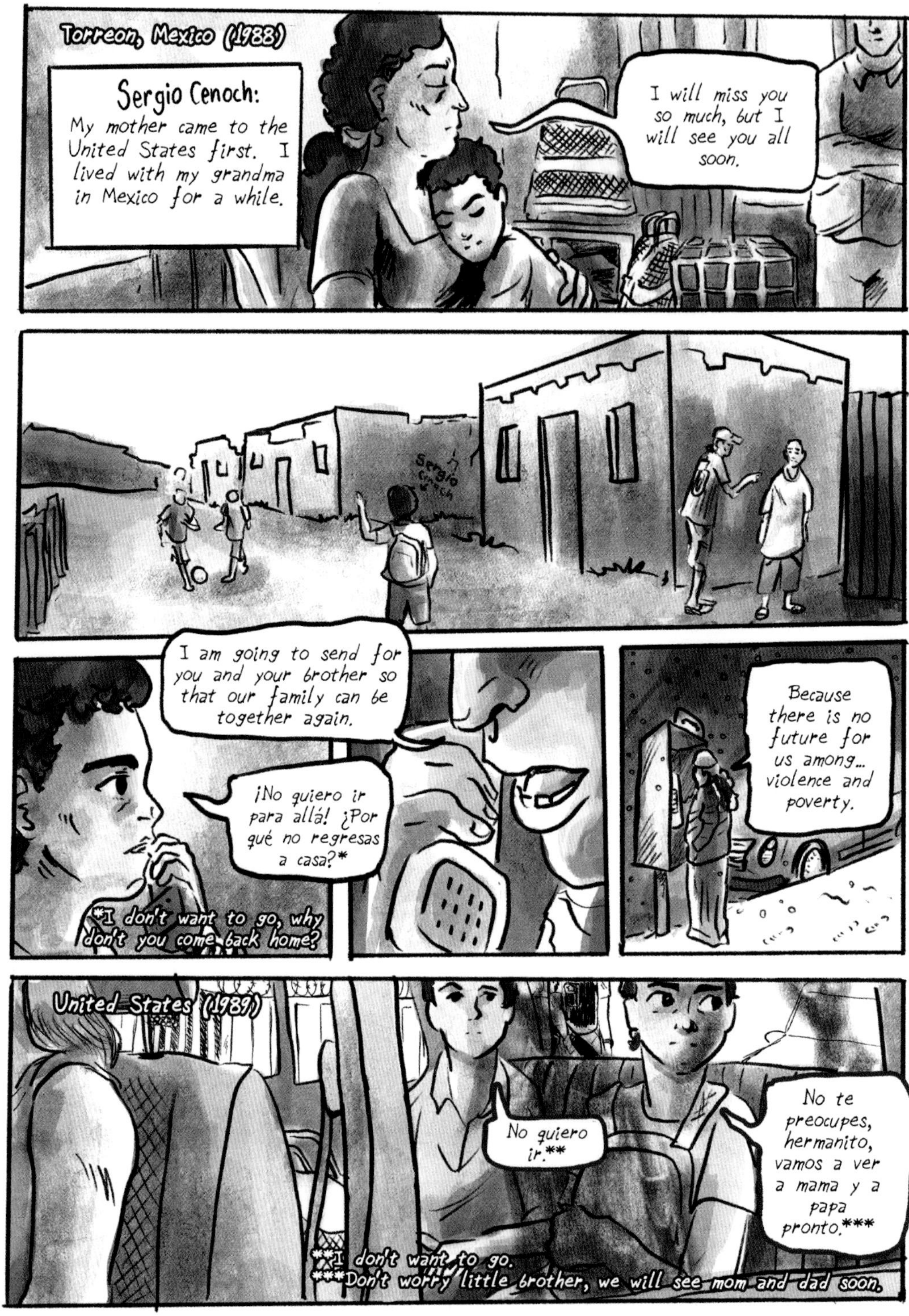
Torreon, Mexico (1988)
Sergio Cenoch: My mother came to the United States first. I lived with my grandma in Mexico for a while.
I will miss you so much, but I will see you all soon.
Sergio Cenoch
I am going to send for you and your brother so that our family can be together again.
¡No quiero ir para allá! ¿Por qué no regresas a casa?*
*I don't want to go, why don't you come back home?
Because there is no future for us among... violence and poverty.
United States (1989)
No quiero ir.**
No te preocupes, hermanito, vamos a ver a mama y a papa pronto.***
**I don't want to go.
***Don't worry little brother, we will see mom and dad soon.

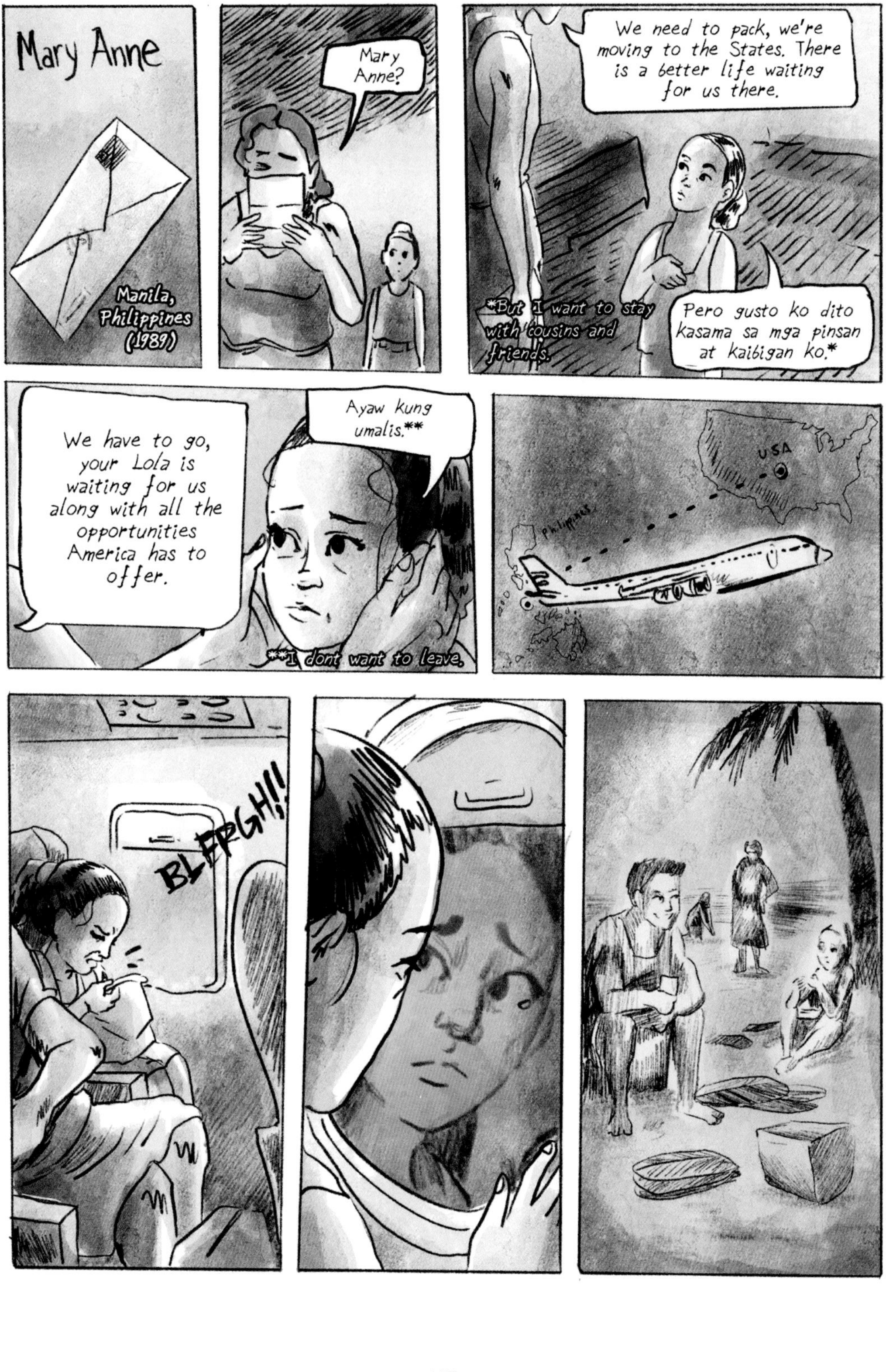
Mary Anne
Manila, Philippines (1989)
Mary Anne?
We need to pack, we're moving to the States. There is a better life waiting for us there.
Pero gusto ko dito kasama sa mga pinsan at kaibigan ko.*
*But I want to stay with cousins and friends.
We have to go, your Lola is waiting for us along with all the opportunities America has to offer.
Ayaw kung umalis.**
**I dont want to leave.
USA
Philippines
BLERGH!!

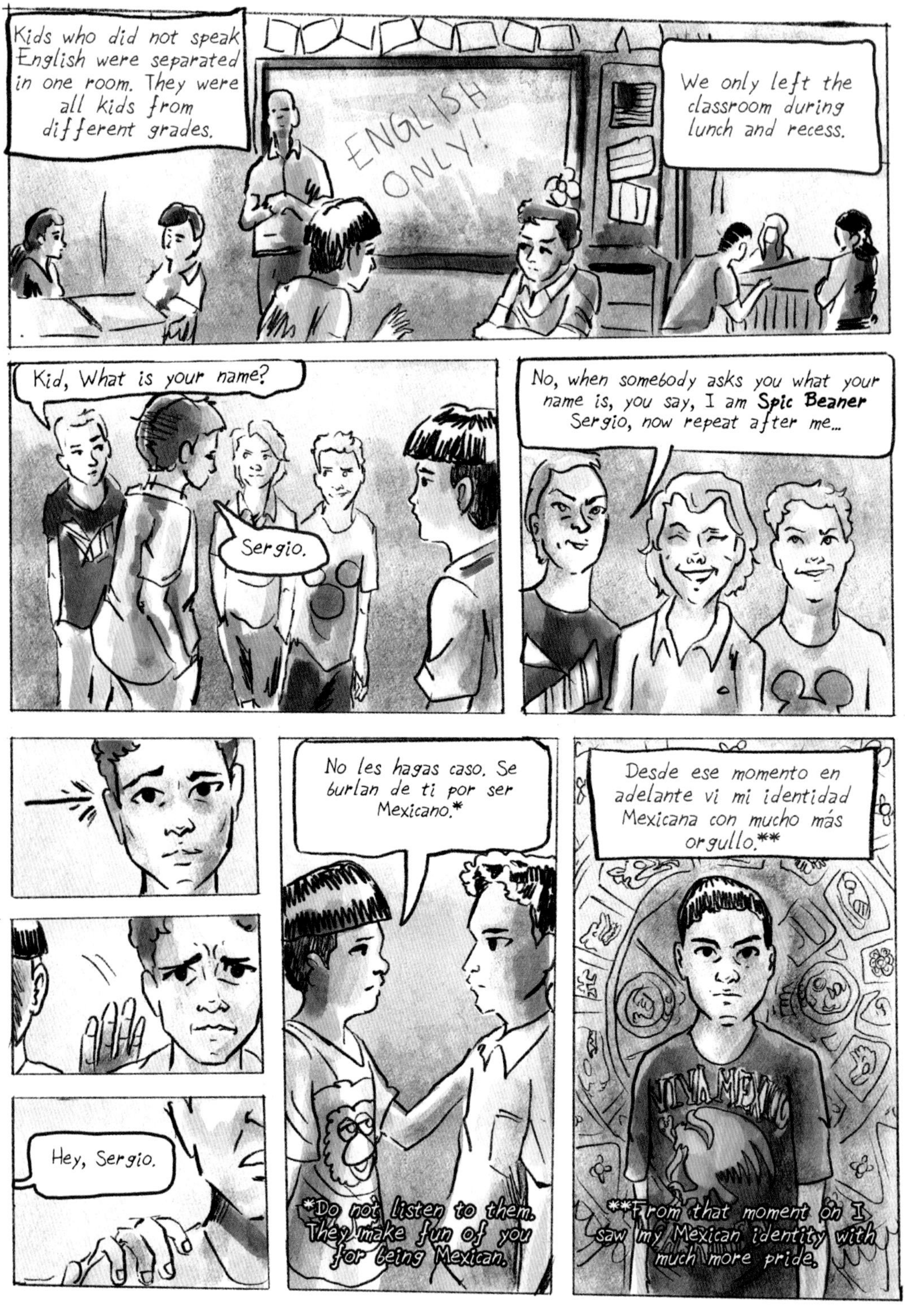
Kids who did not speak English were separated in one room. They were all kids from different grades.
ENGLISH ONLY!
We only left the classroom during lunch and recess.
Kid, What is your name?
Sergio.
No, when somebody asks you what your name is, you say, I am Spic Beaner Sergio, now repeat after me...
Hey, Sergio.
No les hagas caso. Se burlan de ti por ser Mexicano.*
*Do not listen to them. They make fun of you for being Mexican.
Desde ese momento en adelante vi mi identidad Mexicana con mucho más orgullo.**
VIVA MEXICO
**From that moment on I saw my Mexican identity with much more pride.

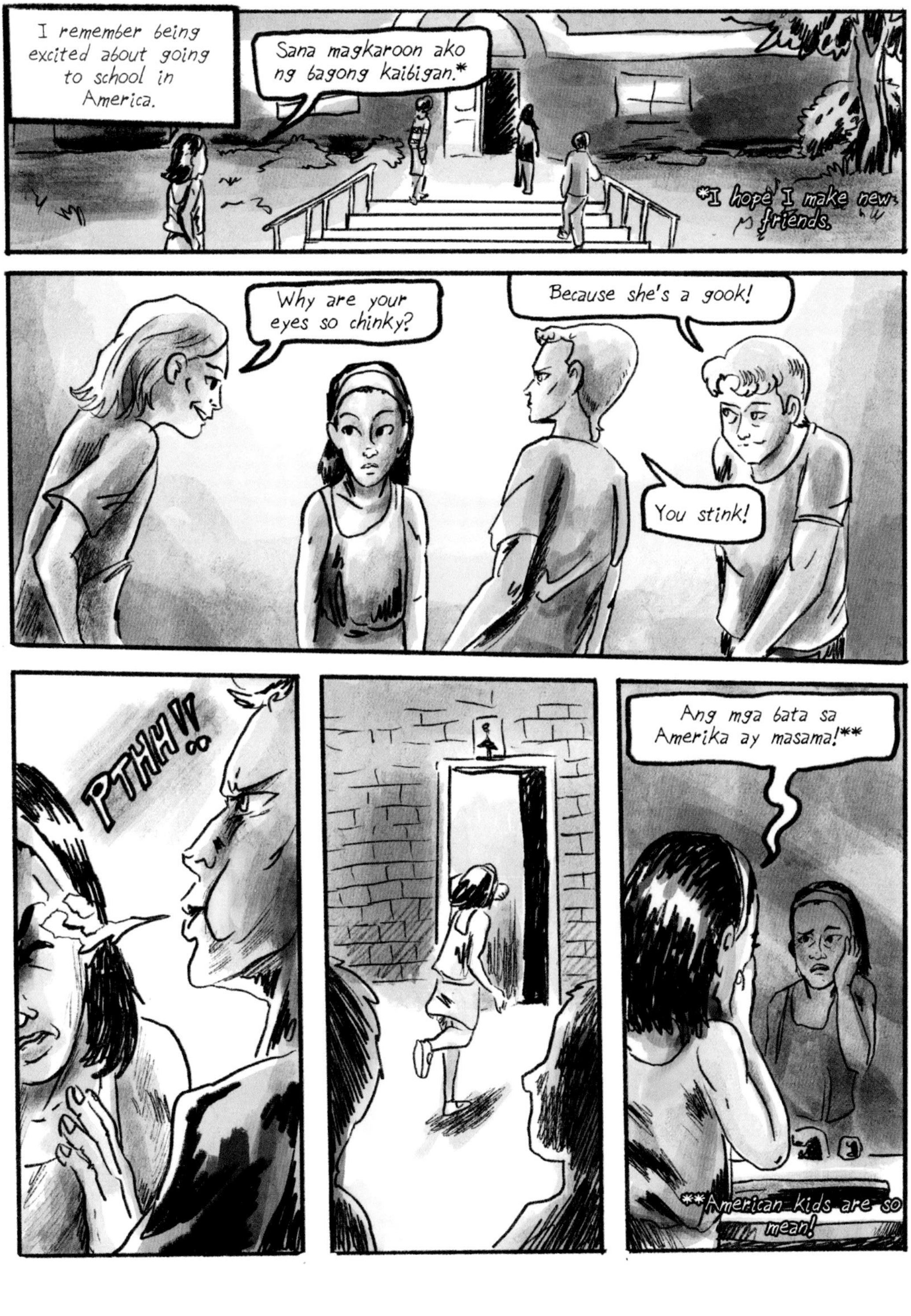
I remember being excited about going to school in America.
Sana magkaroon ako ng bagong kaibigan.*
*I hope I make new friends.
Why are your eyes so chinky?
Because she's a gook!
You stink!
PTHH!!
Ang mga bata sa Amerika ay masama!**
**American kids are so mean!

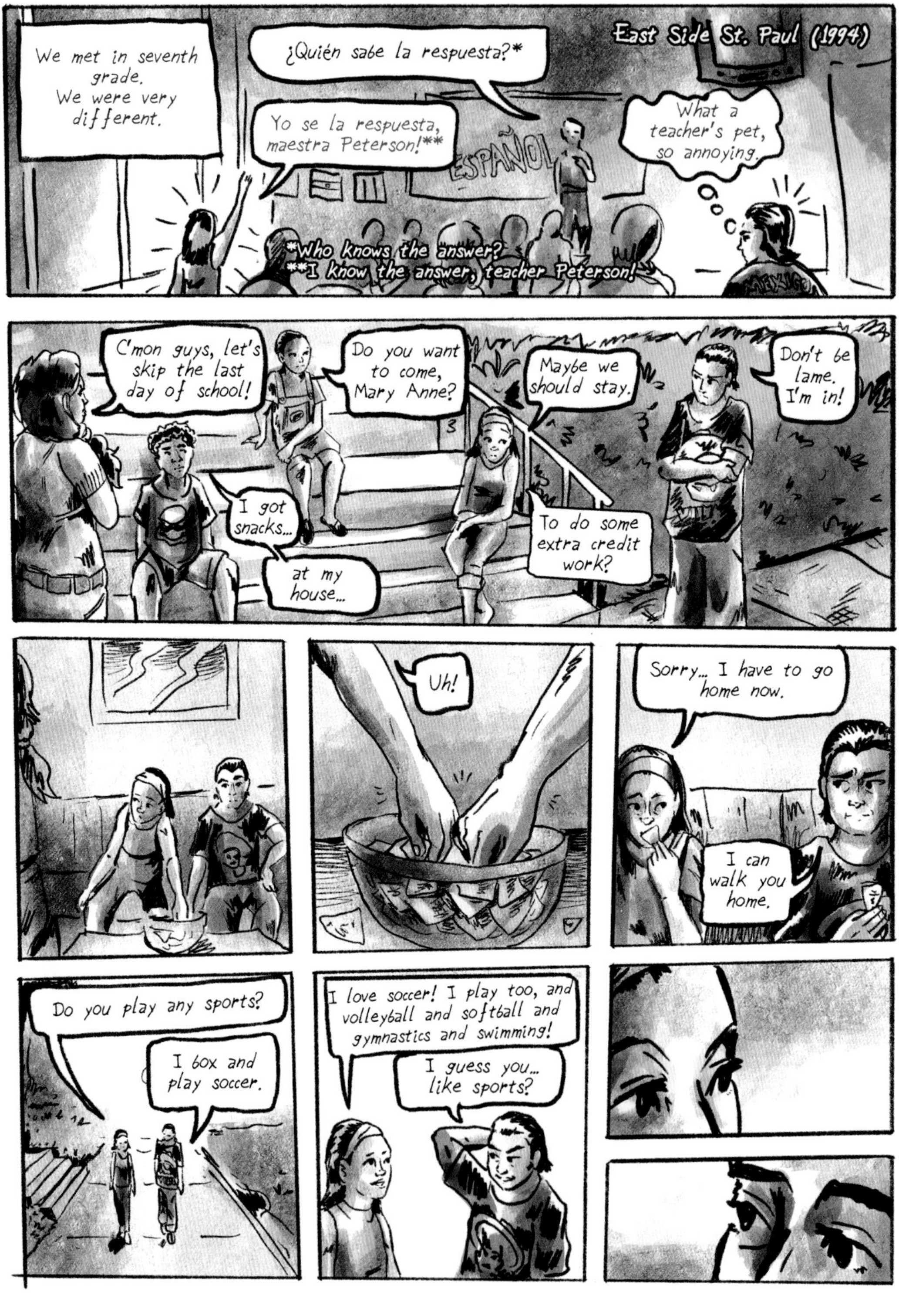

We met in seventh grade. We were very different.
¿Quién sabe la respuesta?*
East Side St. Paul (1994)
Yo se la respuesta, maestra Peterson!**
ESPAÑOL
What a teacher's pet, so annoying.
*Who knows the answer?
**I know the answer, teacher Peterson!
C'mon guys, let's skip the last day of school!
Do you want to come, Mary Anne?
Maybe we should stay.
Don't be lame. I'm in!
I got snacks...
at my house...
To do some extra credit work?
Uh!
Sorry... I have to go home now.
I can walk you home.
Do you play any sports?
I box and play soccer.
I love soccer! I play too, and volleyball and softball and gymnastics and swimming!
I guess you... like sports?

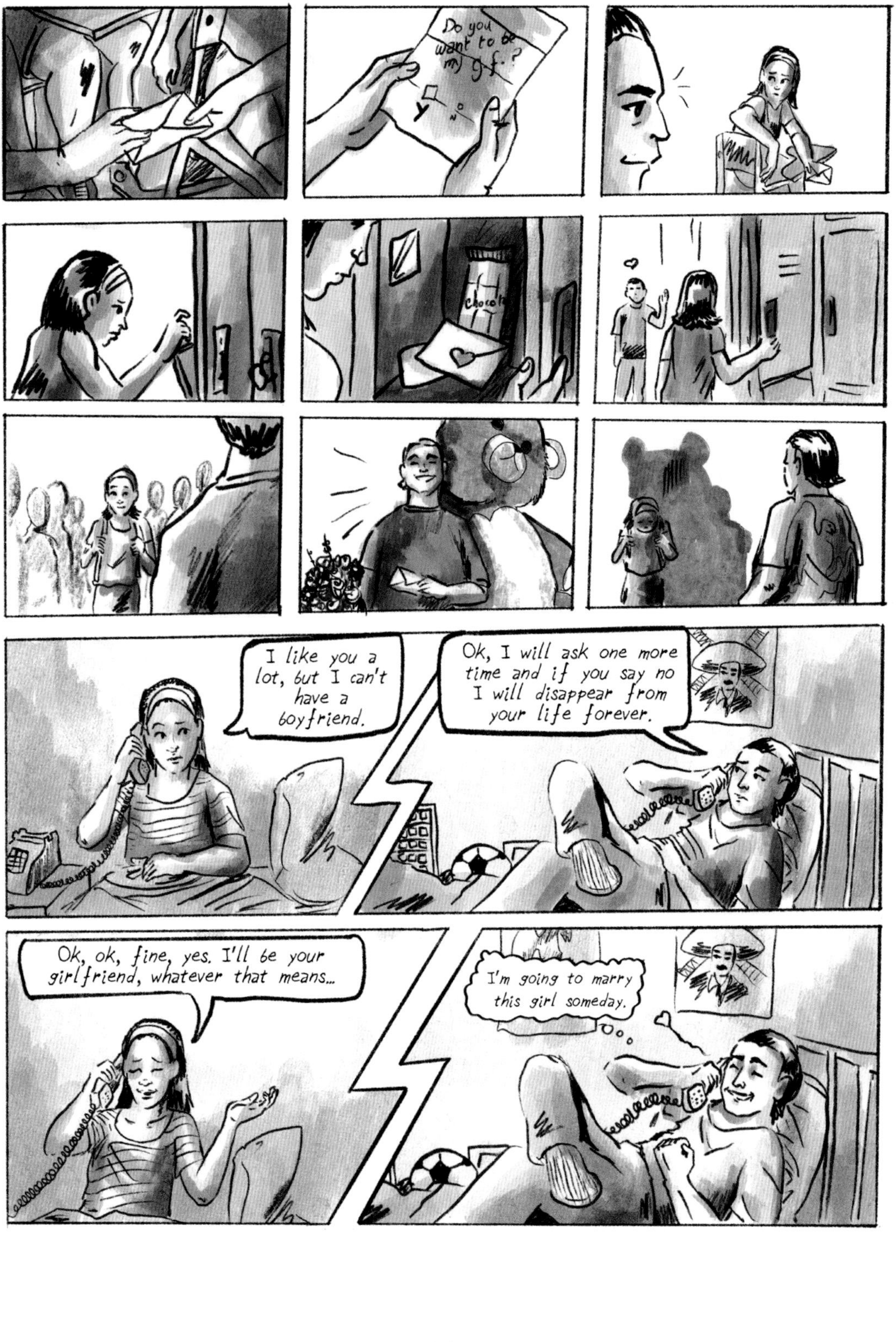
Do you want to be my gf.?
Y
N
chocol
I like you a lot, but I can't have a boyfriend.
Ok, I will ask one more time and if you say no I will disappear from your life forever.
Ok, ok, fine, yes. I'll be your girlfriend, whatever that means...
I'm going to marry this girl someday.

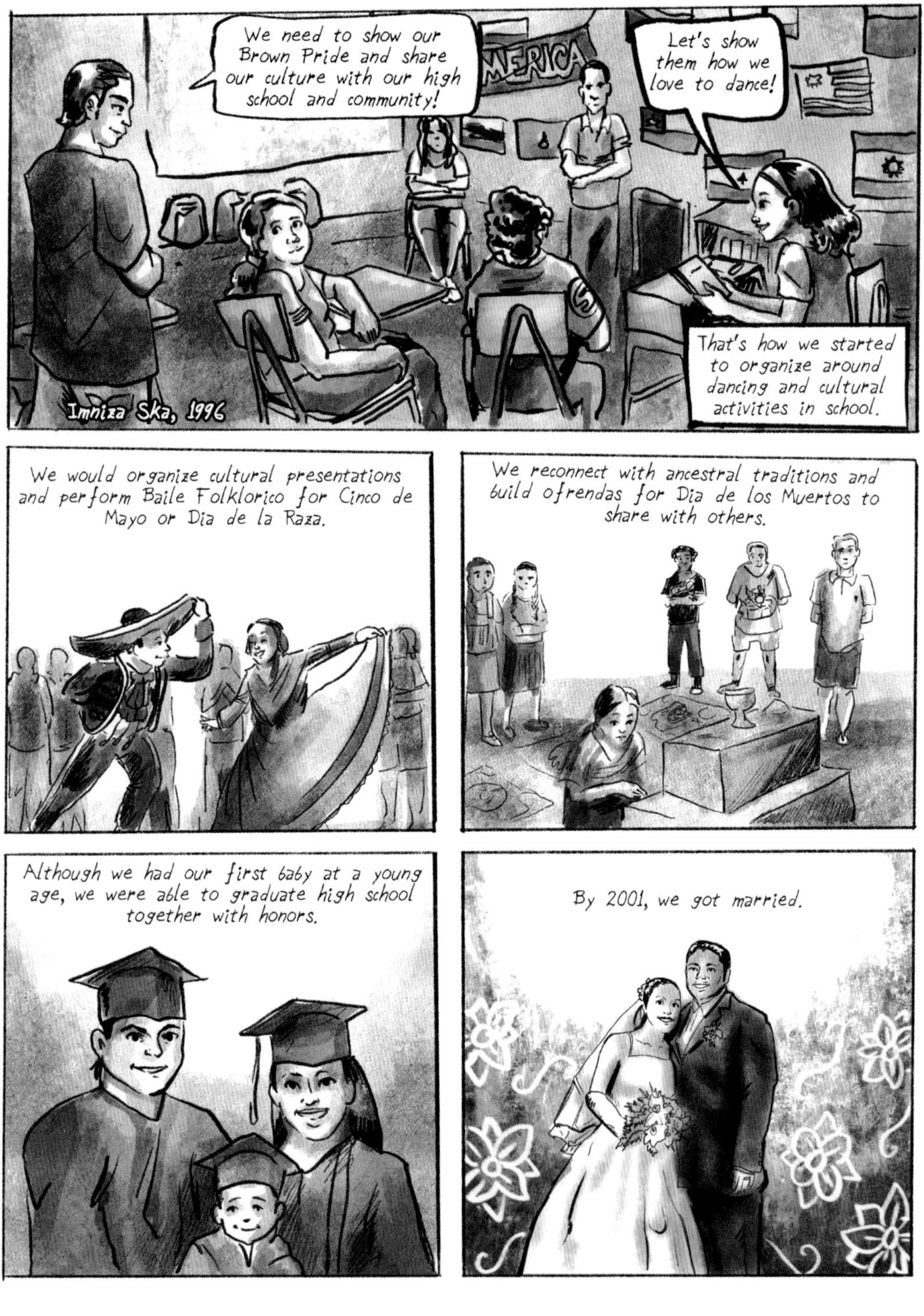

We need to show our Brown Pride and share our culture with our high school and community!
MERICA
Let's show them how we love to dance!
That's how we started to organize around dancing and cultural activities in school.
Imniza Ska, 1996
We would organize cultural presentations and perform Baile Folklorico for Cinco de Mayo or Dia de la Raza.
We reconnect with ancestral traditions and build ofrendas for Dia de los Muertos to share with others.
Although we had our first baby at a young age, we were able to graduate high school together with honors.
By 2001, we got married.

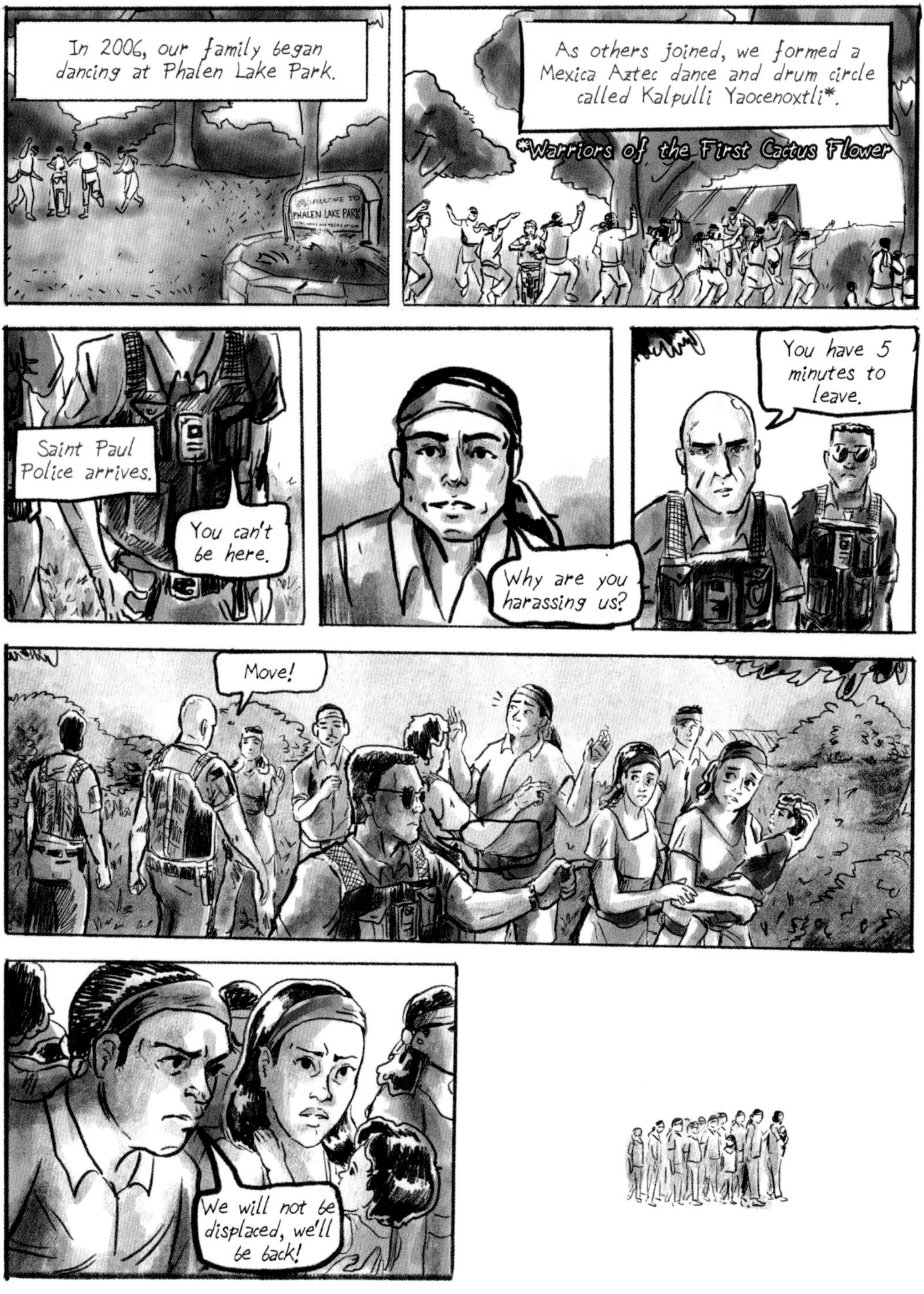
In 2006, our family began dancing at Phalen Lake Park.
WELCOME TO PHALEN LAKE PARK
As others joined, we formed a Mexica Aztec dance and drum circle called Kalpulli Yaocenoxtli*.
*Warriors of the First Cactus Flower
Saint Paul Police arrives.
You can't be here.
Why are you harassing us?
You have 5 minutes to leave.
Move!
We will not be displaced, we'll be back!

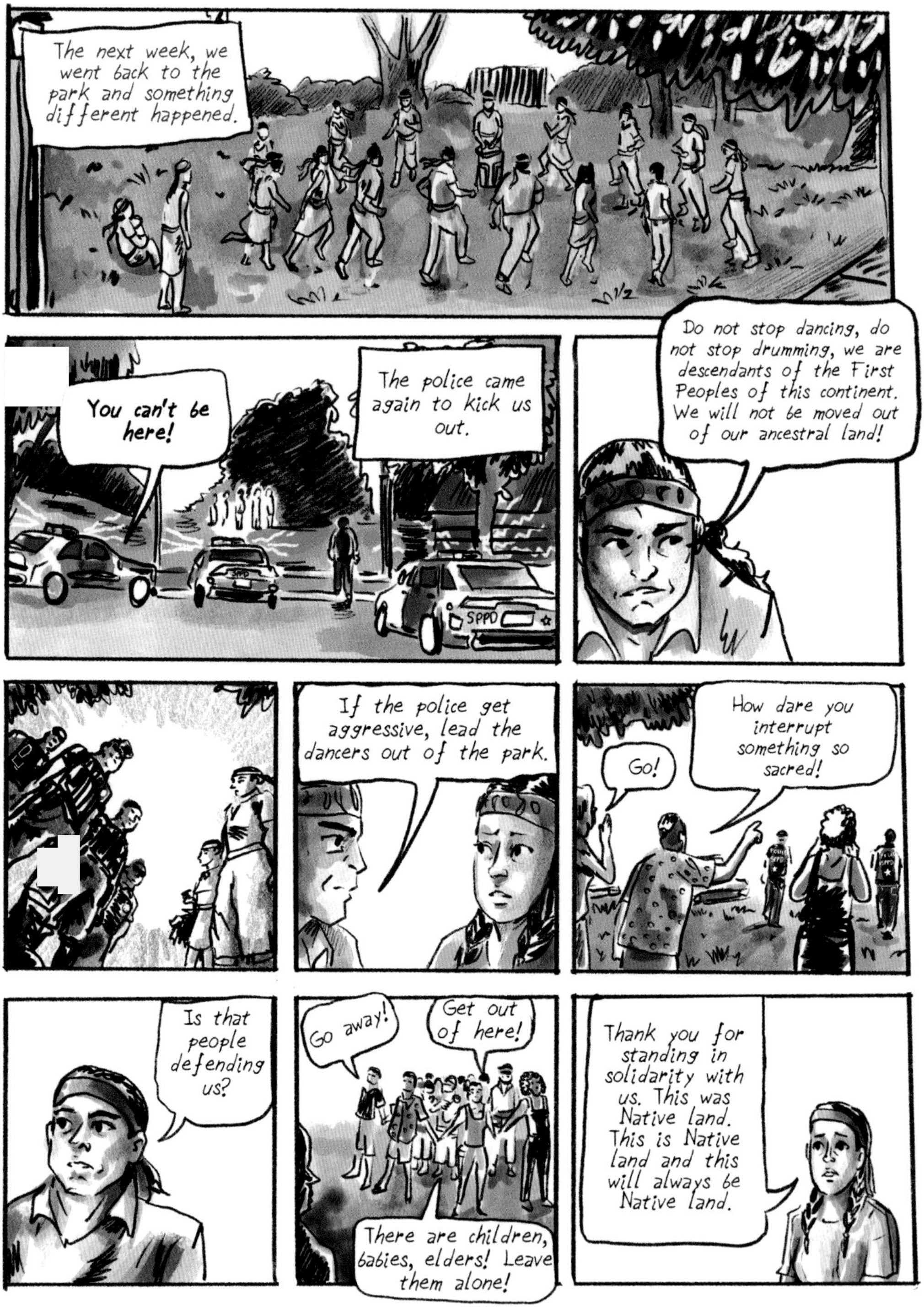
The next week, we went back to the park and something different happened.
You can't be here!
The police came again to kick us out.
SPPD
SPPD
Do not stop dancing, do not stop drumming, we are descendants of the First Peoples of this continent. We will not be moved out of our ancestral land!
If the police get aggressive, lead the dancers out of the park.
Go!
How dare you interrupt something so sacred!
Is that people defending us?
Go away!
Get out of here!
There are children, babies, elders! Leave them alone!
Thank you for standing in solidarity with us. This was Native land. This is Native land and this will always be Native land.

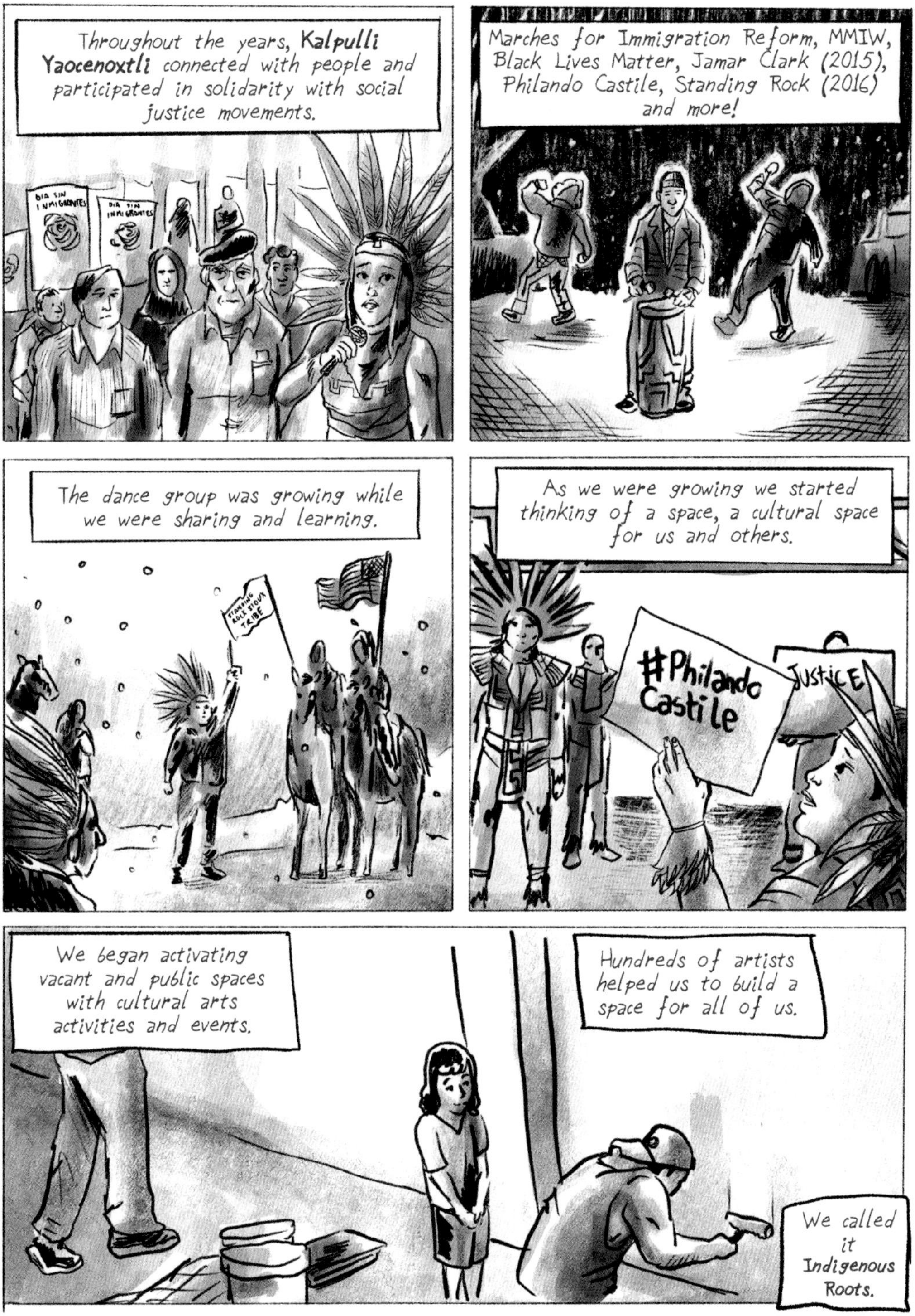
Throughout the years, **Kalpulli Yaocenoxtli** connected with people and participated in solidarity with social justice movements.
Marches for Immigration Reform, MMIW, Black Lives Matter, Jamar Clark (2015), Philando Castile, Standing Rock (2016) and more!
The dance group was growing while we were sharing and learning.
As we were growing we started thinking of a space, a cultural space for us and others.
#Philando Castile
JUSTICE
We began activating vacant and public spaces with cultural arts activities and events.
Hundreds of artists helped us to build a space for all of us.
We called it **Indigenous Roots.**

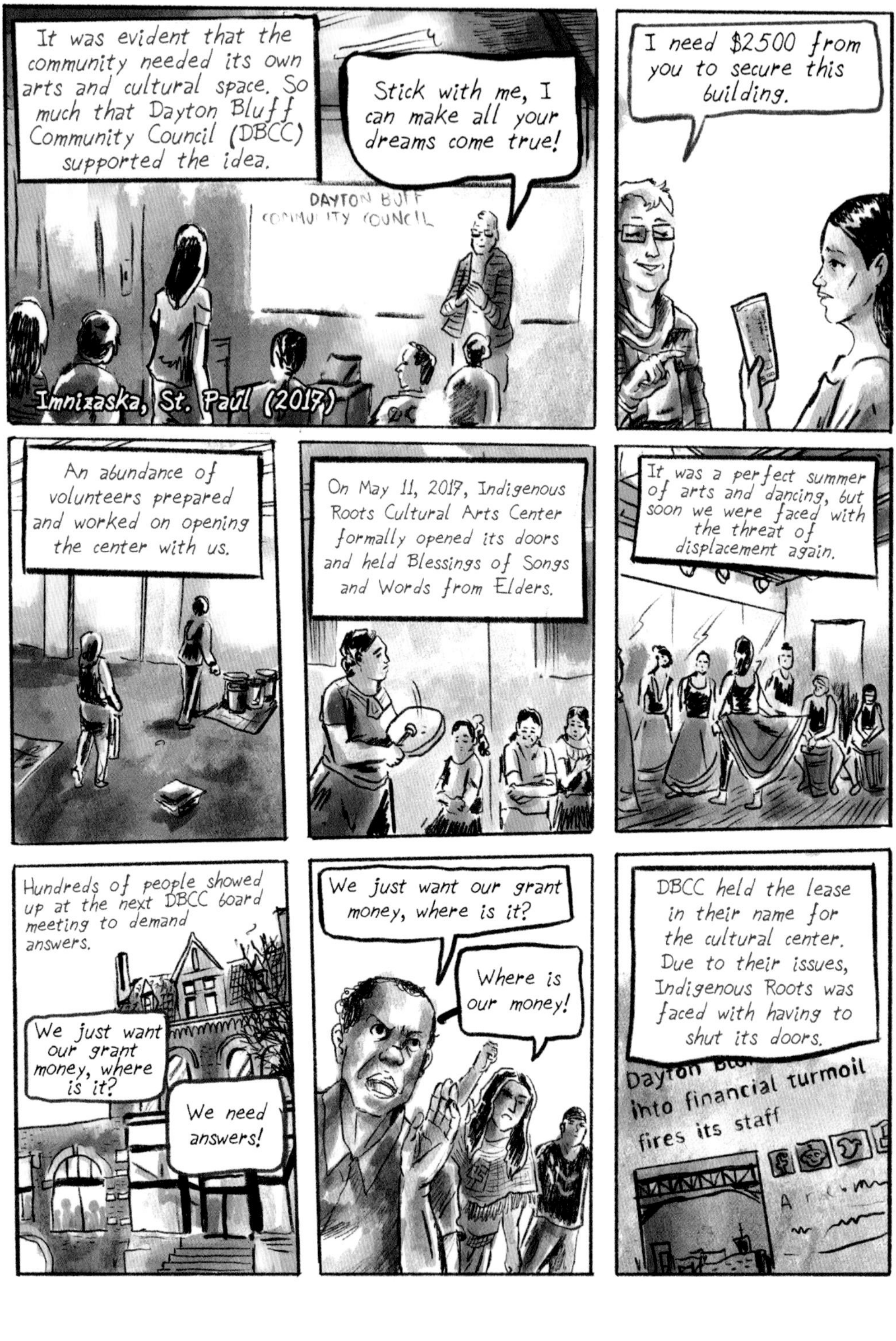

It was evident that the community needed its own arts and cultural space. So much that Dayton Bluff Community Council (DBCC) supported the idea.
Stick with me, I can make all your dreams come true!
DAYTON BLUFF COMMUNITY COUNCIL
Imnizaska, St. Paul (2017)
I need $2500 from you to secure this building.
An abundance of volunteers prepared and worked on opening the center with us.
On May 11, 2017, Indigenous Roots Cultural Arts Center formally opened its doors and held Blessings of Songs and Words from Elders.
It was a perfect summer of arts and dancing, but soon we were faced with the threat of displacement again.
Hundreds of people showed up at the next DBCC board meeting to demand answers.
We just want our grant money, where is it?
We need answers!
We just want our grant money, where is it?
Where is our money!
DBCC held the lease in their name for the cultural center. Due to their issues, Indigenous Roots was faced with having to shut its doors.
into financial turmoil
fires its staff

Although there were financial issues with DBCC, we were able to secure the lease after meeting with the property owner. And we celebrated because we got to keep **Indigenous Roots** as our home.

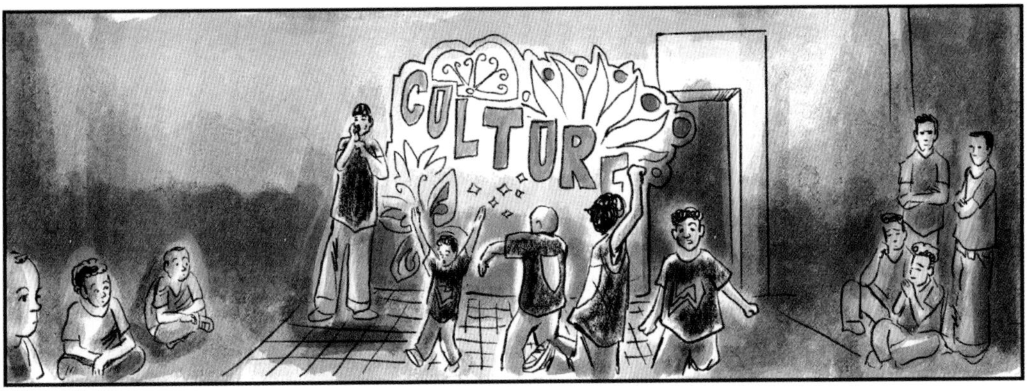
CULTURE

We continued thriving and creating murals inside our building and outside onto the 7th Street Cultural Corridor.

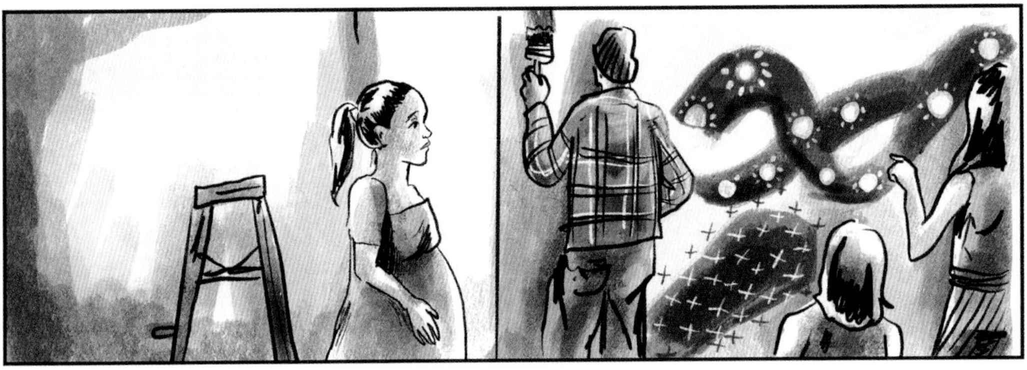

We began supporting artists with their exhibits and business plans as artist entrepreneurs.

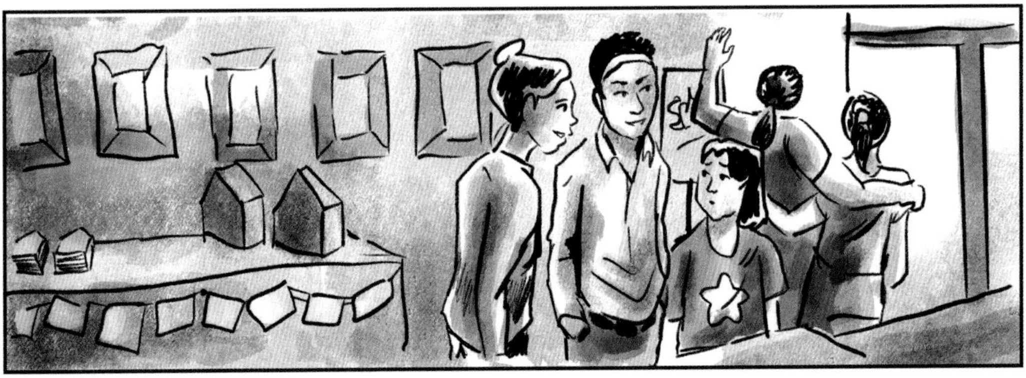

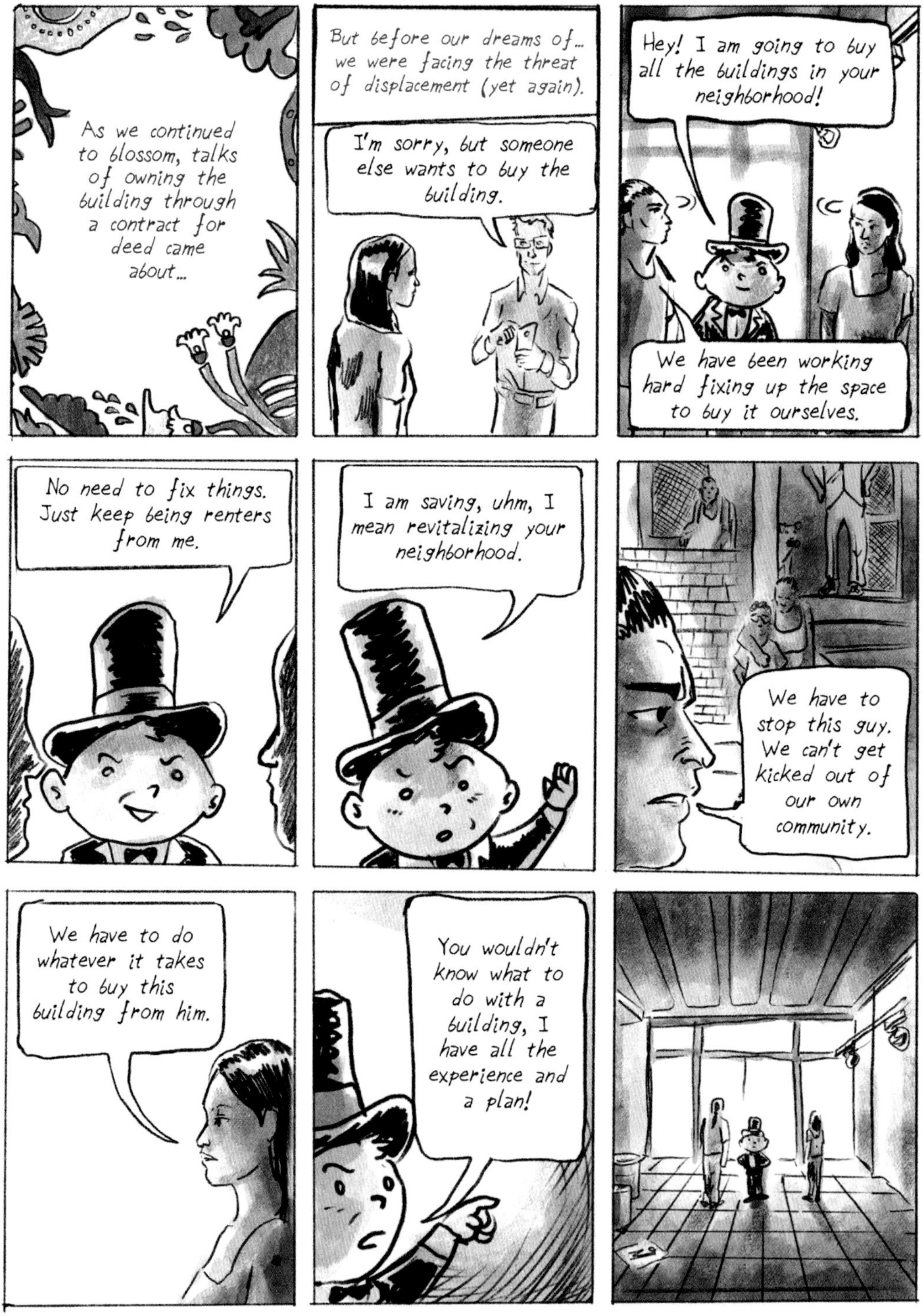
As we continued to blossom, talks of owning the building through a contract for deed came about...
But before our dreams of... we were facing the threat of displacement (yet again).
I'm sorry, but someone else wants to buy the building.
Hey! I am going to buy all the buildings in your neighborhood!
We have been working hard fixing up the space to buy it ourselves.
No need to fix things. Just keep being renters from me.
I am saving, uhm, I mean revitalizing your neighborhood.
We have to stop this guy. We can't get kicked out of our own community.
We have to do whatever it takes to buy this building from him.
You wouldn't know what to do with a building, I have all the experience and a plan!

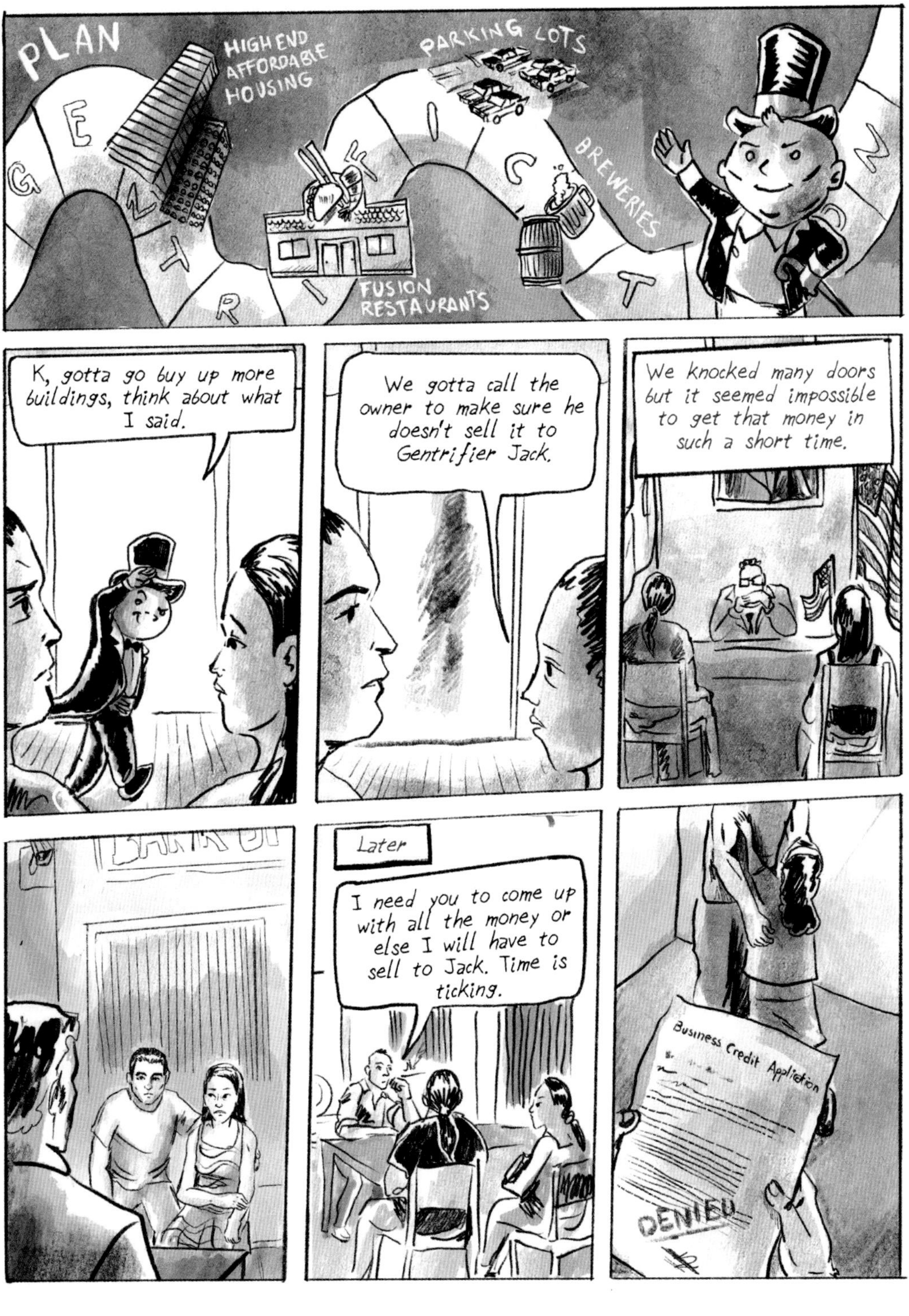
PLAN
HIGH END AFFORDABLE HOUSING
PARKING LOTS
BREWERIES
FUSION RESTAURANTS
K, gotta go buy up more buildings, think about what I said.
We gotta call the owner to make sure he doesn't sell it to Gentrifier Jack.
We knocked many doors but it seemed impossible to get that money in such a short time.
Later
I need you to come up with all the money or else I will have to sell to Jack. Time is ticking.
Business Credit Application
DENIED

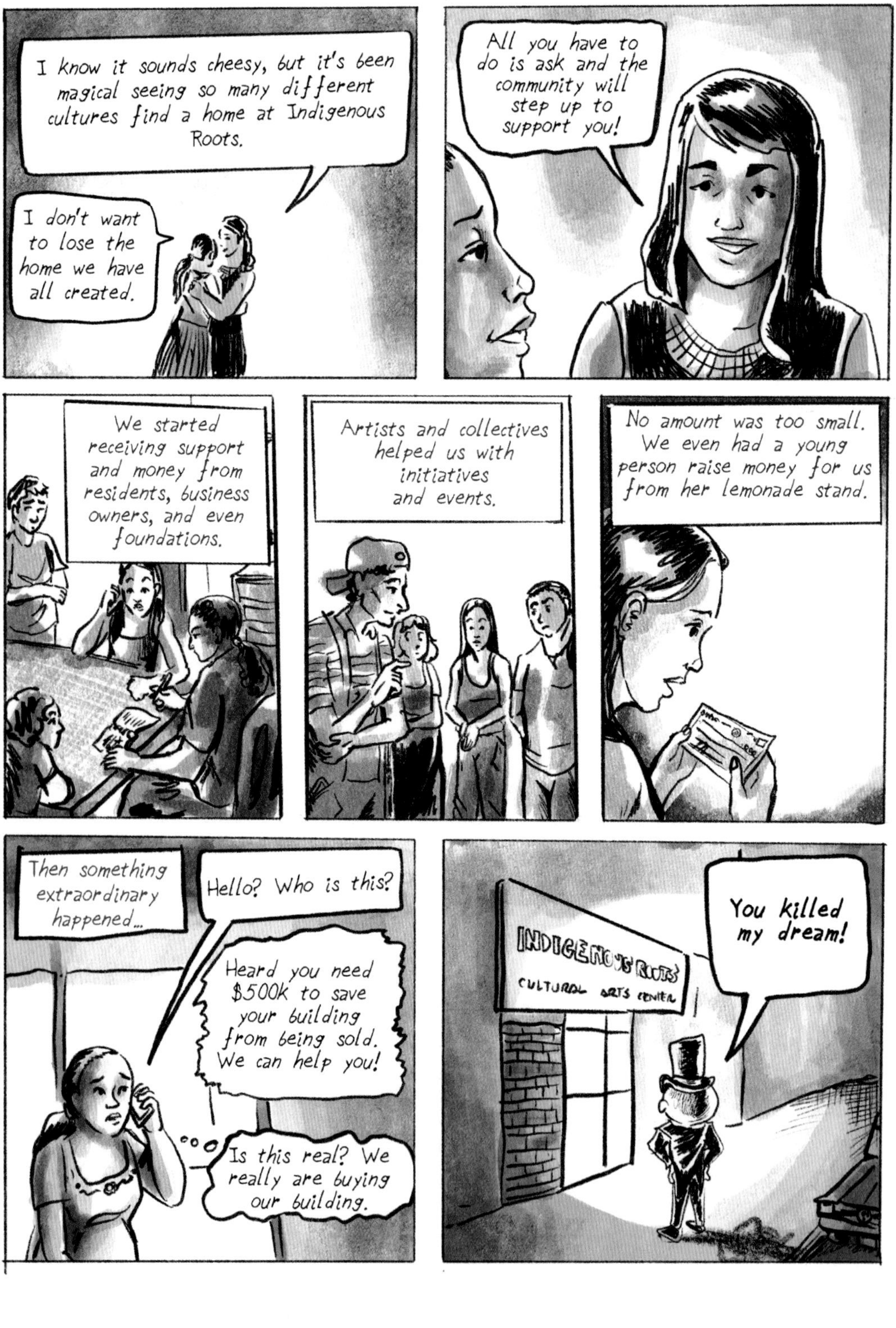
I know it sounds cheesy, but it's been magical seeing so many different cultures find a home at Indigenous Roots.
I don't want to lose the home we have all created.
All you have to do is ask and the community will step up to support you!
We started receiving support and money from residents, business owners, and even foundations.
Artists and collectives helped us with initiatives and events.
No amount was too small. We even had a young person raise money for us from her lemonade stand.
Then something extraordinary happened...
Hello? Who is this?
Heard you need $500k to save your building from being sold. We can help you!
Is this real? We really are buying our building.
INDIGENOUS ROOTS
CULTURAL ARTS CENTER
You killed my dream!

Since buying the building, we continued providing accessible space for Native, Black, Brown and Indigenous artists and organizers.

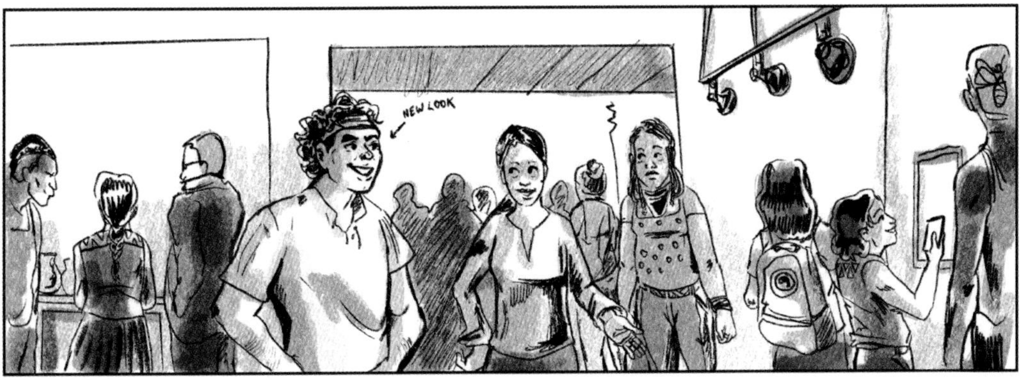
NEW LOOK

Long held conversations about organizing and building stronger partnerships between artists, neighbors, cultural groups, business owners and funders were now in full action mode.

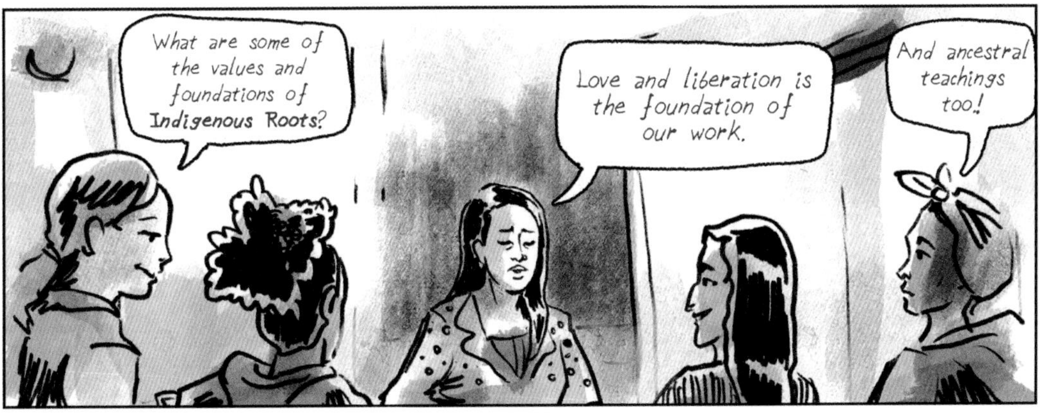
What are some of the values and foundations of Indigenous Roots?
Love and liberation is the foundation of our work.
And ancestral teachings too!

As indigenous roots grew so did our family...

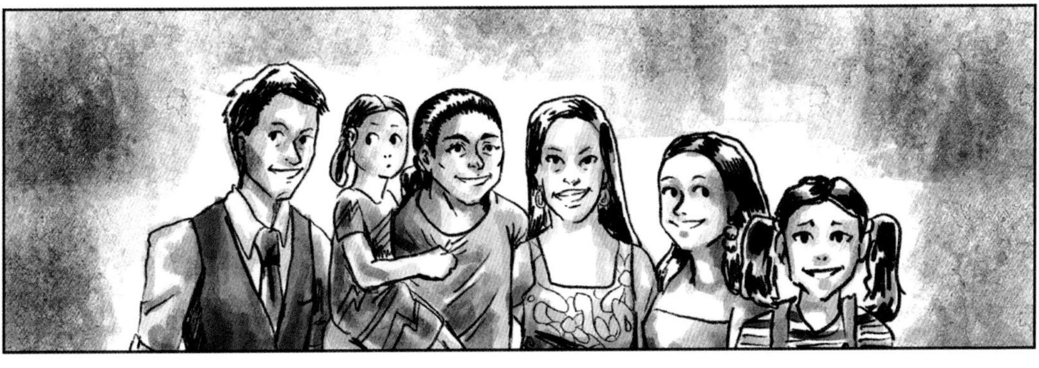

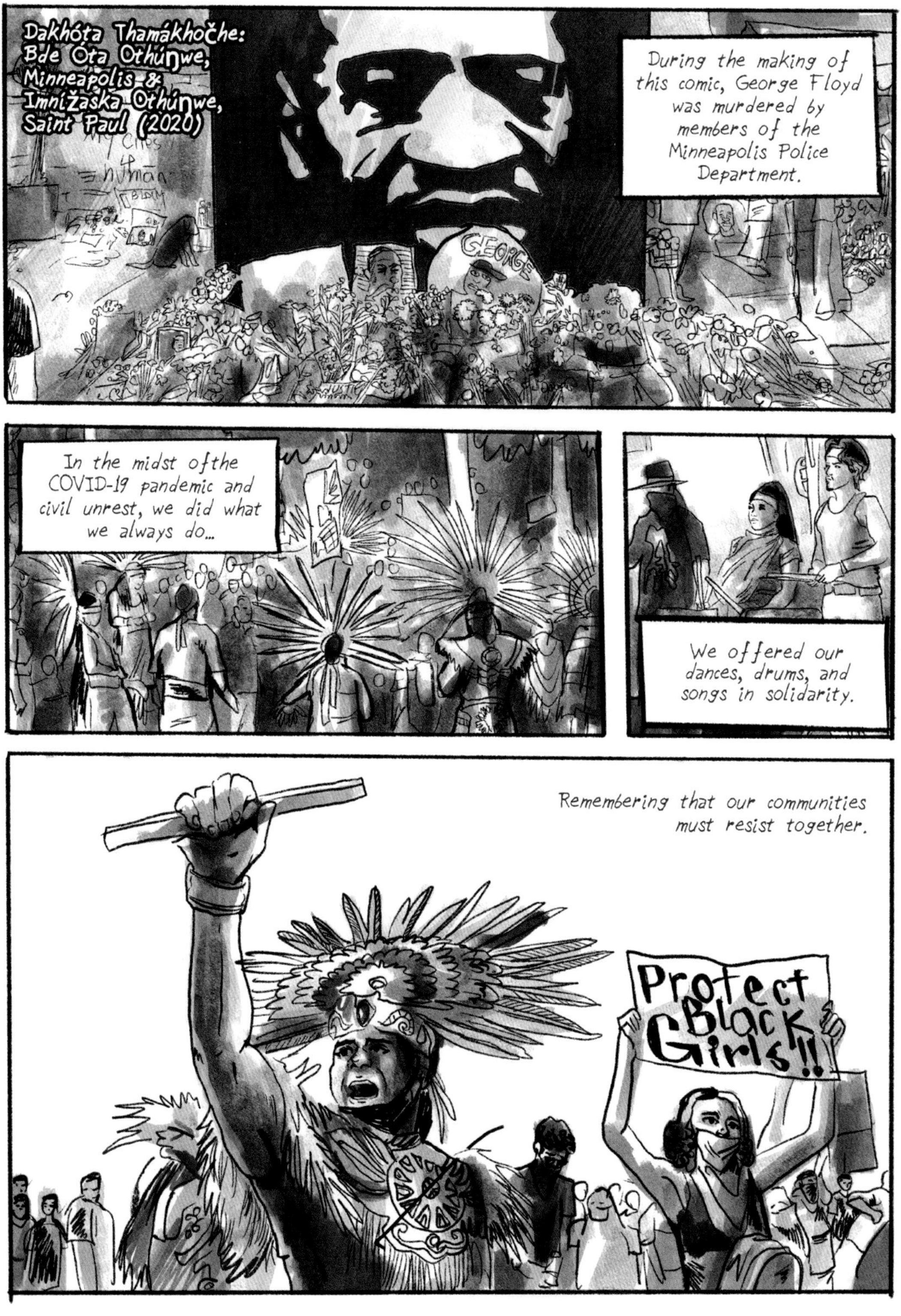

Dakhóta Thamákhoče:
Bde Óta Othúŋwe,
Minneapolis &
ImníŽaska Othúŋwe,
Saint Paul (2020)
During the making of this comic, George Floyd was murdered by members of the Minneapolis Police Department.
GEORGE
In the midst of the COVID-19 pandemic and civil unrest, we did what we always do...
We offered our dances, drums, and songs in solidarity.
Remembering that our communities must resist together.
Protect Black Girls!!

We also effectively mobilized Mutual Aid and Community Rapid Response, distributing food and personal items and helping small businesses board up windows to protect their stores.

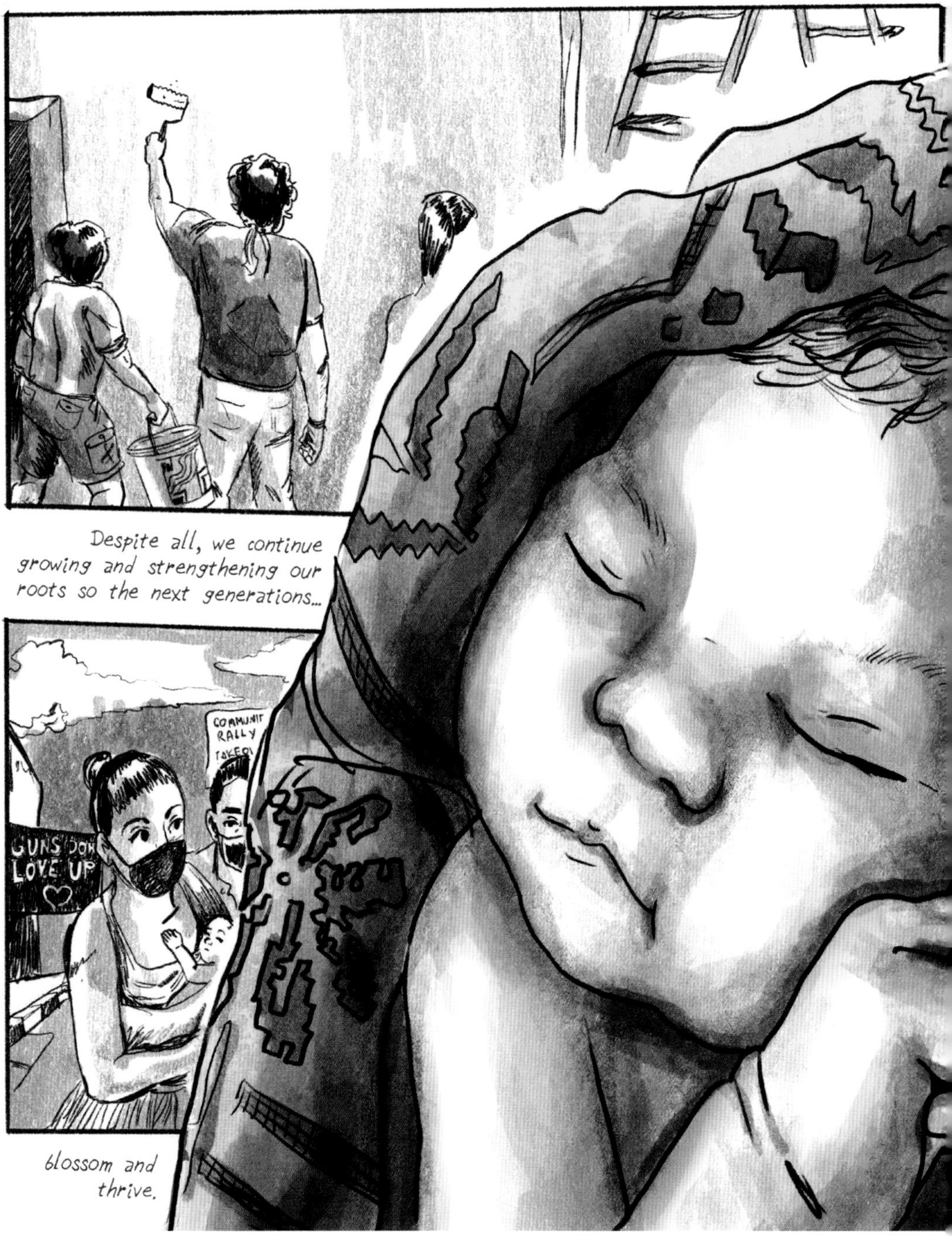
Despite all, we continue growing and strengthening our roots so the next generations...
RALLY
LOVE UP
blossom and thrive.

GLOSSARY

7th Street Cultural Corridor, Dayton's Bluff: In 2016, 7th Street was recognized by Local Initiatives Support Corporation as a business and cultural corridor in partnership with Dayton's Bluff Community Council. In 2017, Indigenous Roots installed its very first series of murals on the 7th Street Cultural Corridor, in partnership with several organizations. In 2019, residents, artists and businesses began to call 7th Street the Intertribal Cultural Corridor to honor the Indigenous Dakota peoples of this land while honoring the many immigrants who have made the East Side of St. Paul, Minnesota, their home in the Twin Cities.

Baile Folklorico: Means "folkloric dance" in Spanish, also known as ballet folklórico, a representative term for traditional Mexican dances that emphasize local folk culture and costumes with ballet characteristics—pointed toes, highly choreographed, exaggerated movements and footwork.

Beaner: A derogatory slur for Mexicans or people of Mexican background. The term originates from the prevalence of pinto and other beans in Mexican cuisine.

Brown Pride: Being proud to be brown. Brown Pride Mentality concerns Mexicans as well as other Latinos (Cubans, Portoricans, Salvadorians, etc.), Arabic people who live in the US, and South Italians (Neapolitans, Sicilians). The Brown Pride Movement concerns Chicanos, Chicanas and Mexas only (Chicano Power).

Cinco de Mayo: An annual celebration held on May 5, which commemorates the anniversary of Mexico's victory against the defeat of Napoleon and the French Empire at the Battle of Puebla in 1862.

Chinky (cinky, chinkies or chinkie): A term of racial offense/abuse. A derogatory slur for Asian background.

Community Rapid Response: A community-centered service that offers fast and responsive requests based on community needs such as providing space, food, safety, and distribution programs with partnerships.

Dayton's Bluff Community Council (DBCC): A vibrant community in St. Paul, Minnesota, which embraces their rich culture, diverse in ethnicity and industry, with growing opportunities for all. It strives to connect Dayton's Bluff residents to their community at large; to their neighbors, parks, restaurants, organizations, councils, businesses, schools, everything this historical neighborhood has to offer.

Día de la Raza: A national holiday known as "Day of the Race" to honor the heritage and cultural diversity of all the Spanish speaking and Latin America countries against the arrival of Europeans in America.

Día de los Muertos: A Mexican holiday also known as "The Day of the Dead" where families welcome back the souls of their deceased loved ones for a brief reunion by creating an ofrenda with their picture, and offering food, drink, and present so they can enjoy them in the afterlife.

Fusion restaurant: Combines elements of different culinary traditions that originate from different countries, regions, or cultures. Cuisines of this type are not categorized according to any one particular cuisine style and have played a part in innovations of many contemporary restaurant cuisines since the 1970s.

Gentrification: The process whereby the character of a poor urban area is changed by wealthier people moving in, improving housing, and attracting new businesses, typically displacing current inhabitants in the process.

Gook: A derogatory term for people of Asian descent. The term may have originated among US Marines during the Philippine-American War (1899–1902). If so, it could be related to the use of "gook" as a slang term for prostitutes during that period. Historically, US military personnel used the word to refer to non-Americans of various races.

Ofrendas: A home or community altar with a collection of objects placed on a ritual display during the annual and traditionally Mexican Dia de los Muertos celebration.

Spic (also spelled spick): An ethnic slur used in the United States for people from a play on a Spanish-accented pronunciation of the English word "speak."

VY LUONG

Born: Châu Thành, Vietnam
Current: Madison, Wisconsin

Vy Luong is a sophomore at the University of Wisconsin-Madison studying biochemistry in the College of Agricultural and Life Sciences. His long-term goal is to finish medical school and become a family physician. His hope is to bring adequate health care to developing and underdeveloped countries. He currently serves as an undergraduate lab assistant at the Mark Mandel laboratory at the University of Wisconsin. He is also a part-time Certified Nursing Assistant (CNA). In his free time, Vy enjoys working out, cooking, napping, sewing, and being a plant dad of four.

www.greencardvoices.org/speakers/vy-luong

CORI NAKAMURA LIN

Born/Current: Chicago, Illinois

Cori Lin is a Midwest-based Japanese/Taiwanese-American illustrator and designer specializing in portraiture, watercolor, food illustration, and culture-centered storytelling. By visualizing narratives and illuminating concepts, she makes art that fuels action. Her editorial work has been published in the *LA Times*, *Eater Chicago*, *WBEZ Curious City Chicago*, and *Twin Cities Daily Planet*.

www.corilin.co

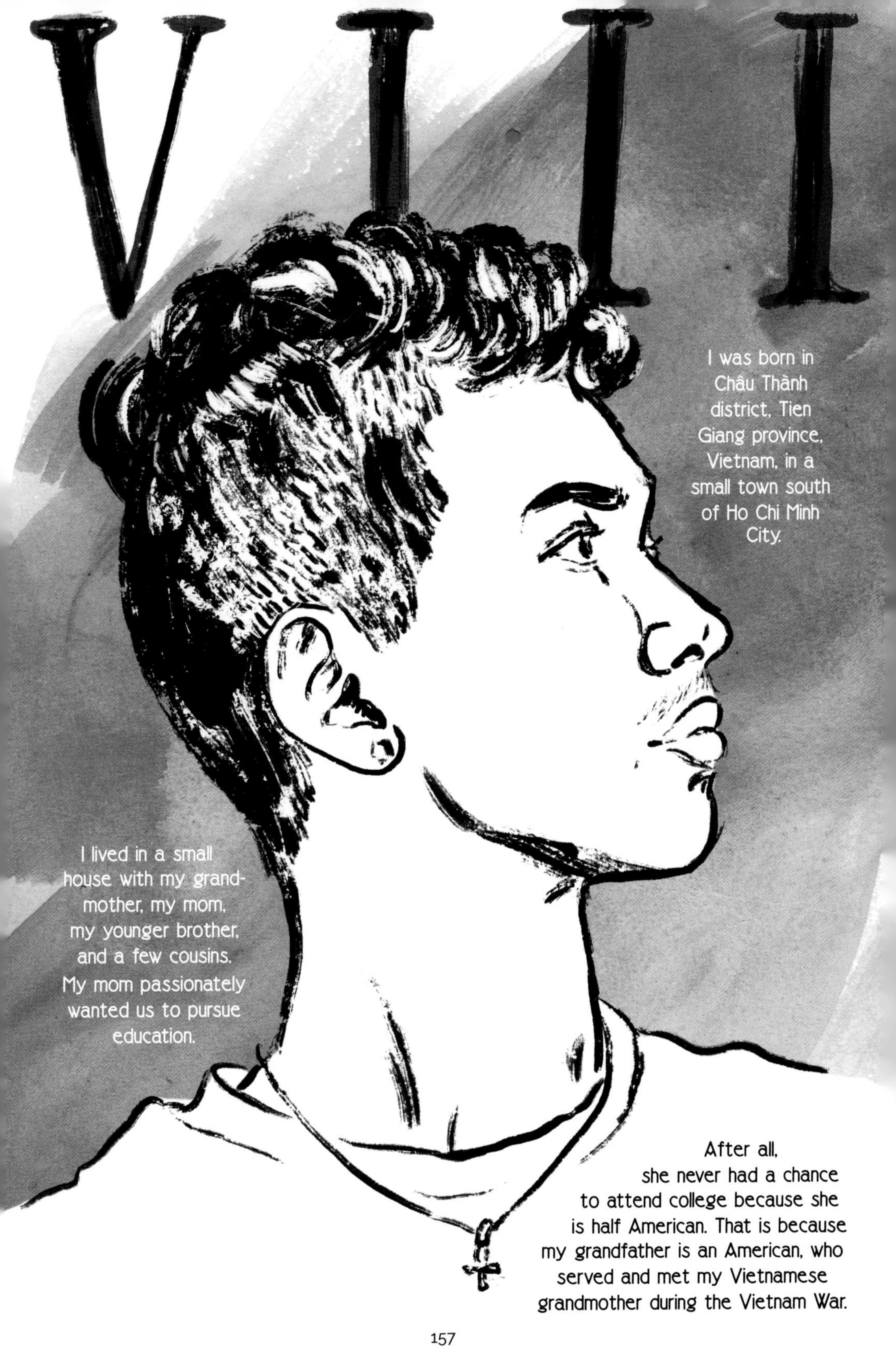
VIII
I was born in Châu Thành district, Tien Giang province, Vietnam, in a small town south of Ho Chi Minh City.
I lived in a small house with my grand-mother, my mom, my younger brother, and a few cousins. My mom passionately wanted us to pursue education.
After all, she never had a chance to attend college because she is half American. That is because my grandfather is an American, who served and met my Vietnamese grandmother during the Vietnam War.

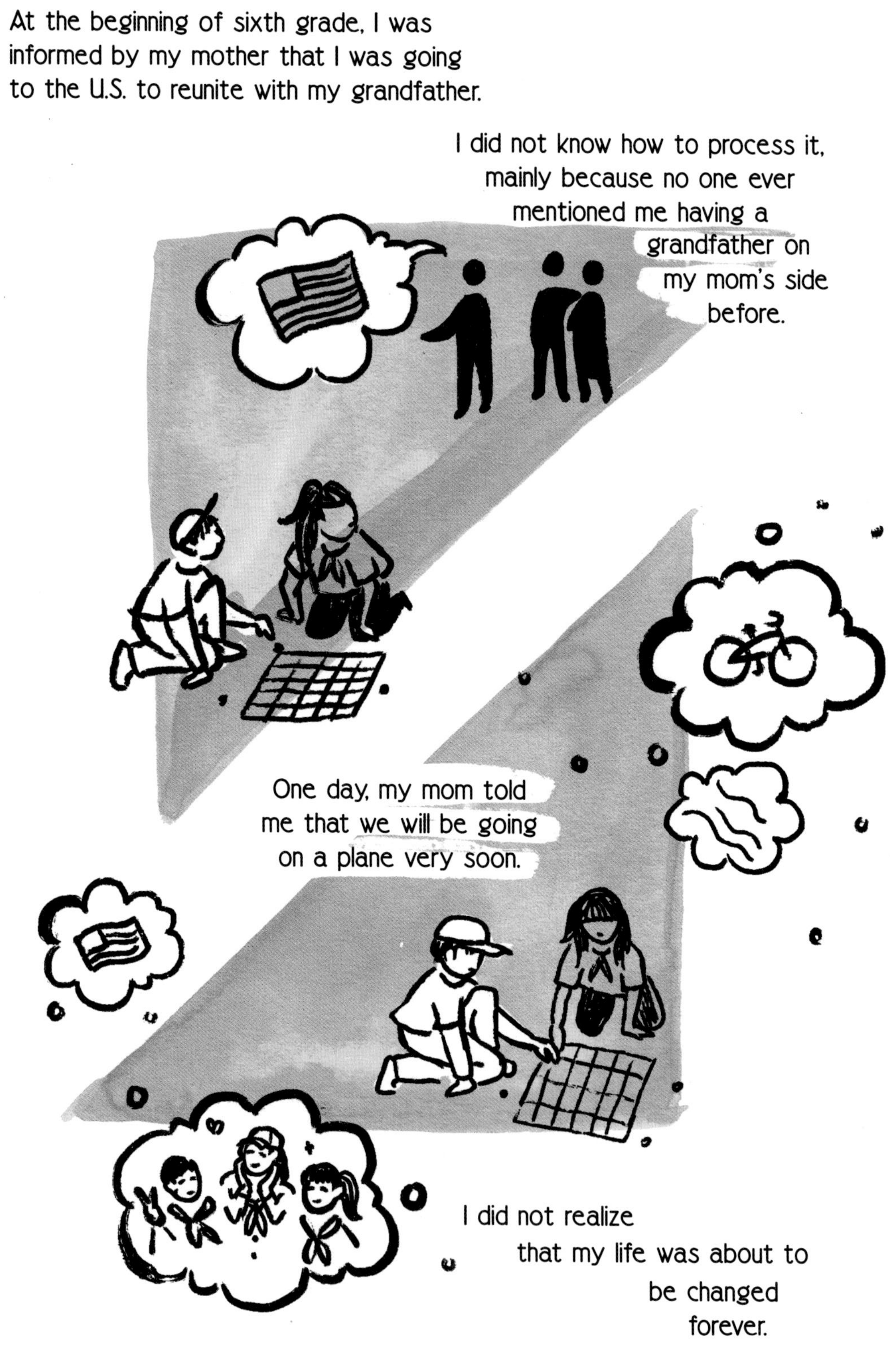
At the beginning of sixth grade, I was informed by my mother that I was going to the U.S. to reunite with my grandfather.
I did not know how to process it, mainly because no one ever mentioned me having a grandfather on my mom's side before.
One day, my mom told me that we will be going on a plane very soon.
I did not realize that my life was about to be changed forever.

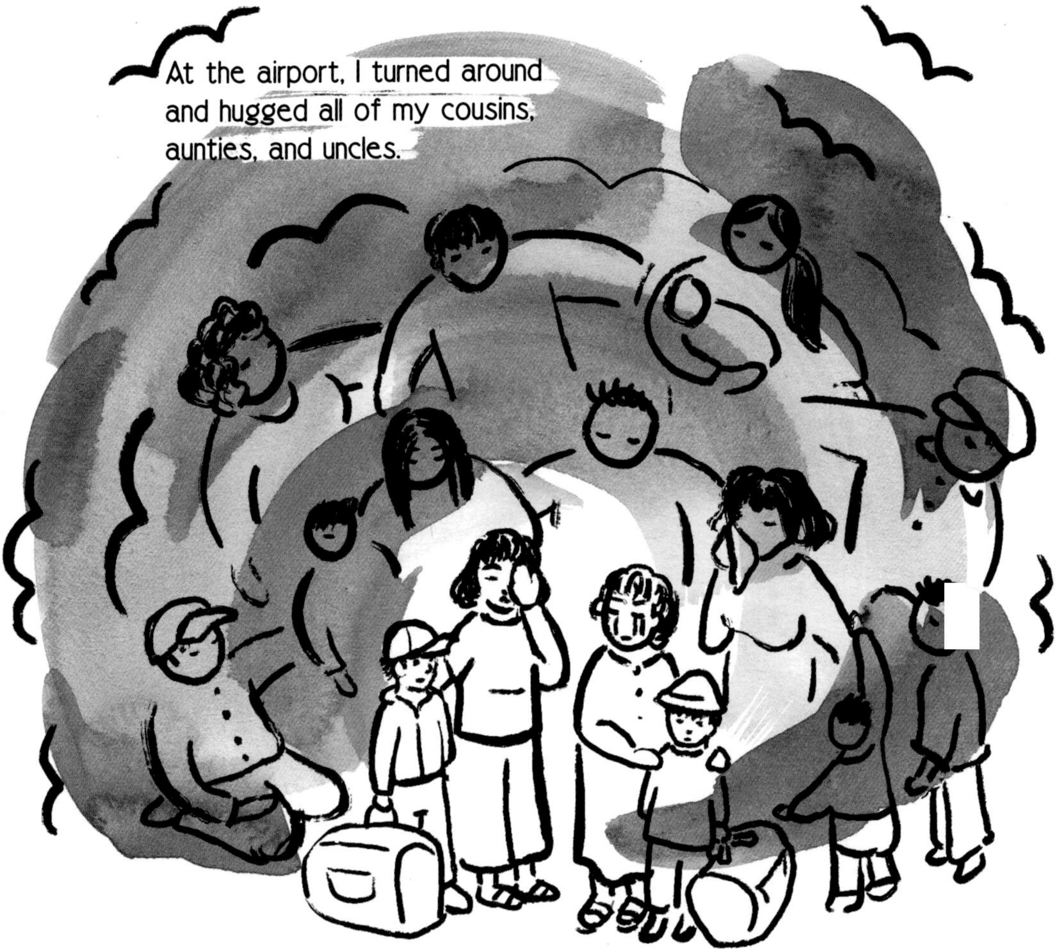
At the airport, I turned around and hugged all of my cousins, aunties, and uncles.

Tears were streaming down their faces.
Everybody was crying, except for my brother and me.

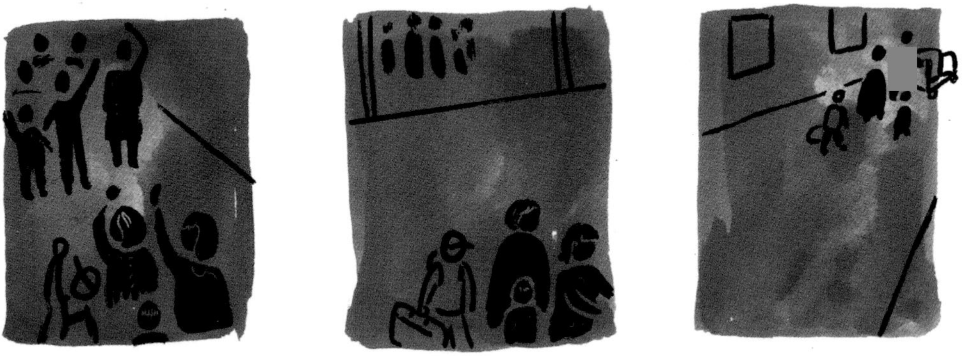

I understood nothing. I felt nothing.

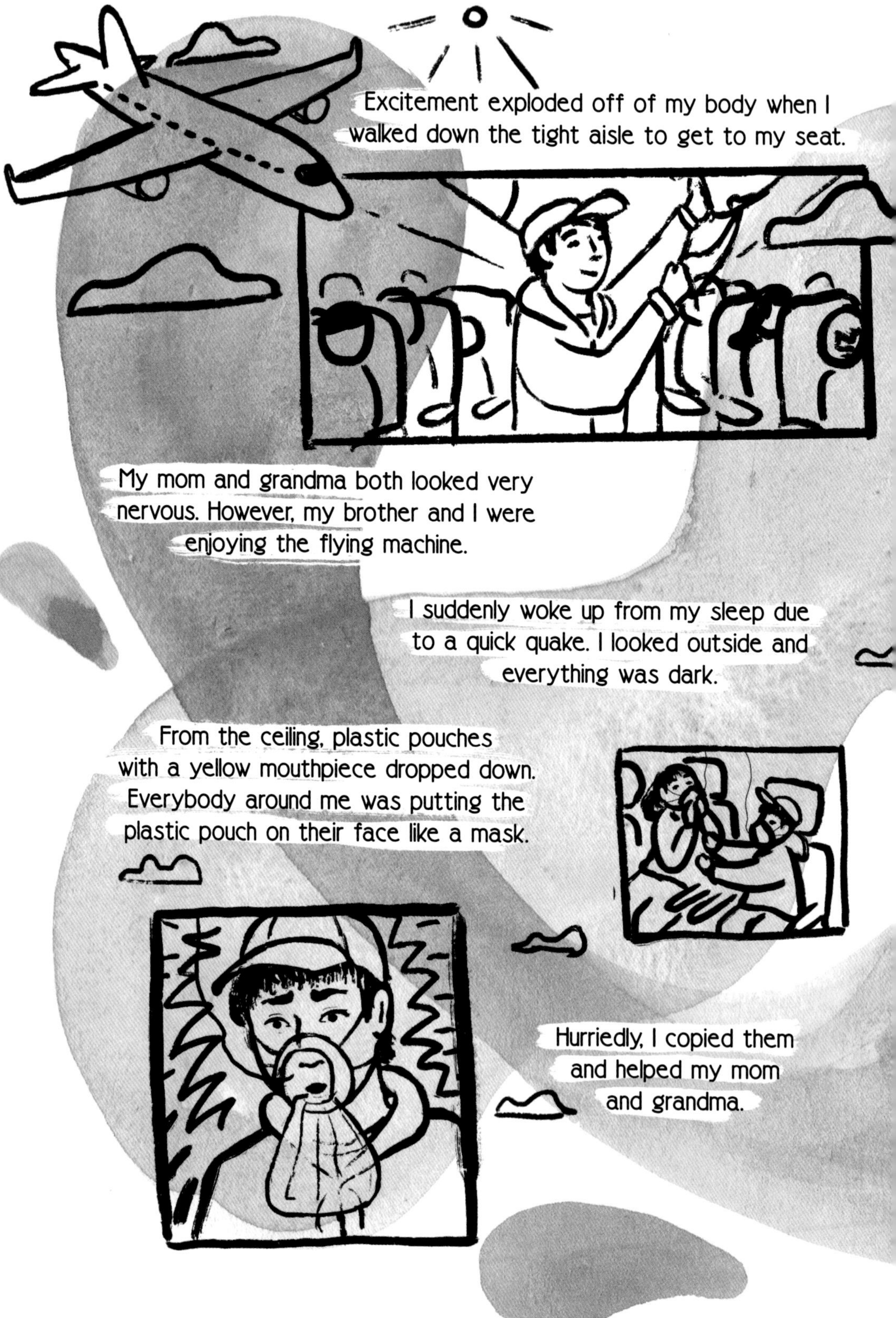
Excitement exploded off of my body when I walked down the tight aisle to get to my seat.
My mom and grandma both looked very nervous. However, my brother and I were enjoying the flying machine.
I suddenly woke up from my sleep due to a quick quake. I looked outside and everything was dark.
From the ceiling, plastic pouches with a yellow mouthpiece dropped down. Everybody around me was putting the plastic pouch on their face like a mask.
Hurriedly, I copied them and helped my mom and grandma.

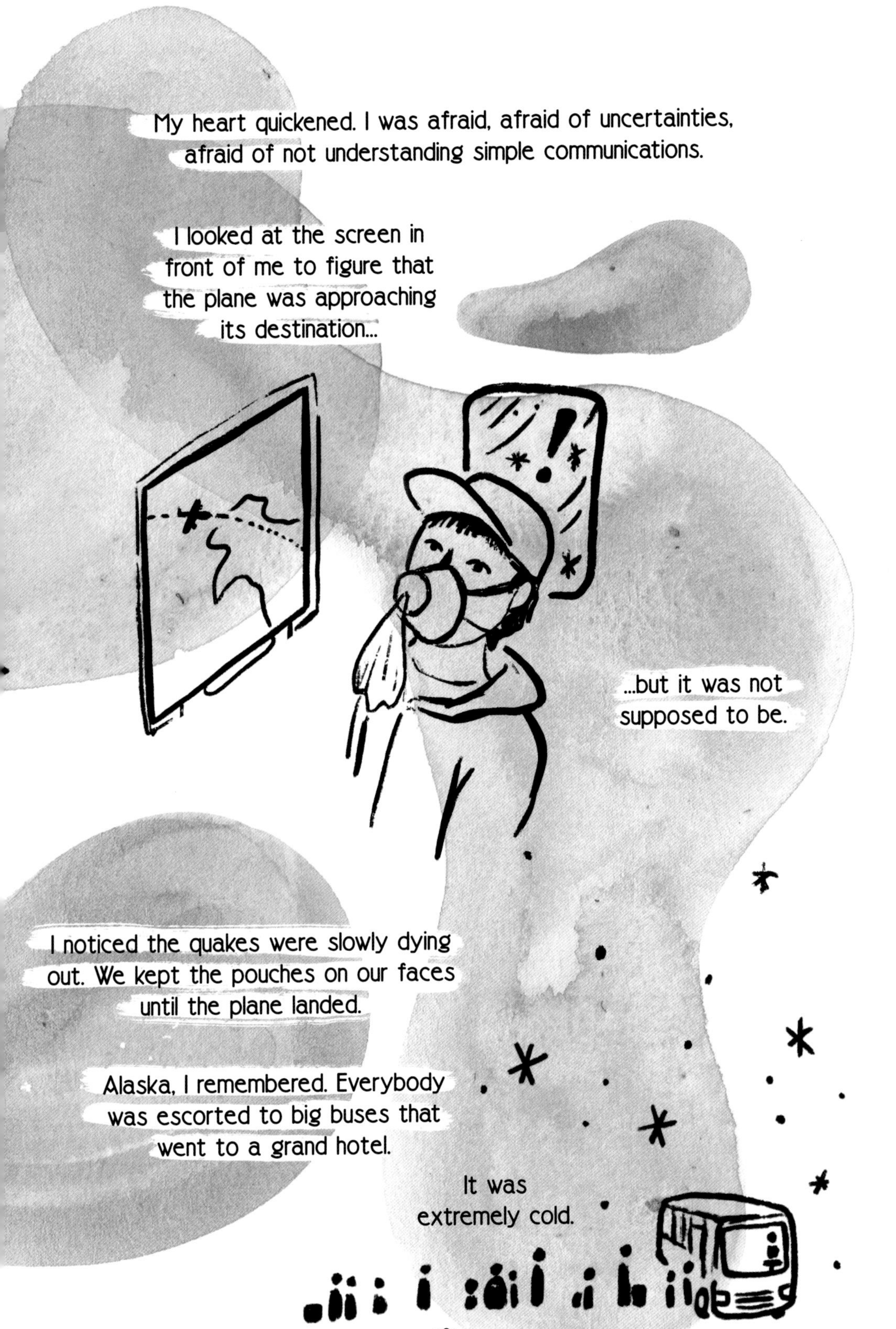
My heart quickened. I was afraid, afraid of uncertainties, afraid of not understanding simple communications.
I looked at the screen in front of me to figure that the plane was approaching its destination...
...but it was not supposed to be.
I noticed the quakes were slowly dying out. We kept the pouches on our faces until the plane landed.
Alaska, I remembered. Everybody was escorted to big buses that went to a grand hotel.
It was extremely cold.

After wandering around at the hotel lobby, we
managed to find an old couple that spoke Vietnamese.
They helped us get our room keys and information
regarding our flight early the next morning.

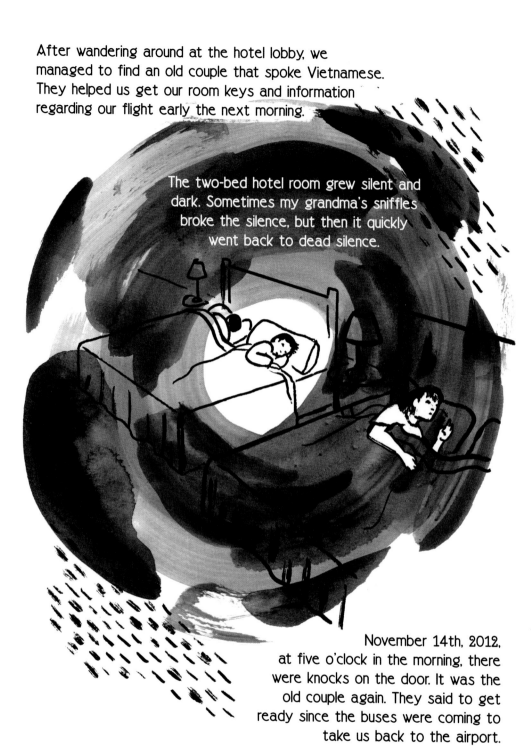

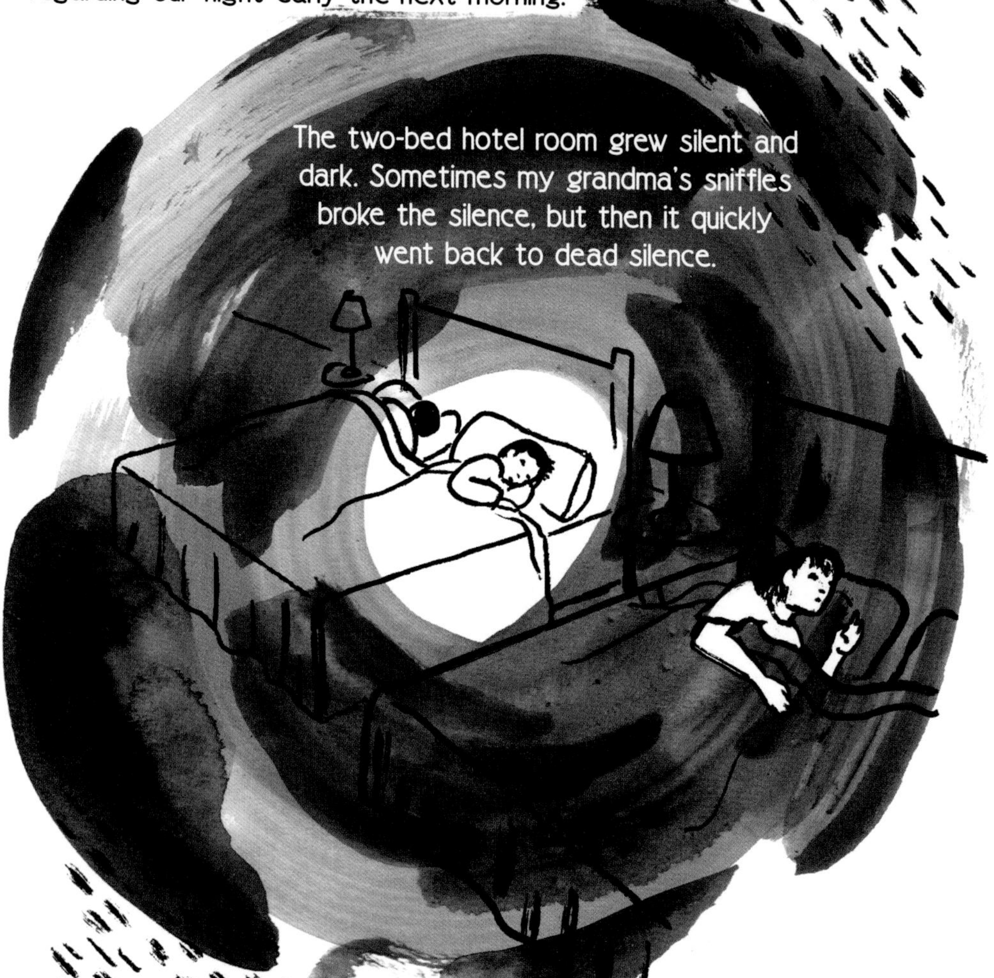
The two-bed hotel room grew silent and dark. Sometimes my grandma's sniffles broke the silence, but then it quickly went back to dead silence.

November 14th, 2012,
at five o'clock in the morning, there
were knocks on the door. It was the
old couple again. They said to get
ready since the buses were coming to
take us back to the airport.

I noticed my mom did not sleep at all the previous night.

Around noon, we boarded the next plane.

I sat back and looked out the window again.

Roughly four hours later, we landed in Los Angeles, California.

It felt much brighter and happier
compared to being in Alaska.

There was also Chinese
food at the airport.

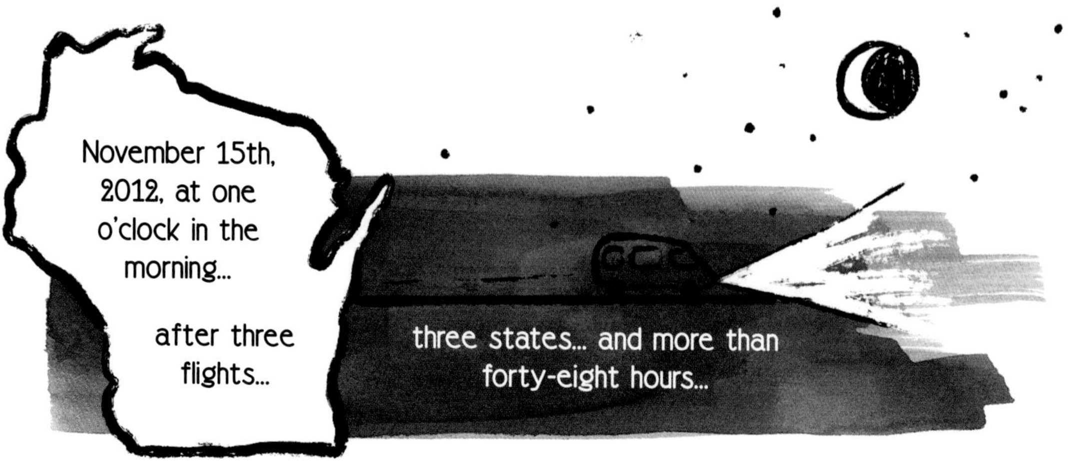
November 15th, 2012, at one o'clock in the morning...
after three flights...
three states... and more than forty-eight hours...

...we arrived at our apartment on the Southside of Madison. We knocked like someone was already inside.

The door opened and my mom gasped.

From the door, a tall, late-sixties white man with blue eyes, a broad frame, and no hair smiled. It was my long-lost grandfather from the Vietnam War.

I felt nothing.

My mom ran up and hugged him. They hugged for a very long time.

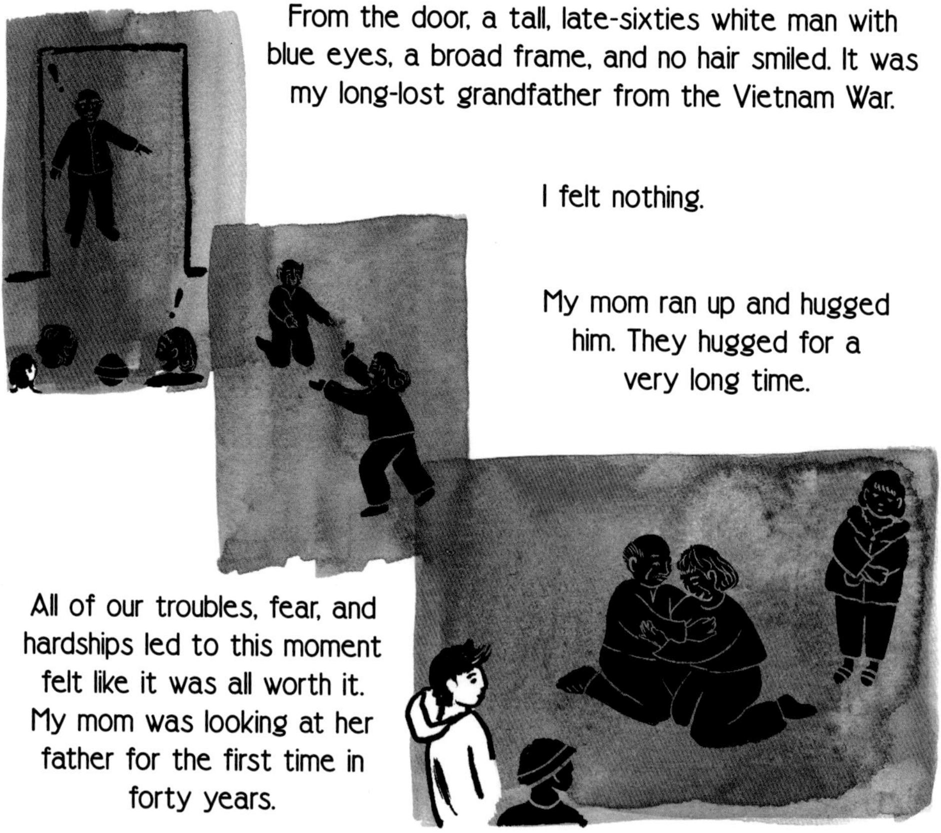

All of our troubles, fear, and hardships led to this moment felt like it was all worth it. My mom was looking at her father for the first time in forty years.

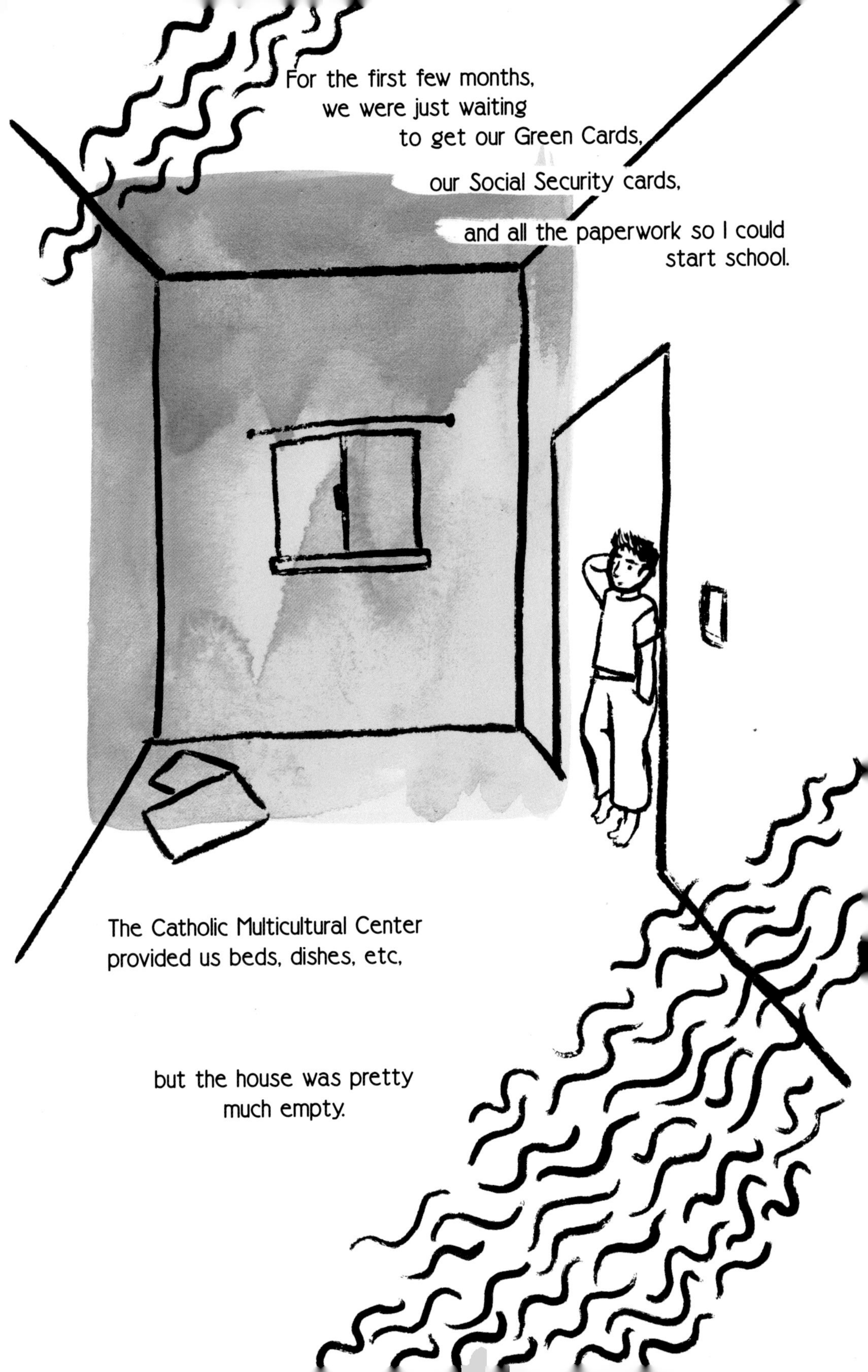
For the first few months,
we were just waiting
to get our Green Cards,
our Social Security cards,
and all the paperwork so I could
start school.
The Catholic Multicultural Center
provided us beds, dishes, etc,
but the house was pretty
much empty.

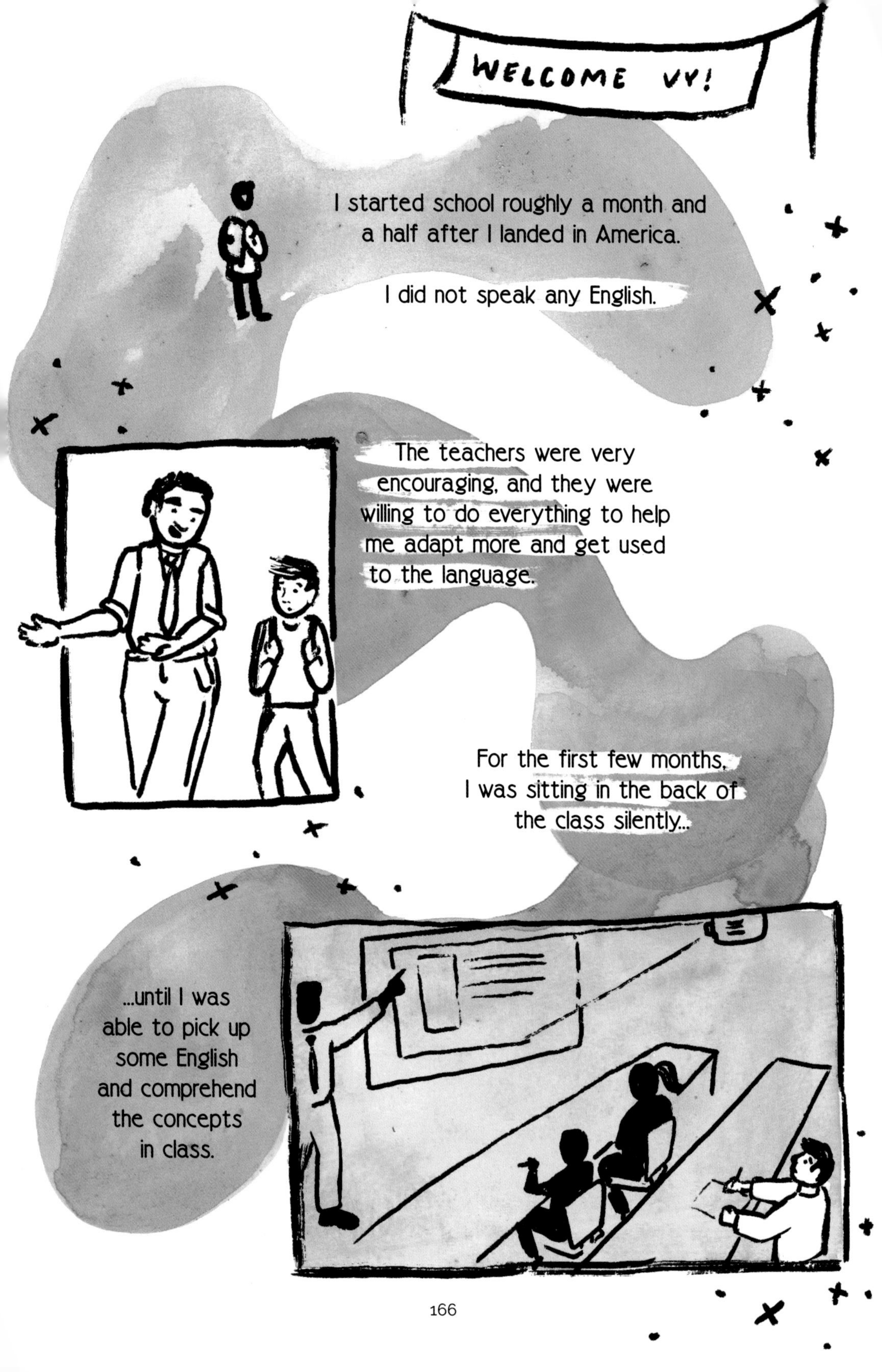
WELCOME VY!
I started school roughly a month and a half after I landed in America.
I did not speak any English.
The teachers were very encouraging, and they were willing to do everything to help me adapt more and get used to the language.
For the first few months, I was sitting in the back of the class silently...
...until I was able to pick up some English and comprehend the concepts in class.

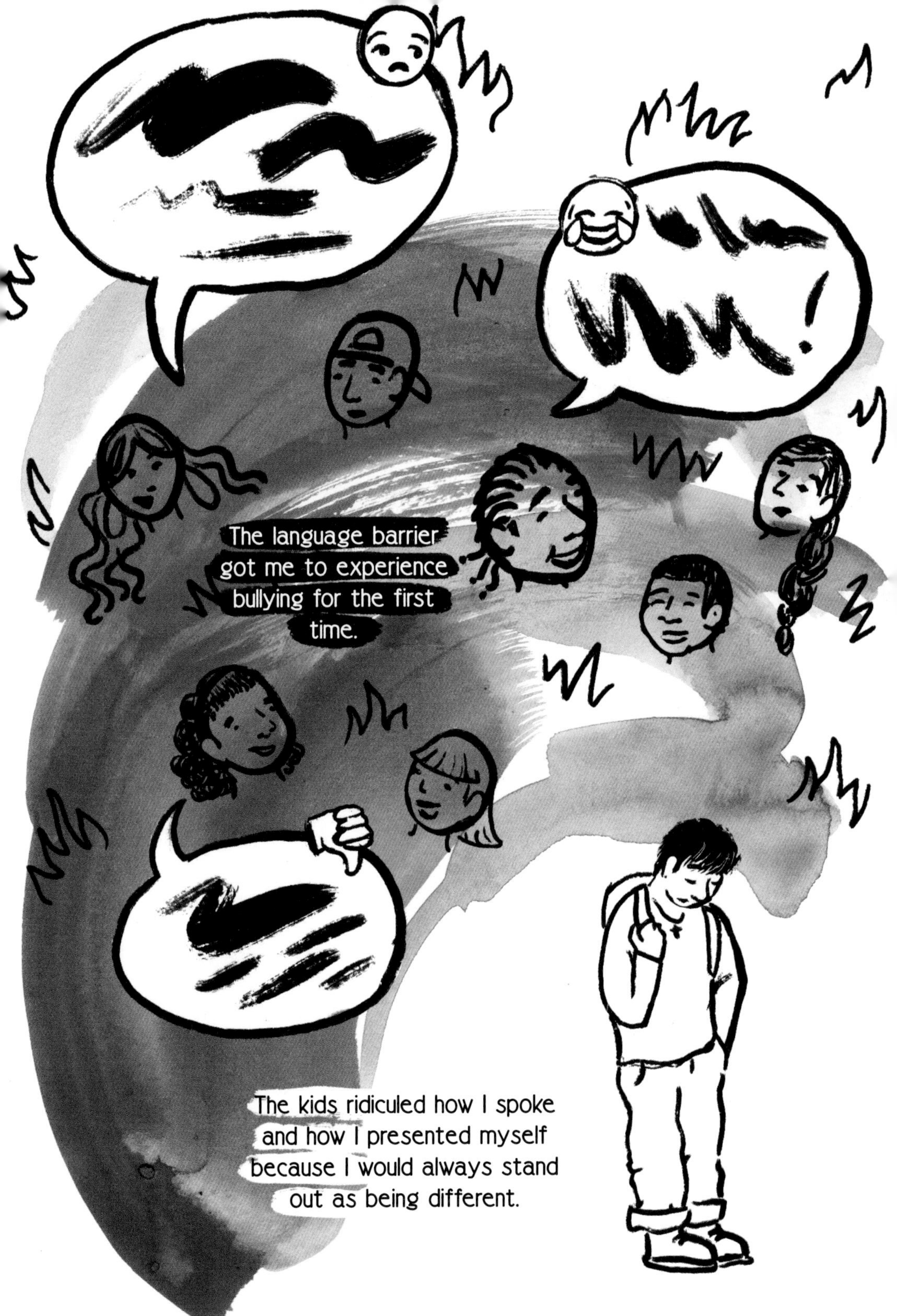
The language barrier got me to experience bullying for the first time.
The kids ridiculed how I spoke and how I presented myself because I would always stand out as being different.

Things were quite the opposite when I started high school at Madison West High School. I felt very comfortable with my surroundings in and outside of school.

I felt like I was just going through the motions in my classes and with my friends. I didn't have to try so hard to receive good grades and fit in.

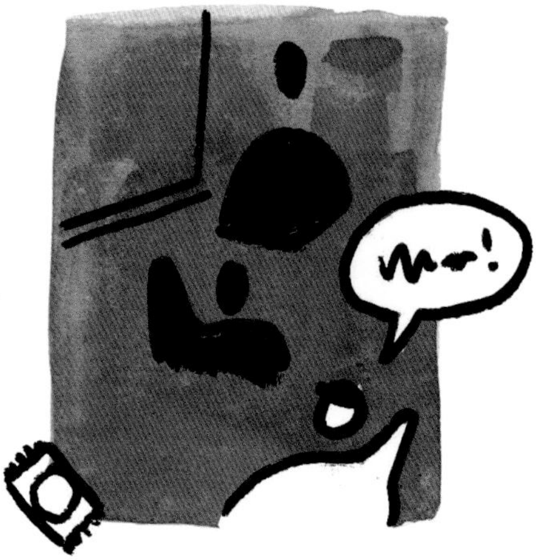

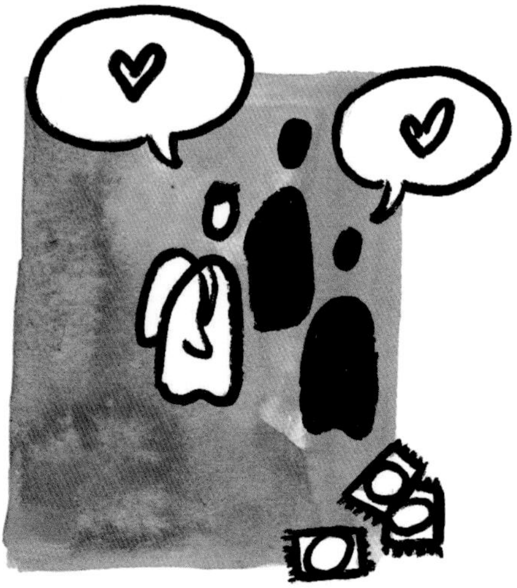

At the end of my sophomore year, I decided to transfer to a new high school.

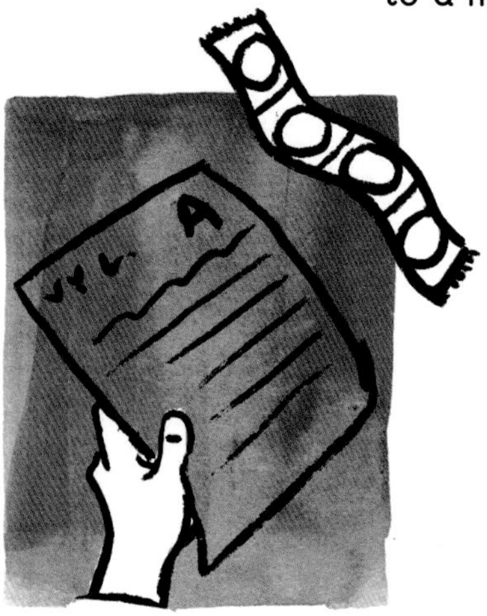
A

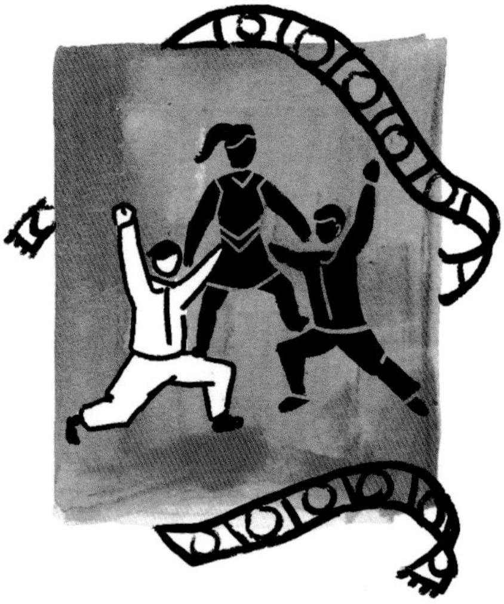

I transferred to improve my high school experience, challenge myself, and prepare for college. I had many breakdowns due to loneliness and uncertainties. However, by the end of the school year, I became the best version of me.

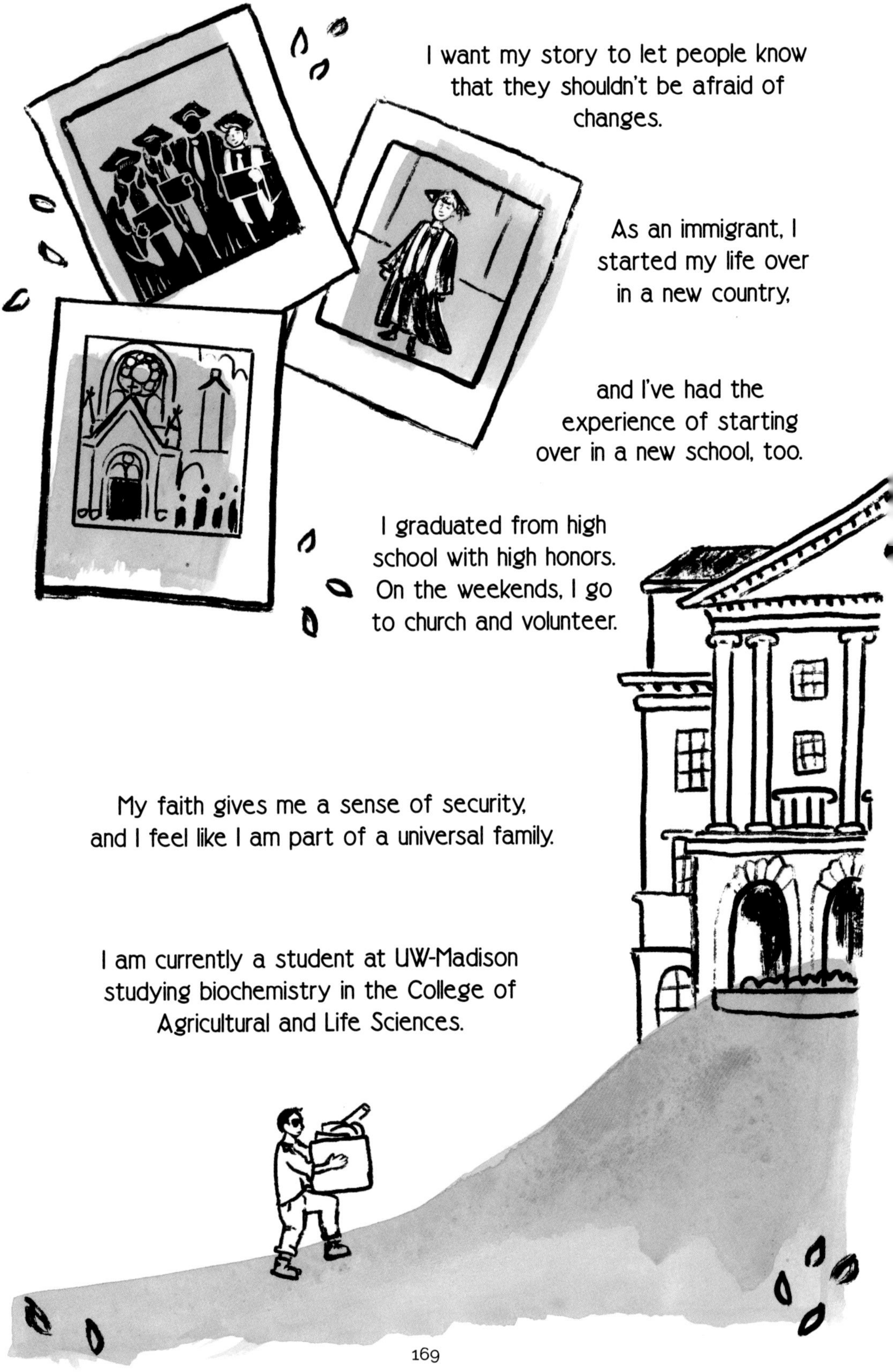
I want my story to let people know that they shouldn't be afraid of changes.
As an immigrant, I started my life over in a new country,
and I've had the experience of starting over in a new school, too.
I graduated from high school with high honors. On the weekends, I go to church and volunteer.
My faith gives me a sense of security, and I feel like I am part of a universal family.
I am currently a student at UW-Madison studying biochemistry in the College of Agricultural and Life Sciences.

Now, I have realized that I would still have to earn the riches everybody in Vietnam assumed all Americans have...

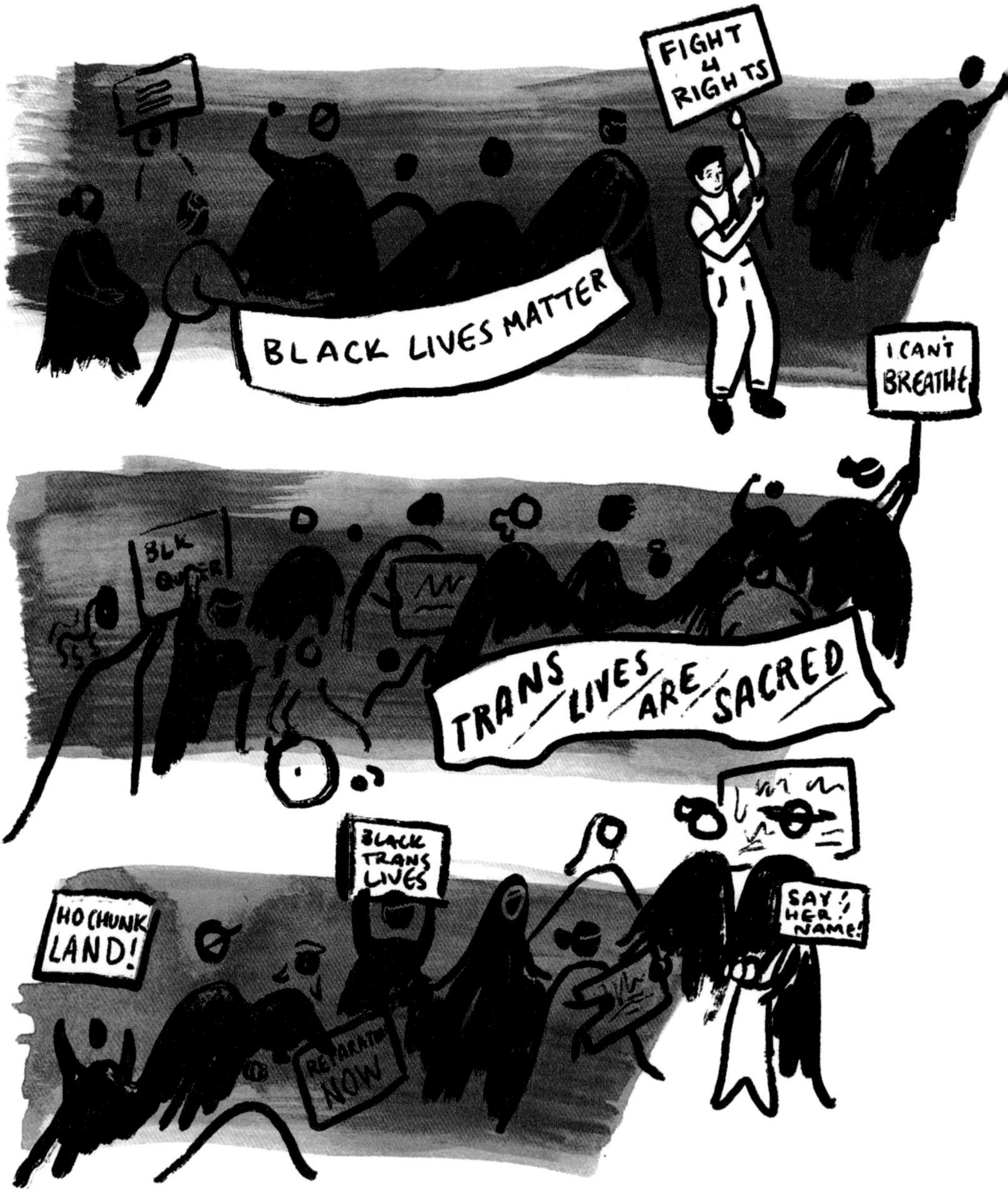
FIGHT 4 RIGHTS
BLACK LIVES MATTER
I CAN'T BREATHE
BLK
TRANS LIVES ARE SACRED
BLACK TRANS LIVES
HO CHUNK LAND!
SAY HER NAME!

...and many groups of people are still fighting for human rights.

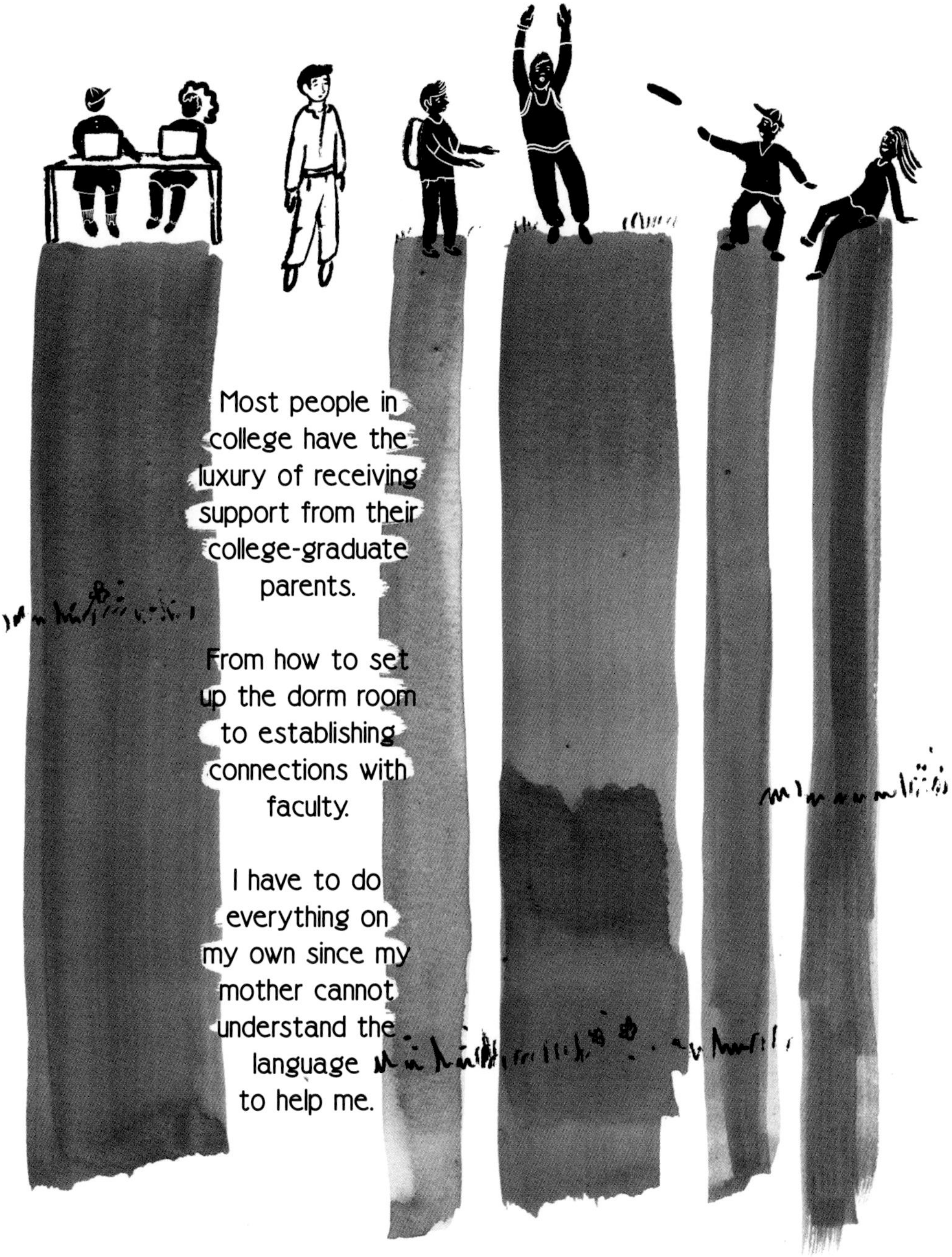
Most people in college have the luxury of receiving support from their college-graduate parents.
From how to set up the dorm room to establishing connections with faculty.
I have to do everything on my own since my mother cannot understand the language to help me.

I learned to keep myself afloat in all circumstances through hard work and perseverance.

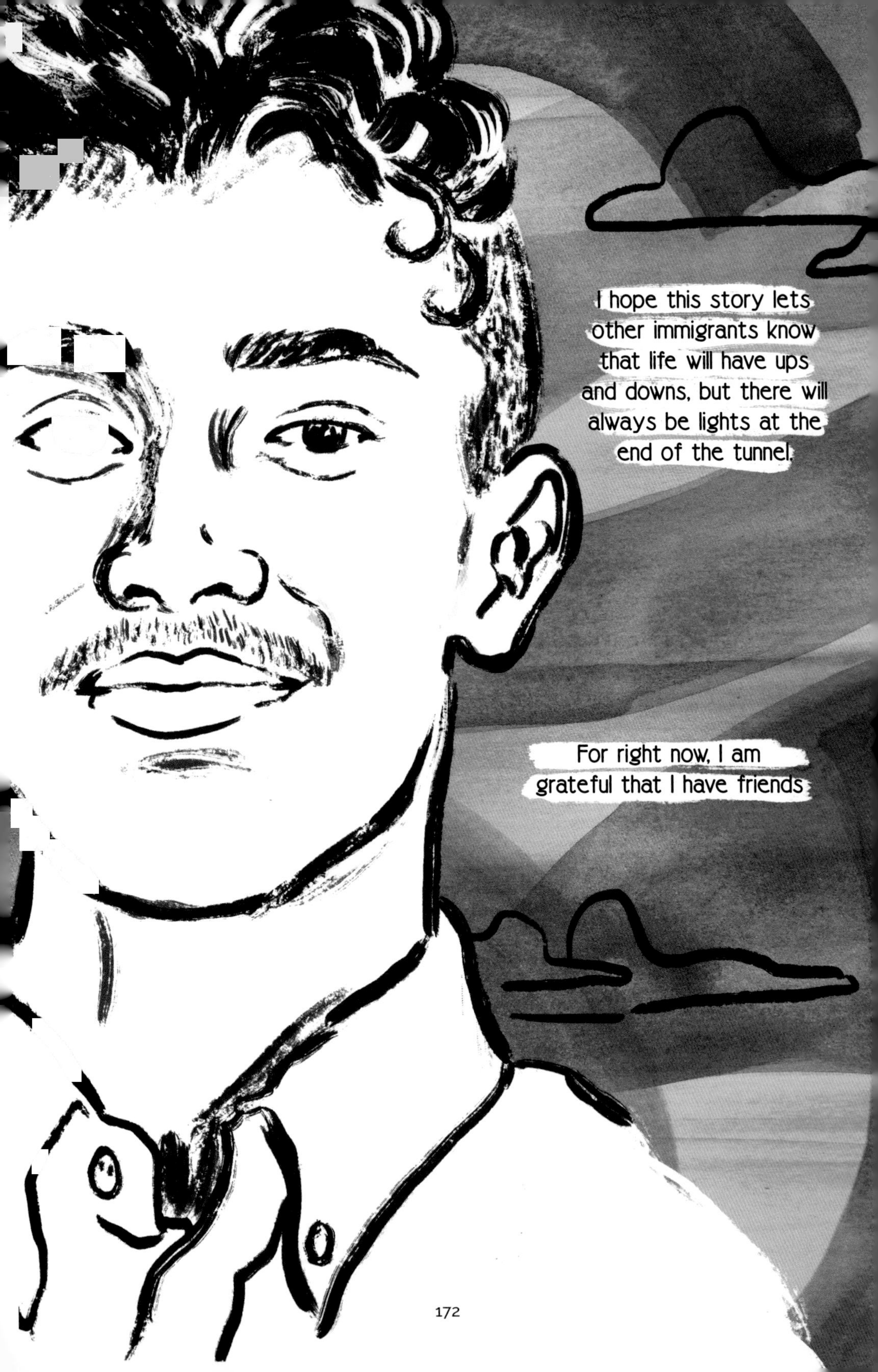
I hope this story lets other immigrants know that life will have ups and downs, but there will always be lights at the end of the tunnel.
For right now, I am grateful that I have friends

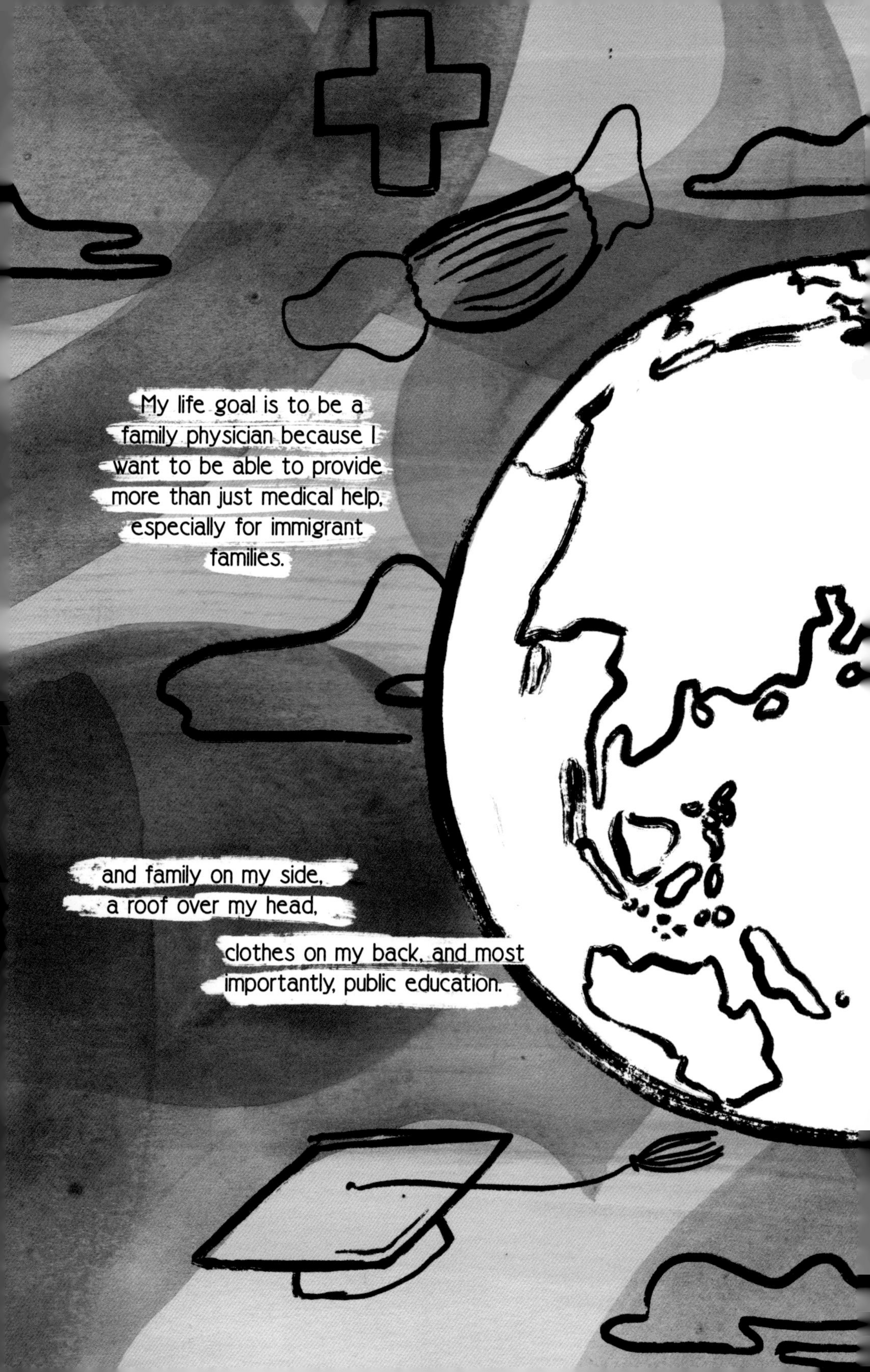
My life goal is to be a family physician because I want to be able to provide more than just medical help, especially for immigrant families.
and family on my side,
a roof over my head,
clothes on my back, and most importantly, public education.

AMARA SOLOMON KAMARA

Born: Salayea, Liberia
Current: Minneapolis, Minnesota

Amara Solomon Kamara left Liberia before the civil war in 1989. Amara came to the U.S. as a refugee in 1994 with the help of his then fiancée, Connie Hederington. He attended Tulane University in New Orleans and graduated with a bachelor of science in sports and exercise. Amara is passionate about physical fitness, fashion, and community empowerment. In his free time, Amara enjoys volunteering and is a strong member of the Liberian Mandingo Association of the U.S.A. He is also a member of the Minnesota Dandies Project, whose mission is to highlight the positive influence that men have in their community that people are not aware of, especially the media.

www.greencardvoices.org/speakers/amara-kamara

HAMID IBRAHIM AND THE KUGALI TEAM

Born: Uganda
Current: London, United Kindgom

Hamid Ibrahim is a creative director from Uganda but resides in the UK. With a background in arts and visual effects, Hamid is a computer graphics (CG) generalist specializing in character rigging and modeling. He originally worked at MPC (a multi-award-winning visual effects production house). There, he worked on films like *Dumbo* and *Lion King*.

Hamid is also a public speaker, having attended several panels at various conventions. At Kugali, Hamid runs a team of art and visual effects artists on CG and anything art related. He is nicknamed, the Machine.

www.kugali.com

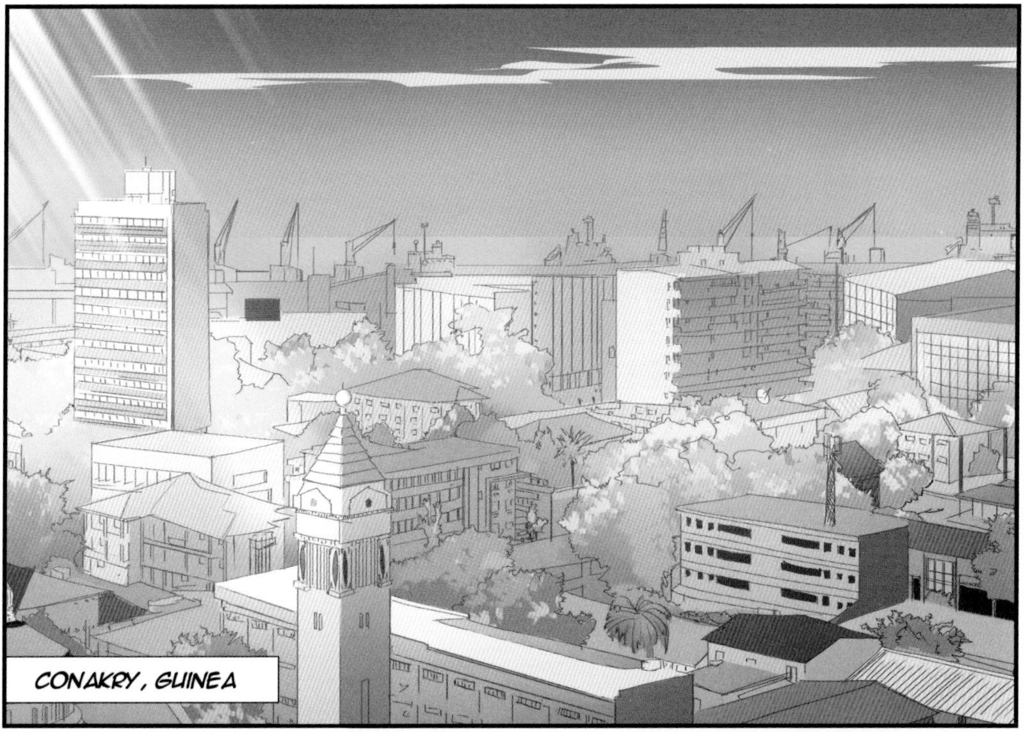
CONAKRY, GUINEA

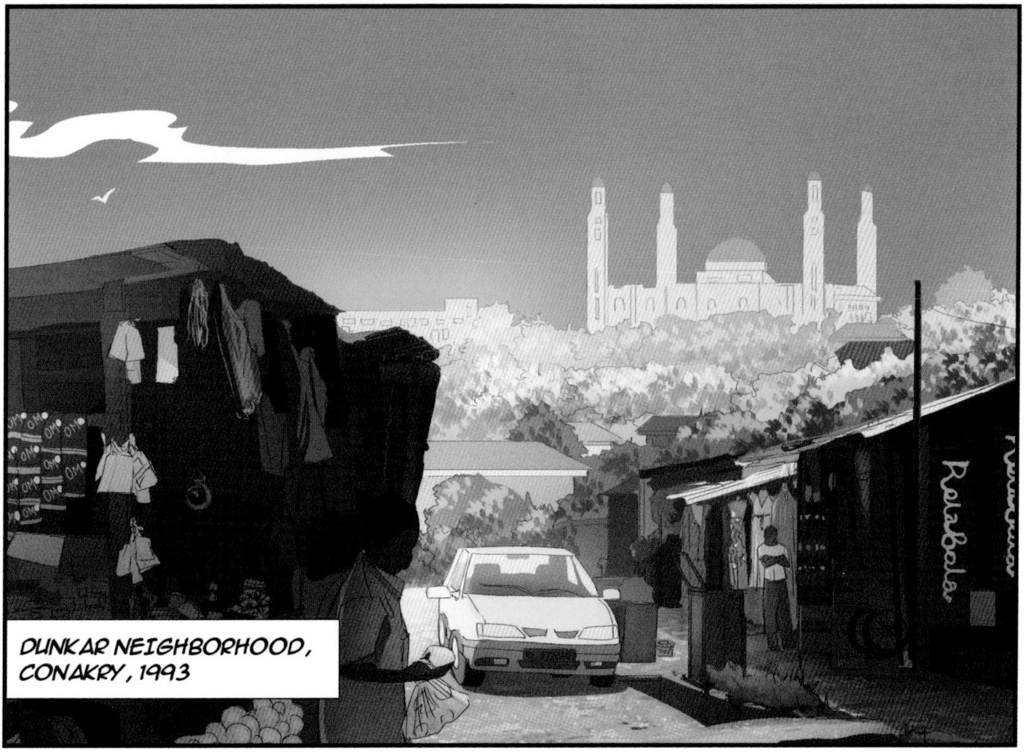
DUNKAR NEIGHBORHOOD,
CONAKRY, 1993

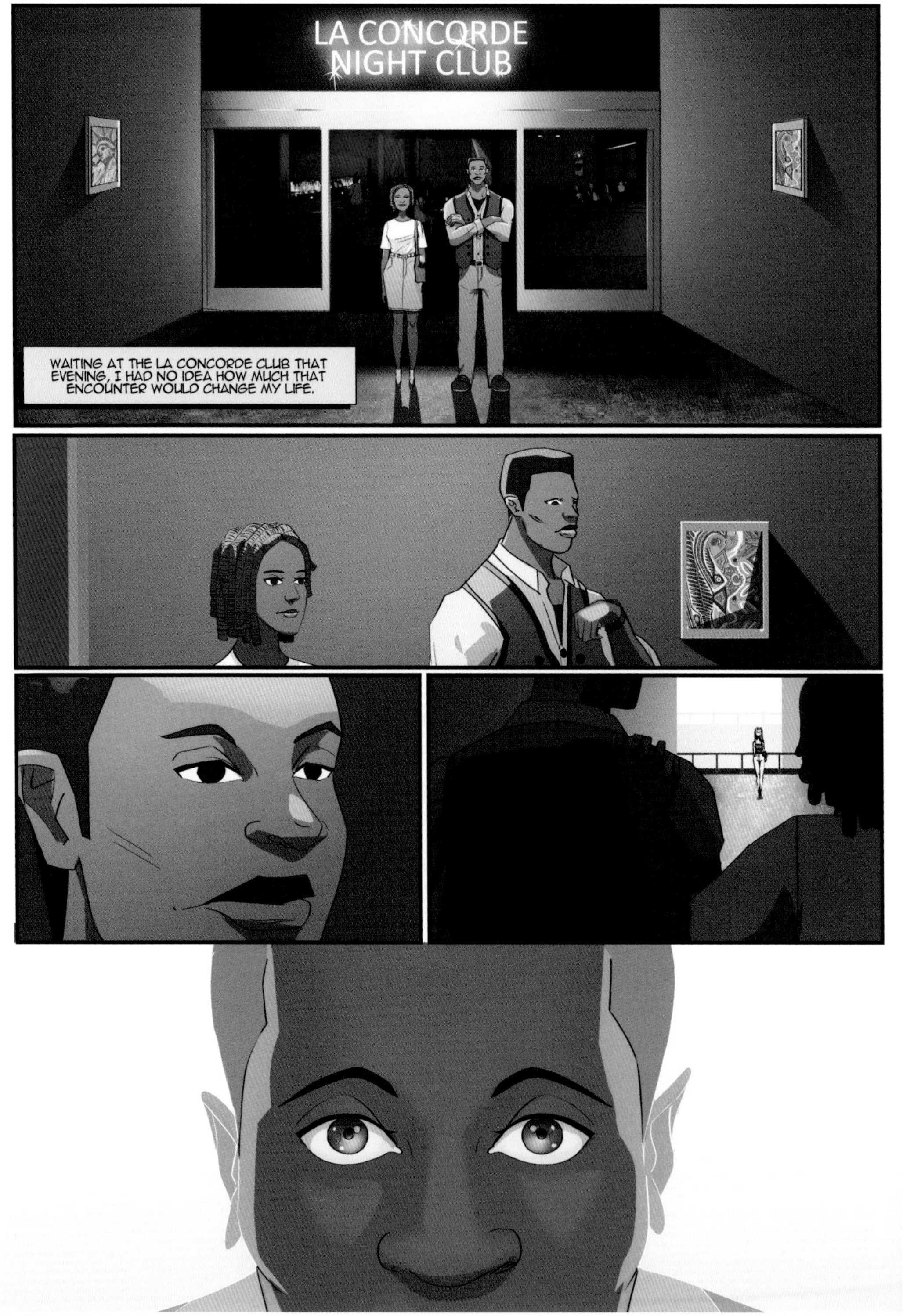
LA CONCORDE NIGHT CLUB
WAITING AT THE LA CONCORDE CLUB THAT EVENING, I HAD NO IDEA HOW MUCH THAT ENCOUNTER WOULD CHANGE MY LIFE.

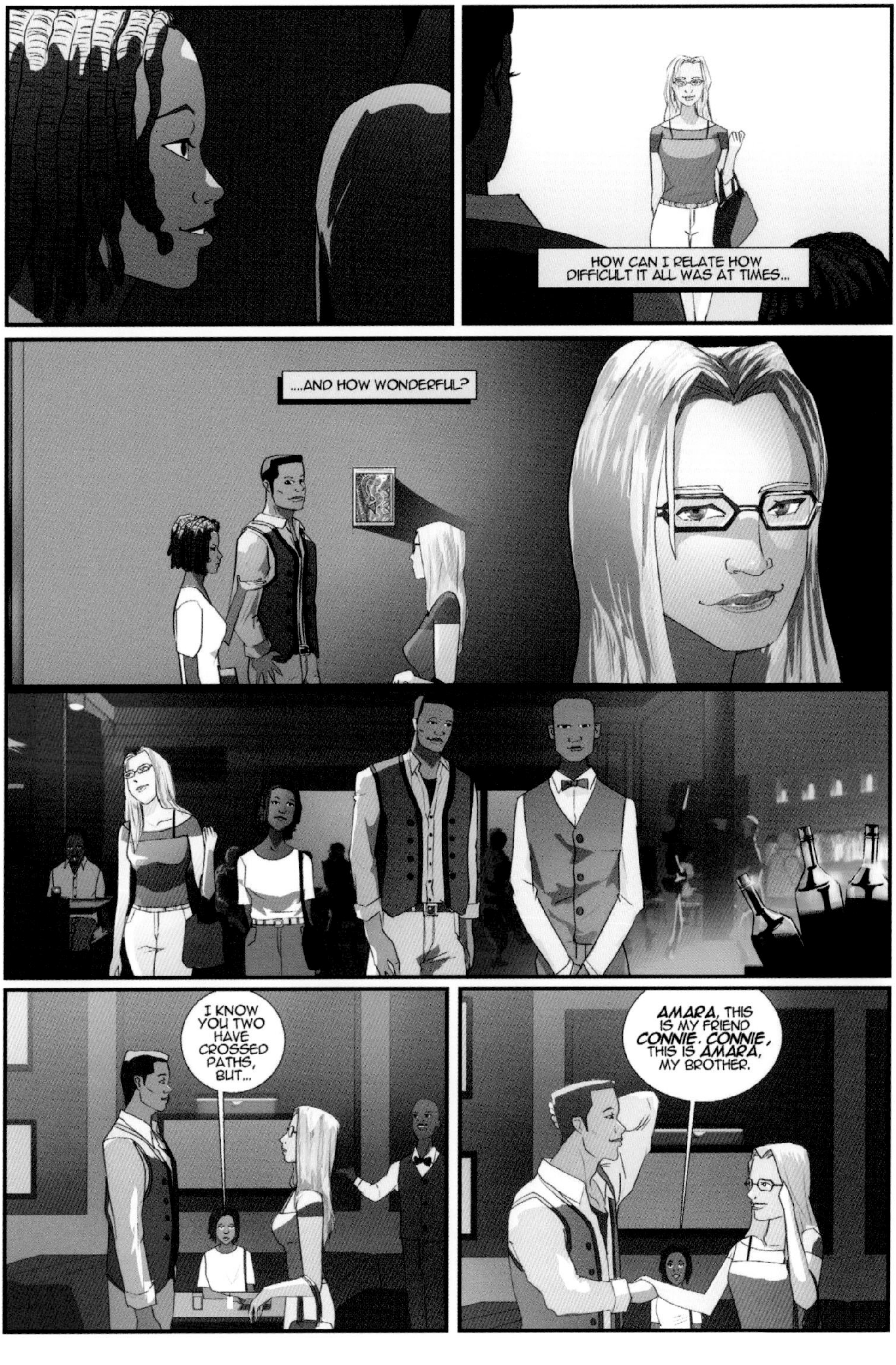
HOW CAN I RELATE HOW DIFFICULT IT ALL WAS AT TIMES...
....AND HOW WONDERFUL?
I KNOW YOU TWO HAVE CROSSED PATHS, BUT...
AMARA, THIS IS MY FRIEND CONNIE. CONNIE, THIS IS AMARA, MY BROTHER.

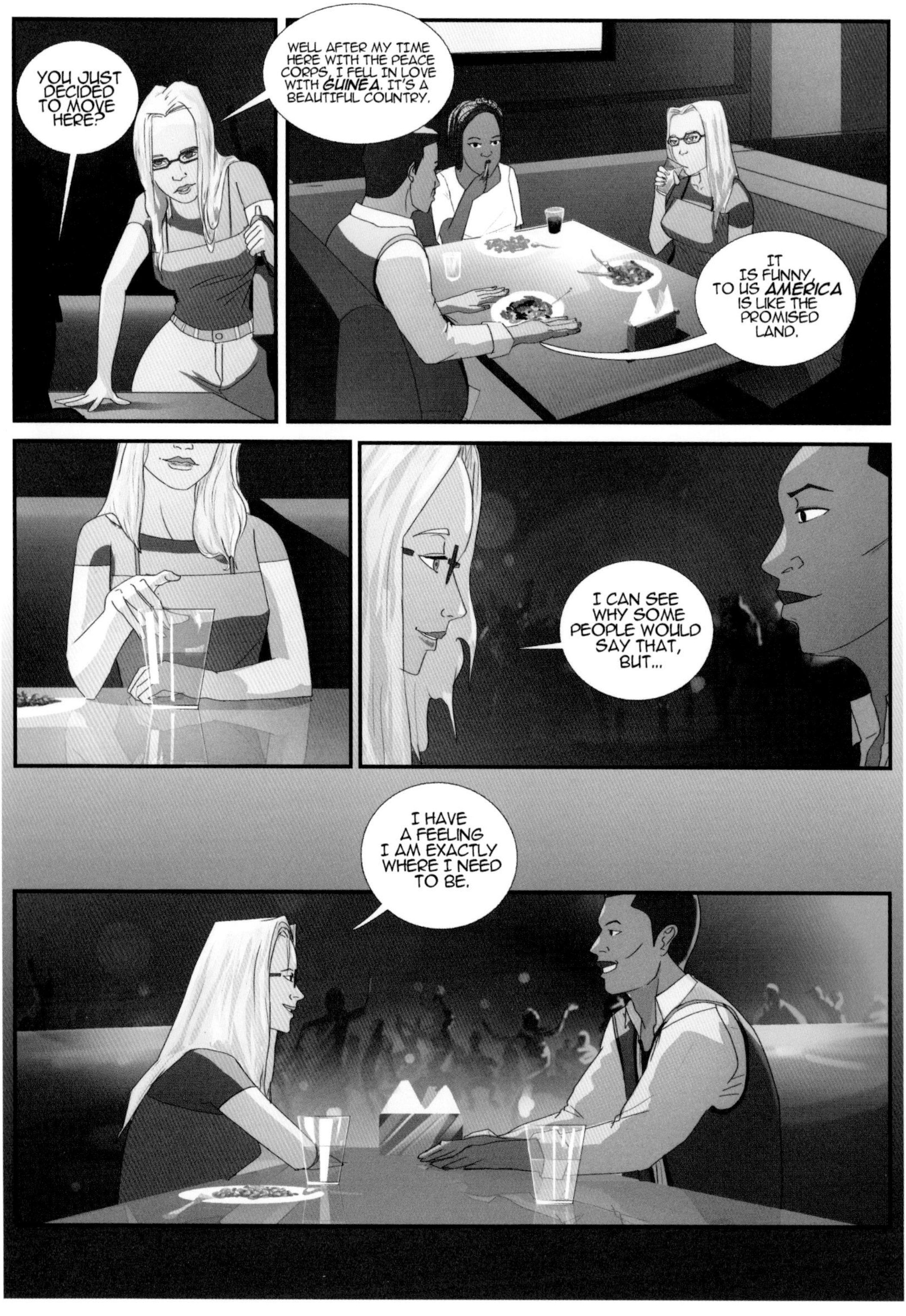
YOU JUST DECIDED TO MOVE HERE?
WELL AFTER MY TIME HERE WITH THE PEACE CORPS, I FELL IN LOVE WITH GUINEA. IT'S A BEAUTIFUL COUNTRY.
IT IS FUNNY, TO US AMERICA IS LIKE THE PROMISED LAND.
I CAN SEE WHY SOME PEOPLE WOULD SAY THAT, BUT...
I HAVE A FEELING I AM EXACTLY WHERE I NEED TO BE.

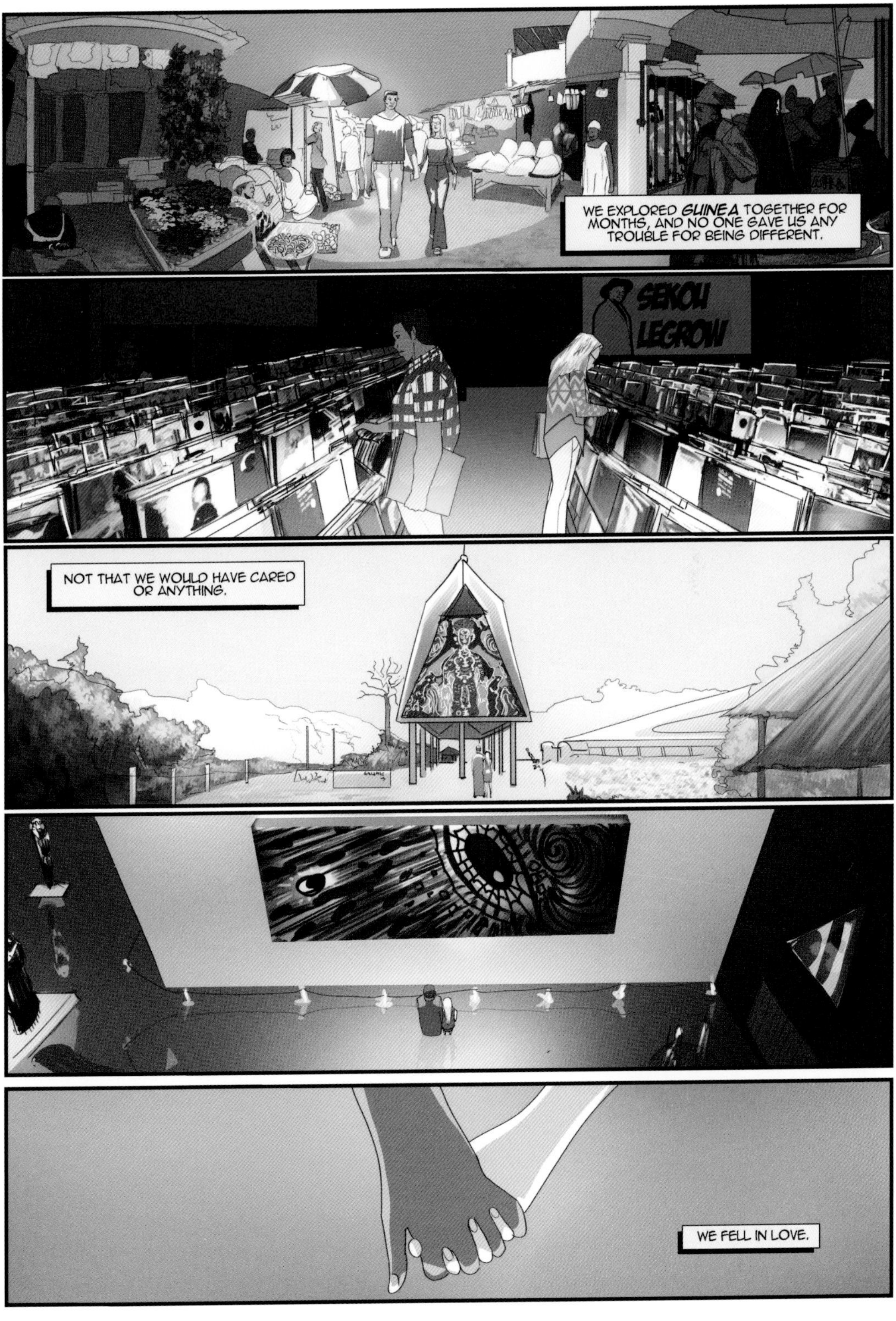
WE EXPLORED GUINEA TOGETHER FOR MONTHS, AND NO ONE GAVE US ANY TROUBLE FOR BEING DIFFERENT.
SEKOU LEGROW
NOT THAT WE WOULD HAVE CARED OR ANYTHING.
WE FELL IN LOVE.

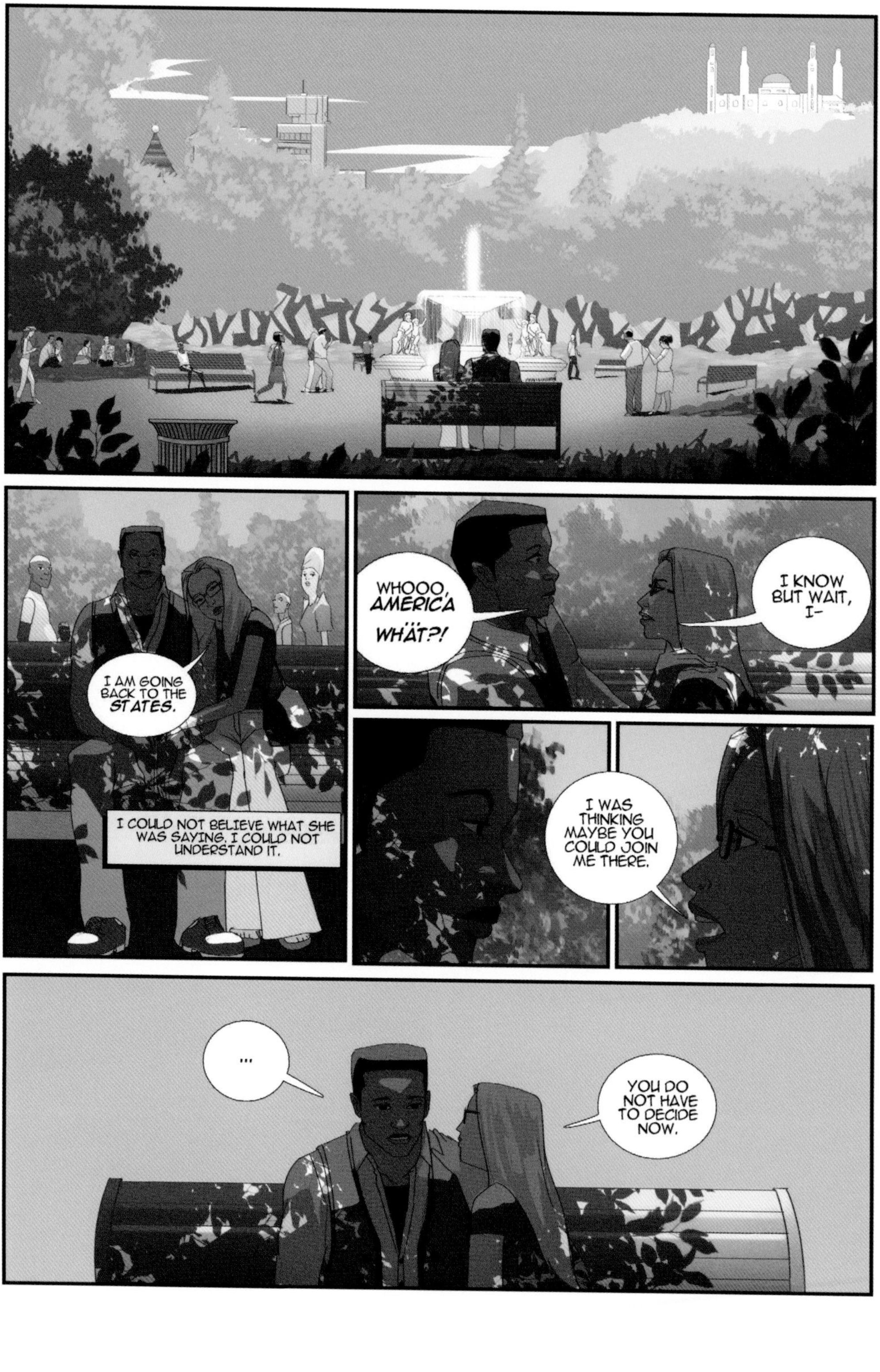
I AM GOING BACK TO THE STATES.
I COULD NOT BELIEVE WHAT SHE WAS SAYING. I COULD NOT UNDERSTAND IT.
WHOOO, AMERICA ... WHAT?!
I KNOW BUT WAIT, I-
I WAS THINKING MAYBE YOU COULD JOIN ME THERE.
...
YOU DO NOT HAVE TO DECIDE NOW.

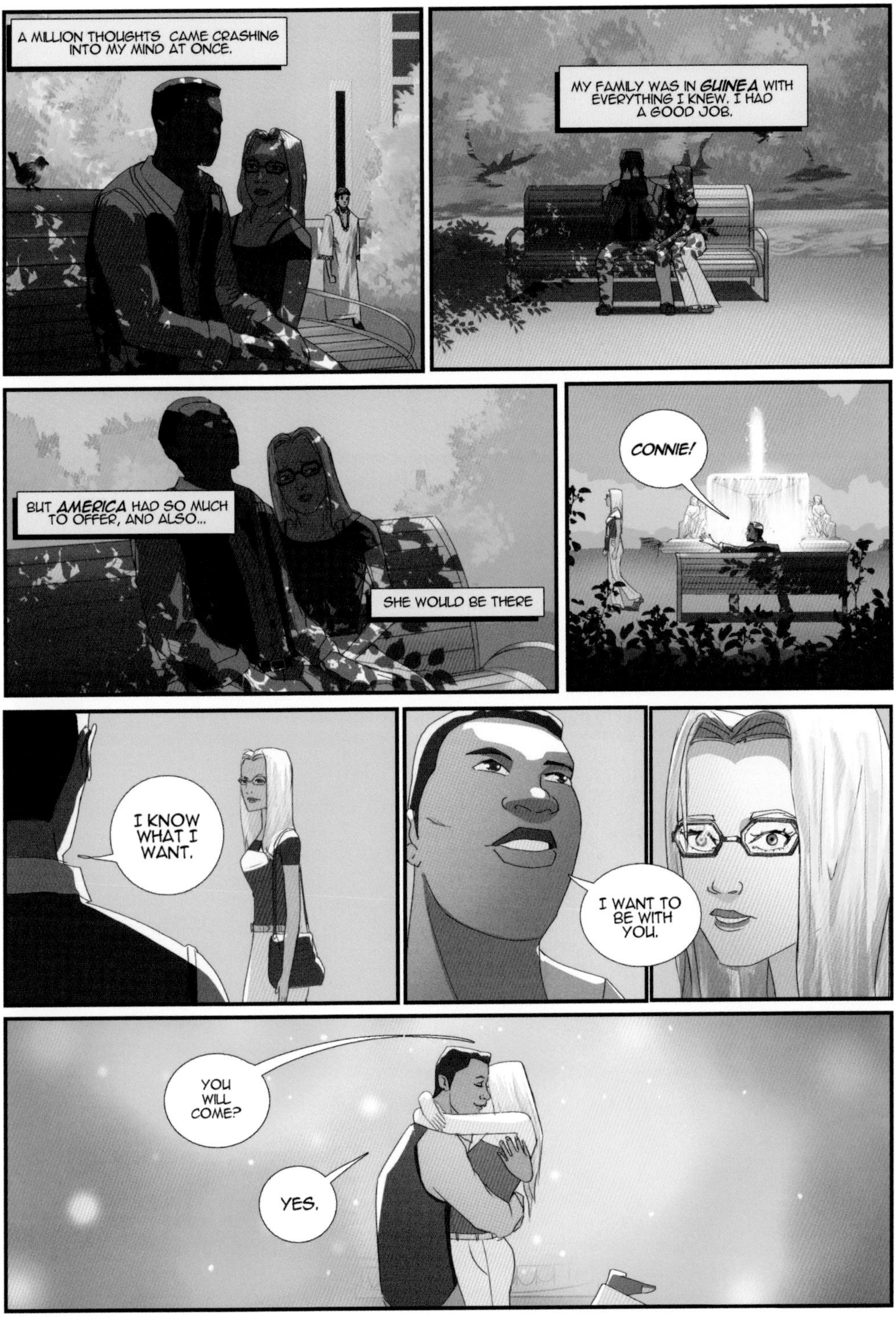
A MILLION THOUGHTS CAME CRASHING INTO MY MIND AT ONCE.
MY FAMILY WAS IN GUINEA WITH EVERYTHING I KNEW. I HAD A GOOD JOB.
BUT AMERICA HAD SO MUCH TO OFFER, AND ALSO...
SHE WOULD BE THERE
CONNIE!
I KNOW WHAT I WANT.
I WANT TO BE WITH YOU.
YOU WILL COME?
YES.

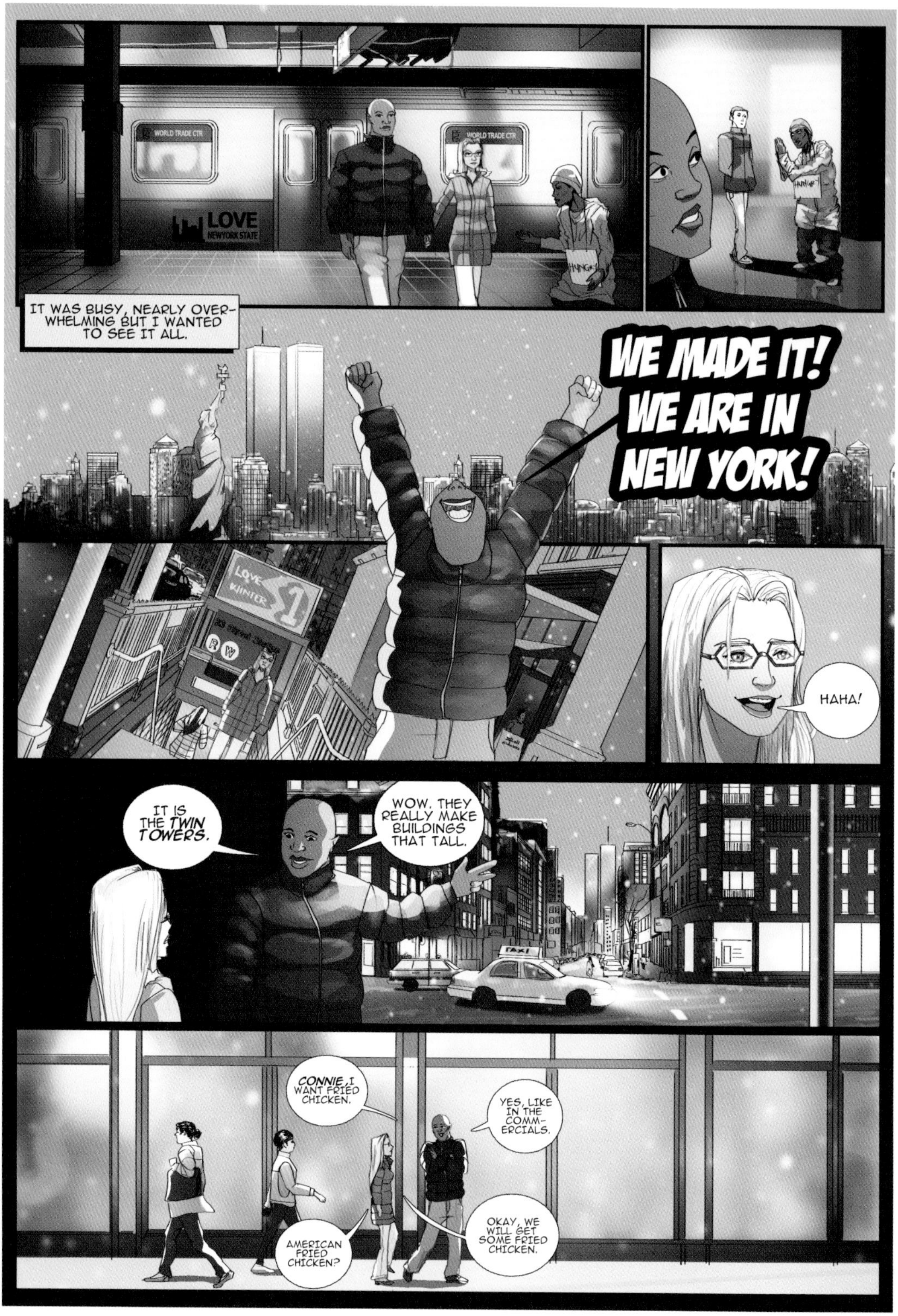
WORLD TRADE CTR
WORLD TRADE CTR
LOVE NEWYORK STATE
HUNGRY
IT WAS BUSY, NEARLY OVER-WHELMING BUT I WANTED TO SEE IT ALL.
WE MADE IT! WE ARE IN NEW YORK!
LOVE WINTER 1
HAHA!
IT IS THE TWIN TOWERS.
WOW, THEY REALLY MAKE BUILDINGS THAT TALL.
TAXI
CONNIE, I WANT FRIED CHICKEN.
YES, LIKE IN THE COMM-ERCIALS.
AMERICAN FRIED CHICKEN?
OKAY, WE WILL GET SOME FRIED CHICKEN.

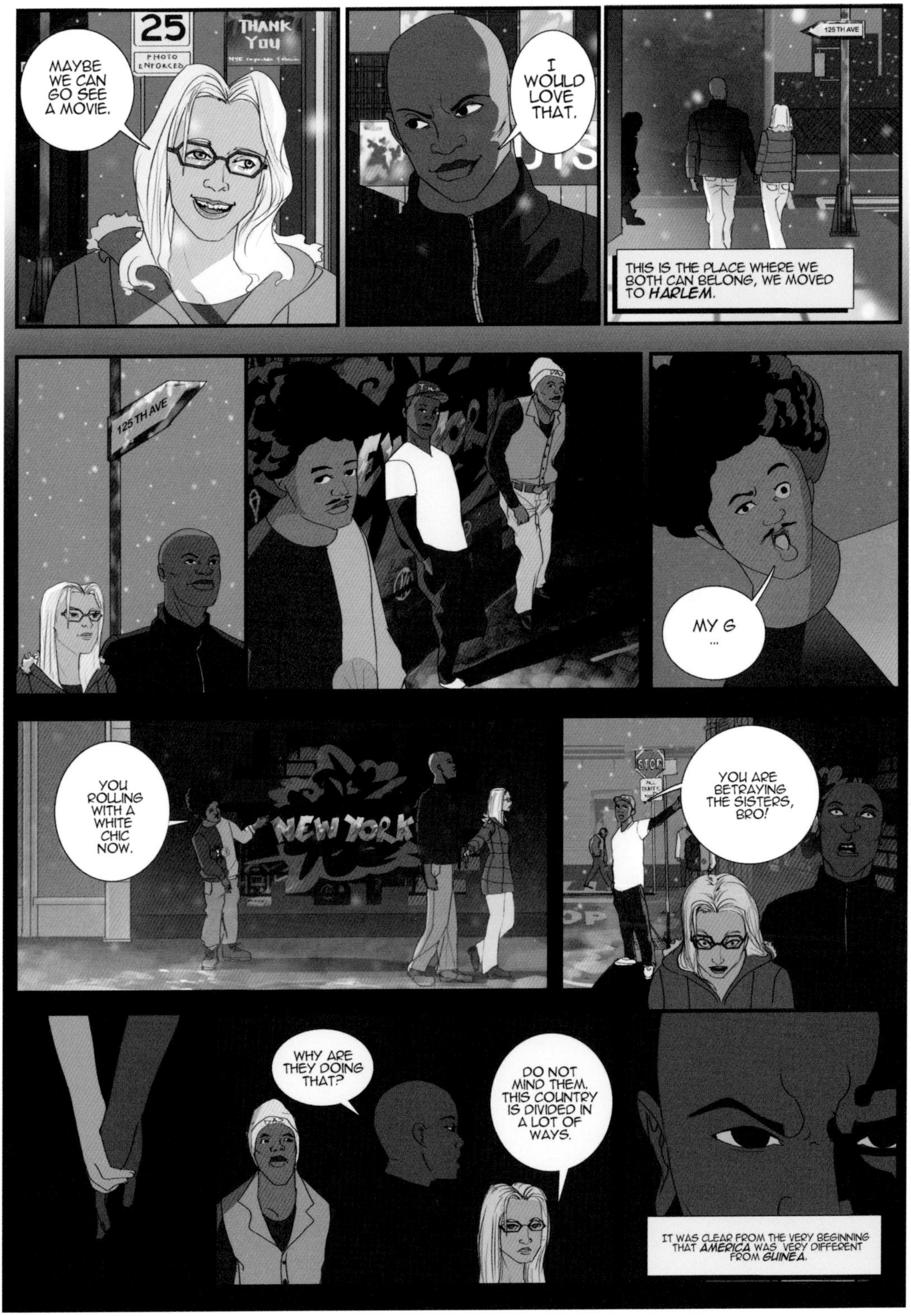
25
PHOTO ENFORCED
THANK YOU
MAYBE WE CAN GO SEE A MOVIE.
I WOULD LOVE THAT.
125 TH AVE
THIS IS THE PLACE WHERE WE BOTH CAN BELONG, WE MOVED TO HARLEM.
125 TH AVE
MY G ...
YOU ROLLING WITH A WHITE CHIC NOW.
NEW YORK
STOP
YOU ARE BETRAYING THE SISTERS, BRO!
WHY ARE THEY DOING THAT?
DO NOT MIND THEM. THIS COUNTRY IS DIVIDED IN A LOT OF WAYS.
IT WAS CLEAR FROM THE VERY BEGINNING THAT AMERICA WAS VERY DIFFERENT FROM GUINEA.

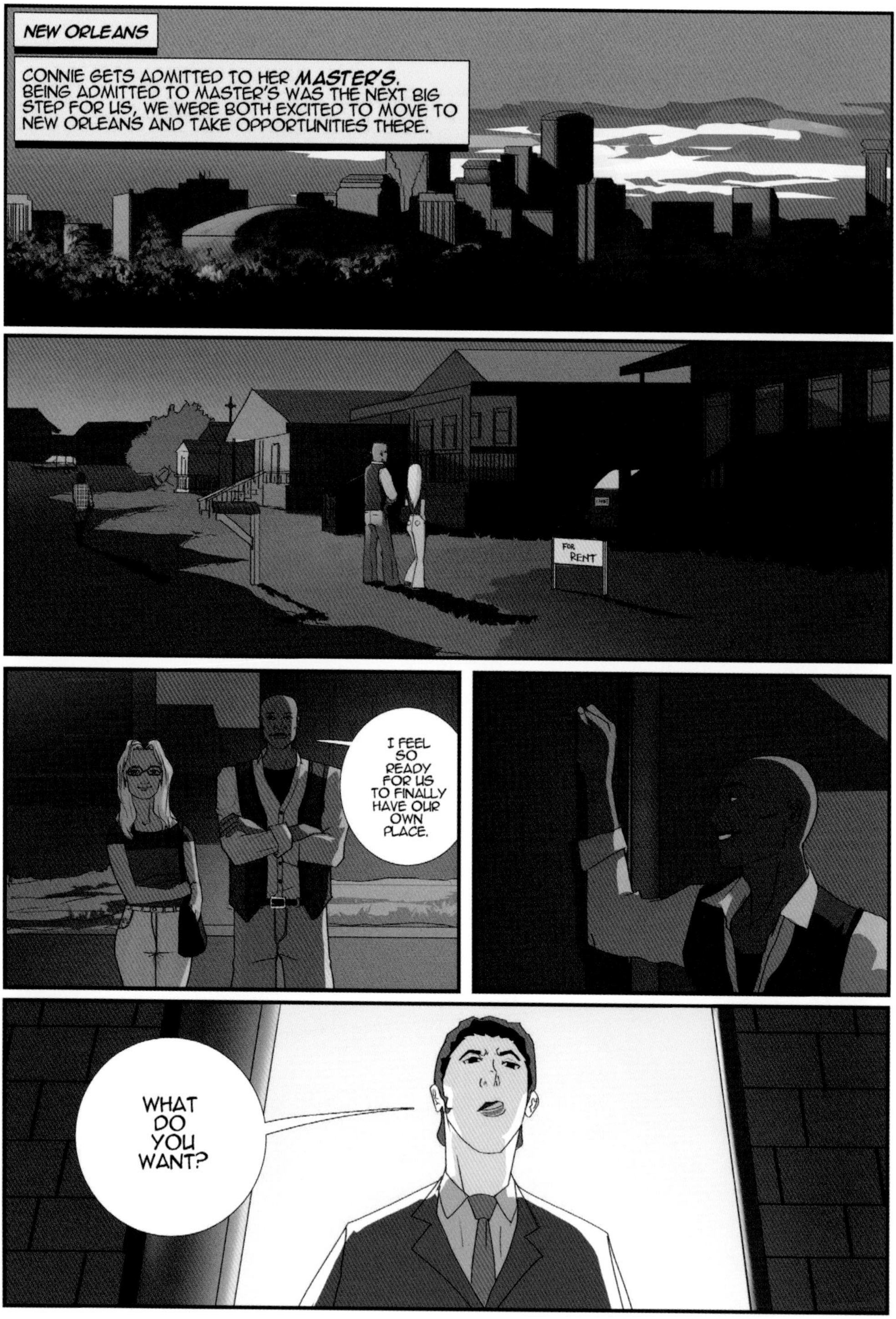
NEW ORLEANS
CONNIE GETS ADMITTED TO HER MASTER'S. BEING ADMITTED TO MASTER'S WAS THE NEXT BIG STEP FOR US, WE WERE BOTH EXCITED TO MOVE TO NEW ORLEANS AND TAKE OPPORTUNITIES THERE.
FOR RENT
I FEEL SO READY FOR US TO FINALLY HAVE OUR OWN PLACE.
WHAT DO YOU WANT?

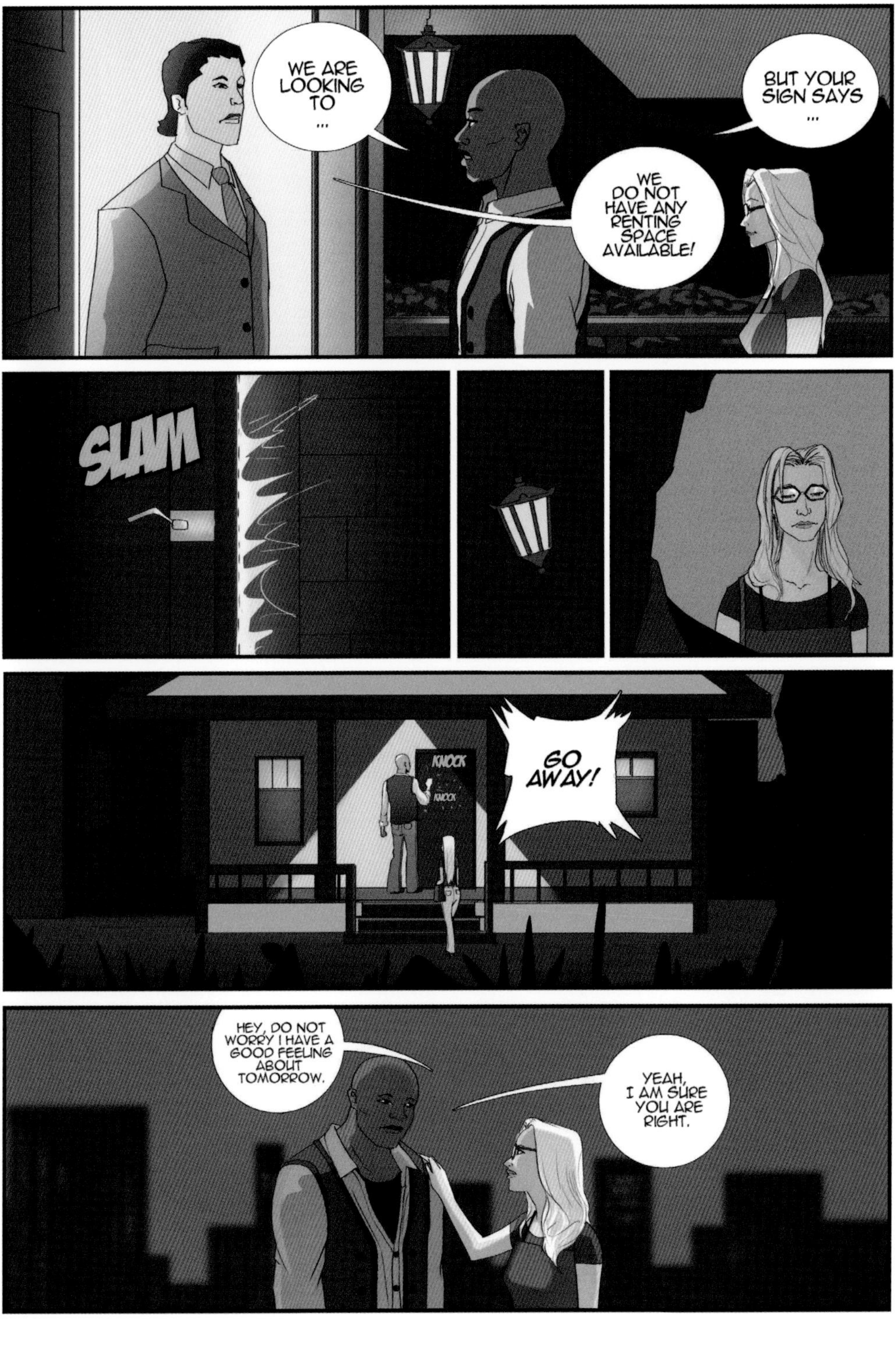
WE ARE LOOKING TO ...
BUT YOUR SIGN SAYS ...
WE DO NOT HAVE ANY RENTING SPACE AVAILABLE!
SLAM
KNOCK
KNOCK
GO AWAY!
HEY, DO NOT WORRY I HAVE A GOOD FEELING ABOUT TOMORROW.
YEAH, I AM SURE YOU ARE RIGHT.

A WEEK LATER, WE WERE GETTING WORRIED WE WOULD NOT FIND ANYTHING.

KNOCK

KNOCK

WE ARE LOOKING FOR A PLACE TO RENT.

OH, COME IN! COME IN!

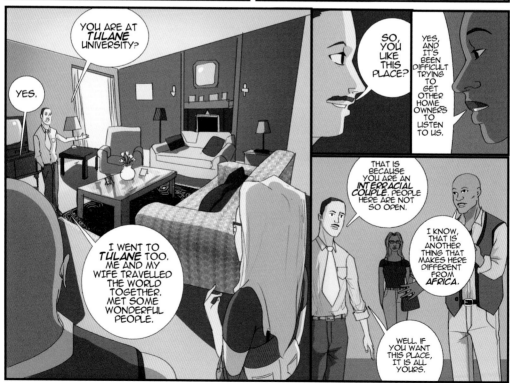

YOU ARE AT *TULANE* UNIVERSITY?

YES.

I WENT TO *TULANE* TOO. ME AND MY WIFE TRAVELLED THE WORLD TOGETHER, MET SOME WONDERFUL PEOPLE.

SO, YOU LIKE THIS PLACE?

YES, AND IT'S BEEN DIFFICULT TRYING TO GET OTHER HOME OWNERS TO LISTEN TO US.

THAT IS BECAUSE YOU ARE AN *INTERRACIAL COUPLE*. PEOPLE HERE ARE NOT SO OPEN.

I KNOW, THAT IS ANOTHER THING THAT MAKES HERE DIFFERENT FROM *AFRICA*.

WELL, IF YOU WANT THIS PLACE, IT IS ALL YOURS.

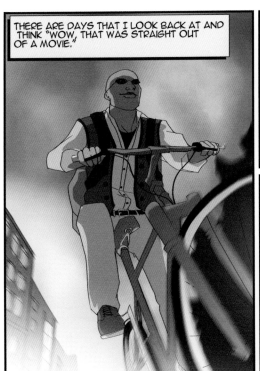

THERE ARE DAYS THAT I LOOK BACK AT AND THINK "WOW, THAT WAS STRAIGHT OUT OF A MOVIE."

I WAS ON MY WAY HOME FROM CLASS ...

THINGS ARE FINALLY LOOKING UP.

DAYS THAT MADE ME REALIZE WHY SOME *AFRICAN* FATHERS WORRY WHEN THEIR SONS GO TO *AMERICA.*

POLICE
RLEANS

PUT YOUR HANDS UP!

WAIT, HE SAID 5 FOOT 4...

THIS GUY IS OVER 6 FEET TALL. THIS CANNOT BE OUR GUY.

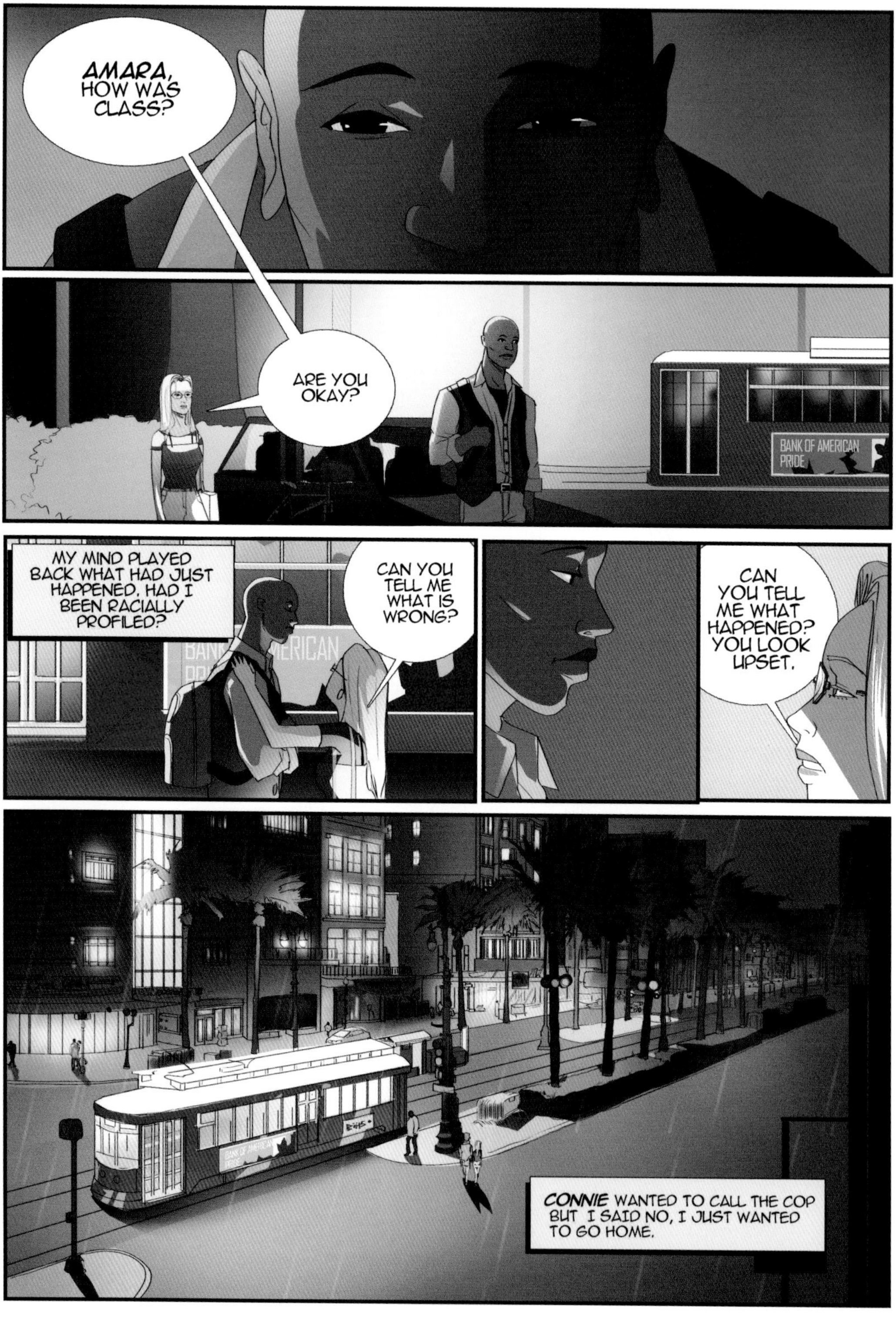
AMARA, HOW WAS CLASS?
ARE YOU OKAY?
BANK OF AMERICAN PRIDE
MY MIND PLAYED BACK WHAT HAD JUST HAPPENED. HAD I BEEN RACIALLY PROFILED?
CAN YOU TELL ME WHAT IS WRONG?
CAN YOU TELL ME WHAT HAPPENED? YOU LOOK UPSET.
CONNIE WANTED TO CALL THE COP BUT I SAID NO, I JUST WANTED TO GO HOME.

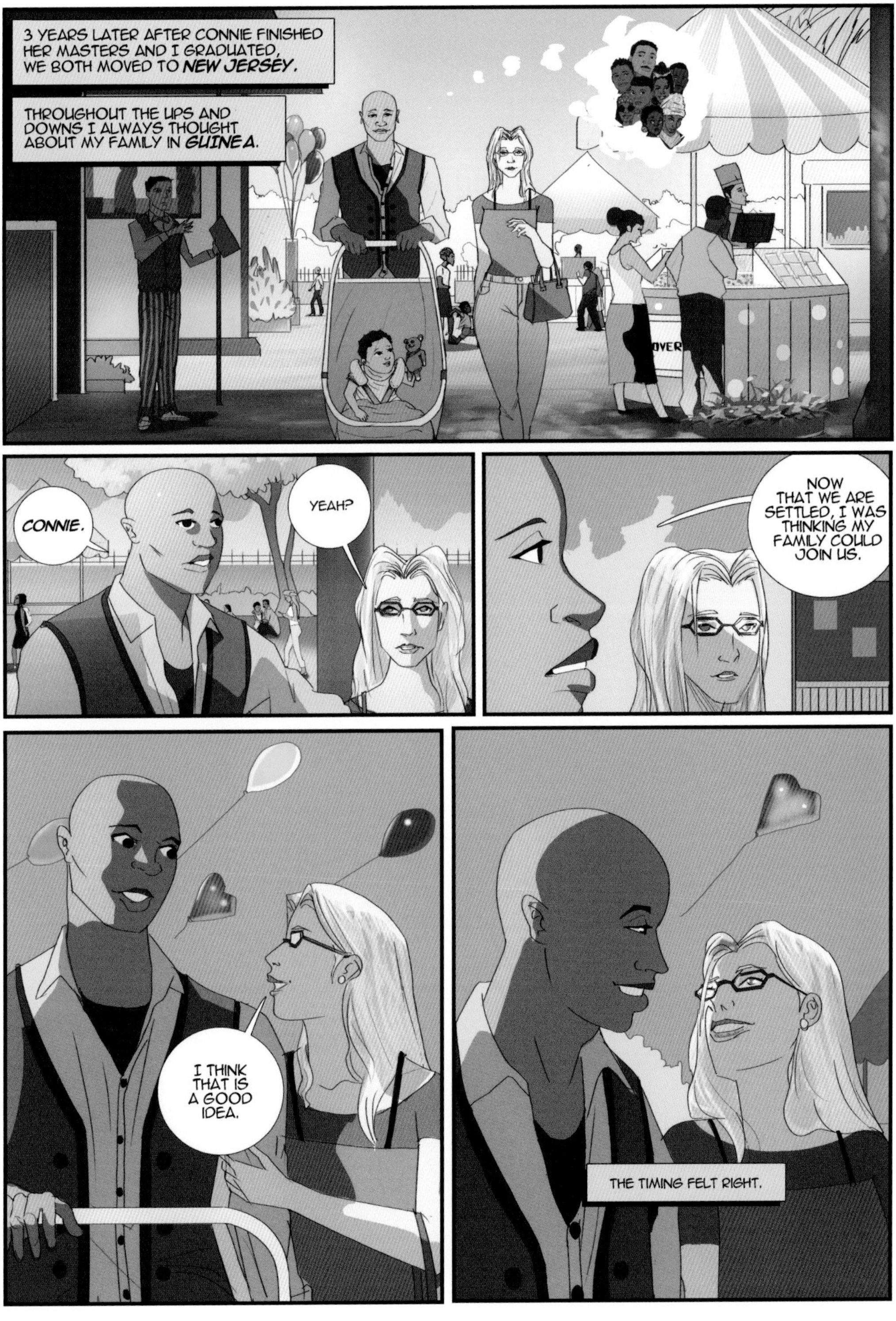
3 YEARS LATER AFTER CONNIE FINISHED HER MASTERS AND I GRADUATED, WE BOTH MOVED TO NEW JERSEY.
THROUGHOUT THE UPS AND DOWNS I ALWAYS THOUGHT ABOUT MY FAMILY IN GUINEA.
CONNIE.
YEAH?
NOW THAT WE ARE SETTLED, I WAS THINKING MY FAMILY COULD JOIN US.
I THINK THAT IS A GOOD IDEA.
THE TIMING FELT RIGHT.

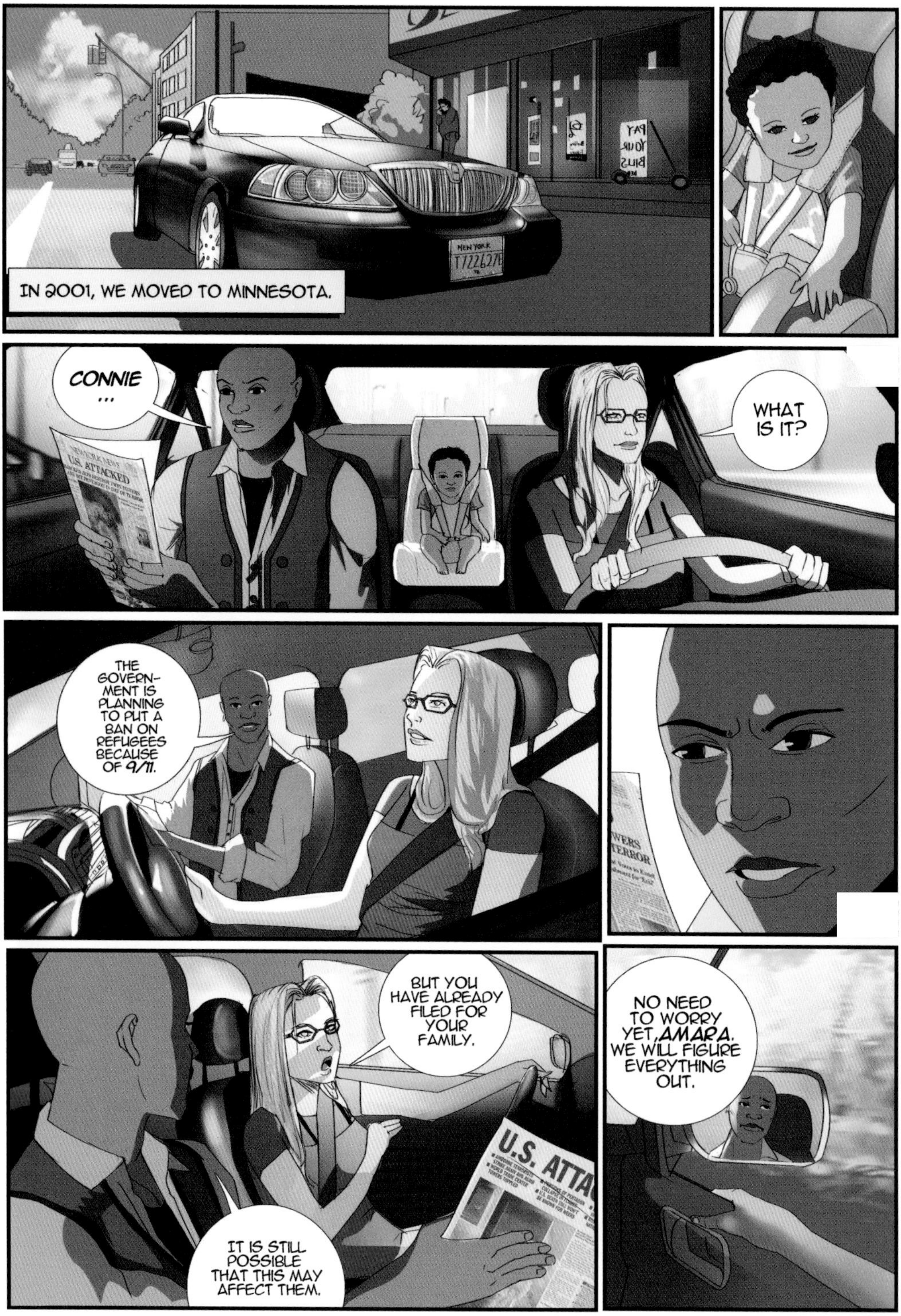
IN 2001, WE MOVED TO MINNESOTA.
CONNIE ...
WHAT IS IT?
THE GOVERNMENT IS PLANNING TO PUT A BAN ON REFUGEES BECAUSE OF 9/11.
BUT YOU HAVE ALREADY FILED FOR YOUR FAMILY.
IT IS STILL POSSIBLE THAT THIS MAY AFFECT THEM.
NO NEED TO WORRY YET, AMARA. WE WILL FIGURE EVERYTHING OUT.

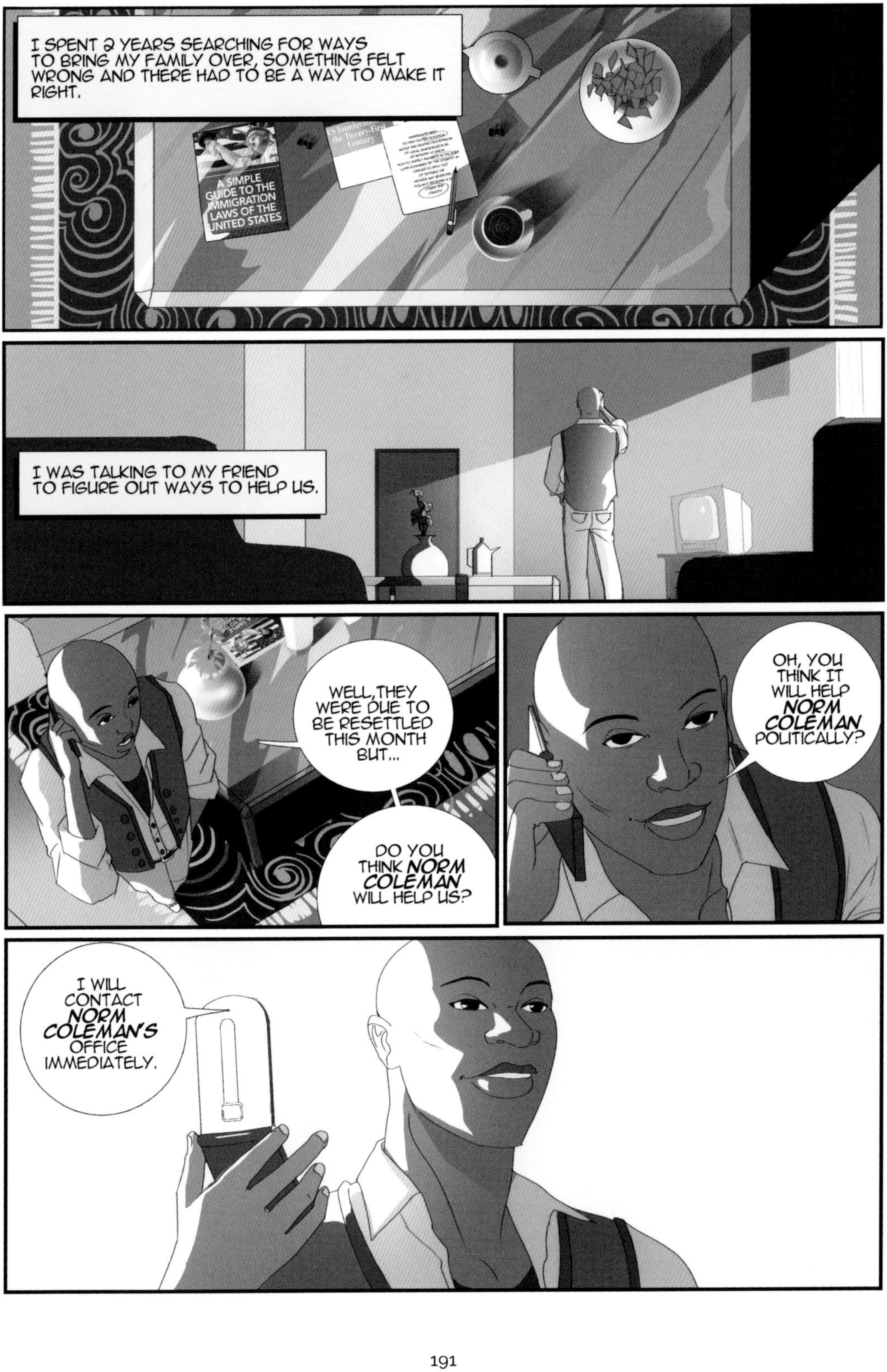
I SPENT 2 YEARS SEARCHING FOR WAYS TO BRING MY FAMILY OVER, SOMETHING FELT WRONG AND THERE HAD TO BE A WAY TO MAKE IT RIGHT.
A SIMPLE GUIDE TO THE IMMIGRATION LAWS OF THE UNITED STATES
I WAS TALKING TO MY FRIEND TO FIGURE OUT WAYS TO HELP US.
WELL, THEY WERE DUE TO BE RESETTLED THIS MONTH BUT...
DO YOU THINK NORM COLEMAN WILL HELP US?
OH, YOU THINK IT WILL HELP NORM COLEMAN POLITICALLY?
I WILL CONTACT NORM COLEMAN'S OFFICE IMMEDIATELY.

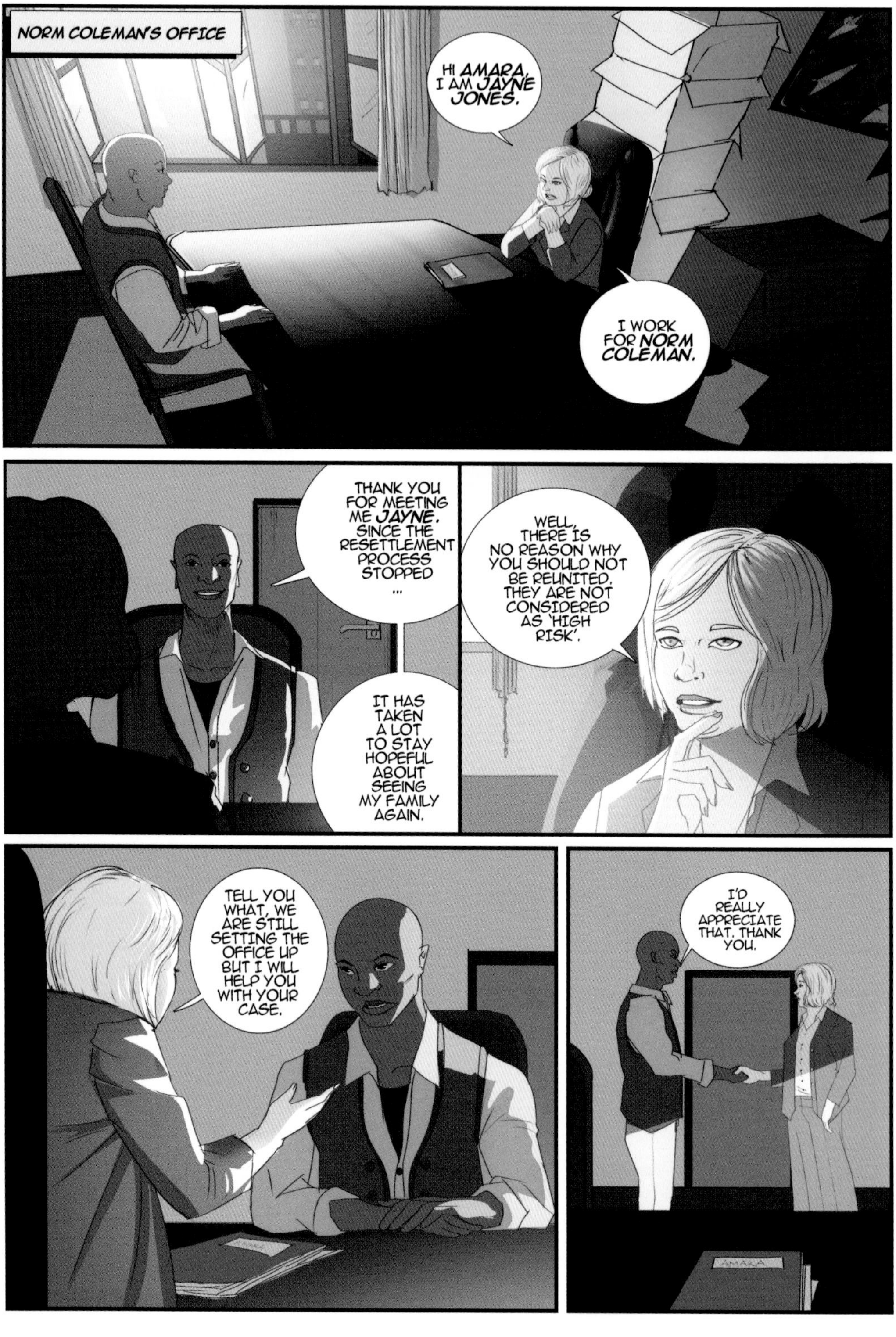
NORM COLEMAN'S OFFICE
HI AMARA, I AM JAYNE JONES.
I WORK FOR NORM COLEMAN.
THANK YOU FOR MEETING ME JAYNE. SINCE THE RESETTLEMENT PROCESS STOPPED ...
IT HAS TAKEN A LOT TO STAY HOPEFUL ABOUT SEEING MY FAMILY AGAIN.
WELL, THERE IS NO REASON WHY YOU SHOULD NOT BE REUNITED. THEY ARE NOT CONSIDERED AS 'HIGH RISK'.
TELL YOU WHAT, WE ARE STILL SETTING THE OFFICE UP BUT I WILL HELP YOU WITH YOUR CASE.
I'D REALLY APPRECIATE THAT. THANK YOU.
AMARA

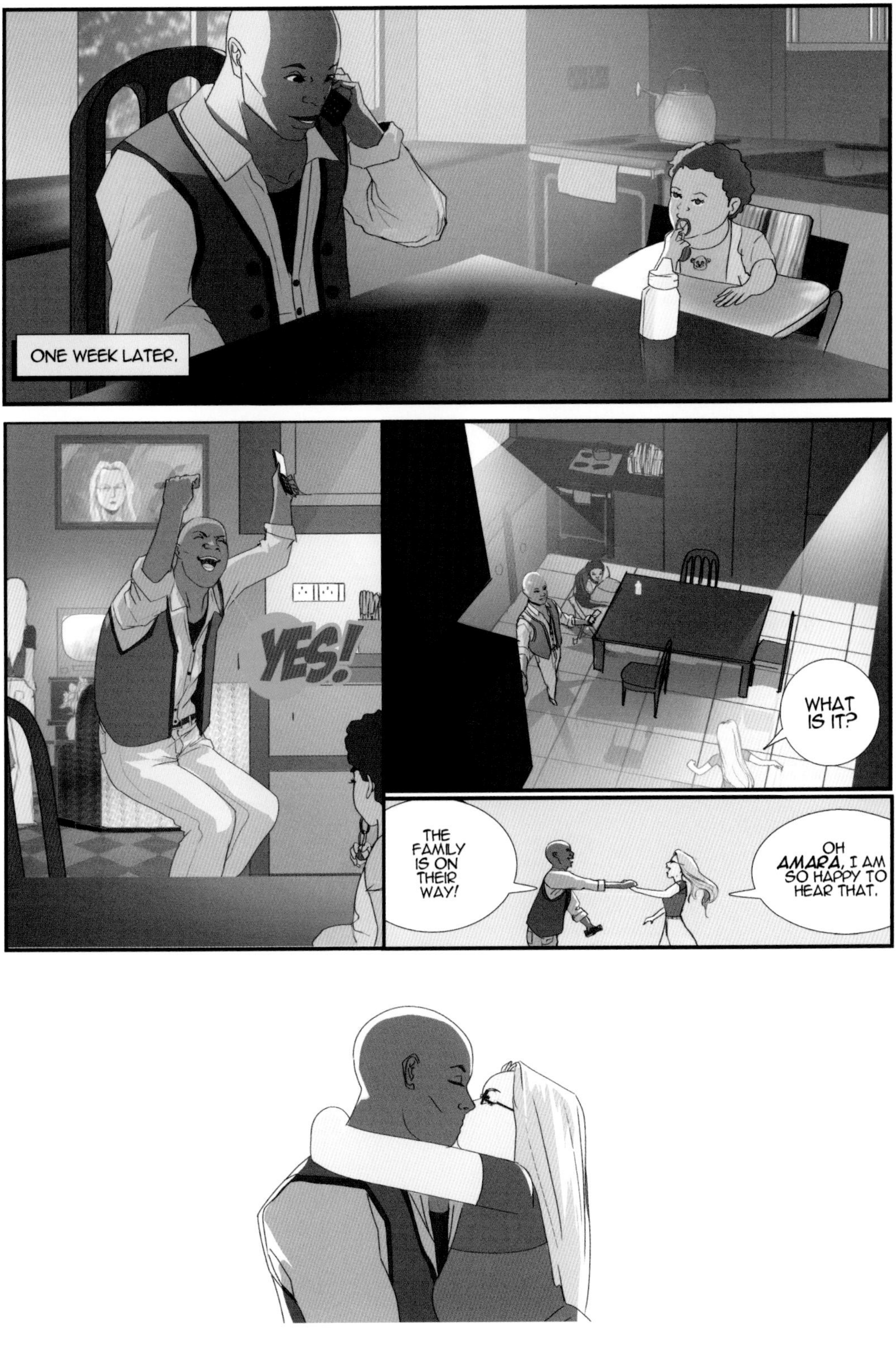
ONE WEEK LATER.
YES!
WHAT IS IT?
THE FAMILY IS ON THEIR WAY!
OH AMARA, I AM SO HAPPY TO HEAR THAT.

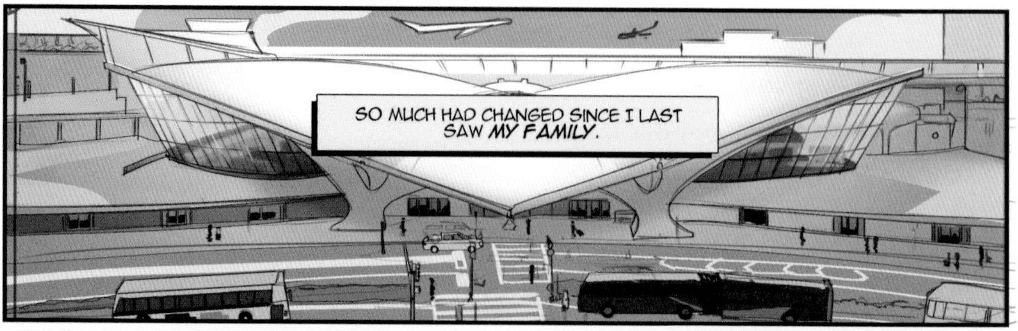
SO MUCH HAD CHANGED SINCE I LAST SAW MY FAMILY.

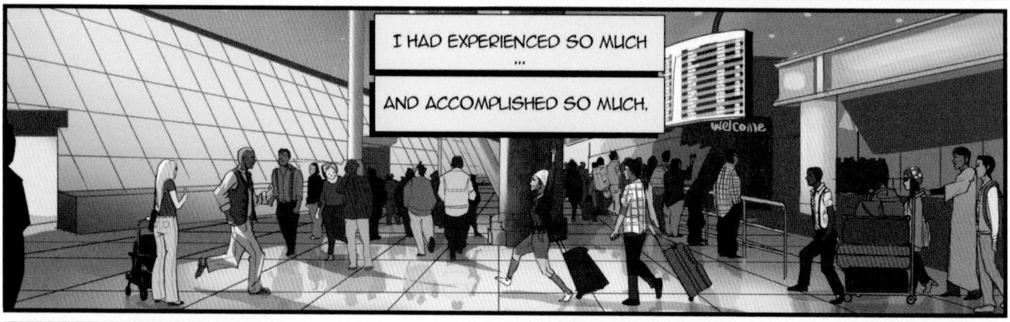
I HAD EXPERIENCED SO MUCH ...
AND ACCOMPLISHED SO MUCH.
welcome

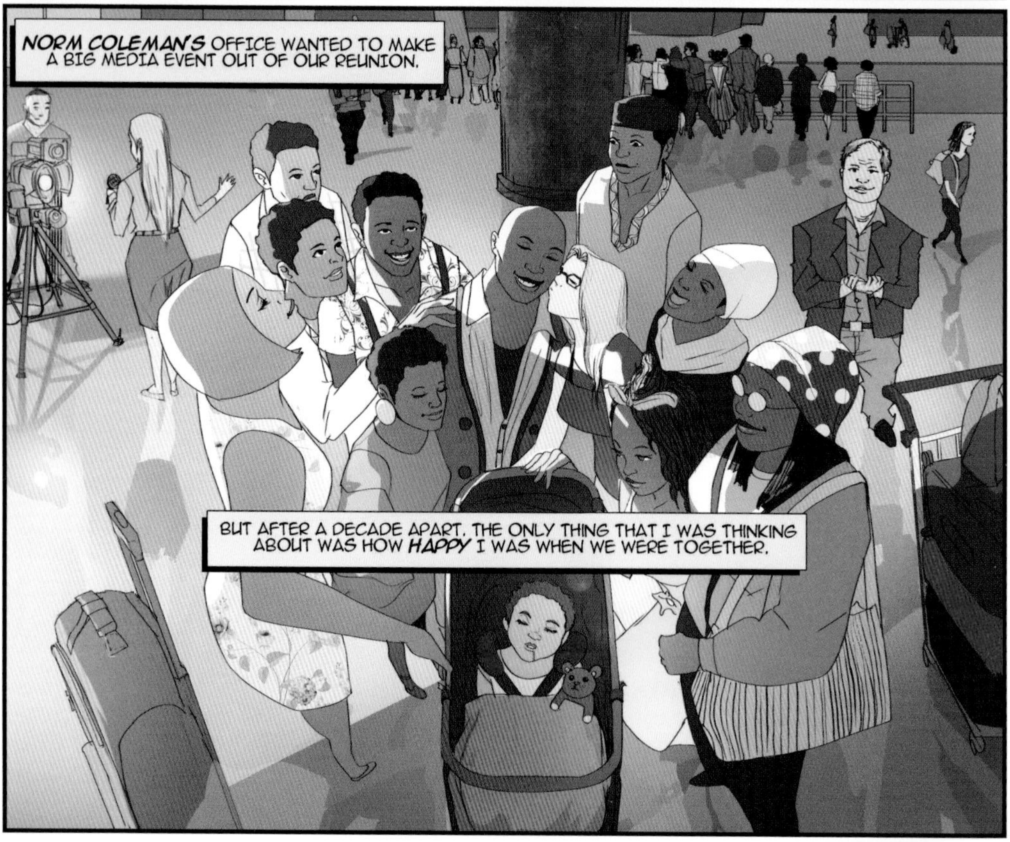
NORM COLEMAN'S OFFICE WANTED TO MAKE A BIG MEDIA EVENT OUT OF OUR REUNION.
BUT AFTER A DECADE APART, THE ONLY THING THAT I WAS THINKING ABOUT WAS HOW HAPPY I WAS WHEN WE WERE TOGETHER.

GLOSSARY

Ban on refugee resettlement (after 9/11): After 9/11, a freeze on refugee admissions was put into effect for over two months while a comprehensive review of procedures was undertaken. A number of new security measures were adopted as a result of this review, including conducting additional security checks of applicants against existing databases, verifying in new ways the identity of all refugee travelers before they board flights to the US, and fingerprinting all approved applicants either before departure to or upon their arrival in the US. The freeze and the enhanced security measures that followed significantly cut into the number of refugees that were admitted in 2002. (Only 27,000 refugees were admitted out of a Presidentially authorized ceiling of 70,000.)

French Quarter: A neighborhood in New Orleans's historic heart, famous for its vibrant nightlife and colorful buildings with cast-iron balconies. Crowd-pleasing Bourbon Street features jazz clubs, Cajun eateries, and raucous bars serving potent cocktails.

Interracial couple: An intimate relationship in which the partners belong to different races or racialized ethnicities.

Peace Corps: An independent agency and volunteer program run by the US government, providing international social and economic development assistance. Volunteers work abroad for a period of two years after three months of training and work with governments, schools, non-profit organizations, non-government organizations, and entrepreneurs in education, youth development, community health, business, information technology, agriculture, and the environment.

Racial profiling: The act of suspecting, targeting, or discriminating against a person on the basis of their ethnicity or religion rather than on individual suspicion. Racial profiling often involves discrimination against minority populations and is based on any negative stereotypes of the targeted demographic.

Refugee resettlement: A global system of governmental and non-governmental actors that helps resettle refugees to a safe third country. Many refugees cannot go home because of continued conflict, war, and persecution. In such circumstances, they are transferred from one country to another that has agreed to admit them, and ultimately grant them permanent residence. Refugee resettlement to a safe third country is considered for only a small fraction of refugees: those whose conditions are so perilous or whose needs cannot be met in the country where they first sought protection. Only a small number of countries take part in resettlement programs— among them are the United States, Australia, Canada, the Nordic countries, and increasingly some countries in Europe and Latin America.

White chick (White girl): Informal and sometimes offensive name for young Caucasian female, sometimes stereotyped as vapid materialists.

ACKNOWLEDGEMENTS

We are writing these words in very precarious times. May 25, 2021, will mark the first anniversary of George Floyd's murder. It woke up the nation and reignited the fight for Black lives. The uprising that followed reflected historic frustrations with the criminal legal system and anger at the systemic racism prevalent in policing that far too often leads to a disproportionate number of Black men, women, trans, and children being killed by law enforcement. Almost a year later, our government buildings are once again fenced off and our stores are boarded up. Two weeks ago, the Minneapolis City Council unanimously approved the historic pre-trial civil settlement of $27 million with the family of George Floyd, a Black man murdered in police custody. Last week, the final jury was selected and in a matter of days, the trial of former Officer Chauvin will begin.

We now stand—a few blocks away from where George Floyd was murdered—in the shadow of his memorial, which is visited by people from across the world, and emphasize that immigrant justice has always been inextricably linked to racial justice. We also want to pause and acknowledge the rise of xenophobia and racism targeting Asian American communities, as well as acknowledge the Native Americans, our original storytellers, whose land we now inhabit.

While we work tirelessly to respond to the immediate needs of our community, we are also committed—more than ever—to continue co-creating Green Card Voices (GCV) books. We know that these stories matter deeply…and more than ever in these times. Our indie and immigrant-led publishing work is an important contribution to the much-needed systems-level, essential change. By sharing stories and creating authentic immigrant-centered resources, we hope to pave the way for a more inclusive and supportive society and, in this critical moment, empower the immigrant authors and readers alike to address issues of racial inequity and develop deeper racial and cross-cultural understanding.

Over 15 percent of the US population, just over 50 million individuals, are not born here (United Nations 2019 Immigrant Population Report). GCV and our collaborators work every day to lift up their stories, whether immigrants or refugees. In this case, we produced a bold and unconventional anthology where we paired storytellers and illustrators from the same linguistic, cultural, and regional backgrounds to create a unique blend between story and illustration. The anthology centers on complex and difficult issues: the ways in which identities and bodies are marked by race, religion, class, education inequality, systematic displacement, discrimination, mental health, disability, activism, and more to reclaim the narrative that has so often been shaped by hate, fear, and xenophobia.

Our Stories Carried Us Here: A Graphic Novel Anthology marks a milestone as GCV's tenth published book and full of firsts:

- First graphic novel—the graphic novel/memoir genre makes these stories flow with creative artistry and authentic emotion.
- First national anthology—ten stories from authors living across the US.
- First co-created novel—storytellers and illustrators from the same linguistic, cultural, and regional backgrounds.
- The first time we've included bilingual storytelling, capturing more realistic dialogue.

When we started this journey two years ago, we wanted to bring forward a graphic novel that focused on amplifying the voices of immigrants and refugees and illustrating the variety of stories, situations, and journeys that come from our new neighbors. In this format, we are able to not only engage with a variety of readers but also evoke empathy and understanding that drive thoughtful and inclusive discussion. The use of both text and imagery enables students to build and develop context that promotes comprehension.

Today, graphic novels are one of the most popular media for young and adult readers. In libraries, the graphic novel sections have the highest circulation rates. For these reasons, it's both engaging and accessible to young and adult readers. *Our Stories Carried Us Here* acts as a mirror and a light to connect us all with immigrant and refugee experiences that inspire both hope and empathy.

For making this book possible, we have many individuals, organizations, and entities to thank for working tirelessly amid this really unprecedented time.

Our heartfelt gratitude goes to the eleven storytellers: Zaynab Abdi, Aziz Kamal, Craig Moodie, Karelin, Ruth Mekoulom, Alex Tsipenyuk, Zurya Anjum, Sergio Cenoch & Mary Anne Quiroz, Vy Luong, and Amara Solomon Kamara. Without your courage to share your story with the world, this book would not have been possible.

Equally important are the illustrators: Ashraf El-Attar, sunshine gao, Ana Hinojosa, Hop (Guy Bertin "BG" Beyem Gouong, Sandjock Likinè, Gérard Nyunai Ngan), Mike Centeno, Tom Kaczynski, Toufic El Rassi, Camilo Aguirre, Cori Nakamura Lin, Hamid Ibrahim and the Kugali Team. We honor your incredible artistry and talents.

Our deepest gratitude goes to Nate Powell, who illustrated the wrap-around book art, and Thi Bui, who wrote a very powerful foreword. We thank Bambi Lambert, a deaf/hard of hearing interpreter for providing interpretation, translation, and transliteration services in American Sign Language (ASL). We would also like to thank Shiney Her, graphic designer, who designed the interior of the book, Wise Ink for copyediting services, and our distributor, Consortium Book Sales and Distribution.

We believe this book is an important, timely, and necessary project that will raise awareness of immigrants and refugees and beyond to engage with society's complicated social and political context, through distinct and diverse perspectives.

Thanks to our funders: the Marbrook Foundation, the RaiseMN Campaign Institute, and the Minnesota Twins. We especially want to thank the tremendous support we received through our Kickstarter Campaign. Without our Kickstarter backers, this publication would not have been possible!

We thank the GCV Board of Directors and staff for supporting us, and all others who have helped our mission along the way. And finally, and most personally, we would like to thank our partners, children, families, and friends for helping each of us put our passion to use for the betterment of society. With the above support, GCV is truly able to realize its mission of using the art of storytelling to build bridges between immigrants and their communities by sharing first-hand immigration stories of foreign-born Americans. Our aim is to help the collective in the US see each "wave of immigrants" as individuals with assets and strengths that make this country remarkable.

Julie Vang, Tea Rozman, Tom Kaczynski
Co-Editors
Minneapolis, MN

AFTERWORD

Learning from the stories featured in this book is just the beginning. The more important work starts when we engage in the difficult, essential, and brave conversations about the changing face of our nation.

Immigration plays a significant role in modern America—and our work since founded in 2013 utilizes the art of storytelling to build bridges that facilitate rich conversations and understanding between immigrants and their communities. Consider, one in five Americans speak a language other than English at home—what a powerful opportunity for new connections and cultural growth. From classrooms to book clubs, from the individual interested in learning more about his immigrant neighbor to the business owner looking to understand her employees and business partners, this book is an important resource for all Americans.

You can also further engage with your communities and learn more about contemporary immigration through *Story Stitch*, a card-based guided storytelling activity which connects individuals across different backgrounds by encouraging them to share and connect through stories. In addition, Green Card Voices (GCV) has **traveling state and national exhibits** to allow for a visual experience with our authors' journeys. These interactive exhibits feature QR links to video narratives and are designed to expand the impact of a published collection of personal narratives.

To date, the GCV team has recorded the life stories of over 450 immigrants coming from more than 130 different countries. All immigrants that decide to share their story with GCV are asked six open-ended questions, as well as share personal photos from their birth country and in the US. These video stories are available on our website and YouTube (free of charge and advertising).

Our aim is to spark deep, meaningful conversations about identity, appreciation of difference, and our shared human experience. To learn more about our dynamic, video-based platform, book collections, traveling exhibits, *Story Stitch*, and other ways to engage with Green Card Voices stories, visit our website: www.greencardvoices.org.

Purchase at our online store: *www.greencardvoices.org/store*

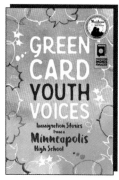

GREEN CARD YOUTH VOICES
Immigration Stories from a Minneapolis High School

Immigration Stories from a Minneapolis High School

ISBN: 978-1-949523-00-3

EISBN: 978-1-949523-01-0

GREEN CARD YOUTH VOICES
Immigration Stories from a St. Paul High School

Immigration Stories from a St. Paul High School

ISBN: 978-1-949523-04-1

EISBN: 978-1-949523-06-5

GREEN CARD YOUTH VOICES
Immigration Stories from a Fargo High School

Immigration Stories from a Fargo High School

ISBN: 978-1-949523-02-7

EISBN: 978-1-949523-03-4

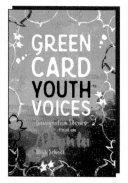

GREEN CARD YOUTH VOICES

Immigration Stories from an Atlanta High School

ISBN: 978-1-949523-05-8

EISBN: 978-1-949523-08-9

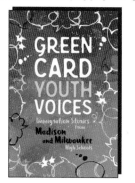

GREEN CARD YOUTH VOICES
Madison and Milwaukee

Immigration Stories from Madison & Milwaukee High Schools

ISBN: 978-1-949523-12-6

EISBN: 978-1-949523-13-3

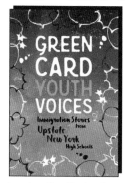

GREEN CARD YOUTH VOICES
Immigration Stories from Upstate New York High Schools

Immigration Stories from Upstate New York High Schools

ISBN: 978-1-949523-16-4

EISBN: 978-1-949523-19-5

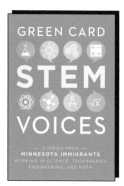

GREEN CARD
STEM
VOICES
STORIES FROM
MINNESOTA IMMIGRANTS
WORKING IN SCIENCE, TECHNOLOGY, ENGINEERING, AND MATH

Green Card STEM Voices: Stories from Minnesota Immigrants Working in Science, Technology, Engineering, and Math

ISBN: 978-1-949523-14-0

EISBN: 978-1-949523-15-7

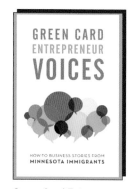

GREEN CARD
ENTREPRENEUR
VOICES
HOW-TO BUSINESS STORIES FROM
MINNESOTA IMMIGRANTS

Green Card Entrepreneur Voices: How-To Business Stories from Minnesota Immigrants

ISBN: 978-1-949523-07-2

EISBN: 978-1-949523-09-6

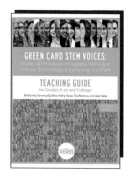

GREEN CARD STEM VOICES:
Stories of Minnesota Immigrants Working in Science, Technology, Engineering, and Math
TEACHING GUIDE
for Grades 6-12 and College

Green Card STEM Voices: Stories of MN Immigrants Working in Science, Technology, Engineering, and Math - Teaching Guide for Grades 6-12 and College

STORY STITCH

Telling Stories, Opening Minds, Becoming Neighbors

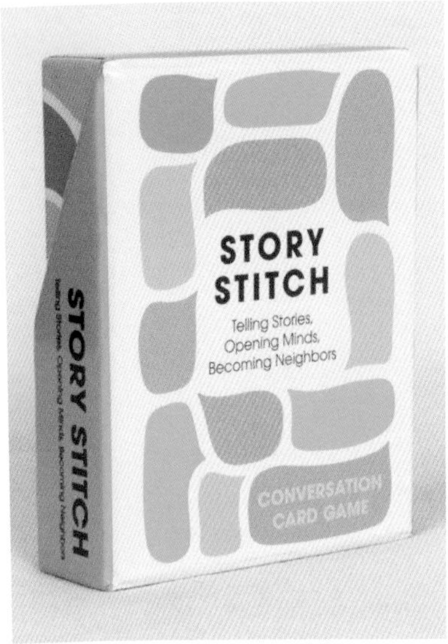
STORY
STITCH
Telling Stories,
Opening Minds,
Becoming Neighbors
CONVERSATION
CARD GAME
STORY STITCH

Story Stitch is a guided storytelling card activity that connects and builds empathy between people of different cultural backgrounds. It was created by the diverse Minneapolis/St. Paul community in a series of co-creating game sessions led by the Green Card Voices team. This card game is perfect for: classrooms (ages 10+), diversity training, workshops, work places, leadership / fellow retreats, conferences, elderly homes, and more. Available as a deck (ISBN: 978-1-949523-11-9).

Contents:

- 55 full color, laminated cards
    - 33 story cards
    - 22 stitch cards
- 1 four-sided accordion of instructions

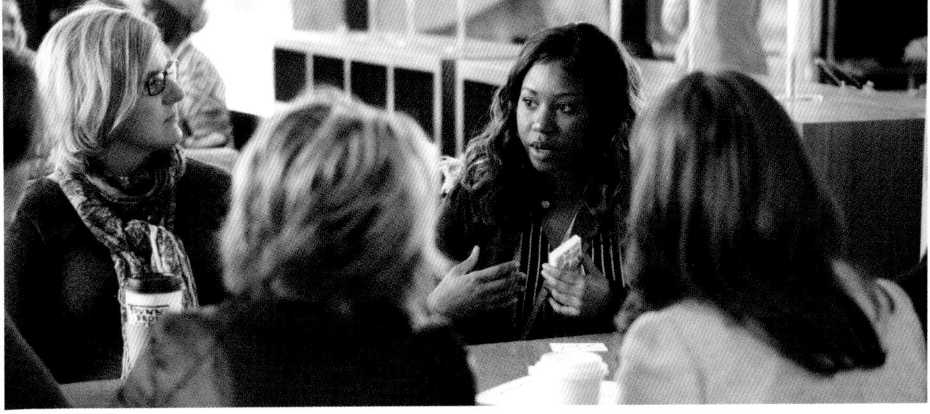